OF
CHAOS
AND
BEAUTY

ELEMENTALS OF CHAOS
BOOK 1

First published by Chaotic Press, LLC 2023

First paperback edition October 2023

ISBN 9798988991137(paperback)

www.meghanrhine.com

Cover design by Alerim

Editing by Rebecca Faith Heyman

Line Edit/Proofreading by Jennifer Murgia

CONTENTS

AUTHOR NOTE

O F CHAOS AND BEAUTY is an intense, action-packed adventure fantasy, set in a harsh and war-riddled world of elemental warriors. Within these pages, you will find elements regarding war, battle, hand-to-hand combat, slavery, blood, intense violence, injuries, and death, all of which are shown on the page. This book contains mature sexual content shown on the page. Readers who may be sensitive to the mentioned themes, please take note, and prepare to enter a world of chaos...

For my guys.
Marlon—who loved, supported, and believed in me.
Hendrix, Maverick, and Onyx—who gave me a reason to pursue my dreams.
Without you, there would be no story.

Chapter 1
Kara

B<small>EFORE THE *SIEGE*.</small>

I am not my mother. I cannot take responsibility for the lives of my faction members. The blood of another friend will not stain my hands. I am through with war. Let someone else shoulder the burden of so much death and failure.

The air in my room feels thick. It clings to my throat as I struggle to take deep breaths, hoping it'll calm my racing pulse. I close my eyes and concentrate on the smell of aged cypress. The scent is synonymous with home. The wood makes up our walls and doors, and I indulge in its comfort one last time.

Walking over to the window I plan to escape through, I open it to let in the nighttime breeze. Tonight's wind flows into my room, bringing with it an unusual chill. Although autumn is upon us, the temperature shouldn't be cool enough to raise chill bumps and shake bones. Despite the cold crisp air breezing through, my breathing doesn't ease.

I hush, sticking my head outside to listen for a disturbance. The streets beyond my house are desolate. None of my faction members wander or carry on after a long night of merriment. I scan the space, looking for any animals—like stray ferncats—that might stir and draw attention to me as I escape.

I hear nothing.

The night is eerily silent, as if waiting to amplify any rustle or creak I might make when leaving and running from my home.

Absently, I clutch the obsidian pendant hanging like a millstone around my neck. The rock is cool with jagged edges that sting my palm the tighter I grip it. I am preparing to fail my faction on two fronts. With one desperate decision, I will rob them of their planned successor and expected marriage alliance.

I think of Cinis, imagining the betrayed rejection he'll feel upon waking to find me gone. My heart begs me to search for an alternative, if only to protect him from this grief. He is the son of a strong fire faction's leader, and I already mourn the loss of his warm embrace. Jealousy is an ugly, visceral thing that rages in my chest at the thought of him marrying whoever they will choose to succeed instead of me.

Regardless of my feelings for him, I cannot hold my faction back. Cinis will give them a chance in this all-consuming war. Stepping down to make way for a more capable and seasoned match will give my people an opportunity for survival. It will give him the opportunity to rule alongside a lead he won't need to carry or clean up after. It's a chance to marry someone who could truly love him in the way he deserves.

While the fire of his kisses still burns on my lips, I can imagine his deep obsidian eyes narrowing in disappointment. I wish I had the time to explain. To let him know that the weeks he's spent in my faction have brought happiness while there should be none. Still, they aren't enough to convince me that marrying him is the right choice. They're not enough to commit to him—to this—forever.

Heat encircles my wrist where the bracelet Rae gave me burns a warning, as if it's her gripping my arm, telling me not to go. My chest tightens at the thought of never seeing my fire-wielding friend again, of never meeting the small life that grows inside her. She will wake in the morning, ready to join me in the turning of the leaves, as we do each Autumn Equinox. Then she will know that I've abandoned her.

I peer outside my window. The path below me is lit by the glowing lotus and ivy indigenous to my faction. They glow especially brightly tonight. Bold greens and neon reds will illuminate my escape for anyone to see.

I reach for the jatoba tree outside my bedroom. She extends a merciful branch down to my window for me to grasp. Holding my breath, I pray to Gaia that the rustling leaves or the creak of my window seal will not wake my parents. My heart hammers against my chest as I wrap my clammy hand around the jatoba's sturdy branch.

I'm so focused on looking behind me, I don't see the vine viper creep toward my wrist, sinking its pointed thorns into my forearm. I yank back, tumbling from the window.

Holding my hand to my mouth, I pray to Gaia that the sound of my fall did not travel, as I press my back against the cypress wall. I heave air in and out to calm myself, squeezing my eyes shut for several heartbeats. When I finally pry my eyes open, I look down at the puncture wounds, touching them to assess for venom.

They're clear, thank Gaia. The viper didn't have the time to poison me, adding just one more hurdle to my flailing attempt at escape.

The thunder of my pulse drums in my ears so loud that I don't hear the door as it opens.

I don't realize that all is lost until the stern voice reverberates through the room.

"Kara, where are you going?" My mother's brown eyes burn into me.

I open my mouth to start a lie but shut it as soon as I see my dad. It's no use.

"Kara, were you leaving?" Dad's brows pull together. His words come out as a genuine question rather than accusation, and for a second, I don't know what to say.

Mom's thin lips pinch together in a tight line. She still wears the dirt-smeared tunic and pants from yesterday, and I wonder if she knew I'd run all along. Shame burns my cheeks and sinks down to a lump in my throat. I can't open my mouth to say that I am going to leave—that I am abandoning my people. It's not something I even want to admit to myself, but staying is so much more frightening than leaving ever could be.

Shock widens her eyes, stretching the crow's feet that gather at their corners, brought on by age and the stress from a faction she looks to hand down to me. "You would leave your people?"

With my escape plan foiled, shame pushes my gaze to the floor. "I'm not leaving them undefended. They have you."

"We are at war. Should something happen to me, our faction needs a successor. They need you." Anger and incredulity lace her tone.

I turn to my father. "Then Dad can take over."

"Sweetheart, you know I can't do that."

My face heats. Suggesting that was a mistake. Only the strongest can lead, and my dad is only a Level One wielder. His elemental powers are the weakest of the three levels, though that is more than made up for in his hand-to-hand combat skills. Aside from my mother and grandmother, I'm one of the few Level Threes in our faction, the strongest of wielders. It's why the faction heads approved my appointment as our successor.

"Mom, I can't lead. I can't marry Cinis."

Her nostrils flare. "This is your duty. We do not have the luxury of doubt. Of waiting until we are ready." She spits the words like something rancid. "I've indulged this foolish indecision long enough, hoping you only needed the space to decide for yourself. You must stand for your people. You must lead." She clenches her teeth as her voice rises.

My dad wedges himself between us, taking a softer tone. "Besides, you seem to like the boy well enough. He is a respectable young man, and a strong match."

"Liking him well enough does not justify marrying him." This isn't about liking—or loving—him at all. I don't love him, I can't.

My mother's patience wanes. "Enough with the childish antics. You are not a little girl anymore. You are of age, and this is what's expected of you. We need his faction's alliance."

"That's no reason to marry someone."

"It is for us."

The ground trembles, and she's exactly three seconds away from losing her shit and releasing a tremor strong enough to split the floor beneath us.

Dad grips her now green and thinning fingers. "Let's not be hasty, Zimara. We may not need to rush into a marriage."

I fill my lungs as if breathing in hope, waiting for him to continue. "Cinis is rather young as well. I'm sure his father will not object to an extended engagement."

I release the breath, deflating, and weighing my options. Could I promise myself to Cinis?

Yes.

I know I could lose myself in his obsidian eyes and generous smile for the rest of my days. But he comes at a price.

Accepting Cinis would not mean accepting only him. He comes with the weight and responsibility of the thousands of people who live in my faction. I'd tie him to a leader who cannot overcome the paralysis of her indecisiveness and guilt. I would doom his rule before it begins.

In my mind, Caelum's sightless eyes look up at me. I'm the reason my cousin no longer walks among the living. I'll never escape his dead gaze. I couldn't save him. It's a constant and unwavering reminder that I am no leader. The blood of a hundred elementals drips from my fingertips. No matter how many times I wash them, my hands are never clean. The guilt of every life I've taken and every mistake I've made strangles me until I cannot breathe.

Accepting Cinis would be selfish, saying yes just to keep him in my life. I can't agree to the succession, only to maintain the Nadir bloodline as lead family. Accepting would mean giving my people a leader who has not delivered victory when it has truly mattered. I couldn't protect the ones I've loved the most, and the rest of my faction will be no different.

"The answer is no," I say. "I will not accept."

A thundering boom quakes the room. I assume it's my mother finally losing control of her anger and element until an icy wind blasts through. It shatters our windows and throws us to the ground. Before we can lift ourselves from the floor, water pools around us.

We are under attack.

CHAPTER 2
SORREN

I WATCH THE SLEEPING town from my vantage point in the forest outside the terra faction. The trees shift around us to make way for my brigade, their leaves rustling as they drag massive roots through the soil to shift themselves in place. Ice prickles along my palm at the disturbance they are causing.

I will freeze every shrub in this forest before allowing them to alert the terras of our presence.

Once my unit is settled in their places, the foliage settles back into stillness. Serpentine vines slither to hang from branches. Small rodents covered in leaves rather than feathers or scales scurry around my brigade. The climbing plants that crawl along the thick trees and creep across the forest floor emit a glow that is only bright enough to cast my soldiers in shadow.

It's the eve of their Autumn Equinox, a ridiculous holiday, where the terras behave as though they alone bring forth the autumn season. They scatter to the forests, changing the colors of any leaves they can touch, pretending that the foliage won't naturally turn on its own due to the changing weather.

Everything is quiet. In the dead of night, the town sleeps, but my soldiers shuffle through our camp, preparing for attack. I swat at a tree that brushes its curious branch along my head and shoulders. The intrusive timber reads me, assessing if I'm a threat. The unsolicited touch feels abrasive as the branch's leaves and twigs scrape against my frame. Although the terra flora is beautiful, I can do without the sentience.

Calix, my lead scout, moves into my peripheral, slipping from the shadows like spilled ink. It's unnerving how effortlessly the man can go undetected. He has been scouting since my father's first term as prime policymaker, back when we were a lesser region, still reliant on the Lower for things like medicinal and agricultural exports.

Calix served the Upper even before the great Prime Nero broke the chains of codependence that bound us to the Lower, and his skill level shows it. As a young corporal, I made the mistake of questioning his stealth. Calix followed me for five days, taping notes to my back that said, *I see all.*

By day four, I had grown so infuriated by the practical joke—and my inability to detect the scout who had literally gone under my nose—that I ripped my officer's coat reaching to snatch another note from my back.

I can still hear Kai's rolling laughter as he pulled the thirty-second sign from my uniform after, Aelious knows, how long it'd been there.

Following his lesson in humility, the scout trained me in the art of stealth and observing my surroundings. I learned more from him about using all my senses to be aware than I had from years at our realm's top military academy. It is an honor to have him serve in my brigade.

Calix's two subordinate scouts flank each side of him as he relays their report.

"We've secured the perimeter." His flat voice feigns indifference, but the clench of his fists let me know that disapproval simmers beneath. I ask no small thing of my soldiers. The ground we tread is morally gray, but our duty is clear. We are loyal to the Upper Region, and today we will do its bidding.

This is how I honor my father. As Nero's only child, my contribution to his legacy is paramount. I have trained tactically since I was a boy. He shipped me off to military school as soon as I could walk and form coherent sentences. I contribute through my strategic mind. I lead his armies, strengthening the military he built in his time as prime. I make my contribution by aiding in the capture of the Lower elementals. I avenge his death by putting in chains those who killed him.

"How many have we captured?" I ask, wanting to know the damage we have done.

His jaw tightens, discreetly pulling down the corners of his mouth and stretching the age lines in his deep brown skin. "There were approximately five hundred elementals occupying the town borders. We captured all but seventy-six."

"Escaped?"

"No."

I swallow to keep my facial expressions schooled and stoic. Seventy-six elementals already lost to a battle that has not yet begun.

My elemental essence seeps from me. It freezes the surrounding air, and I clench my fists to rein it back in before the unsolicited chill reaches the town.

Ceil stands nearby, listening to the scout's report, readying herself for my command. She runs a heavy hand across her head, pushing back the loose strands of blond hair that escape her top knot. The officer only keeps the top layers of her hair at medium length. Even that, she constantly ties up in a tight bun atop her head. She shaves the rest of her hair, from the tips of her ears down to her nape, cutting it to the scalp, closer than any military barber could boast of having done themselves.

Ceil is a decorated admiral and Level Two air wielder. Last year, I appointed her to lead a special ops unit focused on reconnaissance. She's equipped with enough knowledge about our enemy to lead the last line of defense against any escapees. "Admiral, take your troops and secure all exits. Ensure no member of this faction escapes."

Her nostrils flare as she says through clenched teeth, "And what do you command we do with any elementals who make it to the border?"

Ceil is physically incapable of hiding her opinions. Her headstrong determination is a quality I appreciated when making her an officer, but now I cannot allow the challenge. Although I believe no commander is above reproach, at this moment, I am not sturdy enough in my resolve to withstand it.

"You will subdue and load them into their respective transporter, just as the Council has commanded we handle the others."

I step closer to her, keeping my tone firm, daring her to question my command.

"Yes, sir. And if they are unarmed, or of inconsequential level?" Her voice is tight, doing little to hide her disapproval. She means an untrained Level One wielder. A weak elemental who can neither wield their element nor engage in physical combat to defend themselves.

I meet her disapproving tone with feigned indifference. "Then they will be all the easier to subdue."

The words taste bitter as I take immense care to keep my face focused and impartial before turning to administer the rest of my orders.

I can never leak my apprehension. My soldiers cannot know that my gut twists in knots with each order I give. Not when so many hold the same hesitations I do.

We all know what future awaits these elementals. They will serve in our capital and build up a stronger city. They will fulfill my father's vision of an elite Upper Region.

Today, I will do his work. I honor and carry on his legacy.

Nero had a grand vision for the Upper. When he did speak to me, it was all that would cross his lips. His vision for the future, a region not dependent on Lower elementals. A great Upper that is self-sufficient and thriving—continuously advancing. To make his dream a reality, we need more laborers, and who better to serve than those who saw fit to dishonor our contracts and still seek to sabotage us?

I wait for the militant in me to take over. I ready my body to slip into the sub-consciousness that battle brings on. It is the adrenaline rush of a raid that sends me into the automated skills mode that is so familiar and perfunctory.

The feeling never comes. This is no ordinary raid. We are not attacking enemy soldiers.

Tonight, we attack civilians.

I check again to confirm the transport ships are secure and ready for their impending cargo. I walk among the towering metal cages, unsettling and quiet as they wait to swallow our enemy. The aeros on guard will air control the pyro transporters. This ensures there will be too little oxygen to wield fire unless the pyros intend to suffocate themselves. Though, knowing their kind, the fire wielders might be spiteful enough to use up all the air and allow everyone to smother.

We have already stripped the terra transporters of natural land elements. It's protocol to replace any accessible material with magroginite, a manufactured metal that infuses magnetite with plastic compounds. This leaves even the strongest terras unable to wield it. The material makes an ideal restraint for the land wielders. Once we lift from the ground for travel, the terras will further disconnect from the land, leaving them incapacitated. Additionally, we coat the pyro transports with ice to remove any excess heat from the hot-headed elementals.

The outlying civilians already occupy some of our ice and magroginite chambers. A scoff sounds from behind me. I turn to see my second-in-command leaning against a supply crate, wordlessly studying me. The fine strands of his bone-straight black hair slip from his loose ponytail. They fall past his ears to frame the sharp edges of his angular face that always make him look so austere.

To others, it may appear as though I'm simply adhering to protocol. It seems I am taking particular care to ensure we are prepared to attack, but my second knows better. His already narrow eyes squint at me in a knowing glare. My closest friend since we were young boys attending the academy, Kai, knows I am stalling.

"You've checked the transporters already. You know they're secure. If we wait much longer, we will lose the optimal level of surprise," he says.

I know his words are truth. At daybreak, each terra will awaken, wide-eyed and smiling, ready to turn the green leaves to golden, brown, and red hues. Every second brings us closer to compromising the mission. Still, I cannot force myself to give the order.

"Aside from that," he says, "Admiral Malakai watches you."

I scarcely suppress an eyeroll. The prime policymaker's lackey reports my every move back to her.

"Prime Morgana does not need a reason to question your loyalty."

My second is right, as usual. The prime waits for me to slip up. She counts my days and has sent her minion off in battle to babysit. From the time I received the commander designation, I've been saddled with the depraved admiral.

"Patience, Lieutenant." I use his title, reminding him I have the last word. "There are still several hours until sunrise, and we both know none of those indolent terras or pyros will wake before then."

I force the insult from my lips, reminding myself they are the enemy. Hoping it will make engaging with the civilians more bearable, relying on it to deflect from my apprehension.

This is retaliation.

Only a few days ago, a group of warriors from this faction attacked an Upper transport. They stopped our enforcers en route as they were transferring captives to the Outer Region, our prison region. The group killed both Upper soldiers and the Lower captives.

Cannibalistic in their reckless rage, the imbeciles killed some of their own. The group they attacked were not combat soldiers; the prisoners were not theirs to execute. Even so, in true Lower fashion, their ignoble behavior heightened.

It was not enough that they reneged on our original trade agreements, the ones my father fought to secure. Nero pulled our region from the trenches of subservience, and into a place of preeminence through monumental breakthroughs in technology and medicine. His work to bring forth The Age of Innovation, rendered the Lowers essentially obsolete, and they've hated us for it. But because he was also a generous leader, Father allowed them to trade us labor for the services they still needed from the Upper.

Nero gave the Upper independence, and the Lower the opportunity for survival. Still, they have undermined us by trying to steal away those who voluntarily agreed to serve, and they continue to show their lack of honor at every turn. As much as I cannot stand the thought of attacking a civilian town, how else are we expected to respond to such blatant aggression?

The group of Lower warriors clearly saw an easy target and decided to make a statement. They were unconcerned with harming their own unarmed and vulnerable elementals in the process. If this faction has no regard for their own, why should I?

I walk to the edge of the glowing field that stretches before our camp like a living sea. In the night, while the world sleeps, their plant life awakens in a burst of luminescent colors. There is nothing like this in Central City. The floating city sits almost entirely on water. The walkways are nearly all manufactured glass or stone. There are too many buildings and too few terras to cultivate the garden-like landscape I see here. When I am out on the grounds, it never ceases to captivate me.

My battalion uses the sap to camouflage themselves among the trees and shrubs bordering the town. They wait for my signal. It is a command I struggle to give, no matter how I try to convince myself it is necessary.

Along the tree line, I spot a small stick doll, no doubt some terra child's plaything. I pick it up to inspect the fragile twig arms and stiff leafy hair. It's a reminder that we will capture more than just civilian adults today.

Small children from the bordering groups already cry and whine in their tiny cages of magroginite and ice. The thick transporter walls trap all sound within, but their cries ring in my ears, regardless.

These are my enemies. I remind myself so much that it becomes a mantra. The Lower elementals have stolen everything from me. My father would not hesitate in their capture, and neither should I.

The prime's voice cackles in my mind. *You will never be your father.* A harsh reminder that I will never live up to the great Prime Nero. An unnecessary admonition coming from Morgana.

My father did more in his time as Prime Policymaker of the Upper Region than any other in our history. There isn't a piece of tech or medicinal cure we do not owe to him. Apparently, I am the only unremarkable thing that has come from his life, and he never missed an opportunity to let me know it.

I could not earn his pride in life, the least I can do now is avenge his death.

One of my corporals gives me a sidelong glance. Her eyes cut in my direction, then back toward the town with a grimace. Anxiety settles over many of my finest soldiers, who fidget and shuffle in place, waiting on my command. Typically, stone-still, and robotic in their militant focus, they shift—uneasy—glancing to and from me, as if to speak up. As if to challenge the orders even I know are wrong. But we are soldiers. We respect the command. We understand our place.

They look to me for direction, and I cannot waver. My orders are explicit. I must take the terra faction. I will bring all surviving elementals back to Central City. There can be no opportunity for their retreat, and no option for our failure.

Activating the small comm unit embedded in my forearm, I project the screen and view my soldier's coordinates. With the push of a button, I let them know we are ready to move in. I signal for the soldiers behind me, still hiding in the shrubs, to move forward. They creep along the forest floor like shadows, never making a sound, never entirely visible. Tactically painted, they camouflage into the moving and swaying foliage of the terra forest.

Once we've infiltrated the town, the silence that welcomes us is eerie and off-putting. I give the command to begin our raid. One by one, we take the small houses over. Our strategy is to capture the elementals quickly and peacefully before the others become aware. If we can keep the panic at bay, we will spare more lives. If we can take them off guard, there will be fewer unprepared civilians we're forced to fight.

As my soldiers remove civilians from their homes, they envelop the captives' heads in water to mute their shouts. It is a slow process that requires an aero to attend each extraction to supply the captives with breathing air while they're transported to the ships. I estimate at least five dozen homes infiltrated before the first blast of fire whizzes by.

"Incoming!" Kai shouts from his place several feet away from me, leading his own band of hydros.

The flame flies over my head, so close its heat stings my skin, and hits a water wielder behind me. With one of our soldiers down, Kai springs into action. My second pulls water from the ground, whipping it in the air and throwing it at the attacking pyro who screams to alert his neighbors.

Healers race from their beds to investigate the chaos, and more lights illuminate the once quiet homes.

Our cover is gone.

CHAPTER 3
KARA

PANDEMONIUM ENSUES OUTSIDE OUR home. Streams of water rush the ground like river currents while the air cyclones around us. My mother springs into action. Before I realize what's happening, she's already extended her vines to wrap around two Upper elementals, strangling them in an instant.

She draws deeper into the battle, as I stand dumbstruck in our doorway, observing the mayhem. Upper soldiers attack her from every angle. She erects walls of stone to protect herself from the ensuing elements. Air and water assault her with unrelenting speed, but she skillfully darts each attack.

I'm tempted to stay close to my dad. He's only a Level One wielder. He pushes past me and through the door. Looking down at his hands, I see they already hold magsidian axes. This is not his first battle, and he can hold his own. Running into the turmoil, he wields his axes like they are extensions of his own limbs. Seamless in his movement, he is deadly with his strike.

Before engaging, I try to understand what's happening. Amidst the fighting, I see Upper elementals dragging our faction members from their homes. There are children caged in ice and magroginite—elders dragged along the floor.

I shake my head, sure this is a nightmare. We are at war, but this isn't right. These soldiers shouldn't be here. Our realm has rules. There's a code we uphold, even in war. This goes against it all.

A ribbon of water whips around my head, pulling me from the doorway and starving me of air. I don't know from which way the element is cast, so I look to disrupt everyone in my vicinity. Reaching to the ground, I dig into the soil and force it to turn. With a powerful push, I bear down on the floor, whipping the dirt beneath me, causing it to ripple and knock over all who stand nearby.

Once the helmet of water has dropped, I can focus in on the nearby Uppers. Two hydros and an aero. With my hands still buried deep in the dirt, I command roots from the soil to wrap around their falling bodies, ensnaring them.

"What are you doing here?" I demand. "Why have you come?"

I understand this is retaliation, but to attack innocents? People of honor take retribution on the battlefield, not in the homes of unsuspecting civilians.

The Upper elementals scowl, sealing their lips and thrashing against their root bindings. The middle aero locks eyes with mine, his narrowing in a glare. I feel the air pull from my lungs as he extracts his element from me. These Uppers will tell me nothing. Before he can suffocate me, I push my hands further into the ground, opening it to swallow the three elementals whole. Once they're buried, I sprint away to find Rae.

She's a Level One wielder, and unlike my dad, she doesn't stand a chance in battle. I can't leave my best friend defenseless against these trained soldiers. I cannot let them harm the child that grows inside her.

I rush across the town square. Elementals claw and crawl over each other like ants erupting from a disturbed mound. Frenzied men and women run in every direction while element-made weapons soar through the space. When I reach Rae's home, the front door gapes open, and water trickles down her steps.

I am not surprised when I search and find the house vacant.

Rae is gone.

The space illuminates in a flash as a lightning bolt pulls from the sky. Striking the ground, it incinerates a group of air wielders, leaving a pile of ash behind. Only a Level Three fire wielder can command lightning. Cinis is nearby.

"Kara!" His voice comes from behind me. By the time I turn around, he's already at my back. "Are you alright?" Cinis bends his head to look at my eyes, appraising me, searching for any hint of injury.

"I'm fine," I say, putting my hands against his strong chest as he pulls me in. "What's happening? Why are they *here*?" I ask, praying he can give me some answer.

He shakes his head. "I don't know. I saw them loading elementals into transporters."

We look around at the battle enclosing us. Although we have the numbers, our opponents have the skill. They brought a handful of soldiers to fight a sleeping town of civilians. We're overpowered and do not stand a chance.

Cinis looks down at me as if he can read my very thoughts. "We have to get as many out as we can."

"My grandmother," I say. She'll know how to get the faction away.

Grandma was our faction's last leader before my mother succeeded her. She's a powerful land wielder who can lead our people to safety.

We search for her, locating her almost instantly. At the edge of town, she wields a garganthian tree. Fighting through the colossal timber, she wields large branches that swoop down to knock away her opponents. Massive roots lift from the ground and slap down around Upper elementals, snapping them in one swipe.

A group of faction members surround her, mostly children, with some adults and elders. I look for Rae among them, but she's not there. They stand behind my grandmother, wielding their own elements in defense. The pyros only produce pitiful sparks that flicker in their shaking hands. The terras cannot wield their fingers into vines. They're all Level Ones. She protects them, her plans aligning with ours.

There are still a dozen Upper elementals closing in on her and the small piece of our faction she is trying to save.

"Open the soil," Cinis says.

He needs my help quickly accessing the elemental device terras and pyros share. *Magma*. It is both the most destructive and fruitful device available to wielders, equally accessible by terras and pyros. I stoop to part the dirt, reaching deep, until I can feel the heat rise from its core. He pools molten lava from the soil and wields it around the line of enemies.

As the lava boils to the surface, it scorches my sleeves and burns my skin, but it's a pain I can handle, connecting with my element in the magma. I'm steadfast in holding the ground open, ensuring we incinerate our enemy before I yield.

"Kara," Grandma says.

I rise, shaking the magma from my hands before running to her. We collide in an embrace, and I find a moment of solace in her arms, however fleeting.

"Grandma, you have to get them out of here."

"Yes, there are more waiting outside the town," she says, and I exhale. "But we have nowhere to go."

"Take them to my faction." Cinis steps to my side. "The Smithers will take you in. Tell my father I've sent you and give him this."

He removes the obsidian pendant from his neck, handing it to my grandmother. I clutch the matching stone hanging to rest atop my chest. It's the one he gave me only two nights ago when he asked me to be his.

Panic speeds my pulse. "Cinis, go. You can't stay here. There's no way for us to win this. Lead them back to your faction and return home."

He grabs my hand in his. "I'm staying right here."

Shock hits me and reverberates against my core. His deep onyx eyes bore into mine, and the air escapes my lungs as shame thickens my throat. He's choosing to stay. The man I was so ready to leave is choosing to stay behind in a faction I was going to abandon only minutes ago.

I don't think I can atone for the dishonor I've done to my faction. And as a wall of water slams into us, I realize now is not the time. More Uppers have drawn in, focusing on the spectacle of elemental wielding that caused the magma eruption.

"Go now!" I yell to my grandmother as a hydro pierces the ground with jutting streams of hot water.

Geysers erupt all around us, effectively hiding the water wielders who manipulate them. Cinis heats the streams until they're nothing but steam. Icicles whiz past my head, nicking my eyebrow as one grazes me. I leave Cinis to deal with the hydros and set my sights on a Level Three aero that's effectively taking out half my faction single-handed.

I can tell from his uniform that the aero is an officer. From the ornaments that adorn it, I know he's high ranking.

He turns to look at me and pauses, his icy gray eyes flickering with curiosity. I use the opportunity to strike. Lifting my hand in the air, I slam it down to the ground, parting the land beneath him. Thrown off balance, he falls, and I erect walls of stone to box him in.

The moment I enclose him in the terra prison, he uses his element to blast through it. The walls of stone crumble, falling in a heap. I wield the rocks and aim them at his head. I feel the winds whip around me in a cyclone and am swept up in their current. I call to the roots in the soil that lift and wrap themselves around me, ending the spinning. I pull myself closer to the dirt and throw it into his twister. Though dust flies and clouds his vision, I can see clearly.

Suddenly, the cyclone stops and with it goes all the surrounding air. I choke on *nothing,* my lungs burning to be filled.

I extend a vine from my hand and whip it around the aero's arm. From it, I push thorns and feel his blood trickle down the lianas as if it rolls across my own fingers. He cries out, his eyes narrowing into a vicious glare.

Again, he cuts himself free, slashing through my vines. I hiss at the pain, angered even more. At my full strength, I wouldn't feel the hurt of injury to my elemental devices. The battle's depleted me, and after all the essence I've spent, I'm working on little more than reserves. So entwined with my element, I feel every nick and break as if it were truly my own.

Everything around me shatters into a million unsalvageable pieces. Chaos and carnage overwhelm my senses. The stench of burned flesh bombards my nostrils, while the screams of my despondent cohorts claw at my eardrums.

I can taste the salt of water hanging heavy in the air, out of place in an area so far from the sea. Heat wraps around me, oppressive in its embrace, as flames climb up the walls of the houses behind me.

It is always a risk to build homes of wood anywhere pyros might wield, but the Mining Faction's allegiance with the Upper has hindered our access to stone for fire resistant construction. Though they belong to the Terra Clan, the Golds have turned their back on our region, aligning themselves with these monsters.

Icicles fly from the officer's hands, aimed at my feet. They pierce the ground around my body, and I see he does not mean to injure me. He grows the icicles from small spikes to large bars, closing me in. Pushing my hands into the ground, I disrupt and move the surrounding soil, causing them all to fall. I whip the soil again, turning it into a huge wave that I aim to cover him with, when another cry rings out.

I look to see my father fighting another air wielder. His axe whizzes through the air, tipped black with poison. A blast of wind throws it off course, barely nicking the aero he's engaging with. He lifts the other axe to follow, but before it can leave his clenched fist, an icicle pierces his neck.

Everything stops. I drop the soil I've been wielding and run to my father.

Before I can reach him, ice encloses around me. I fall to the ground, unable to move my arms and legs. A cloak of ice becomes a straitjacket and only inches from my father, I'm forced to lie there and watch him bleed out.

CHAPTER 4
SORREN

I T'S NOT LONG BEFORE I connect the deep green eyes and matching brown locks. The word "Dad" need not leave her mouth before I realize who she was crawling toward.

My core tightens and I cringe as she screams.

Just a moment ago the woman before me stood, commanding the surrounding turmoil. Her natural aptitude for her element apparent in the uniquely chaotic and utterly genius manner she wielded her attack. Seeing the elemental force fall—crumbling like an autumn leaf—should bring me joy. It should bring me triumph, but all I feel is guilt.

I remind myself that I must show strength. These people are not like us. They do not know mercy. These terras are not like the Gold terras, who've maintained our favor and aligned with our cause. They do not understand kindness. We must meet these Lowers with force and aggression. It is all they will respond to. It is all they have displayed.

I call for a soldier to cart her up with the rest of them, leaving her father lying dead on the ground.

"You're a pretty thing, aren't you?" I hear Malakai sneer behind me. "I'll make sure you're my personal servant. You'll pay for every drop of blood your dear father took from me."

I turn to see him carting off the terra I've captured. Before I can stop myself, I snatch the air from his lungs. Malakai drops the girl, and I throw an air pocket beneath her before she can hit the ground.

Malakai falls to his knees, clutching his throat. I bend to meet him. "You will do well, Admiral, to mind your tongue." His thick fingers claw at his neck as he kneels before me. It is a unique torture for an elemental to be cut off from their element. "I think you've had enough battle for today. See your way to a medic. Your wound is festering."

Once I've released the air, the aero fills his lungs with his element, murder blazing in his eyes. I am not surprised that Malakai so liberally taunts the terra with her fate. All Lower captives of the Regional Battles serve the Upper. Malakai grew up with servants. Kai and I grew up in the military academy where there were none. For Malakai, it is as conventional as commanding the wind, but for me it is as innate as eating fire.

"Lieutenant," I call Kai. "Please see this one to the terra transport."

He gives a wary nod, looking between Malakai and me. Although my rank is superior, he knows it is not wise for me to have made such a public spectacle of undermining the prime's watchdog.

In true hydro form, Kai is practical above all else. Hydros are notorious for their even temperament. It is both their most admiral and most annoying trait. Even their sexless deity, Hydris, cannot bother with such impracticalities as gender distinctions, remaining fluid in all things. Hydros are as pliable and keen as the element they wield.

In this moment, I wish I could disregard the practicalities. I should have released the captured terra on Malakai. Let him make those threats while she was volatile and unbound.

I might have if I weren't uncertain in my own abilities to subdue her. Fighting her alone has drained most of my essence, and I will likely fail in a challenge to her until it is regenerated.

We cart more Lower elementals from the battle. They range in age, size, and wielding capability. The defeat that plays on their bloodied faces mirrors the defeat I feel. A feeling that baffles me because there ought to be triumph in its place.

This faction's people never stood a chance against my brigade, and there is no honor in this victory. I've sold my soul to win this fight and will leave this field a lesser man for it.

Now that battling is all but done, the town settles, and we prepare to depart. As Kai takes care in lifting the girl from the ground, a comm notification comes through from the scouts we'd sent out to make sure there are no stragglers. I accept the call, casting a hologram of Calix's face into the air before us.

"Commander." His words are breathy in their urgency. "They're escaping."

The terra girl's head snaps to the hologram, but I am silent, allowing him to continue.

"A group of Lowers has made it out of the town. They've evaded Ciel's soldiers and are heading west."

Damn it, Ciel.

I know better than to believe the admiral's group of special operatives could not constrain the fugitive elementals. Only a few years my senior, Ciel's battle skill and strategic mind have also progressed her through military rank more rapidly than our peers. Her obstinateness and recalcitrant nature are the only attributes keeping her from exceeding her station.

She is skilled, and a group of unprepared civilians evading her is laughable. This is a mercy release. She has defied my orders and allowed them to leave.

The terra's mouth opens to say something, then quickly shuts as she thinks better of it. The crease of her brow deepens as she pulls air in and out with her quickening breaths.

Malakai pushes forward. "How many?" he says.

"Maybe a few hundred."

"We must send soldiers out at once," the admiral commands where it is not his place.

"Stand down, Admiral," I order.

The large group will be difficult for the terras to move, and even more difficult to defend. Capturing them will be like plucking grapes off a vine. They didn't stand a chance before and certainly don't now. But going after them will reveal Ciel's insubordination, and I truly have no desire to continue this fight.

Malakai's teeth grind as he waits for my order to continue. The terra at Kai's side sends me a silent plea for mercy. I look over to see tears brim her eyes and know that this is the very last thing there is to take from her.

"Let's gather what we have and move out. We have won."

Malakai's face reddens. The soldier flanking him opens then shuts her mouth in a challenge she dares not follow through with. I feel the air release from the terra's lungs in a deep sigh and am solidified in my position.

"Our orders—" Malakai pushes through clenched teeth. I raise my hand to stop his rebuttal. I know our orders. I know I am to return *every* surviving Lower, but this is madness.

"It is likely only a group of lower-level elementals, children, and the elderly." I know that is what my strategy would be, should I have been on the receiving end of this attack.

I clench my jaw as the battle roars unabated. There is so much screaming, so many sobs.

Battle is loud. The guttural yells and throaty moans of soldiers fading from this life are as inherent to me as the whoosh of a breeze.

These are not battle noises. The screams I hear are too high pitched, holding a terror that grates me. The sobs that spring forth from the battlefield and transport carriers hold the truest heartbreak I have ever encountered. The sounds drive me insane, and it is all I can do not to claw them from my ears.

I must finish this.

"It does not matter who they are," Malakai returns.

"Our transports are already full, we have enough—"

"We have orders," he says.

"Remember your station, Admiral, and stand down." I can no longer ignore the moral questions that flag at us taking a civilian town.

When given the order, I was uneasy. I did not agree with it, but I continued, as was my duty. Here and now, watching children, elderly, and the weak, fall—bleeding—ripped away from our grasp just to be imprisoned again, shakes my fantasies of nobility and duty.

Kai comes behind me, still holding the terra. He puts a hand on my shoulder, opening his mouth to speak; no doubt more practicality. Malakai pushes forward, interrupting him, "Why, your father would have—"

"My father would have killed you for insubordination." I stand chest-to-chest with Malakai. My eyes are level with his, and our faces are so close that I can see each angry scar that mars his skin. They are not delicate or discreet. The scars fall in deep red gashes that leave indents throughout his aged face. He deserves each one, and I would love nothing more than to add to his collection.

"He would've run an ice pick through your skull to make an example of you." I press my hand to Malakai's bloody temple to illustrate, allowing an icicle to emerge from my palm, just enough to cut his skin. "Would you still like for me to emulate my father?"

He is silent.

I cannot suppress the predatorial smile that stretches my lips to show my teeth, as I watch a bead of sweat roll down his forehead and nose. He swallows, his glare burning into me, before falling to the ground.

I release the aero, turning my back on him, not willing to spend any more time and energy justifying my decision to the Level Two admiral.

"Prepare the fallen for interment," I say to the officer as I walk away.

We must freeze our fallen soldiers. The aeros will remain in their crypts of ice, while the hydros will be returned to the sea.

I look at the mass of Lower bodies littering the battleground. There will be no honor in giving them an aero's burial, so I leave them for their Lower brethren to lay to rest, should they return. There is nothing more I can do for our enemy.

I hear Malakai snarl as he obeys my command.

This is not over.

CHAPTER 5
KARA

G RIEF CHOKES ME AND trips my steps as they move us into the transporters, pushing me into a space with other terras. I struggle against the ice, still encasing me. It burns against my skin and slows my heartbeat as a deep lethargy seeps in. Still, I search the bare magroginite walls for a weakness in our ship.

I have to get out. I have to save my people. I can still salvage this.

If I could just find something to grasp—even metal would do.

There is nothing.

Although most of my people are unable to manipulate metals and stones, the Upper went through the trouble of removing even that from the transporters. The extensive area is barren of any implements for escape. Thousands of terras pack the space, crammed together like florets in a sunflower, leaving room for nothing else.

Raging against the magroginite wall, I slam my body into it, hoping to shatter the ice restraining me.

I will end these Uppers. I swear that—before I take my dying breath—they will all pay for what they have taken from me.

For all my useless thrashing, I don't even chip the ice. I stop struggling and turn to lean against the unnatural metal wall.

As the transporter lifts, my element pulls farther and farther from my grasp. It pulls from my core and out through my fingertips in reluctant snapping tendrils. Each one breaks, until there is nothing left. And when I am achingly empty, grief wraps its thorny arms around my chest, squeezing me until I cannot breathe.

There is nothing I can do for my father, or my people. I have lost it all.

My throat tightens, and I struggle to pull in the air I need. Tears pour over my eyelids to fall on the ice that encloses me, freezing with the rest of my bindings.

When we are at an ungodly altitude, the aeros allow our icy restraints to melt, replacing them with thick magroginite shackles.

Whimpers and fervent whispers rumble throughout the room. Across from me, Calla frantically smooths her daughter's curls. She clutches Tilly to her chest as if the tight grip could stop an Upper from snatching her away at will.

"Mommy, I'm cold," Tilly whines, as fat tears stream down her cheeks and fall from her tiny chin.

Calla quickly shushes her, whipping her head back and forth to see if any guards are watching them. "It's okay, baby. It'll be over soon."

Calla buries her mouth in Tilly's messy ginger locks, shushing against her scalp. The four-year-old is a pyro and should not be on a ship with terras. The soldiers must have mistaken the young fire wielder and assumed she was a terra like her mother. I thank Gaia for her mercy.

Vacant stares line the faces of many terras, while some foolishly pound on the transport walls, unwilling to accept defeat. Others look to find me.

I want to hide from the eyes that beseech me for guidance. The Upper has destroyed my faction. And just as I'd always suspected, I could not save it.

I gave everything I could—used every skill and tactic I've spent my life refining. Still, it wasn't enough.

I was not enough.

In the same way I'd failed Caelum, and Emi—and so many others—I have failed my people.

As I sit here on the transporter floor, my faction town lays in ruin. The wooden homes likely still burn, if they are not warping under the tide of water the damned hydros unleashed on the only home I've ever known.

This faction was my responsibility, and for all the elemental level and skill Gaia has blessed me with, I could not protect it.

I search the crowd for my mother and pray to Gaia that she does not lie on our town's ground like my father.

My father is dead.

I couldn't go to him, couldn't hold his hand while he lay there dying. I couldn't even say goodbye.

I squeeze my eyes shut, but all I can see is him lying on our town floor, looking up at *nothing*, as his life flowed from his neck and into the soil beneath him.

I don't have anything left to give to the people whose eyes ask me to lead.

In the few hours of twilight, before the first rays of day reached across our world, the Upper took everything.

I can't meet the eyes that ask for more than I have left to give. Every pitiful look or tormented stare reminds me of just how much I have failed—just how much I have lost.

So, I sag against the wall behind me, and bury my head in my knees.

I can't look at them anymore.

CHAPTER 6
SORREN

O NCE WE HAVE SETTLED in on our journey, I survey the ship. Many of my soldiers cannot meet my gaze, nor can they meet one another's. I see a corporal's eyes squeeze shut in a brief reprieve, as if he can block out the moans and sounds of defeat reverberating from our captives.

I remind myself that we are victorious. In doing what we must to progress the region, we are righteous. Capturing the Healing Faction is a tremendous boon for my people. Bringing the healers to my region will only compound my father's tireless work.

The medical advancements that he led ensure that no Upper will be subject to a terra's prejudices or arrogance when seeking healing. We are no longer exposed to the possibility that the terras could cut our supply to medicine, rendering us helpless to fight illness and injury. Now the same terras who inspired such innovations will serve to advance them.

I have honored my father and region immensely.

As my soldiers progress through the crowd of terras, releasing them from their ice restraints, I hear the shriek of a little girl, followed by a woman's wail. I turn to see one of my soldiers rip a child from the arms of a Lower who must be her mother. As the young child kicks and screams in one soldier's arms, her mother claws at the back of another, carrying her away.

"Soldier, halt!" My tone holds all the chilling intent that I try to keep from escaping my palms and freezing the cargo bay floor. "Explain yourself," I order, unable to comprehend why he would cause the captives any further distress.

He quickly dips his head, still holding the terra woman. "Commander, she is a terra, and the child is a pyro who will need to stay in a chilled space."

The woman's eyes widen as the little girl begins to cry. Bile collects at the back of my throat at the sight of her little lip trembling. "The child remains with her mother."

The woman scrambles toward her daughter as my soldier speaks up.

"But—"

I raise my hand to stop him before he can earn the consequence associated with questioning a superior.

"A child cannot melt magroginite. She remains with her mother." I glare at the soldier who is only following protocol, rage festering in my chest like a cyclone grasping for momentum. I clench my fist, tensing my muscles then releasing them, attempting to quell my misguided fury with each breath.

The soldier nods, following my command, and I turn to leave the cargo deck.

The rest of our flight is turbulent. Carrying so much cargo, at such a high altitude, is a precarious feat, but we must take such measures. When transporting terras, we must lift them as far away from their element as possible.

My mind races through the entire voyage. Anticipation that I never let bubble to the surface festers in my chest. I have no doubt the prime is aware I've disobeyed orders, and I know the consequence will be severe.

Once we arrive in Central City, I give the command to unload our prisoners. As my soldiers corral the captives, I exit the transporter, the familiar scent of salt and sea wafting into the ship as I open the exit hatch. Although we are not hydros, this is my father's city. He changed the destiny of our region through the work he did in this capital, and every facet of this place holds his ghost, ominous and condemnatory, haunting me beyond the grave.

When I descend to the landing field floor, a line of Capitol Enforcers awaits me, each standing stiff and at attention. Anticipation prickles across my skin as I force my facial expressions to remain cool and unfazed, though wind swirls in my palms, breezing up my arms and driving a chill through my body.

The prime emerges through the gates, trailed by her usual entourage of guards, and select policymakers. My soldiers follow me down from the ship, and as she approaches, we each stop to slam a fist against our chests, bowing in respect.

Prime Policymaker Morgana appears aloof as she walks past us to appraise the cargo, we have en tote. "Very good, Commander, I see you've completed your mission, but are these all the survived elementals from the faction?"

Malakai's back straightens, and a discrete smile plays on his lips. He's already reported to the prime.

I look at the captives and back at her. "No. A group of a few hundred escaped."

She appraises me, pinching her lips together in a sneer that does little to conceal her excitement.

"Very well." She lifts her hand, and in the next moment, I am surrounded by water. It cuts off my entire air supply, leaving only the tiniest hole for me to breathe, but not wield.

She leans in and I can barely hear her through the water. "You are under arrest, Commander."

Kai pushes through the crowd. "What is his charge?"

I am taken aback by the practical hydro's challenge of our prime policymaker.

Morgana's eyes lock with mine as her lip curls up to reveal her canines. "Treason."

CHAPTER 7
KARA

I DIDN'T LIFT MY head until I felt the transport slow. My fingertips stung as my element grew nearer, signifying our landing. The Upper elementals carted us from the transporter like herded cattle.

There's a disruption up ahead, and I wonder if one of my faction members has attempted to escape. I know it is useless.

The soldiers push us forward, past the gate and toward a transporter train. I frantically scan the crowd for my mother. My eyes touch each body standing before me, and none belongs to the only parent I have left. I accept she has passed on, like my father, and anguish knowing there is no one left to bury their bodies.

Will my grandmother go back to enact our burial ritual? Lay to rest the fallen terras of our faction? That is the only way for their essence to recycle and move on to bring life to the trees and foliage we are so connected to. Who'll burn the fallen pyros who could never find peace buried in the soil? Will my entire faction suffer in eternal unrest?

The soldiers don't relent in their corralling. They shove us forward and push us together. I catch sight of thick black curls and can't snap my mouth shut before calling out to her. "Rae!"

I spot my best friend and a mixture of joy and grief overwhelms me in knowing that she is alive but did not escape with my grandmother and the others.

"Kara!" she shouts back, pushing her way to me. The soldiers surrounding her force her away, loading her into a separate boxcar.

"No," I whimper as they separate us again and load me into a car of terras.

I hear a soldier shout, "Put the pyro over here! He'll cause less trouble among the terras."

Cinis.

His face is bloody and bruised, with the beginnings of frost burn forming on his cheek. They shove him into our car, and he stumbles against me, unable to bear his own weight. I work to keep us stabilized as he trips over me.

"Cinis, are you alright? You should have gone back."

"I won't leave you or this faction. Whatever happens, no matter what, I'm here." He struggles to keep my gaze as his heavy head sways.

I worry over his injuries. His forehead swells, blood dries and crusts where it's poured from his wounds. His eye is already blackened and swelling shut. I do my best to brace Cinis, as he is unsteady on his feet. The man before me has given up everything for my faction, and I'm more acutely aware than ever of how little I deserve him.

We spend the ride swaying back and forth, trying to maintain our balance as the transport bumps and turns. Time morphs, making it feel as though we ride for hours, and yet in no time at all. Our bodies pull forward in unison as the vehicle comes to a halt.

The side wall lifts, and we are once again ushered out into single file lines. The car opens to a massive field. Thousands of people line in neat rows behind dull magroginite fencing. They are all that remain of my faction.

Latticing magroginite encloses an area large enough to encompass our town's harvesting garden. It's out of place in a space that only holds sand and grass, as if it serves this purpose alone.

Holding us.

My line progresses forward, and as we inch to the front, I glimpse a holding station just before the fence entrance. There, I can see one person after the next twist their head to the side. They're forced to lay it on their left shoulder, exposing the right side of their neck.

Emrick is next. He jerks his body away from the soldiers, thrashing against his binds and toward the next line. I look over to see them processing Rae.

"This one is too weak," an enforcer says to another. "Put her with the others."

His words are so dismissive, as if he's talking about a farmed traelu being rejected from the slaughter. The enforcer at his side grips Rae's arm, jerking her from the line.

"Get your hands off her! *Don't fucking touch her!*" Emrick thrashes his body against the enforcer holding him. "*Rae!*" he screams.

Two more enforcers join, grabbing Emrick's shoulders and pushing his head to the side. The chief officer lifts what looks like a syringe, plunging it into the terra's flesh. He lets out a cry, and I see the veins of his neck blue and bulging.

They bring a magroginite collar around him and snap it shut. These are the same collars the captives wore. The same collar I tried to pry from Caelum's neck before he fell to his death, attempting to flee me. The other enforcer grips Emrick's arm and carts him across the fence line. My heart quickens with my breathing, each step I take toward the station heightening my panic. I can't break my gaze from Rae, as they cart her off, away from the rest of us. I scan the space, looking for a way to get to her.

"Don't, Kara." Cinis's eyes are heavy on mine as he shakes his head, already aware of what I'm thinking. "It'll be okay," he coos behind me. Lying to me, as if I'm a child.

It won't be okay. Things will never be okay.

His eyes do not leave Emrick as they drag our comrade to his place behind the fencing. The terra is a reminder to us of just how futile resistance is.

Our pointless struggle against the Upper has ruined us. They have stomped us out at every turn, blocked every recovery attempt, and stolen the Gold Faction's allegiance. Working from the inside out, they crippled our entire region through a single strategic alliance. Cutting our trade from the mining faction, our region's defeat began long before we realized. With limited access to metal, the Upper crippled our infrastructure and weaponry. By cutting our coal imports, they rendered our intricately laid out power grids useless, along with all the tech that relied on it.

We were grossly outmaneuvered from the start, continuing to fight while all we had to gain was damage. We never stood a chance, and this will be no exception.

When my turn comes, I do not stall or hesitate. I turn my head and feel the bite of acid pierce my skin. When the collar of manufactured metal closes around my neck, I gasp at the sharp pain of two interior needles biting into me. As I'm pulled from the line and carted past the fence, my mind begins to haze, confusing my thoughts and dulling my anxiety.

Behind me, Cinis stumbles along. They collar the last of our group and usher them into the magroginite cage. As the gate closes, panic speeds my pulse, working past whatever injection they gave me to mute it. My throat tightens as claustrophobia makes me frantic. I grasp at my element, but it evades me. I cannot access my wielding abilities, and my mind grows unsure of how to even command them. The elementals around me mirror Caelum and the other captives we tried to rescue—dazed and unable to wield.

"Kara, what are you doing?" Cinis presses against me, his brows clenched.

"We have to get out." My words jumble together as I heave in air, trying to fill my lungs, dizzying from hyperventilation. Cinis's eyes squint, the obsidian of his irises softening on me. His face cracks with overwhelming pity, but I don't want it. I just want to escape.

The air whips around us, and I look to see who's controlling it. Hovering in the sky, above the cage's open top, an aero stands commanding the wind. He is no ordinary elemental. The sight of him is terrifying, and a shiver shakes my spine at the thought of him entering our space, like a vine viper into a kibblet hole.

I squint to make sure I am seeing correctly. The man's skin is an icy shade of blue, almost gray. Frost covers his arms and neck and I push forward from my place in line to take a better look, Cinis scrambling behind me. The aero's eyes stare ahead at the air he wields, and I see they are devoid of pupils. No color center's the monster's eyes, they are iced over and white as the brittle hair whipping around his head.

A woman flanks his side, standing on the invisible platform of air. Her features are equally terrifying, but in an elegant and almost beautiful way. I cannot tell if her skin is simply pale or completely translucent. Pointy fins protrude from her head where ears should be. Long tendrils of bright green sea-weed flow from her crown like a mane of hair. Iridescent scales outline her sharp-boned face and cluster down her collarbones to cover her chest. There I see a delicate chain, draped across her collar and twining down to cross around her abdomen. It is thin and doesn't seem to be composed of metal or any other land material. The chain glows a bright coppery gold, and pulses around the woman.

She opens her mouth in an O that frames needle-sharp teeth. It appears as if she's singing, but water pours from her mouth instead of melody. Still, I can see several elementals transfixed to her, swaying to her silent song.

I've never seen anything like this. These perverse creatures do not belong in the natural world. I fear that Aelious and Hydris have come down to imprison us, then realize what they truly are.

"Immortals," I gasp, looking at the god-blessed elementals of every fable told to us in youth and intertwined into all the songs and festivals of our culture. I gawk at the imminently powerful beings I'd always thought to be figurative rather than literal, only metaphors to emphasize our gods' favor.

"That's impossible," Cinis says, his mouth hanging open while he looks at the same beasts as me. "They're not real. Immortals don't exist."

I don't waste time trying to convince him otherwise.

Fear holds a tight grasp on me as saliva gathers in my mouth, the contents of my stomach preparing to erupt. I kick off my shoes, grasping at the power in the sand and soil beneath. Beside me, Cinis's face does not draw from our immortal captors.

"What could they want with us?" he murmurs, and I'm too busy grasping at my element to guess.

Cinis draws into himself, taking in all the heat he can muster. A blue vein bulges from his forehead and he falls to his knees. With a loud crack, I see sparks fly from his fingertips. He shouldn't need to exert any effort to kindle a flame, but this minor act has taken everything from him. He moves his fingers to my binding, pushing more heat into his blaze. Although he focuses on the chain in between my wrists, the flame is scorching and burns my skin. Once it's hot enough to melt the plastic, I pull at the shackles until they break apart.

With free hands, I waste no time trying to break his binds. I attempt to push vines through my fingers to use as a picklock, but I can't grasp the essence that is as ornate to me as the blood running through my veins.

"The tubes. See if you can remove them." Cinis looks at my neck, and I feel for the vials connected to the needles biting into my neck.

I pinch and pry at them until they wiggle free. My fingertips sting as my essence flows from them. Like blood flowing back into sleeping limbs, I feel my abilities awaken.

I dislodge the needles from their tubes. This metal is pure, and not the plastic infused magroginite used in the collars and bindings. Although my abilities remain minimal, when I grip the needles, they bend and conform at my command. I use them to pick the lock on Cinis's collar. The others around us see what we're doing, and try to follow suit, but none of them can summon the aether needed. They cannot free themselves. We must work fast.

I fumble with Cinis's collar, pulling it apart with as much care as my trembling fingers can manage. He does not wince when the needles, dripping with blood, pull from his flesh.

Before we can move on to free the others, the spinning air quickens, forcing us to bear down and stabilize our balance. It pulls at our flesh, tugging at the essence within. I yelp as the aether flowing in me begins to jerk and force its way to the surface of my skin.

The immortal's silent song cascades from her mouth in a waterfall of liquid. A high pitch emits from her, and it takes a hold of my focus, threatening to separate me from conscious thought. I feel my essence lull away, as if it's being tugged by tiny strings from my chest and through my fingertips. I clutch my hands into fists, refusing to relinquish any piece of my gift to the monsters more akin to gods than elementals.

The wind whipping around us picks up speed, throwing us off balance. The high-pitched sound coming from the woman blackens our vision, and I lose all hope of escaping this cataclysm.

I crash into Cinis. His arms wrap around me so tightly, I can steady my breathing against the thunder of his heart.

"Don't be afraid, it'll be okay." He moves his lips across the crown of my head.

Do these creatures want to kill us? My entire faction, decimated in a matter of hours.

With our senses evading us, resistance is futile. The only thing I can do is pray.

I call out to Gaia, the sacred deity of my people. I pour my soul out, praying for her protection. I beg the mother of all land wielders to show mercy to Cinis and Rae. I pray for the child still growing in Rae's womb, and I beg for the deity to spare my people.

When the rushing winds swallow the sound of my desperate prayers, I think I hear a buzz, but the frequency is so high I can't be sure. I bury my face into Cinis's chest as he weaves his fingers through my hair. The people around me gasp as the wind seems to pierce through our flesh and wrap itself around our insides. It pulls at the elemental essence within me, and pain radiates through my core. A rush of energy flows into me, overpowering each of my nerve endings until it feels like every cell of my body implodes.

Cinis grunts, gripping me tighter to him as silence falls upon us.

I can't see, but his body—along with everything else — seems to slip away, until all that is left for me to hold on to is the thump of his beating heart.

CHAPTER 8
SORREN

TEN WEEKS LATER

The bars of my cell ping as I run an icepick across them. I fling it into the makeshift bullseye I've carved into the wall of dirt, closing me in. One after another, I drive picks into the center, each crushing the one that lay before it. I try to fill my days with anything to busy my mind. I've lost track of the time I've spent down here. I stopped trying to count somewhere around six weeks, and still more time has passed.

I assess my guards. Four hydros and two aeros cramped in the small room outside my cell, dozens of feet underground. No matter the precautions they take, no matter how far they bury me below the surface, we all know I can still escape. The moment I attempt a breakout, the hydros will surround me with water, and the aeros will work to regulate the air—trying to limit my access to the element. But I can still best them.

This is all rather unnecessary. I'm not going anywhere.

If I were to escape, I'd have to leave the region. It's the region my father built, the one he gave his life for. There isn't an elemental in the Upper that won't recognize the only child of the great Prime Nero. There is nowhere left for me to go.

It's no secret that, if left up to her, Prime Morgana would let me rot in this magroginite barred tomb. She sees me as a threat. The love for my father was so great that the Upper elementals cried out for me to take office after his assassination.

It was out of the question. I was much too young, and our political structure doesn't work in that way. We are not like the Lower, who name successors to offices. Their successors are supposed to be impartial. They say the strongest will lead, but what they really mean is the strongest of their bloodline. Each faction replaces their leader with the strongest son or daughter competent to head. There is no objectivity in their process.

The Upper maintains a superior society because our leaders are truly the best, chosen in honest impartiality. We hold elections so that our people can decide who makes policy, and enforce terms, so that no policymaker is above reproach. We function as one unit, unifying the entire Upper Region under the Council of Policy, where the Lower remains fragmented.

The factions' insistence on remaining independent of each other is the very flaw that allowed us to advance past them. Their political structure allowed for our alliance with the Golds. Though, as perfect as our system is, it isn't for me. I have no interest in policy.

This fact is evident as I sit, awaiting my trial. I have failed my father, his vision, and my region, but I will not compromise in this. Of the thousands I have laid to rest on a battlefield, I sleep well knowing they chose. We each have the choice to walk into combat and defend what we believe in.

Civilians do not choose. Children cannot choose. I will not be the one to make the choice for them, consequences be damned. Nero gave the Upper independence, and although it's been my life's mission to promote this advancement, even I have limits.

I hear the thumping of footsteps descending the stairs, moving toward my cell. Ice prickles at the tips of my fingers, ready for whatever may come. They're not the footsteps of a timid servant here to bring me food or water. These footsteps are loud and haughty.

"Restrain the prisoner." I hear the timbre of his voice as I take in one last breath of air.

In an instant, I'm surrounded by water, cutting off my air supply. Malakai comes into view, sneering as he looks down at me through the watery cage. I push the air that fills my lungs out, bursting through the walls of water just enough to take another breath in. I send the wind of my cell whirling, causing the water to fly across the room, never touching me, just to show him that I can.

Malakai and the other aeros struggle to wield it, but I am too strong. I revel in the frustration that contorts his face, knowing I have truly gotten to him. After weeks of confinement, I take no small joy in upsetting the smug admiral.

He calls out for backup, and more hydros rush into the room. A sheet of water wraps around my head as more band across my body moving in a rapid circle, binding my hands and legs together.

55

Malakai extracts what air flows through the water. I know struggling is useless. Where would I even go from here? I may have sympathized with the Lowers, but I would never bring myself so low as to live among them. The longer I am cut off from my air supply, the weaker I grow.

Malakai looks at me through the liquid sheet. "Settle down, boy. It's time for you to plead your case. The council has formed and will see you."

My mouth falls open and fills with water. The shock of it allows me to forget that I still cannot breathe. This means they are ready to decide. It means I am one day closer to sealing my fate.

Good or bad—treason or not—the end is near.

He must detect that I'm no longer a threat, because Malakai allows small bursts of air to pass through the water and fill my lungs. Not enough for me to wield, but enough to breathe.

He reaches through the water to cuff my hands behind my back and connect them to the shackles on my feet. Gripping my biceps, he hurls me out of the cell block and up the stairs, which lead directly into the capitol building.

The echo of our footsteps on the stone floor fills the otherwise silent corridor. My lungs burn as they wait for each bubble of air Malakai allows me. As we approach the massive council room doors, my pulse quickens. I straighten my spine and lift my head, rolling my shoulders back. They cannot see me weak. I cannot falter. No matter what.

I stride into the council room, both arms held by a soldier and even more flanking me at each side. Malakai walks before us, ushering me to the podium centering the room as he bows to the Council of Policy. The members of the council stretch out in a massive row of twenty-three that curves into a crescent to surround me. Centering them, and directly in front of me, is the prime policymaker, Morgana Ellis.

Her almond eyes narrow and squint. Red mixes with the yellow undertones of her skin as I step forward. She snaps her fingers to release the mask of water, unceremoniously dropping it to the floor with a loud *splat*.

She speaks, never breaking eye contact. "Sorren Astley, we charge you with the high crime of treason. How do you plead?"

"Not guilty."

Her lips press into a thin line as she looks down at the documents before her. She calls out, "Insubordinate conduct, misconduct as a prisoner, conduct unbecoming of an officer, misbehavior before the enemy, aiding the enemy, willful disobedience of a superior commissioned officer, sedition, and treason."

The list of accusations spins my head and rolls around in my mind. I maintain my composure so as not to feed into what she likely hopes—a fit of rage, an outburst of some sort. I am no pyro.

I calmly take on each charge, talking through my defense. "As I was the highest-ranking officer on the field, no superior commission officer commanded I go after those particular elementals."

My years at the academy were all spent studying tactical strategy and our political structure. I know our laws well.

"Once the Lower elementals escaped our soldiers, they were no longer *in the terra faction*, therefore outside my dispatch." I can handle my defense.

"According to our bylaws, sedition requires an individual to incite others to act in opposition to the Council of Policy. My orders were not in opposition of the council, rather in the best interest of my brigade."

The sun is visible through the wall of glass behind the council. Its slow descent toward the sea marks the time I spend defending my innocence.

"Intelligence prior to this mission estimated only six thousand elementals occupying the Healing Faction. I have delivered that to you, and more. We did not prepare to exceed that number."

"So, you admit to incompetence, inadequately planning for the mission?" Morgana counters.

My muscles tense as I grip the podium so tightly that I crack the clips that hold my list of transgressions before me.

"There are limits to all planning. We cannot account for every possibility while still carrying out an efficient mission." My words come out measured and calm, not losing grip of the anger, waiting to lash out. "I believe that accommodating one thousand additional elementals was sufficient."

I continue to paint a picture of the hostile takeover to the row of policymakers. I remind them of the code that expands across our realm, which applies to all elementals, even in times of war.

"The command was unethical and should not have been given. As Commanding Officer of the Western Territory, it was my duty and right to evaluate the situation and make that call." I allow the flow of my words to pass over the judging body.

The council grills me in their gruesome cross examination. Questions of my experience in combat, in leading my brigade, are all brought forward.

"Was it your intention from the beginning to defy your orders?" a policymaker asks.

"Are you accusing me of sabotage?"

"We are simply trying to decipher truth from falsehood. You seem to be so resolute in your assessment of the council's inability to give orders. I wonder if you'd gone in the entire time with intentions of following your own rules."

Another council member joins in on his statement. "I had imagined you'd be most eager to help us. You should aim to see this region built up to the full potential your father envisioned it."

"This is not the Upper my father envisioned. He did not seek to create a region beyond rules and reproach."

The words are a lie. My father wanted to rule at all costs. For all his idealistic talk of a superior region, he would let nothing stand in the way of attaining it.

The prime policymaker's small hands ball in tight fists until the blood drains from her knuckles and her nails bite into flesh. "You seek to defend the very faction which attacked a prison transport, killing unarmed prisoners?" she says in a challenge.

"I will not defend them. But neither will I defend an order I know was wrong. If we become mindless and lawless in our desperation for revenge, then how are we any different from the rash pyros and terras we fight? The Upper is a righteous region. We have ethics and standards by which we abide, and it is my duty as an officer to uphold them."

"It is your duty as an officer to follow orders," Morgana seethes.

A policymaker speaks up from his place beside her. "The prime is correct. These were decisions made by the council, through deliberation and voting. No one person has the power to override the decision of the council. And although your intentions may have been noble, you do not have the foresight, experience, or authority to contradict what we order."

When the officials turn to each other in deliberation, they prepare to seal my fate. Hushed voices carry whispers I cannot make out. They are fervent in their closed-off discussion. When the murmurs cease, the prime clears her throat, ending the cross-examination.

Prime Morgana stands, and the rest of the council follows suit. She turns to me, jaw clenched and her fist still tight. "Thank you for your testimony. That will be all."

She looks at Malakai. "Restrain and escort the prisoner back to his cell. The council will now deliberate. You will be called for sentencing by day's end tomorrow. Dismissed."

Just as quickly as the veil drops, the blanket of water wraps around me once again. Malakai reaches through to grab my arm, his fingers digging into my triceps, pulling me out of the council room. Taking long strides, he knows my shackled feet cannot keep up as he drags me down to my cell.

"Open the damn cell," he barks at a nearby hydro.

The young guard scrambles to comply, pulling the magroginite bars open. Unlocking my shackles, Malakai throws me into the cell. My head cracks against the stone floor as I stumble down, the water mask doing nothing to protect me. Once the metal bars clink behind me, the veil of water drops, and I can breathe easy again. I gasp my element fully into my lungs, basking in the abundance of it.

I bring my hand to the back of my head, feeling the sticky wetness of blood. *Bastard.*

Malakai crouches down so that his eyes level with mine through the bars. His lips curl back in a sneer as he spits out, "I will see you again tomorrow, boy. I look forward to watching you sentenced to death. Nero's name won't save you this time."

As he stands and walks away, I rush the bars. No sooner do I slam against them than a wall of water lifts a few feet before me. A warning from the hydros against any thoughts of retaliation. I temper my rage. I know these soldiers are only following orders. They do not wish to guard me any more than I wish to be trapped in this underground cell. Although they answer to the prime, they are still my soldiers. This is still my territory. Until death.

I sag against the dirt wall of my cell, trying to decide what to make of tomorrow's sentencing. I hear the light tap of feet cautiously making their way down the stairwell. These footsteps are too light to be Malakai's again. Likely just a servant here to dole out my daily rations. I don't bother looking up. I don't care.

"I'm here to provide any necessary medical treatment." The soft hum of the servant's voice differs from the usual rotation of capitol workers that have made it down here before. I look up to see who it belongs to and am struck by dark brown waves of hair and deep emerald-green eyes.

"The prisoner has a head abrasion. See to it," a guard says.

The terra woman from the raid stands before me. I find myself dumbstruck at how they could have possibly tamed such a capricious elemental and brace myself for her wrath.

I welcome it, every bit deserving of whatever she cares to throw my way.

The girl looks at me, pausing in a moment of recognition that flickers across one emerald eye and dies in the next. She goes to work unloading the food from the basket she carries and preparing her bandages. I gawk at her composure. It appears she will not confront me at all.

It is a strange feeling, watching someone I've captured live out their punishment. Until today, I've never recognized an elemental I've captured serving in Central City. In part, this is due to how little time I spend in the city. One battle usually leads into the next, leaving little to no time in between. But more so, it's because no other Lower has caught my attention the way she has.

"It's you," I say, but she just looks at me, green eyes wide.

"Excuse me?" she says, placing the tray of food down and moving to examine my wound.

"What I did . . . to you . . . your people." I search for a way to explain. "I'm sorry for what happened to your faction." The words seem insufficient for all that I want to convey. I hush my tone so as not to illicit too much attention from my guards. They are lenient, but they have limits.

The terra's brows furrow, and her mouth pulls into a deep frown as she continues to clean my wound, my shaggy and outgrown hair muddling her efforts. "I'm sorry. I don't know what you're talking about."

"Don't you recognize me?" I know that my time spent in this cell may have changed my appearance. I must have lost weight. My facial hair has overgrown, but I am hardly unrecognizable.

"I'm sorry, sir. I don't know who you are."

This is wrong. Even if she doesn't know me, mention of her faction sparked no recognition on her face—no anger or grief—only confusion. It is as if the whole thing never happened. I try with simpler questions to see if she's only playing a part to avoid interacting with me further. "What's your name?"

"Medical Land Forty-seven." This is her identification. Since the start of the war, they assigned all servants identification to indicate which building they serve, their element, and servant number.

"No, your name. Who are you?"

Her mouth parts as she goes to say something and then closes, as it seems to slip her mind. Her eyes cast down and her brows furrow as if she's trying to work some imaginary puzzle out in her head.

She bites her lip and looks up at me. "I—I don't know."

I believe she's playing with me. This must be her discrete way of letting me know I have no right to ask anything else of her. And in truth, she is correct.

She fumbles with the bandages in her hands, putting more attention and focus than necessary into tearing a square for my injury. She looks up at me, then down again as red fills her cheeks, her brows furrowing once more in frustration. Almost as if she truly doesn't remember.

I do not press the question. The thought seems ridiculous, but I don't want to be cruel. I don't know if this is a twisted game she's playing. Maybe she simply does not want me talking to her. I know I wouldn't. She couldn't possibly have forgotten. Not the warrior I met only weeks ago.

When she lifts the bandage to my head, I catch sight of the talisman dangling from her wrist and grab it. Her skin feels warm under mine, and I recognize the smooth hum of power that lies beneath. Something in her connects to me, and I know she can feel it, too. She does not pull her arm away. She continues to look up at me, holding my gaze, challenging and defiant.

I struggle to tear my eyes away from hers, turning her wrist so that the talisman faces us, and I see it is honoring the water deity, Hydris. "You wear another deity's talisman?"

"What do you mean, *another deity*? Whose talisman should I be wearing?" she says.

"Gaia's." I feel ridiculous, needing to even say it.

"I know of no Gaia," she says, and the firmness of her words shocks me. I no longer believe this is a petty game. This is blasphemy.

"She is the mother of all land wielders. You honor her." I tread lightly, for I'm coming to realize this is no act. Something is seriously wrong.

Her eyes squint with suspicion. "I don't know of any Gaia. We serve Aelious or Hydris. Depending on our house."

"You would rebuke the deity that made you a Level Three land wielder?"

Her mouth falls open in a snort. "Level Three? You're delusional. Land and fire wielders don't have levels. Even the strongest among us are no match for a Level One air or water wielder."

I wince at the collar around her neck and remember that it neutralizes their abilities. But to believe but she does not have a level or forget that she's an L3 is absurd.

"That is enough. Servant, back to your duties. Prisoner, stand down," the hydro guard calls to us, already wielding a sphere of water.

The terra needs no excuse to escape me, she scrambles back as if she cannot get away quick enough. Hurried footsteps clink up the stairs as I wonder if this is the last time I will ever see her.

CHAPTER 9

KARA

MY HEART BEATS IN time with my feet pounding on the marble floor. A sharp pain slams against my skull and I press my fingers into my hair, trying to dull it. The pain stops me in my tracks. It pulses in tempo with my heart. My skull feels as though it may crack, splitting in two. The stabbing intensifies, spreading from the crown of my head, shooting through my fingertips.

Although the prisoner riled me, I can hardly blame this episode on him. The pains are coming more frequently now. I don't know what's causing them and I'm helpless against the hurt. It isn't a dull ache. It's a knife that presses against my skin from the inside, pushing to carve its way out. In my fingers there are needles, wiggling tiny holes in the tips, waiting for whatever is building up inside of me to pour from them.

And oh, how I wish it would pour out. The pressure's unbearable. I take deep breaths to calm my nerves. I press my back flat against the wall I've stopped at, allowing my body to slump into it and continue to breathe. I draw in deep, purposeful breaths until the pain subsides and my pulse slows.

Who is he? The prisoner was so confident he knew me, but I'm sure I've never met him. For a face so unfamiliar, it awoke feelings of rage in me I can't explain. I almost want to hate the stranger. Still, there is something familiar about him. Something in his words ring true.

But the man spoke nonsense. Talk of factions and levels, even some mystical land mother. He is mad, though I'm not sure what else I would expect from the inmate. He's been locked down there for as long as I can remember.

Until today, Medical Land Fifty-three has rotated with ML Seventeen, attending to the prison's occupants. This morning she was gone, like so many others, never returning from maintenance. I think she grew too weak to serve, but they take others from the city for misconduct. Fifty-three doesn't seem like the type. Though I don't really know her well enough to judge. Whatever the reason, I was told ML fifty-three will no longer be with us, and I'm to assume her duties.

My stomach twists at the thought of seeing the prisoner again. Although I'm sure he's done nothing to me, I can't negate the gut feeling of hating him. Such a strong emotion surprises me, and I chastise myself for being so harsh. As the policymakers we serve say, 'It is in the pyro's nature to rage, and the terra's nature to nurture.' That is why terras serve the council more directly. We work in nicer buildings such as the capitol while they generally assign pyros to more laborious tasks such as smithing.

I make my way down the capitol's marbled halls. The empty corridors echo every step in an uncomfortably loud crescendo as

I hurry to the infirmary. ML Twenty-three leans over a mortar and pestle, throwing her weight into grinding some herb into medication. Its aroma fills the air with a pungent, fresh smell, woodsy and thick. It makes me long to immerse myself in the land. I try to place a name to the herbs she processes, but none comes to me. She focuses all her attention on the stone, as if it is the only thought in her head. I lay the inmate's leftover ointments down on the countertop with a *clink* that draws her attention.

"Forty-seven, you're back. Good, I need you to go down to the smith's building and retrieve today's package." She stops grinding the herbs and focuses on me. Her eyes narrow as she continues. "Now that you're taking over Fifty-three's responsibilities, you will go there more often."

The faintest smile creeps across my lips. I find it pulling at the corners of my mouth as I think of the handsome fire wielder who works in the smith's building.

Twenty-three's mouth pulls down in a scowl as she continues. "You can wipe that little smirk off your face. I don't want you getting mixed up with that pyro. You go in, you pick up the package, and you leave. Is that understood?"

"Yes, ma'am."

"Those pyros are no good. He will only get you into trouble. The next thing you know, you'll be working down at the smiths, or with the other ill-mannered terras harvesting. Or worse yet, they'll cart you to the Outer."

I shudder at the thought and jerk my head side to side, reassuring her I will be on my best behavior. She sends me on my way, and I scurry across town toward the metalsmith.

It's where the aeros and hydros bring their waste. Dead fish accumulate, belly up to the sun before sinking to the depths, to allow whatever bottom-feeders hang about to feast on their remains. The smell directs me better than any trail sign could. When the stench of stale water puckers my lips and crinkles my nose, I know I've arrived. Still, the route is a treat to travel.

Although I regret Medical Land Fifty-three's absence, I can't deny my excitement at inheriting this duty. Aside from the handsome pyro, the trek to his building is magnificent. It's easy to keep my head down while walking the crystal-clear pathways, with an open view of the sea life that lies beneath. Albeit manufactured glass, which is no more than an indestructible plastic, the roads are completely transparent, allowing a glorious view of the sea below. I don't even mind when the streets flood with the daily tide, washing cold salt water all the way up to my ankles. As long as I'm allowed outside the stuffy capitol building, it's enough for me.

By the end of my journey, late autumn winds redden my nose and freeze my fingertips. I sniffle, grateful for the heat radiating from the smithing building. The thunder of a mallet to metal greets me before I even reach the door. I knock on the large metal slab, but the sound is lost among the noise.

I push it open and call out, "Pyro!"

The hammering stops, and he looks up at me through thick golden curls. A wide grin creeps across his face, brightening his obsidian eyes, as he stands at the massive hearth, surrounded by clay bricks. The furnace's mouth gapes open, spanning the length of a medical cot. The hearth's opening breathes flames that dance and rave, climbing toward the ceiling. The fire fights to be free of its clay confines, restricted and controlled by the pyro that tends it.

"Terra." His voice is smooth as silk.

I stand for a second, forgetting to speak, happy to simply admire the flame bronze hue of his skin, decorated with fine swirls and patterns of raised flesh. "Brands" I think he calls them. My gaze falls on a large patch of red covering his arm. Angry and rough, it's blistering.

"Frost burn?" I ask, gesturing toward the fresh injury.

He shrugs. "Damn aeros. So touchy."

I'm sure that every time I see him, he's sporting fresh evidence of a recent punishment and am reminded of Twenty-three's warning. "I'm here to get today's package."

"Ah, what happened to Medical Land Fifty-three?"

"I don't know. She's gone." He grimaces. The pyros know better than anyone what it means for a servant to go missing.

The pyro swaggers toward me, box in hand. When he is just inches away, he slowly bends his head toward mine. "Well, I hope that means I'll be seeing more of you then."

His gaze moves down my face, falling on my lips, then lowering even further to my chest. He brings his soot-blackened hand to the pendant that hangs above it, and I'm sure he can feel the heavy thud of my heart as his knuckles graze my skin. His eyes pinch together as his face crumples into a pained expression; his lips peeling back to push a wrinkle into his nose and show his white teeth tightly clinched. In a moment, it seems to pass. He shakes his head, still holding my necklace.

"Obsidian," he says. His words come out with an edge of strain that lets me know the pain has not completely receded.

"How do you know?"

He shrugs. "How did you get this?"

"I don't know. I've had it for as long as I can remember." I try to think back to a time when the pendant didn't dangle above my heart, but the heady scent of smoke and spice that always seem to accompany the pyro rushes my thoughts. My breathing quickens. Twenty-three's warning blares like a siren in my ears, but I can't hear it over the rush of my own pulse.

"I—I," I begin to reply, but double over as pain shoots through my chest and slams against my skull like lightning. Pressure builds up in my fingertips and I'm afraid they will split open. The pyro drops his box. Metal collars fall out as they hit the floor. In a second, his hands are on mine.

"Are you okay?" His words rush together, eyes probing me for an injury he will not find.

"I'm fine," I say as I struggle to stand upright, pushing through the pain that has me stumbling.

"What is it? What's the matter?" He pushes me to answer, desperate to help.

"I don't know. I don't know what's wrong with me. It just hurts sometimes." I bring my hands to my head, digging my fingertips into my temples.

The pyro brings his hand up to meet mine, brushing his fingertips across my hairline. "Here?" Then he reaches to my hand, his thumb grazing the pads of my fingers. "And here?"

I nod, shocked that he can so easily pinpoint my pain.

"I get them, too. Like a dagger trying to pry its way out? Like an explosion stuck inside you, unable to expand, just waiting to be released?"

I nod, unable to find any words that could explain how I feel listening to someone describe my torment so perfectly. As much as she's tried to help, Twenty-three doesn't experience the pain I do. None of the servants we work alongside have this gnawing hurt that increases with each passing day. It's strange to discover I'm not alone.

"Yes. How do you stop it?" I'm desperate to know.

His eyes soften and fill with pity. "I don't. It's there for a reason. I take it, and let it fulfill its purpose until it is through. I don't know why, but one day I will."

My shoulders sag at the disappointment of coming so close to a solution and still being so far. I give him a half smile, grateful he shared this much with me.

Crouching down, I pick up the box that was dropped on the floor, gathering the collars inside of it. "I better be going."

He smiles. "I look forward to seeing you tomorrow."

I move backward toward the exit, bumping into a wall on my way out before awkwardly turning around. Looking at him over my shoulder, I open the door and leave.

Once I make it back to the capitol building, I seek out the head of maintenance. The collars go to him. Each day, the department runs maintenance on all the servant collars. He'll switch out any defectives or give collars to any new servants arriving. The implements are our lifeline. Terras and pyros aren't suited to live in the aquatic environment of Central City. The collars secrete a serum that stabilizes us.

I search for his office but can't quite remember where it is. I wander the halls of the capitol building for what feels like ages, frustrated that my mind is in such a fog.

I turn down another hall, and it looks familiar. I chastise myself. I should know where the maintenance office is. The location sits in the corner of my mind behind a veil that I can't lift. Just as when the prisoner asked for my name, I could almost feel my mouth forming it, but my mind wouldn't allow me to speak. The word that is at home on my tongue is locked behind a door in my psyche that has no key.

I continue to wander down the hallway until the shrill of some creature's voice stops me cold. It booms from behind a half-open door toward the end of the corridor. I know I should not pursue it. Everything in me screams to turn around, but the sound persists.

"Gone!" it yells. "All of it, gone!"

Its voice is cold and alien. It screeches like ice scraping across glass. I shake as I peer through the partially opened door. "You will find it!"

The scream is piercing and if the windows were not made of indestructible glass, I'm sure they'd shatter.

"How does the essence of seven thousand elementals simply vanish?" he says.

I slap a hand over my mouth, stifling a gasp as I take in the sight of him. His skin is an icy shade of blue, almost gray. Thick frost spotted with patches of solid ice covers his arms and neck. He is devoid of pupils. No color centers the monster's eyes; they're iced over and white. I've never seen a creature so terrifying. I jerk my face away from the door before he catches sight of me.

A woman's voice speaks up in defense. I recognize it belongs to the prime policymaker, though it doesn't hold the haughty confidence I've grown to associate with her. "I do not know. But we have all our finest soldiers on it. We will find the missing aether."

Her words rush together as she seems desperate to reassure the monster that whatever he seeks, he will have. Who is this *thing* that can command the prime policymaker in such a way?

"I cannot contain her without it." His words are just as frantic as they are furious. Who is he referring to? What could be powerful enough to concern this terrifying creature? "You will release him. *He* will locate it."

"My Lord, he is a traitor—"

"Silence!" The creature booms with so much force, tendrils of ice fly from the room. I peek over to see the prime policymaker, bowed over her bent knee. "You will release him. I will have the essence. Whether it comes from the Lower elementals, or yours, matters not. But trust me, Morgana, I *will* have it."

I don't hear him leave, but he takes the cold with him. I hadn't realized I was shivering or that the temperature dropped so deadly low until I no longer hear the creature's voice. As I tiptoe away, a rope of water wraps itself around my neck and drags me backward.

"Prying ears get cut off, girl." It is the prime policymaker. She has discovered me, and will no doubt make me pay. I choke on the water, desperate to breathe again. The liquid hand lifts me up and pulls me closer to her face as she looks into my eyes, snarling. "Never bother. You won't remember this, anyway. Let's get you to maintenance."

There's a break in her hold and I use it to gasp in precious air before she wraps her liquid hands around my throat once more, dragging me down the hall. By the time we make it to the maintenance room, my eyes water and feel like they will soon bulge right out of my head.

I gasp in air with each quick break of her hold, filling my lungs with precious oxygen. As we enter the sterile room, it feels oddly chilled. Enforcers huddle over a maintenance chair, arguing with each other.

"Fucking idiot! How many times do I have to tell you to pay attention to how much you're taking?"

"I did, I swear," a younger enforcer says.

"Well, I think this guy would have to disagree." The older enforcer slaps his hand down on the slumped over servant, shoving him from the chair. The aggressive jolt causes the man to tip over and flop onto the ground with a loud slap.

"That's the fourth one this week!" he shouts, rolling the servant over with the nudge of his boot. As the enforcer flips the servant over, the man's head tilts to the side, his eyes open, and unseeing.

He's dead.

Terror rakes icy fingers down my back, sending a convulsing shake through my entire body. It sets all my nerve endings on edge and pushes my pulse to race. I can't hear what the prime says to the officers above the loud whooshing of my heartbeat pounding in my eardrums.

They're going to kill me.

As the prime allows a break in her hold for me to breathe, a scream bubbles in my throat and releases in an ear-piercing screech. The enforcers' heads snap to us.

The prime whips another ribbon of water around me, stifling my screams as I thrash against her, struggling to break free.

They killed him.

The ribbon of water grips me tighter and lifts me off the ground, my legs frantically kicking out. This doesn't seem to faze the prime, as she ignores me and addresses the enforcers.

"Explain yourselves."

The enforcers slam their fists against their chests and jerk their heads down into a bow. The older enforcer steps forward. "It appears Officer Reymen extracted too much from the servant."

My lungs spasm as I fight to breathe, my heart banging against my ribcage and spinning my head. What have they done?

The prime rolls her eyes, her upper lip curling as she glares at the young enforcer, then back at his senior. "Hydris almighty. Now, more than ever, we need to be efficient with our extractions," she seethes. "And we cannot extract from dead elementals, can we?"

The enforcers shake their heads.

"Get them both out of here," she orders, gesturing to the dead elemental and the young enforcer. "Now, can I have an officer who knows what they're doing?"

She drops me on the floor as the senior enforcer rushes over. "Strap her down and be generous with the serum. I need to ensure she remembers nothing."

My pulse quickens as I fight my spasming lungs to take in more air. When the prime releases her watery hold, I gasp, choking on the air as it squeezes through my windpipe. As soon as my lungs fill, I scream, jerking from the senior officer. Large hands grip each of my forearms as two more enforcers strap me into a chair and secure bands across my arms, legs, abdomen, and forehead.

"What are you doing? I'm sorry. I didn't see anything," I cry as tears stream down my face, mixing with the water dripping from my hair. "I won't tell anyone. I swear."

My earnest pleas go ignored as a bite at my neck silences the sputtering protests.

The maintenance enforcer pushes a tube into my collar, and I feel burning liquid pour into the veins of my neck and travel down my shoulder. As the liquid sears through me, it connects with an energy swirling in my core. A jolt of power rumbles inside of me and I feel it spinning, connecting with the burning liquid coursing through my veins.

The pain causes me to cry out, but the sound never leaves my throat as my body goes limp and my senses start to dull.

It's not long before I can no longer remember why I'm struggling or thrashing. I no longer wish to buck or pull at all.

My pulse slows and my breathing evens.

I feel calm—almost serene—as my vision fades in and out.

When I open my eyes, there is a maintenance enforcer by my side, where I am seated in a chair. I rub my head, not knowing where I am or remembering how I got here. I must have fallen asleep.

Oh, no.

I'll get in trouble for sleeping while I'm supposed to be working. I try to remember how this could have happened. I frantically retrace my last actions so that I can explain the slip to my superiors.

I remember walking from the smithing building, but where was I going? What was I doing there?

I dropped something in the water along the main pathway. A sea lizard had flown up from the water to grip my hair, but what did I drop as I shooed the creature away?

None of this brings me any closer to an explanation. I look up at the maintenance enforcer at my side. "I'm sorry. I didn't realize—I wasn't napping," I sputter. "I don't know how I got here. I didn't mean to fall asleep."

The enforcer looks at me, then to the prime policymaker.

"Finished," he says.

I recognize the prime and immediately stand to bow, bumping my hand against my chest. My limbs are not prepared for the swift movement. Once I lift from the chair, my legs give out beneath me, causing me to fall back down.

I push myself up, trying to show our prime the respect her station is owed. It is an honor to be in her presence. I brace myself to be reprimanded for sleeping while I should be working, but she simply waves me off and addresses the maintenance enforcer.

"Thank you. Have her escorted to the servant's quarters," she says, leaving us.

Pain ricochets through my head, stabbing at my skull. The niggling of a memory tries to claw its way out but is suffocated by the haze that has overcome my mind. I push it back, clinging to the enforcer as he leads me to my quarters.

I desperately need to sleep.

Chapter 10
Sorren

I FORCE ICE OVER my fingertips, letting it run down my hand, up my arm, and across my shoulders. What starts as thin frost grows into a thick layer of ice that coats my entire body. I let it build on itself until I've formed a cocoon at least half a foot thick. I leave tiny holes that allow air through and sit in my chilled casing to await sentencing.

Time passes—or not at all—I can't tell either way. I sit and bask in the cold numbness I have surrounded myself with. Preparing for my judgment. I do not know if I've wielded the thick sheet of ice so that I may feel its essence course through my body once more. So that I can harness the raw cold power of my element flowing through me one last time. Or if I've prepared a crypt for myself in anticipation of today's sentencing.

They do not give prisoners a proper burial. They will not lay my body to rest in a tomb of ice as my deity, Aelious, would have it. They will likely sentence me to the Outer, our prison region, to either live out the rest of my days incarcerated or be executed. One thing is for certain. No one returns from the Outer.

It's a fate I may very well deserve, but not for the reason the council would sentence me to it. As I said on the stand, in front of the council, I do not regret letting the terras go. I do not wish I could go back in time to capture the hundreds more that fled our grasp. If I could go back, it would be to abort the mission altogether.

I am even more resolved in my sentiment now that I've come across the terra girl. Such a display could not be genuine. She acted the part of a nescient servant girl so expertly. I had to go over our last encounter several times in my mind to make sure I wasn't fabricating the idea of it all together.

I think back to the holidays of my childhood, the few times I would return home from the academy. My father loaded his manor with servants, and I always found them quite odd. The Lower servants always seemed distrait and forgetful, but nothing compared to this. My stomach sinks at the thought that all the elementals I captured in my raid have been altered in the same way the powerful Level Three terra had been.

Lines crack and split my makeshift prison. As the ice breaks down, I do not attempt to maintain it. I know it is time, and I have accepted my fate.

No sooner does the last shred of ice fall than water overtakes me. Burning chains of iron slap across my wrists, binding them behind my back. The liquid that surrounds me heats and burns as my body temperature rises.

I look to see a redheaded pyro controlling his own element. The man does not use machines to heat the water. Tech does not feed the iron chains their relentless burn. The pyro does not wear a collar. He is free.

He sticks a freckled hand through the water that surrounds me to better regulate the heat. Pushing me forward, Malakai speaks. "Let's go asshole. It's time you get exactly what's coming to you."

He pushes me forward and I take several steps to keep from stumbling over the burning chains that shackle my feet. They escort me to the council room, where massive glass doors are the only thing separating me from my fate.

The hydros who stand guard heave the large doors open and Malakai again pushes me through, aiming to have me stumble in front of the Council of Policy. This time, I prepare my footing, and take great care in recovering my steps. They will not see me fall, least of all by his hand.

As I approach the podium center of the crescent-shaped table, all twenty-three of our region's policymakers watch me. Their eyes track my movements, like birds of prey stalking their target. Morgana sits directly across from me. She seethes as her glare remains locked on mine.

When I have settled into my position, Morgana stands, smoothing her bone-straight hair behind her ears. Inky black strands, streaked with gray, sit atop her scalp in a sharp diagonal cut. It appears as if a blade sliced straight through, from the base of her skull down, falling just below her chin, framing her round face in a style as severe as she is. Her fingertips turn white as she clutches the parchment paper, holding my fate in her grasp. I brace myself as she brings it up to read.

When I approach the council, she lists my infractions. "Sorren Astley, for the crime of insubordinate conduct, we find you guilty. For the crime of misconduct as a prisoner, we find you guilty."

Each verdict is like a punch in the chest. A tightening of the burning chains which will drag me to the Outer before the day's end.

"Aiding the enemy . . . not guilty."

I release a sharp exhale at the first sign of hope.

"Willful disobedience of a superior commissioned officer, not guilty. Sedition, not guilty." Morgana's lips purse as if the words cause her physical pain, her face twitching with each verdict. The tightening coils in my chest unfurl as breathing comes easier with each exoneration.

Morgana glances from her paper to me, raising her voice haughtily. "Conduct unbecoming of an officer, guilty." My reprieve is short-lived, my victory seemingly false. It appears all my clever defenses will not save me.

"Misbehavior before the enemy, guilty." She lists charge after charge, each winning a guilty verdict.

I brace myself, awaiting the prime to announce my last charge.

"For the high crime of treason," She clenches her teeth so tightly, I think they may break. I catch the smear of ink as the paper dampens along with the surrounding air. Morgana is losing control of her element, unable to hide the fury that bites at her. Her jaw remains firm and closed as she pushes the sentence through her teeth.

"Not guilty."

Shock slams against me as I shake the water from my ears to ensure I've heard her correctly. I only need to look over at Malakai's dumbstruck face to confirm they have not charged me with treason. The myriad of relief and disgust etched on the policymakers' faces gives me hope I will live to see another day. I know many have rallied behind me, but even I am surprised and awestruck at the turn of events.

Morgana does not skip a beat, flowing straight into my sentencing. "For the crimes we have found you guilty of, we hereby strip you of your title, Commanding General of the Western Territory."

Though expected, the news hits me, blowing the wind from my lungs. Every snide comment made about my unworthiness of the station plays through my mind. All I have worked for, taken in an instant. I have nothing if I do not have my title to validate what everyone will now only attribute to Nero.

"We sentence you to rehabilitation by reconditioning. The Torcher, Jarek, will administer your sentence." She gestures to the pyro at my back. "The Admiral will oversee it."

As Malakai stiffens at my side, I know a fresh new hell awaits me at his hands. But I do not care. As a military officer, I know how to withstand pain. I welcome it as a cleanse and purge of weakness from the body.

"Your office as Commanding General of the Western Territory may only be reinstated upon successful rehabilitation and reconditioning." A wicked smile curves the corners of her lips before she continues, "and upon the successful completion of your next mission."

"Which will be," I say.

"To locate and capture the escaped elementals and anyone aiding them. At which time, you will return them to Central City, where they have rightfully belonged since your first failure."

She punctuates the last word with an intended force. Reminding me of the series of events leading me to stand before them now.

"We have shown you ample mercy here today, but let us be clear, we will show no mercies should you fail this mission."

This knocks the wind from my lungs as the weight of all that has plagued me slams down on my chest. I could never have imagined being forced to relive the mission that has tormented my conscious thought in such an acute and cruel way. I know this is a chance for redemption, a shot at doing right by my father's legacy. It's an opportunity to make up for the botched mission I so thoroughly screwed up. But this is wrong.

Policymaker Aquil stands. "Your reservations are not lost on us. We understand you may feel *conflicted*," he says the word as if it is dirty. "But the council has decided it is necessary, and you must display the capacity to follow orders." I nod. "However you may feel, your loyalty is to this region, without waver or question."

I lift my fist to my chest in respect for all that he says.

I suppress the guilt and anxiety, reminding myself that I do not owe these Lowers anything. This is a second chance, an opportunity to right my wrongs and honor my region. I cannot hold my enemy in higher regard than my own people. I cannot put anything above the success of my father's vision.

I force my grip on the podium to loosen, allowing blood to flow back and color my white knuckles. I look at the floor, counting my breaths, slowing them to temper my apprehension. Morgana watches me, and when I raise my eyes to meet hers, she allows the corner of her tight mouth to stretch into a smirk.

She addresses Malakai. "Admiral, take him away. His sentence takes effect immediately."

As she gives the command, the binds that held me before wrap around me again. The pyro throws more heat into the water. It's more tolerable, now that I know I'm not being escorted to my death.

I look over to Malakai, who rushes us forward, and rescind my last thought. He leads us out of the room and to the conditioning arena. We pass back the way we came, taking the long and winding staircase deep below the capitol building. The conditioning arena lays deep underground along with the capitol prison cells. Buried below enough stone that none of the fine, law-abiding citizens can hear what occurs beneath them.

Once we reach the arena, Malakai wastes no time having the guards prepare me. Shoving me forward, he moves to the prep table. From it, he picks out a solid black apron and gloves. He locks eyes with mine as he dawns the protective ware.

"Saved again, I see," he says, pulling the elastic of his glove until it snaps against his forearm. "Never bother. I will do right by our region. I know what you've done, and I will see you punished."

The hydros that escorted us work together to lift me. One stands on a platform, locking my wrists in a pair of chain shackles hung from the ceiling. Another encloses my ankles, so I am held in midair at an angle not quite horizontal.

"Understand, boy, this will not be easy. You will suffer. I will expose you for the weak entitled urchin you are. You may have Nero's protection out there, but in this arena, I own you. And before your sentence is through, I will see you broken."

CHAPTER 11

KARA

*I*F HE DIES, YOU'RE *going with him.*

Admiral Malakai's threat makes sense once I see the dire state in which he's left the prisoner. Blood mingles with the sweat that cascades down his dangling body. The man's shirt has been ripped to shreds. The only thing left covering him are the tattered pants, barely hanging on by their blood-soaked waistband. I fumble my fingers across the shackles that cuff his ankles. They are the only ones I can reach.

I look for a latch, or any release mechanism that might allow me to free him. When the guards ordered me to tend his wounds, not even Hydris could have prepared me for the gory scene I'd walk into.

When I opened the door, my eyes drew straight to his dangling body. It is not until I look around, hoping to find a key of some sort, that I take in the full extent of all that has happened. Red sprays and splatters coat the wall where a bloodied chain hangs, still burning hot. The floor is a mess of ash and blood, and I can only assume a fire blazed below him. Fresh blood pools on the ground beneath his body.

He's losing too much. It's a wonder the man is still alive to receive treatment.

"I'm going to get help. I'll be right back, I swear." I place my hand on his chest, if only to confirm his pulse is still there. He doesn't nod or give me any sign that he's conscious, much less has heard my words. I dart from the room, skipping over the mess of shattered ceramic and glass that I dropped upon entering. The wasted remedies are of no consequence. None of the superficial antidotes I brought will do anything more than irritate the wounds of a man so close to death.

I race down the corridor, hoping to stumble across someone who will help me get him down. When I turn the corner, I run straight into another terra, slamming into his chest like I'd run into a brick wall.

"I need help. Hurry, in the conditioning arena." The words stumble from my lips, and I am sure by the look on his face, I don't make a bit of sense.

"What is it? What's happened?" The terra holds me by the shoulders to steady me, looking for some clarity in the message I'm trying to convey.

"They asked me to tend to the prisoner receiving conditioning, but he still hangs by chains. I'm afraid that if we don't get him down soon, there'll be nothing I can do."

There may be nothing I can do, regardless. This is honestly a task for Twenty-three. She is the best healer among us. What she can do with the medicines and salves the Upper has manufactured is amazing. I only wish I possess a fraction of her ability, especially now. Of all the days for her to be away sorting through the harvest.

The other terra follows me as I race down the stairs toward the conditioning area. I know there is no time to send for Twenty-three. As unlikely as I am to provide any help to the man, it is even less likely that she'll arrive in time to do him any good either. The best I can do for him now is get him down and into the infirmary.

I burst through the doors of the conditioning room, heading straight for the platform set aside by the wall. As I push it to align with the prisoner, I catch the other terra standing in the entrance, frozen and dumbstruck.

"Get over here and help me. I need to get these cuffs off. Do you see anything that can pry them open?"

As if snapped from his trance, the terra springs into action, rummaging through the horde of devices meant to inflict harm rather than provide aid. I place my hands on the prisoner's cheeks. They burn hot, although he is an aero. This isn't good. He should never be this warm.

"I've got something." The terra runs to me, handing over a small pry bar. I busy myself wedging it into the cuffs, holding his wrist, trying not to concentrate on the life slipping away beneath my fumbling hands. I let out a sharp yelp when the right cuff breaks open, releasing him. His body jerks and the terra below me scrambles to catch him.

Once we've stabilized the right side of his body, I go to work on the left cuff. The terra holds his arms, prepared to catch the full weight of his upper body as the left cuff releases and he tumbles down face first. I take no time at all in freeing his ankles and my heart leaps at the sweet sound of his groan.

He's alive.

"We have to get him to the infirmary," I say to the terra as he wraps his arms around the aero's chest and hauls him out. I hold the man's waist so he's not totally dragging and help the terra transport him quicker.

The Admiral's threat isn't the only reason I'm desperate to help the aero. I know this man. We've met before, I'm sure of it.

Somewhere in him are the answers to questions my hazy mind forgets each morning after a long night's sleep.

But dead men don't tell secrets, and there is no mistake that death looms near for the battered aero. The pitiful sight of him, debilitated and broken, spikes my urgency, and as much as I wanted to hate him before, those feelings are lost to me now.

Once we're in the infirmary, the terra places him on the first open bed. I peel off the scraps of clothing, now sticky with blood, to assess the damage.

I suck in my breath with a hiss upon seeing the full extent of his injuries. There's little of his body that is not either scratched, bruised, or bloodied. The only thing helping us is that many of his wounds are cauterized. Only the largest gaping gashes bleed. *And oh, do they bleed.*

"Hydris, grant me the strength I need to heal this man." I send a quiet prayer up to the deity of the house I serve. The deity of our prime policymaker, for I know my meager abilities alone will not help him. Pain, sharp and fierce, slams against my skull and into my fingertips as I try to recall the best methods for healing him and assess what injuries to focus on first.

"Get the hemoxi," I say to the terra, still fumbling around the infirmary, doing his best to assist. I lather the salve onto his cuts, hoping it will help with the clotting and cleansing of his blood.

"Pass me the avulki." This should bind his wounds, but no matter how much I slather on, the bleeding does not stop. His face reddens as more sweat beads across his brow, dribbling down his hairline.

They assign serving terras tasks their element is naturally inclined to. Terras can more easily manipulate the salves and ointments we use for healing, but our inferior powers extend only so far. His life is slipping away like the beads of sweat that run down his skin, and I cannot stop it. I place my hands on his neck, pushing my fingers into his jugular. My pulse races as his dies.

I knock over canisters in my haste to find something that will help him. Frustration clouds my mind, and I can't think straight. I should know how to help this man, but I cannot access the knowledge that should be second nature to me.

I slam my fist on the table when the avulki salve proves to do nothing more than mix and create a mess of the blood still pouring from his wounds. Anger forces a growl from my throat. I feel helpless to heal him.

I am not helpless.

He *must* live. I have so much to ask the aero who seems to know more about my past than I do. In one last desperate attempt, I send a prayer to the land mother the prisoner told me of. What was her name? *Gaia.*

If there is such a deity, it is her blessing I need most. I grab the hemoxi once more, pushing all the essence I have into this simple task. He will not die.

Pain ricochets through my body, more intense than I have ever felt. My head begs to burst open. A knife may as well have wiggled its way through my temple and slashed itself across my skull. My fingertips burn as if the hottest coal sears beneath my skin.

I do not let the pain waver my focus. I must help him. The pounding in my chest beats like a war drum, so intense that it may throw me back. When I place the salve on his wounds, a burst of energy rips through me, strangling a scream from my throat.

A floodgate has opened and raw burning aether surges through my veins, pouring from my fingertips in a blinding green light. I do not stop to marvel at the impossible phenomenon. The energy that overtakes me is in control. The essence wields me, rather than the other way around, and it presses me on. I work the salve into his gaping wounds, cleansing the blood that flows through them. This time when I bind them with avulki, they seal.

Once I have stopped the bleeding, I rise, taking the mortar and pestle in hand, gathering the herbs I need and mashing them into a paste. I am in a trance. I do not have control of my body or my mind. The essence that has engulfed me is stronger than either.

When I return to him, I take the gooey mixture at the tips of my still glowing fingers, pushing them into his mouth. I coat his cheeks and under his tongue, without a care that the aether burning and flowing through my fingertips could do anything but heal him. In this moment, I am so very connected to the herbs and plants I cultivate, we may as well be one entity.

My adrenaline calms as I work over the rest of his body, searching for what I must heal. By the time I've tempered myself, regaining control of the body that seemed possessed, the energy no longer surges through my veins. Though it is still there, rather than a rushing pulse, it ebbs and flows, steady as my now calm breathing.

The prisoner's mouth gently parts as I press a sponge soaked in water, mint, and gymsen against his dry and split lips. His recovery is miraculous. The rhythm of his heartbeat is strong and steady. The skin of his forehead and cheeks are cool, as an aero's should be.

Now that things have settled, I remember the terra, standing back pressed against the corner of the room. His jaw hangs slack. His wide-open eyes stare at me with a burning curiosity that borders fear.

"Leave us," I command, where I have no authority. But he listens anyway, scrambling to open the door and make his escape.

Alone with the aero, I allow myself liberties I would have never taken in front of the fellow terra. I take my time working skava serum over his closed wounds. This will help with scarring, maybe even eliminate it. I take particular care with his face. He has a beautiful face. It'd be a shame to leave it marred.

I gingerly brush the black locks of hair, sweat soaked and matted, from his forehead. I move my fingertips across the sharp planes of his cheekbones and jaw, reveling in the now cool feel of his alabaster skin. Brushing the pad of my thumb along his swollen lips, I linger longer than it takes for me to rub in the salve. I jump as his hand reaches up to touch mine and watch as he pries open his blood sealed eyes. The swelling has receded, but when they open, they are a red veined mess.

He parts his lips to speak, and they crack as he pushes a hoarse whisper from his throat. "Thank you."

"Shhh." I place a finger over his freshly bleeding lips, reaching for more hemoxi and avulki to reseal the irritated wound. "You took quite a beating. For a second, I thought you weren't going to make it."

I cut the malba plant with oil and water, mixing it into a thin serum I can drop into his eyes. Then I give him more of the water gymsen mix from the sponge.

"I shouldn't hav—" His voice cuts off with a cough. He brings his hand to squeeze mine. "It *is* you," he says.

I don't know what he means. He must still be a little delirious from the fever. I pat his head, sponging the water mixture across his hairline.

He drinks more of the gymsen mix, putting extra care into forming his words. "You saved me."

Though hoarse and only a raspy whisper, his voice grows stronger.

"Sorren." He brings my hand to his chest, introducing himself. Something pulls in the pit of my stomach at the intimacy of his touch.

"Sorren," I repeat, rolling the name around in my head, deciding that I like the sound of it on my tongue. The smile he gives me lets me know he feels the same.

"Your name?" he says.

Though incomplete, I know it's a question. The same infuriating question he had for me before. "I've told you the only name I know."

Taking another sip of the mix, he carefully speaks. "You have a name."

His words are slow and no louder than a whisper, but he presses on. "What you just did should be proof enough that you are so much more than you seem." He coughs, and I can't understand why this is so important to him. "Try to remember, please."

His eyes beg me to give him something I do not have a grasp on. I don't know why I so desperately want to please this stranger. I have no idea why I have any desire at all to see him well or to make him happy. Maybe it's because he's the only person who's ever thought I deserve a name more than an identification. Maybe it's because he's the first person who ever thought that I'm something more than a servant.

Until I met him, I hadn't realized that I even wanted to be. It's the way he looks at me, as if I'm powerful, as if I'm strong—something to be admired—adored. That is a kindness I am determined to repay. An honor I am desperate to earn.

I shut my eyes, forcing myself to concentrate on the recesses of my mind that are closed off and fragmented. It feels like a maze with trapdoors and false exits. While the energy from before still flows through me, I use it to knock down the barriers, keeping me from remembering what I know is mine.

I have a name. It sits behind a wall in my mind that I find myself afraid to breakdown. It sits among a pain more severe than any splitting headache I may have gotten in the past when a memory seems to wiggle its way to the forefront of my psyche.

The pain that sits locked away behind this wall lies deep and rooted. It is a severe and debilitating ache that will consume me if I give it even the slightest bit of opening. A pain I don't want to remember. So, I leave it be. I let it stay quiet and dormant. My life is simple without it and that's how I'd like it to stay.

But when his crystal gray eyes bore into mine, waiting to hear the word that I know feels at home on my tongue, I search for it. I creep past the wall just enough to reach out and grab the simple name that has belonged to me since birth. And when it rolls from my tongue, I know it without a doubt to be true.

"Kara."

Chapter 12
Sorren

"To defeat our enemy, we must first recognize our enemy." Malakai recites the famous words of my father's last address. Words I've heard repeatedly over the years. Words that never fail to turn my stomach.

"We have given the elementals of the Lower region countless opportunities to thrive. We have been generous to our Lower counterparts, but our generosity has limits. We can no longer allow the inferior elementals of the Lower to hinder our progression. I envision a great nation. One no longer dependent on Lower scum." He parrots my father's words with such cold distance, I can almost imagine Nero standing before me.

As the flames burn hotter, they pull sweat from my pores in such abundance, it feels as if they cascade down to the floor in a waterfall.

"Sorren, tell me what three characteristics make the Lower elementals inferior to Uppers?"

I ignore him, retreating further into myself. I refuse to delineate the words that have bred life to the idea that Lower elementals are better off serving than autonomous. I will not play into the pointless game that will earn me pain no matter what answer I give.

The fire of the pyro's chain wraps around my abdomen, tearing skin as he yanks it back.

Malakai answers for me. "They are lazy."

Another lash drags against my back, ripping open the already butchered flesh.

"They are intellectually inferior."

Another lash, but with this one, I lock eyes with the pyro that punishes me. I drive with my expression that the Lower elementals my father spoke of include him. If he's fazed, he does not show it. His focus remains locked on me, cracking his heated chain, aiming to rip my flesh. Does he not believe he is one of them?

"Tell me, Sorren, is the truth of Nero's words not validated through the Lower's primitive living?" Again, I do not dignify him with an answer. "Do you agree that our advancements in tech and medicines have exposed the Lower's true nature? Without their aid we thrive, mere machines replacing their contributions to our survival. But without us, the Lower has fallen, reducing them to their rightful place, beneath us."

Still, I give no answer to the heinous question. Instead, I focus on the pyro, rather than the pain he inflicts. Has his time or status in the Upper allowed him the fantasy that he isn't seen as a lesser? I don't know what he's done or what he has given to attain this illusion, but I do my best to let him know that's all it is.

"They are dangerous. But you already know that don't you?" Malakai says.

The pyro punctuates his statement, driving in just how dangerous he can be. The chain slaps against my abdomen, one lick after another so rapidly I do not have time to recover from the blows. Each contact empties my lungs of air until I cannot breathe, I cannot speak, I cannot cry out.

Malakai chuckles, "Ignore me again, boy, and you will not make it to see tomorrow's session." When Jarek lowers the chain, he dons a pair of brass knuckles that light up with the heat he channels to them.

"The Lower elementals killed your father, and you did nothing. Yet, you believe yourself worthy to command the entire Western Territory?" His voice is casual and taunting, and no matter my training, I cannot keep myself from reacting.

I thrash against my chains. "I was fifteen."

"Yes, and after so much time, you are still that same scared child, riding your father's fame and profiting from his death. Unable to execute the severe force this war requires." Malakai's words reach a place Jarek's weapons cannot. His words creep into the mental space I've occupied throughout this session. It cracks the armor I've built, and I want nothing more than to lash out at him. Remind the arrogant bastard that I am the single most talented wielder the region has seen in generations. My abilities are unparalleled in their raw skill. I want to boast of my victories on the battlefield and the numbers of Lower soldiers I've defeated.

But I cannot. None of that matters. Because no matter how desperately I've wanted to prove to the world I am worthy of these accolades, I cannot even convince myself.

"You are pathetic. You had the greatest source of knowledge at your disposal. The great Prime Nero handing you the world, and you don't even believe in what he's built enough to fight for it."

The flames burn hotter until the intensity is suffocating. My throat is dry and swelling from the heat and abuse, preventing any words I could say from ever leaving my mouth. Malakai is not immune to the blaze. The thick strands of blond and brown hair stick to his forehead, as droplets of sweat fall from their ends.

Through the heat, he continues to recite my father's last speech. His voice rises in heartiness as he articulates each word with a sickening superiority that makes him sound as if he were the one to deliver the address. As if he speaks in front of a crowd rather than a chained and tortured man. "It is for this reason . . ."

He stops, waiting for me to answer. He knows I know this address line-by-line, word-for-word. I spit at the floor in front of his feet. Before my insult falls to the ground, the brass knuckles of Jarek's left hook slam against my cheek. The heated metal of his right fist catches my face, pushing it in the opposite direction. The acrid tang of blood fills my mouth as it spills from my lips and pours down my chin.

Malakai repeats his statement, again prompting me to answer, but I do not. Blow after blow rips apart the skin at my cheek bloodying and swelling my eyes until they shut, and my consciousness begins to slip.

"It is for this reason that the Lower elementals . . ." He waits again, and I realize he can do this all night, but I cannot. My torturer has lost grip on his assignment. This is not duty, this is personal. He *will* kill me.

So, I answer. "They must serve."

Another fist lands square on my jaw, for good measure, and the reconditioning ends. Malakai approaches as the pyro extinguishes the bed of flames beneath me.

"You are a disgrace. To your station. To your region. And to your father's legacy. They may not have sentenced you to the Outer but let the knowledge of this imprison you until the day you die."

Sunlight flickers just beyond my eyelids. I squeeze them shut, harnessing a few more moments of peace, before taking on the day. I know what awaits me.

After weeks of rehabilitation, each day begins to bleed into another, all following the same routine. Mornings are dedicated to reeducation where facilitators bombard me with Upper propaganda until my ears threaten to bleed. My reconditioning takes place directly after that, which is only bearable as it is a prelude to my healing, when I can see Kara again.

Kara. The name she'd worked so hard to give. The name I did not deserve rings across my mind and plays through my ears like a canticle. It keeps me sane through the worst of my reconditioning, where I look for anything to focus my mind on so that I don't crack.

Every conditioning session has been one fresh torture after another, and I return to the infirmary every night, a little less whole than the day prior. Still, Kara spends her nights tending to me, healing me beyond the limits of what she should be capable of, showing me a kindness that I do not deserve.

"I know you're awake." The hum of Kara's voice floats into my ears and I tense my jaw to keep from smiling.

Immediately, I regret the movement, as it shoots pain across the cheek that is still bruised from yesterday's reconditioning session.

"You're mistaken. I am so deeply asleep that you might need to confirm that I haven't slipped into comatose." I keep my eyes shut to further my jest.

"Hmmm, well, let's see." The terra presses two fingers firmly against my neck, and I can feel chill bumps rise on my skin in response to her touch. "Your heartbeat seems regular."

Next, I feel the tickle of her hair brush my chest as she bends over, bringing her ear near my lips. "Breathing is good."

Finally, she presses the pad of her thumb against my eyelid, gently lifting it up. "Pupils are normal."

Releasing my eyelid, she clicks her tongue. "I'm afraid you may be suffering from AECN."

I peek an eye open at her, my other eye entirely committed to unconsciousness. "Is there truly such a thing?"

She nods her head solemnly. "Yes, Acute Exacerbation of Chronic Nonsense, and it's more common than you think."

"Hmmm, is it serious?"

"Very. It can often be life threatening," she says, and I can hear the smile in her words.

"Well, what's your professional recommendation?"

"For one, not freezing out the girl who's in charge of putting you back together every night. You dropped the temperature. I'm practically shaking here."

Finally, she lets out a soft laugh, and I open my eyes, unable to resist seeing her smile. I pull back my element, removing the room's chill.

"Here, I've brought you some breakfast." She sets a plate on the side table next to my cot, crinkling her nose. "I believe you'll be pleasantly surprised to find that it is fish . . . again."

I reach over to lift over the plate's cover, my stiff muscles protesting the movement. "Oh, but it's smoked this time."

Although it looks delicious, my face hurts too much to chew anything at the moment. Kara curls her lip, entirely disenchanted with the dish. She's made it clear that she hates fish, which is most unfortunate for someone living in a hydro city.

She sighs, moving in to examine my wounds for progress. "I just wish there were more fruits, or vegetables. I'm practically living on seaweed at this point."

I stifle a gag, thinking of ways I could get my hands on some fresh produce for the terra whose diet was surely plant based prior to arriving in Central City.

She brings her hand up to examine my cheek.

"You've still got a nasty bruise but thank Hydris it was only a fracture. For a moment, I was worried your entire jaw would come unhinged."

"You remember."

She beams at me, nodding.

Her mind has grown stronger with each passing day, as have her abilities. Her healing has become smooth and effortless. I relish each flare of recognition that flickers across her beautiful face as she remembers the amazing things she's done. What starts as small sparks at the tiniest memories from her previous life, burn into the full on recalling of our previous conversations and encounters in the days prior.

Each night has been progressively better and each day I try to figure out what causes her memory to haze. She can recall everything from the day prior, up to maintenance and the hours following. I worry over this, struggling to find answers, though I am limited due to the strict schedule my rehabilitation facilitators have set for me.

It leads me to believe the blockers in the servant's collars could be affecting her memory. They keep the servants from utilizing the full extent of their elemental essence. This neutralizes them so they aren't an immediate threat, but maybe it also muddies their memory. Whether an unfortunate side effect or calculated byproduct, I can't know.

Her memory is always worse in the mornings. She often forgets the details of things she's done the night prior, and I hate the temporary grogginess linked to that time of day, but today is different.

"Do you want to see something else?" Her mouth curves into a sly smile as she pulls a few small leaves from her pocket. The leaves lie in her palm as she touches them with the tips of her fingers. She closes her eyes, and her fingertips begin to glow, but quickly flicker out. She gives a frustrated grunt, then peeks an eye open at the limp leaves in her hands.

I place my palm under hers, and her emerald eyes meet mine.

"You have to hold your focus, Kara." Gods, I'll never tire of saying that name. "Hone in on where you want your aether to go. Be patient and find a place in your element to connect."

This time, when her fingers glow with a dull green light, the small leaves deepen in their verdant hue. When she finishes, Kara looks up at me, beaming with accomplishment.

"I did it! I can enhance the herbs." She lifts one of the deep green leaves to me. "Here, try it."

I take a small leaf, plucking it into my mouth. As I chew on the medicinal herb, the pain in my jaw subsides. With each bite, I can feel the medicine seep into my jaw and cheek, soothing the ache left over from yesterday's reconditioning session.

This woman is an amazement. Despite the collar's blockers, she can still wield her element with masterful skill.

I've begun helping her regain her wielding abilities. I know this is incredibly stupid, but I cannot deny her this. To watch her face glow or her smile widen at the flair of essence flowing from her fingertips brings me a boyish joy I have not found elsewhere.

I don't know what possesses me to help her cultivate the power her collar mutes. Maybe it's my guilt for allowing her to find comfort in our conversation and laughter with her enemy.

Even as I go through the torturous reconditioning, I continue to betray my people. I abet the cultivation of her powers, while atoning for the sins I've committed in sympathizing with her faction.

There's something about the girl that draws me. A spark I felt the second I saw her on the battlefield of her home faction.

She is a wild force, an incarnate of Gaia divine, and I find myself enamored.

CHAPTER 13
KARA

I RUSH TO THE reconditioning arena, already running late to
retrieve Sorren. I got caught up helping another medical work-
er with his rounds of treatment in the barracks. The soldiers gain
so many minor injuries during training that it is often easier for
everyone if we attend to them in their barracks. Otherwise, the
infirmary would be in a constant state of overflow, rather than
practically empty as it currently is.

When I push the heavy doors of the conditioning arena open, I
find Sorren dangling from his bounds, head slumped, and his leg
bent at an unnatural angle against its shackle. My throat tightens,
and I want to rage at the men who've done this.

I race to him, quickly working apart the shackles at his ankles
first. In the months he's been suffering through his sentence, we've
developed a consistent routine. I move the platform beneath his
feet, hissing as my eyes rise to the break in his calf. There's a slight
bulge in his skin where the severed bone is pushing to tear through.

Damn them.

"Gods, we need to set this quickly." I step onto the platform to
unhook the manacles around his wrists. Sorren plants the foot of
his good leg on the block, holding on to the chains above him for

support. "You can't bear on your leg, lean on me, and I'll help you down."

I wrap my arms around his abdomen and flinch as he lets out a groan. I can't help but tighten my hold as we've already begun to lower him from the block. I can feel the cadence of his breath change and am sure he has at least one cracked rib. Once he's stable, I release his torso, jumping back to search his face for a hint that he's okay.

He gives me a tight smile that stops mid lift, his eyes shutting in a clear sign of pain. I race to the side wall, scrambling across the assortment of discipline implements I don't want to imagine them using on him. When I come across a long metal bar, I bring it to him.

"Here, use this as a crutch, so I don't have to clutch you as tightly."

He takes the bar and stabilizes himself against it, leaning against me for added support as we climb the stairs. When we make it to the infirmary, I usher him to his private room. We were given explicit instructions to isolate the prisoner. The officers made it seem like the instructions were part of a solitary protocol, but as the one who's tended him every night for months, I know they don't want others to see what they've done.

Not all his days are terrible, though some are worse than others. Today is a bad day. I don't waste time in getting to his wounds, taking care to assess his injuries.

As I prepare my supplies, I ask him about the session. It's a question I ask every day that helps me understand what they did to him during his reconditioning. It allows me to gauge what tactics they used to assail him, which pieces of him need the most care.

"Mental, or physical?" I say, and by the dull look in his eyes, I already know the answer.

"Both."

Heartbreak is a stabbing pain in my chest, and I can only imagine what they've done.

"Do you want to talk about it?" Some days he'll tell me what's happened. I think it helps to have someone other than the three in that room, know the truth. Other days he doesn't. On those days, I think he'd rather pretend that none of it happened at all.

I can't take his melancholy. In this moment, I'll do anything to see him smile. "You're pretty banged up, Sorren. Keep this up, and I don't know how I'm going to keep that pretty face of yours intact."

"Don't be modest. I have the utmost faith in your capabilities." His voice strains on the words that he puts too much effort into making sound casual.

I quickly mix some herbs that I know will ease his pain. I reach for more herbs I've never used before, but innately know will help him. The knowledge slips into my mind like a whisper, and I do not pause to question it.

"You damn well should. I've been a healer all my life," I say, trying to keep him distracted from the pain.

My gaze snaps to his, where I find him wide-eyed and staring at me.

"I'm a healer . . ." not a medic, a *healer*. A memory flashes across my mind of me learning about tonics and toxins. A brown-haired boy with the same emerald eyes as mine sat next to me as an aged terra patiently explained the anatomy of a flower she held in her hand. I remember the flower was black but can't recall its name.

"Sorren, my people are healers, that's what I am!" I repeat the sentiment, flabbergasted at the sudden jolt of memory.

His eyes are wide, just as shocked as I am.

"Wha—What else do you remember?" he stammers, and I seal my lips. I can't trust him. It didn't take me long after being assigned to care for him to decide this. The stronger my memory grows, the more my intuition warns me to keep him at a distance. And although I try to keep my walls high, little pieces of myself slip through the cracks, and we discover them together.

I shrug, absently griping the black stone hanging from my neck. "That's it. But isn't that great?"

Infatuation is a fun game to play, but I can never forget that this man is being punished for a reason. My gut screams at me to be wary of him, and I intend to listen.

"Yes," he smiles, the tense features of his face relaxing. "That is great."

I continue to address his wounds, not wanting to divulge any more of my discoveries until I've completely explored what I can remember.

Once I patch up the gash on his eyebrow, I move down his face, clicking my tongue when I come to his nose.

"It's broken again." What's their deal with the man's nose? "Soon, I won't be able to keep it straight."

I graze my fingers along the bridge of his nose, then pack his nostrils with gauze, shaking my head.

He looks up at me. "I'm sorry. I will try to remember that for tomorrow." He tries to smile, but the curve of his lips stops mid-lift and ends in a grimace.

Gods, I must sound like such an ass. "That was pretty insensitive of me." I look down, biting my lip. "I'd just hate to see your face altered by what *they've* done."

His eyes meet mine, and in contrast to the rest of his face, there is a lightness there. "And why is that?" He challenges, growing greedy with my complements.

Heat floods my cheeks as I dampen my suddenly dry lips. Steeling my resolve, I can feel my nostrils flare as I lift my chin, meeting his gaze and challenge. "Because I like your face. It's a handsome face, and as long as I'm able, we're going to keep it that way."

Feeling bold, I look down at him, allowing my eyes to linger on the broad outline of his strong jaw, still prominent under the dark shadow of his stubble. His gaze heats as I move up to the soft lips I would give anything to press my own against.

I wonder what he'd taste like. How his tongue would feel against mine. Would it be cold, an icy burn against my teeth?

The boyish smile that pulls across his face pushes through the grimace to stretch his lips in a wide grin. My heart flutters against my ribcage, mimicking the rapid swirl deep in the pit of my stomach. Still feeling bold, I bring my hands up to graze his jaw, pushing my fingers against the thick stubble shadowing it.

"How do your sessions work?" I say, breaking the silence. "Do they just hit you the entire time, or is there a point to all this?"

"The pain is supposed to focus me. I am to associate it with the wrong I have done and the consequences I could face. They ask questions. They remind me of things—make me remember."

Remember. What a fickle thing memory is. Each day, my own memories grow stronger. I think of the dull haze I'd felt months ago, the frustrating stupor in which I'd spent most of my day. Slowly, the feeling receded to only nighttime and morning. Now I wake up fully cognizant, flashes to a life before Central City, flickering in my mind.

I've completely overcome the grogginess I once hated, remembering everything from my day, and the days prior, save for maintenance. At maintenance hour my mind flusters in a haze I cannot fight, the entire ordeal turning into a blacked-out memory I cannot access.

Although I wish I could ask Sorren for help, it is up to me to find out what is happening during maintenance. And with each day that I grow stronger, I come closer to my goal. My mind burns with questions I dare not ask the aero. For all our voracious flirting, I know he is dangerous. This man holds so many secrets, and until I discover what they are, I know I can't trust him.

I continue to graze my fingers from his beard to hairline, curling the overgrown locks between my fingers. "And what wrong have you done? What could earn you such severe punishment?"

His gaze darts to mine, studying me. His brows knit together, then release, his eyes dropping to the floor.

More secrets.

"I disobeyed orders."

"Was it worth it?"

"Yes." The word flows from his mouth. His eyes widen as he looks up at me, and I imagine he may not have thought the answer through. I hold his gaze, searching his icy gray eyes for a clue to who this man is, that holds a spot in my memory I can't uncover.

He is the first to break our gaze, and I take the hint to quit probing.

I move my fingers from his hair and get back to my mending.

"When will this all be over?" I ask, looking at the nasty break in his shin. I need to set it.

"When they are satisfied that I've learned my lesson and won't betray them again."

This is going to hurt. "And what do you plan to do once you are free?"

I grip his calf, waiting for a moment of distraction. Instead of answering me, his face goes blank. His gaze darts to the side, and he forcibly pulls a mask of indifference over his face. But I see it. The hesitation—the guilt.

Is there someone else?

Jealousy tremors through me in a raging quake. I swallow the lump lodged in my throat. I have no claim to this man. This insecurity is ridiculous. Of course, there's someone else. He's a gods damned military commander. He's young, and handsome, and smart, and brave, and strong, and . . . *fuck me* . . . I really like him.

For once, I wish he wouldn't bother with suppressing his chill. I'm hot everywhere. Embarrassment blazes through me, as if I'd announced my thoughts to the world.

I continue, gripping his calf, remembering my task.

"Is there a girl? Someone waiting for you when you get out?" I can't help it. I tell myself, I'm only trying to distract him, but truly, I'm a glutton for pain. I need to hear him say it.

"No." He blurts out, eyes wide and sincere.

Relief floods through me in a cool wave that steals my breath and steadies my pulse. I bite my lip to keep from smiling and remember that I still need to set his leg. When he opens his mouth to continue, I grip his leg and twist, snapping it forward and setting it in place.

Sorren coughs, trying to cover the yelp he released at what I know must have been excruciating.

I quickly bind the break in tight gauze soaked with my most recent concoction of enhanced herbs to dull the pain.

"There, not too bad." I look up at him, summoning the sweetest smile I can. He grunts, nodding, taking deep deliberate breaths.

"Your gentleness could use some work," he says, his words still a little breathy. "I'd hate to imagine your enthusiasm, should my answer have been yes."

I feel the corner of my mouth pull up and give him an unshielded wink. His jaw tightens in response, the Adams apple in his neck bobbing below it.

"Help me with my wielding?" I ask with a hopeful grin.

"Of course. Show me what you've got."

I smile and fan my fingers out. Squeezing my eyes shut, I try to do what he's told me a thousand times. I search for the essence within me and pull, huffing a grunt with the effort it takes.

"Kara, what are you doing?"

"I'm trying to push my essence out."

"You're going to push *something* out."

My eyes pop open, and I reach for a roll of gauze to toss at his head. It bounces off his temple before he can catch it.

"Sorry, sorry. Look, let's try this," he says, grabbing my hands, fanning them out above his.

"Aether is in everything. Your element's essence flows through all land material, including you. It's what gives them life and power. Use the essence flowing through you. Grasp and command it. Once you've controlled that, you can call to the aether in the plants and land around."

I nod, unable to truly focus on anything beyond the cool soothe of his large palms cradling mine.

"Close your eyes."

I obey, relaxing my body and opening it to my element.

"Feel your essence in the core of you. Focus on it and pull it through your body. Breathe in as you pull it up to your chest and through your shoulders."

His slow words pass over me, the soft rumble of his voice raising chills on my skin. I breathe out, focusing on the aether that flows through my body just as vitally as blood.

"Now draw it down your arms and into your fingertips."

I can feel the electrifying flow of it lazily winding in my core. Rather than grabbing at it, I coax the essence within me, gently tugging up and out. The aether flows through me in strings of vibrance, shocking every nerve ending from my abdomen, flowing through my chest, and down my arms. I can feel it concentrate in my fingertips, intensifying almost painfully.

"That's it, wildflower, you're doing it."

I bite my lip, trying to suppress the grin that stretches my mouth whenever he uses the endearment. I peek down at my bright fingertips, glowing a dull, luminescent green atop Sorren's palms.

He gives me a smile, warm and indulgent. "Now stretch your fingers out. Envision the essence in ropes of green vines that push through your hands and out your fingers."

As I do, the sting of essence pushes through, finally releasing to flow from my hands.

"Take a look." The deep timber of his voice vibrates through me, and I slowly peek down and gasp.

I watch as my fingers slowly begin to thin and lengthen. The green glow overtakes them completely until they are a deep verdant, budding out tiny leaves. The thin vines creep up Sorren's hand to droop across his wrist and forearm.

"Keep practicing, and you'll be able to move and wield them, just as you are the fingers of your hand."

Gods, I can't believe it.

My chest wells, so full with this gift he's continued to give me. I lift my arms around him, pulling him in for a hug, my new vines slapping across his back. Heat flares where his icy hands lift to press between my shoulder blades and into the small of my back.

I lift my head up, touching my forehead to his as his firm hands wrap around my waist, gently pulling me in. As his broad chest presses against mine, I move to bury my face in the crook of his neck and whisper, "Thank you."

CHAPTER 14
SORREN

I LAY BACK THINKING of the warm, blithe girl who is so different from the one I'd met in battle months ago. Though she is bound mentally and elementally, she is somehow free and unburdened.

I peer out through my open door, watching as she hunches over a potted plant, likely some herb she is cultivating to address my mounting injuries more efficiently. Though her fingers glow green, and the herb pulses beneath her essence, she huffs out a sigh. She has accomplished so much, but it is still not enough. She knows more ability lies dormant within her, as if she remembers her Level Three status, and has just chosen not to share it with me.

I can't blame her. She shouldn't trust me.

After what feels like hours of effort, she pushes the plant away. With a huff, she plops her head on the desk in front of her, defeated.

I sit up in my cot, willing to do anything to turn her grim expression. Holding out my hand, I pull a snowflake from the air. It lays in my cold palm, a delicate web of icy design. I stretch it, enlarging the tiny flake to grow almost quadruple its size, so that the lacey designs are clear and prominent.

Blowing it toward her, the snow crystal lands on her arm. She lifts her head to look at it, narrowing her gaze to focus on the oversized flake. I form another, and another, varying in size and design, sending them over to the slumped girl.

Bringing heavy lashes down, she leans her head back and allows her face to catch the falling flurries that melt on her skin. Parting her lips, the corners of her mouth lift as she inhales the now cold air.

"I don't think I've ever seen them this way . . ." She stands, and the bud of a smile blooms on her lips. Spreading her arms, she spins, as the snowflakes fall like rain all around her. Her movements are so free and graceful, they remind me of a traditional dance my people perform on the ice. The way they glide and flow across the frictionless surface appears almost magical.

I hobble from my cot and into the primary space, empty of any other patients or attendants. Placing my hand on the floor, I push the cold from my core and onto the marble tile. A thick sheet of ice creeps across the ground until it is completely covered. Kara's eyes widen as her mouth parts. I wield the air in the room to form a wind that pushes the cots against the walls, clearing the center space.

Although her remedies are powerful, my leg is still a long way from being healed. I bear down on the metal pole and limp over to her. Taking her hand, I lead her to the ice. "There is a waltz my people perform on ice. Your twirling reminds me of it."

"You have to show me." Her pleading eyes widen up at me. I gesture down to my leg, grateful for the excuse to avoid making a fool of myself. I'm a soldier, not a dancer.

She places her hand on my chest. "When you're better, then." It is a command, not a question, and I can only nod, unable to deny her anything.

My left hand clutches the brace as my right encases hers. She squeezes it, looking up at me, trusting me to guide her. I pull her to glide across the ice. Her fingers intertwine with mine, fitting perfectly like puzzle pieces. My feet are at home on the ice. On their element, they are sturdy and strong. For her—I cannot say the same. Kara sways back and forth, holding her arms out for balance.

When I release her hand, her arms swing in frantic circles in a fit to regain her balance. She turns and braces herself on me. I must bear down on the crutch to keep from toppling over.

"Whoa there. I've got you," I say, wrapping my hand around her waist, gripping her tightly. She stills against my chest, looking up with hooded emerald eyes. I cannot hold the heat of her gaze, so I gently turn her around, keeping my hand gripped on her hip to guide her forward.

"Oh, this is amazing!"

"Okay, Kara, I'm going to let go. Just hold your legs firm and make slow, deliberate steps. Use each movement to propel yourself forward."

"Okay, I've got it!"

I reluctantly release her and watch as she glides down the ice. I guess she panics, because she begins to push back and forth, flapping her arms like a baby bird.

"How do I sto—" her voice cuts off with the thud of her running into a medical cot shoved against the wall.

Twisting and circling her arms, she takes the most ungraceful fall imaginable, landing straight on her backside. Sitting on the ice, she throws her head back and releases a howl of laughter. It's quite possibly the loveliest sound I've ever heard.

The hysterical terra then lifts her body from the ground, only slipping three or four times on the way up, before calling over to me, "Now I know how to stop."

A brilliant smile once again frames her face, and I don't have the heart to tell her that what she's done is more a crash than anything.

She pushes herself across the ice, gaining more excitement with speed. "Look, Sorren, I think I've got it! It feels like I'm flying!" she sings to me. With brown hair waving and whipping around her head, I see an ember spark, and she is beautiful.

Rounding a corner, she pushes herself to keep from falling, but that also increases her speed.

"Wait! I'm going too fast!" she yelps as she rushes toward me, and I know she won't be able to stop herself.

I bear down on my crutch, so that it can hold us both, but must abandon it, as she slams into me, full force. I catch her with both hands, trying to steady us, as we swing in a circle, still playing off her momentum. We fall and I twist us to shield her from hitting the ice.

My back slams down with a thud and she collapses on top of me. Taking a moment to regain our breath, she looks up to meet my gaze. Bright emerald peeks at me through thick lashes, and I see the faintest gold lines streak through her irises. A strange tightening curls in my stomach and pushes an unfamiliar warmth through me. My skin tingles in all the places her slight frame lies on top of mine.

"Thank you," she whispers so low I barely hear it, her breath fanning across my chest.

Everything falls quiet, and the only sound to be heard is the slow and steady rhythm of our breathing. I lift my hand to trace up her arm, feeling the bumps that raise on her smooth skin, then rest my palm on her triceps and squeeze in response. I hold her gaze just a bit longer, warmth taking root in the pit of my stomach, where there was only ice before. We watch our breath turn to white in the air between us, and I lift my hand to tuck a stray wave behind her ear.

Her lashes flutter closed, and her lips move toward mine. I have never wanted anything so intensely as I do this terra. With the heat of her body pressed so firmly against my own, I could be a scoundrel and take what she so willingly offers.

But she won't offer me her lips or affection if she remembers who I truly am. So, I turn my head and look away.

CHAPTER 15
KARA

COLD BRUSHES AGAINST MY lips where I expect for there to be warmth. I blink to see Sorren's head turned to the side. His eyes strain to fall on anything but mine and he looks as if he'd rather be anywhere but beneath me.

I shove myself from him, as if my haste could outpace my shame. As I lift myself to stand, I forget there is a sheet of ice beneath my feet. Slipping mid-rise, I fall again on my backside against the air wielder. I fight the rising heat that creeps up my neck and face. I'm sure I look like an idiot.

"Wait, I didn't—" I raise my hand to cut him off. I don't want to hear any false reassurances meant to spare my dignity.

"Kara . . ." His voice is low and pleading, as he gently pulls my hand down. My breath stops at the sound of that word. The simple name that only he has uttered. The name that grounds me and feels at home on his tongue. My gut wretches at the conflicting emotions raging against my chest.

"Kara, please don't misunderstand." He pulls my hand into his as he lifts into a sitting position. "There is no one in this realm I've ever wanted more."

My heart thumps at the confession, breath escaping from my lungs.

"But not like this." His eyes turn down as my stomach bottoms out. "Your memory is not completely recovered, and—"

I snatch my hand from his. I see what's happened. Mortification blanches my skin, and I can't help but feel like a dimwitted moron. Tears sting my eyelids. Tears I'd rather die than release to fall in front of this man.

"But I can still decide," I say sharply. "I'm not so simple-minded that I'm incapable of identifying and acting on my feelings." In all my self-righteous pride, I cannot keep the pathetic twang of pain from lowering my voice.

Sorren's eyes grow wide. "I never thought you couldn't understand."

But what he must mean is that he believes I'm too dense to realize the consequences of my own actions. That he thought I would do something I won't even remember in the morning.

Maybe this is my fault. I've kept so many of my improvements close to me, afraid to show him my hand. How can I possibly expect him to know that my memory has all but recovered?

I remember everything . . . well from a point. I still don't remember much of my life before coming to this place, but even those memories come back to me daily.

Regret festers at how distrustful I've been of the sweet aero. I've been so concerned with him betraying me, though all he's ever shown me has been kindness. A kindness his superiors would punish him for if our wielding practice is ever discovered. A kindness that could cost him everything.

"I can remember," I say, the defensive edge of my voice making me sound childish.

"It isn't that I think you wouldn't remember this." He gestures between us. "You just haven't regained your previous memories." His words come out in a rush. "Regardless of my feelings, you deserve to have all your memories before deciding if you truly want me."

He isn't making any sense, and my insecurity flares at his illogical words. Why wouldn't I choose him? I can't ask. I can't appear even denser than what he must already think I am.

He really must not know how much I've improved. My chest tightens as I clench my jaw, frustration overwhelming me like a raging sandstorm. I turn my head, knowing that at any moment, the hot tears of embarrassment will fall and seal my shame for good.

"Kara, please . . ." And there it is. The single word that melts me so thoroughly. He says my name and all my anger shatters, falling into despair at something I want so badly, but evades me. Whether I want him, or to simply remember it all, is something I just can't sort out now. "Please trust me when I say whatever feelings you have are more than reciprocated."

I scoff at his pleading attempt to soothe my embarrassment, but he pulls my hand into his and dips his eyes to meet mine. "Let's just give it time. My fate is still so uncertain. I've been through reconditioning longer than is standard. You deserve more than a broken prisoner. Give me time to be someone who could begin to deserve you."

The sincerity in his words shatter me. Fear grips me for the first time as I consider the real possibility of him not making it through reconditioning. Not everyone does.

Not all the pieces they break on him are physical. More and more, he declines to share what's happened in his sessions with me, instead, retreating into himself. They're wearing him down, and each night I see another fragment of him gone.

I pull his hand to my chest, gripping the man that is so humble to think that there is still something he must do to deserve the affection I've already developed for him. Why he feels anything less than worthy, rather than too good, is beyond me. But his pleading eyes beg for me to understand. So, I nod, wondering how I ever thought I could hate him.

"Let's clean this up," he says, raising my hand to his lips where he gives my knuckles a light kiss, then places his palm on the icy floor.

As quickly as the sheet of ice spread across the stone, it absorbs back into his palm, taking the intense cold with it. I reach out my hand to help him from the floor, wincing as he grimaces through the pain of moving his leg.

"I shouldn't have run into you. I'm sure to have damaged your leg, knocking you over just as it's begun to heal," I say, leading him to his cot.

"Doubt it. I've got the realm's best healer, and for some reason, she just keeps fixing me." He winks at me as I help him lower onto the bed, and my stomach somersaults.

"Flattery will get you everywhere, but that may be a bit far reaching."

That's saying the least. ML Twenty-three is a known master of herbal and medicinal healing. I'm constantly in awe of her capabilities. She keeps me close, and has become more than a mentor, but a guardian. I've learned much from her patient teachings, but my abilities to enhance and manipulate herbs and remedies may never meet her own.

"I wait for the day you stop second guessing yourself and your abilities. I've seen what you can do. If they were real, I'd think you were a secret immortal, like the guardians of old."

I can't meet his eyes as he spins the flattering lie. The fullest extent he's seen my powers on display was the first night I healed him. I think back to the overwhelming show of wielding. When the essence broke free from some hidden barrier in my core to flow like a title wave, engulfing me in a fit of power. Since then, the essence has not overtaken me like it had that night, but the steady flow of aether has remained lucid and tangible.

Sorren smiles, lost in his own thoughts. "Humph, my father would have loved that. All his lunatic raving of immortals come to pass."

Something rings true about the mythical beings he speaks of. A memory itches at the back of my mind and I shut it down before it turns into a powerful slamming against my frontal lobe. What's left is a simple feeling, an inkling that feels like déjà vu.

"I think they're real." The words escape my mouth before I can stop them, and I stifle a groan at how ludicrous I sound. I don't quite remember the stories, but I know the immortal guardians are fictitious. *I know this.* But something in my core screams they aren't. Something inside me scurries away and hides behind a locked memory, whispering *they exist.*

I dare a glance at him, expecting either the anxious stare of someone who believes they're speaking to a madwoman, or the smug scoff of someone who thinks I am a joke.

I receive neither. Instead, his sharp gray eyes are inquisitive and respectful.

"You do?" His question is not condescending. Rather, he seems genuinely curious and eager to consider my perspective.

I bite my lip, not willing to say another word. I may not have made a total fool of myself just yet, but I have no solid reasoning to believe in the creatures I know to be a child's tale.

When I offer no reply, he continues. "My father did too. He was obsessed with the idea of immortal guardians. If he wasn't advancing his vision of a supreme Upper, he was caught in the throes of research. Crazed by the idea of gaining so much essence that it turned an ordinary elemental into a god. Commanding their element so wholly that they wield the aether itself." His shoulders shake with a slight shiver, and I find myself captivated by the idea.

"So, I take it your dad was a bit of a control freak?" This earns me an amused snort.

"Are they bad? The immortals." I hate asking the question that makes me look even more mindless than before, but fear grips me at the very thought of the fantasy creatures, and I must know.

Again, his response is not haughty or mocking. He is patient and reflective, thinking before giving me an answer. "Not according to my father. If you'd listened to him, they're god-like beings, created to protect us."

"From what?" I ask without shielded reserve.

His lips curve into a roguish grin. "From the monsters of the Outer."

I can tell he teases me, but it is not at all malicious. My eyes go wide with intrigue as he indulges me with the story.

"Old world monsters, that breathe fire and lure non water elementals into the shadows of the deep." His tone deepens and eyes narrow as he goes on with his facetious ghost story. "Monsters that terrorized the realm, before the deities tasked guardians with their capture and imprisonment." His gaze lifts, looking off in a distant stare.

"Guess the Outer is a prison region to more than just wayward elementals." He muses over creatures that I am sure are purely fictitious.

"Have you ever been there?" I say.

"No. No one goes to the Outer. When prisoners are transferred, our enforcers simply hand them over to the gatekeepers. Once you're stationed in the Outer, it's a lifelong assignment. No one leaves, no matter who you are."

"Then who would choose to accept such an assignment?"

"Many vie for the position. It's extremely prestigious. A soldier stationed there leaves their family with wealth, status, and legacy. Those are no small accommodations." He looks to the side. "It may be the pampered brat in me—" he says the words as if he's mocking himself, but a sad pitch in his voice hints that he may actually believe them, "—but there isn't anything that could tempt me into going to that black hole of a region."

There is something vulnerable and broken about Sorren. He is unlike the other injured soldiers who come into the infirmary. His wounds are deep and vast. He's been crushed by a weight that feels so familiar to me, that I only want to help him bear it.

This weight—this vulnerability that he allows me to witness—feels like a secret shared between us that no one else is privileged to. One that no one else could understand. It links us in a way I've never felt toward anyone else.

I circle back to the immortals, fascinated with the fantastical beings, but mostly to stray from the sentiment that's caused him distress. "So how did the guardians gain so much essence?"

With only the tiny taste of volatile power flowing through my previously numb veins, my heart races at the idea of someone accumulating more.

Sorren shrugs. "Some say it was a gift from their deities, including Gaia." He mentions the land mother that still seems ridiculous to me, no matter how much he tells me about her. "It was a last act of mercy from the gods that have remained otherwise silent since. But even the guardians could not have expected the price they would pay for such a blessing."

I lean in closer to him, bursting with curiosity. I'm seconds from shaking the handsome aero who spins his story like a fine tapestry, holding the final thread to dangle above me until the suspense is almost too much to bear. "Well, what was it?"

"All power comes at a cost. We pay for what we wield with our energy and vitality." I take a slow breath, all too familiar with the spent feeling that follows the flow of essence from my fingertips. The weight of total depletion that accompanied my initial fit of power the first time I healed Sorren.

"With power that far exceeds any Level Three, when the essence can no longer take energy, it demands flesh." He pauses again, watching the grimace flinch across my face. "With each expenditure of immortal power, the guardians sacrificed a piece of themselves to their element. They merged into the waves of the sea. Ice overtook their skin. Molten lava flowed through veins that blood no longer held a place in, and extremities turned to arms and legs of branches and stone."

Skin of ice.

Pupilless eyes and a voice that shrieks like nails on glass blare across my mind. I squeeze my eyes shut as pain ricochets against my skull, doing my best to camouflage my distress. I am unsure what Sorren sees, but he stops his story. I breathe through the pain and rising anxiety of a memory so real I can feel it wrap icy fingers around my constricting throat.

His hands rest on my shoulders, coaxing me to calm. His head dips to level with mine and his voice takes on a soothing tone. "But they're not meant to be frightening. Some are said to be beautiful beyond measure. As ethereal as the flowing sea, with eyes of diamonds, and hair of flowing languid fire." He smiles as if he sees something in me worthy of the comparison. "They are the total embodiment of their element, and nothing is more fantastical."

I choke back a laugh, still covering the receding pain. "And you mean to compare me to these divine creatures?"

The smile leaves his lips, and his hands grip on tighter to my shoulders, gaze baring straight through me. "One day you will see you're so much more than you believe."

And damn him. His icy gray eyes bore into mine, and a sandstorm of emotion rages within me. I find myself suddenly furious with him. Furious about so many things. Because something deep inside me says I ought to be, even though I have no solid reason for it. Furious at him for rejecting me, even when his rationale could not be nobler. But above all, I could hate him for breeding in me a discontentment where there is only sweet complacency.

Before his pale gray eyes looked at me in a way no one ever has, holding more admiration and desire than I've ever faced. Before his full lips whispered tales of a woman stronger and more gifted than I could ever hope to be, lying dormant within me. I never wanted to be more than the simple servant whose whole life lay plain as her set out daily schedule. I'd never wanted to remember anything more than I'd wanted to recall the late-night conversations we'd held every day prior, working through pain and vulnerability to grasp and hold on to memories that no longer leave me with each passing day. I've never fought for anything like I do to harness the essence he's helped me cultivate.

A storm rages within me, and though I'd love to call it fury, I know it's something so much more.

Chapter 16
Sorren

MALAKAI PACES THE ROOM below me. My eye twitches at the loud click of his boots, each time his heavy heal hits the stone. The ring of his steps drums through my mind and keeps me awake at night. The incessant clicking is always accompanied by the forceful cadence of my father's words. Words I cannot escape, no matter how I try to tune them out, or fill my thoughts with other things.

While Jarek inflicts an acute physical torture on my body, it is one I can handle. Malakai seeks to breakdown and destroy my psyche. He plays mind games, seeking to exploit the insecurities and fears I have battled since adolescence, until I'm sure I can take no more.

"You sympathize with the very people who've destroyed so much. Tell me Sorren, what have the Lowers taken from you?" The blaze burns higher. This time the flames lick my skin, leaving behind seared flesh. "Answer me."

I know what he wants me to say. My mouth fights to yell out the truth—that those elementals stole everything from me. But I clench my teeth, refusing to award him with an answer.

135

Malakai's jaw squares as he sets into a glower. The arch of his eyebrow heightens as he moves on to the next question. "Who killed your mother?"

At this I thrash against my chains, lunging forward, seeking to headbutt the arrogant bastard.

"Oh, so there is life left inside you. For a moment I thought you'd perished," he says. "Who robbed the Upper of their Secunde before she could ever be formally presented?"

As I lunge forward again, I am met with Jarek's iron coated fist, throwing my body back with a force that rips my cheek, and rattles my teeth.

Malakai throws his head back in a howl of laughter. "You killed your mother."

The sting of truth hurts more than any lash or strike from Jarek. The reminder Nero served me, with every disappointed look or resentful glower of my childhood, stabs at my heart now that I hear Malakai say it aloud.

I killed my mother.

In giving me life, she sacrificed her own. Since the day of my birth, I have brought only death and destruction to this world. A legacy I continued throughout my life. One that has landed me here, above the relentless flames that seek to cleanse me of my sins, but only remind me of all the damage I have caused.

"Who allowed her to die?"

I do not lift my head as I answer. "The terras."

As the words leave my mouth, they feel like a copout. A scapegoat for the true transgressor. Me.

My father always blamed the terras for not saving her. Whether they couldn't—or wouldn't—remains a mystery. But it doesn't change the fact that she wouldn't have needed saving had I not caused her harm.

If my father was motivated to release the Upper from their codependence with the Lower before my mother's death, he became obsessed by it after. It is what he attributed his immense strides in technology and medicine over the course of the following five years to. I don't know if he blamed the terras to ease the responsibility of her death from me, or if he truly believed the Lower elementals wanted to see her die.

"Very good." The smug smile that upturns Malakai's lips twists my stomach. I seethe knowing he has found satisfaction in my answer. "And who killed your father?"

"The pyros." Without pause, I let the words fall from my mouth.

I remember receiving leave from the academy, traveling back home to prepare his body. The Lower instigated the initial attack that began the Regional Battles. In an attempt to steal their serving elementals, they ambushed Central City. They took my father captive and killed him in the crossfire. When I arrived to prepare his body for burial, it was burned beyond recognition.

A blazing hatred rips through me as I recall the young elemental I was, burying the only parent I had. I'd only just presented as a Level Three, barely passed puberty. I'd never had the opportunity to make my father proud. Never had the chance to show him I was more than just the murderer of his beloved wife and disappointment of a son.

"Yes. The pyros killed your father, and the terras let your mother die. Still, you betrayed your region and disobeyed orders so that you may aid them. In allowing even the smallest fraction of terras to go free, you awarded them the opportunity to grow in strength and numbers against our people. And for what?"

I do not know. I cannot answer him. I can only hang my head in disgrace. Above the hatred that burns inside me, shame sears hotter.

"Why you sympathized with the enemy will remain a mystery to us all. It is a testimony to your ineptitude to retain the office you were given because of your father's name."

I am defeated.

"Again, because of your father's stature, you are given leniencies and liberties afforded to no one else in our armament. Your office will be reinstated, pending the successful completion of your mission. Do you understand your assignment?"

"I do," I say without hesitation.

"What must you do?"

"I must find and capture the escaped faction members. I will bring them back to Central City so they can serve. As is their place." The words are mechanical as they fall from my lips.

"And what mercies will you show them?"

"None."

His eyes narrow as his hands pull back into fist. "Your rehabilitation is complete. Your reconditioning is successful."

As he speaks, the flames that were below me die, and the cuffs that burned my ankles and wrists cool. Without another word,

Malakai takes one last look at me and turns to leave, the pyro following behind.

I wait for what feels like hours for Kara to come. Just as well, it gives me time to sink into my misery. Every word spoken today, though painful, was true. They are all truths I must come to terms with, whether I want to or not.

By the time Kara walks through the conditioning arena doors, my arms have already gone numb. The pretty features of her delicate face turn down in a sullen grimace and she looks at me with a pity I don't deserve. She is the last person who should show me any compassion. The last person who should gift me with any kindness. The only reason she does is because she doesn't remember who I am or what I've done, and I am a miscreant for allowing it.

Her hands quickly work apart the shackles at my ankles. She moves the platform beneath my feet as I test standing on it so that she does not need to catch me as I fall from the chains. My leg has healed enough that I no longer need a crutch, only sporting a modest limp. When she's confident I'm sturdy enough to stand, she climbs on to the platform beside me, tiptoeing against my chest to reach the cuffs at my wrists. Her body presses close to mine as she unlocks them. When she releases me, I lean into her, not quite strong enough to stand on my own yet.

"There we go. Let's get you to the infirmary."

"Yes, this will probably be our last healing." I look down at her, trying to muster a smile.

She looks up as we struggle to climb the stairs to the capitol building's surface.

"That's great news," she smiles. "So, your conditioning is complete? I'm so relieved."

Conditioning, the overly kind way of describing torture, has a humor that's not lost on me. "Yes, but I'm afraid I will miss our encounters."

She looks up at me with a sly arch of her brow. "Well, you don't need to go getting into trouble for an excuse to come see me. Most of my work is around the infirmary. You can drop by anytime to say hi." She looks away, but not before I see the burn of rose on her cheeks.

"I'd like that very much." I smile, my mind straying to ways I could sneak off to the capitol building, knowing very well that it will be impossible.

She helps me through the door of the medical room, and I stumble to my bed, settling myself in while she gathers the herbs and salves needed to heal me. She walks over with an arm full of jars and a mortar and pestle in her hands, continuously grinding the pace she has concocted.

"You seem burdened for someone who was just released from their sentence."

I cannot tell her I war with traitorous thoughts so soon after my reconditioning. As if the punishment served no purpose at all. I cannot tell her that my mind is heavy with the decision I must make of whether to hunt and capture her people once again. So, I give her a different truth. "Today's reconditioning was particularly taxing."

"Well, as I'm not seeing any severed bones or missing fingernails, I'm guessing they hit you pretty hard mentally."

I wince, flexing my hand at the reminder of my prior fingernail extraction. Kara helped me to regrow them, and it isn't the worst punishment, but I still think I'd prefer the swift pain of a broken nose.

"What was it this time?"

"We talked about my parents." I say and her grinding stills.

"Your mom?" She jerks her head back; her voice rises in feigned casualness. I haven't spoken to her about my mother's death. Though it feels like I've shared my entire life with the girl who cannot tell me anything about her own, I don't have much knowledge of the woman who birthed me.

"Yes, he reminded me of my first dishonor to the region in taking their Secunde, before she'd ever been introduced."

"The Secunde, that's the title you give the prime's spouse?"

I nod. "They were married quickly. There was no courtship or engagement period. In one day, he announced his marriage and impending child." I recite the story that's been told to me by others. "My mother was sickly and had a hard pregnancy, so my father thought it best to save her public introduction until after I was born."

Unfortunately, she never made it to see that day. "She died giving birth to me."

Kara's arms are around me in an instant, pulling me into her embrace. "I'm so sorry, Sorren."

"It's fine. I never actually knew her."

It's difficult to receive condolences for someone you've never met. Even harder to receive them for someone you killed. I don't feel like I have a right to mourn her, so I never have.

"My father never really spoke to me about her. I don't even have a picture of what she looked like. No one else actually knew her. So, she is a ghost in the truest sense of the term."

I believe the silence regarding my mother was partly because of my father's resentment for her death. Though he was never one to discuss sentiments, regardless. Unless it was about progressing his vision for the region, the man had nothing to say to me at all.

Kara doesn't press me any further. I think that's my favorite thing about talking to her. She doesn't try to bolster me with anecdotal positivity, doesn't try to *fix* how I'm feeling. She simply listens. And when the memories of what I've done become too heavy to continue speaking, she gifts me with silence.

When her hands move to my skin, I feel the sting of essence flow through them.

"You're even stronger today," I say as she expertly dresses my wounds.

"Yes, I can feel it." She smiles.

The injuries from my previous conditionings have all healed, with only modest scars as evidenced they'd even occurred. When she's addressed the wounds on my head, she moves to my chest. Her deep emerald eyes hold mine as she dips her finger into the bowl of muddled herbs in her hand. She takes her time, dragging her fingertips along my skin, gingerly passing the herbs over the gashes and cuts.

My heart quickens with each slow stroke of her fingers, dancing along my chest. They carry an energy that she channels through the herbs she wields, and I believe she's been holding out on me.

When she comes to the burn rivets made by Jarek's chain, she tsks. Dipping a long strip of gauze in a liquid mixture at her side, she gingerly places it on the long lines of chain marks. Her fingers work to smooth the gauze down, sliding down my abdomen in maddening strokes that I expend all my focus on not reacting to.

"Hmmm, you're still warm." I swallow, not telling her that the heat rising in my core has nothing to do with today's reconditioning. "Can you give me some ice?"

I break my concentration to form the elemental device. I place a pitiful ice skewer in her palm, unable to wield anything more. Her gaze holds mine as she places the ice on my skin, gliding it down my burns. I feel my palms grow clammy and damp, squeezing them into fists to give the tension somewhere to focus.

I cannot take the cold glide of my own elemental device on the hot strips of skin.

"Does that feel okay?" she asks, her voice low and inviting.

"Ye—yes," I cough, as she releases the ice, allowing it to slip down to my navel.

Gods, this woman is going to kill me.

When her fingers touch the gauze again, she closes her eyes. I feel the electric of aether push into my injuries, seeping through my flesh and penetrating to wrap around my core. I gasp in air as her essence connects with mine in a bright glow on my skin.

When she lifts her fingers, she pulls the gauze away. I look down to see smooth skin, only white marks left across my abdomen.

"Gods, Kara." She holds more aether than I knew. She's never been able to do this before. Never been able to heal so quickly—so thoroughly. She's truly regained her level, and she is a marvel to behold.

"Say it again," she sighs, tilting her head back, her lashes fluttering closed.

"Say what?"

"My name. That word on your lips is the only real thing I've felt for as long as I can remember."

I shouldn't give in to the temptation, but I want to bring her comfort. I want to give her happiness, even in so small of a measure.

"Kara," I say the name, desperate to find the relief wash across her face.

She breathes it in like the purest air, letting the hum of her given name linger in the space between us. As she leans into me, I know I should tell her. I should confess all my sins before this woman who so eagerly trusts me.

"Sorren." She looks up at me through thick lashes, whispering my name, and I cannot.

She says my name like a question, requesting permission I am all too eager to give. Her lips press against mine and I shut down every alarm bell that rings in my mind. I toss every ounce of honor I have to the wayside, letting her melt into me.

As her mouth presses against mine, her soft lips part, giving me access inside. I tentatively stroke my tongue along her full bottom lip, pulling it in between my teeth with a gentle tug. When her tongue grazes mine, I can feel the rapid flow of her breathing increase.

She presses herself into me and I place a hand on the small of her back. I run my other hand through her thick brown hair, hungry to feel every inch of her. Needing her body against mine, as if it's the last time she will ever be in my arms.

Her nails dig into my shoulder blades as I leave a trail of kisses from her jaw to the curve of her neck. I linger there, feeling the thrum of her pulse against my tongue. It beats intime with mine, beating like an encased creature crazy to escape.

A breathy moan escapes her lips, sending tremors of need straight through me. As I rise back up her neck, I gently take her earlobe between my teeth. I get high from her scent, that smells of lavender and jasmine with undertones of cedar that intoxicates and enthralls me.

I feel the flush of her skin warm with the rapid rise and fall of her chest, her fingers circling to grip my hair. I'm sick with myself for allowing her to believe I am what she needs. I am a scoundrel and a con, but for as long as she'll have me, I am hers.

The door of my room swings open, and she jumps from me as if I'm a pile of burning coal. Her hand flies to her kiss-swollen lips as an older woman stares her down with a scowl.

I recognize her. She is the leader of the terra faction I'd captured. When the older woman's eyes reach mine, they burn with a disapproval that blazes hot as any pyro. I deserve every bit of her disgusted glare, and for a moment I worry she recognizes me.

Under her disapproving gaze, I am reminded of the wretch that I am.

"Sir, I believe you are healed. It is time for you to go." She orders me to leave as if she is my superior, and I do not buck her unwarranted authority.

I rise, giving Kara one last glance, and take the leave I should have before allowing things to go so far.

CHAPTER 17
KARA

I BRING MY FINGERS up to touch my tender lips. They dampen as they slide across the thin line of frost trailing down my neck. I cannot suppress the girlish grin that forces itself across my face. This only serves to deepen Twenty-three's ire.

ML Twenty-three's eyes burn into me. "You will not serve them in *that* way."

She refers to the servants who trade more than their regular duties to gain favors from the Upper elementals.

Her accusation stings me. I stand, furious that she could even assume such a thing.

"How could you even think—I would never—" I can't finish. That my feelings and actions for the aero are anything short of genuine is insulting.

Her face softens as she sees I am hurt. The deep furrows in her brow release. "Then why? What was that? Did he force himself on you?"

"No." I can't say the word fast enough. "I initiated."

My eyes turn to the floor as I feel my cheeks heat.

She raises her brows, blinking before swiftly recovering herself. I don't know what exactly came over me. Why I felt bold enough to lean in to kiss the aero, especially after his previous rejection.

Maybe I was afraid I may not see him again now that his conditioning is over. Or maybe I found some security in the idea that the worst of his punishment is through and allowing myself to fall for him is not as much a risk. But even as I say it in my head, I know how ridiculous it sounds. A servant with a crush on an Upper elemental, an officer no less. Ridiculous.

"I hadn't realized you two had become . . . close." She busies her hands sorting the harvested herbs, reaching for casual, I guess, to compensate for the fit of anger she originally confronted me with. I know she only has my best interest at heart. For as long as I can remember, Twenty-three has always looked after me, but today I wish she hadn't.

"It was unexpected," I say.

In the weeks that I have cared for Sorren, we've spent countless hours talking and getting to know each other. Unexpected is an understatement. I couldn't have anticipated feeling so strongly about the aero I instinctually wanted to hate. There's just something about him that makes me feel . . . Well, just makes me *feel*.

Kissing him was right. Releasing myself to his touch is the first thing I've done that caused me no confusion. My desire for him is true, more than anything else in my life.

He's awakened something in me. A strange power that feels like it belongs. It's almost impossible not to associate the surge of energy with him. When he's near, I can't tell whether the excitement surging from me springs from the essence I wield or my affections for him. Not even the pyro from the smithing building has stirred such infatuation in me.

Twenty-three continues. "Nevertheless, it ends here. You will not make a fool of yourself chasing after some Upper officer. They are dangerous."

"How do you know? And who are you to tell me what I can and can't do?" She is my superior, but she's not my master.

"I care about you."

"You don't even know me. You don't even know my name."

She opens her mouth to speak, then shuts it, but this springs another question. "Do you even know your own name?"

Again, she opens her mouth, but nothing comes out. Had it never occurred to her she couldn't call her own name? "Don't you find it odd that we can't remember these things?"

There are so many things we cannot recall. It's never bothered me before that so much seems to be locked away in the recesses of my mind. They were never worth the pain that memories brought. It wasn't until Sorren made me believe I was more than what I had been told that I even cared.

Twenty-three stands, eyes cast down as if searching her own mind for answers she cannot grasp. The look on her worry-stricken face pulls me to pity, and I regret bantering at her with a question I knew she couldn't answer.

"We have names. My name is Kara," I offer.

When the name reaches her ears, her eyes flash as she processes it. It looks as though she feels the name on her tongue before releasing it from her mouth. "Kara."

The word comes out slow and purposeful and the sound of it is so true and so familiar that it almost brings me to tears. She has said my name before. She's said it more times than anyone else. My heart knows it, but I cannot recall.

"Kara . . . *Kara* . . ." She repeats the word as if trying to place where and when she said it.

I squeeze my eyes shut as pain wraps itself around my temples. A memory slams against the blockades in my mind. It's a monster banging its fists against the door, so hard that I almost topple over as I press my back against the imaginary barrier to keep it shut. The memories slam so hard against the obstruction in my brain that I'm afraid all the walls will crumble and topple down if I do not settle it.

Whatever this memory holds, it brings pain. A pain I don't want. A pain I can't handle. So, I lock it away and I stuff it deep into the corners of my psyche that see no daylight. Where the ghost of all my forgotten memories lay asleep.

ML Twenty-three crosses the room with a slow tentative stride. She wraps her arms around me in a familiar embrace. I've been held in this embrace so many times, but I can't recall one.

She whispers into the crown of my head as the pain subsides. "I just cannot bear to see you hurt." I pull my head back to look up as she continues. "The Upper elementals—no matter what they may seem—they are dangerous."

Although we both know she has no concrete knowledge to back this statement, we understand it to be true.

The door of the medical room opens again and in walks a maintenance enforcer, come to collect us. We must have lost track of time and not gone on our own. "You two, come with me. The day is over. It is time to maintenance your collars."

It is not unusual for a maintenance enforcer to gather up straggling servants. Many often lose track of time or lose their way to the maintenance room. We follow him through the capitol building until we reach our destination.

Rows of chairs connected to monitors and machines stretch out before us. They process servants through one side of the room and exit them out the other. Each evening we come for our collars' maintenance. They check for bugs, inefficiencies, and give us access to the areas we will need for the next day. They also inject us with a serum that helps us to cope in the hydro landscape that is not naturally hospitable to terras and pyros.

Although this happens daily, something about the process feels more familiar than ever. Maybe it's the enforcer who sits me down in the chair, strapping my arms, legs, and forehead. Is he someone I've seen before?

A memory wiggles its way through my brain, one I cannot subdue before it reaches the forefront of my mind. The memory is of this soldier strapping me down to a chair alongside the prime policymaker. I remember screaming and begging for them to let me go, but they didn't. Why was I so afraid?

Two soldiers stand behind me now, one training the other. He instructs the rookie on how to release the serum, which will put me to sleep. Alarm spikes my pulse, but I try not to show it, fearing they may be too liberal with the sedative. I fight the haze that threatens to overtake my consciousness, hanging on to every word of the soldier behind me.

"When this vial is empty, the servant should be adequately sedated, and you can begin extracting."

He pulls a needle from my neck, then re-punctures it with another. I don't flinch, numb to the pain, but aware of the pressure. The numbness only extends to the surface of my flesh. When the soldier releases his next serum, I feel every bit of it burn through the veins in my neck, shoulders, then chest.

I want to cry out, but my mouth remains sealed. My eyes will not open. I am paralyzed. Still, I fight the black haze that begs to pull me under. I feel the essence of yesterday and every day before, flowing through me stronger than it's ever been. I use it to fight sleep and coax consciousness.

"Now here's the tricky part, so watch close. You only want to take enough to drain them. Never more than can fill this vial."

What is he talking about? What is he taking?

I feel the pull at my neck as the energy which was flowing through me draws toward the needle in my throat. As the essence I fought so hard to wield exits my body, I realize what they steal, and am horrified.

"Why don't we just take it all?" the rookie asks.

"You do that, kid, and they'll die."

The image of a man slumped over in his maintenance chair flashes across my mind. My pulse spikes as I remember him flopping to the ground, dead eyes looking up. I struggle to slow my breathing, though I feel like I'm on the verge of hyperventilating. I desperately beg my heart to steady it's pounding before the enforcers realize I am not sedated.

"With daily extractions, we maintain them at a sub-Level One, so you know there's only enough to fill one vial. That's why regular maintenance is the key."

I want to scream and claw my way out of this hellhole. This is impossible. Our essence is our life force. It is as innate to us as blood and bone. They cannot take it. *Impossible.*

But as I scream the words in my mind, they are drowned out by a high-pitched buzz. The ear shattering frequency seeks to cut me from conscious thought. I feel the energy drain from me. All the power that has rushed to the surface, depleted.

When the needles pull from my neck, another two replace them. When the collar tightens around my skin, and the sting of whatever serum secretes from the needles seeps into me, I can still feel the hum of essence flow through my veins. I know they have not taken it all—not even close. It still runs strong and deep, ready for me to summon.

The enforcers leave me sitting in the chair for a while until the numbness wears and haze no longer fights to take hold. I stay calm, knowing if I give the slightest inclination that I was conscious, they'll ship me on the first transport to the Outer.

A soldier lifts open my eyelid, flashing a light at my pupil. He gives my cheek a few light taps as he says, "Complete. This one is ready to go."

I blink my eyes open as if waking from a long slumber. The other soldier lifts me from the chair that I've already been uncuffed from. I try to slow my pace as I'm ushered out of the room, unable to leave quickly enough. Once I've reached the corridor, I find ML Twenty-three, fresh from her own "extraction". I move in front of her. Her pupils dilate and don't seem to focus on any one thing. I pull her to the side, where I'm sure no one can hear us.

"Twenty-three, do you know what just happened?"

Brows furrowed; she's clearly confused. "Maintenance," she says, as if I am the one out of my mind. She must have been asleep just as I have been for every maintenance prior.

I try something else, hesitant to test the theory that frightens me. "What is my name?"

Again, she looks at me as if I have no mind at all. "You are ML Forty-seven."

The words slam against me, and I lean against the wall to keep from falling. My name flowed from her lips only an hour ago. How could she not remember?

Her eyes soften, and she looks at me like a pitiful sea lizard, stranded on dry ground, lost and out of place. Taking my arm in hers, she gently pulls me from the wall and guides my path. "Come on, sweetheart, let's get you some rest."

I make a silent vow to her that whatever they're doing to us stops now.

Tomorrow, there will be no extraction.

CHAPTER 18
SORREN

THE COOL WINTER WIND dances across my skin as I walk the glass streets of Central City. The daily tide pushes a thin sheet of water over the walkways so that they disappear, giving everything the illusion of floating. I try to focus on appreciating my first steps outside the capitol building as a free man. It is pointless.

I cannot rid my mind of the Healing Faction leader's hate-filled glare. It reminds me of who I truly am and what I have done. Kara's spoiled me with the benevolent smiles and doting laughter she so freely gives. The older woman is the first to look at me and see through the façade. To see a monster.

After hours of wandering, I find myself at the gate of my father's manor. The pretentious monstrosity looms, obtrusive and daunting. It reflects its master, and I have always hated it.

Following my father's death, I have done my best to avoid returning. When in Central City, I always stayed in the barracks with my brigade. After the trial, I moved into a jail cell. Then, during reconditioning, I spent every night in the infirmary.

I am not welcome in the medical wing, and I can no longer avoid the only home I have left. Still, the thought taunts me that if I fail my mission, I will lose even this.

I walk the pathway up to the front door. The heavy slab of glass screeches as it opens. The empty home feels like a mausoleum, void of all life. Although no one has lived here in the years since my father's death, servants regularly come to clean and maintain the house, preserving it as a desolate shrine.

Although conditioning has only just ended, I'm expected to make progress with my mission quickly. Should too much time lapse, my loyalties will again come into question. And the Upper has every reason to question me.

I do not know if I can bring myself to go after the helpless elementals who barely escaped my grasp months ago. The thought of betraying Kara again rips me apart. How could I sentence those pyros and terras to whatever freakish abominations the Upper has been experimenting with?

I owe it to Kara, and to the thousands of other Lower elementals I've wronged, to find out what is happening to them. I cannot go into this blind. Truly understanding what I have done, and what I am prepared to do, is the only way I can consider this mission.

I do not waste time reminiscing and walking through the manor. It has held no joy from my or my father's lifetime. There are no fond memories to recall. It is not home. The word more accurately fits the academy.

I spent every waking moment of my youth at the military institute, aside from the few holidays I spent marooned here. But this is where I'm expected to stay until I complete my mission. That's just as well, for I know my father's ghost holds all the answers I need.

I walk to the study and download the detailed mission briefing from the comm unit embedded in my forearm. Following my release, the council reactivated it with modified clearances. I use it to summon Calix and his subordinate scouts.

I consider soliciting Ciel's help with a sensitive request. Involving her would be a risk, but I know I can trust the wayward officer. She owes me this much and more. If I'm to bide my time, I must keep up appearances. I must send scouts out to at least search for the escaped faction.

I run my hand along the massive desk, stopping at the imposing brown leather chair. Sitting here, I feel like a child trying on his father's oversized clothes. It is a reminder of the shoes I will never fill.

I place my hand on the security unit beside the desk. It pulls a sample of DNA from my palm. This is how my father encrypted all his data. As disappointed as he'd always been in me, he never lost the hope that I would carry on in his footsteps. Our conversations were never personal. They were always an opportunity for him to lecture or teach his beliefs, his aspirations, his vision. I'd always soaked it up, so eager to please, hoping that the son he'd always found such disappointment in, could one day elicit pride. That day never came, and now, as I teeter on the edge of treason once again, I am glad he did not live to see what I have become.

When the desk unlocks, its surface rises to a 45-degree angle, lighting up a screen that takes me to my father's files. I pull up maps of the lower region, knowing I will have to give my scouts some directive. I rummage through survey after survey—plot after plot—piecing together the intricately detailed map my father spent years composing. It has every layout and location of all six Lower factions imaged to scale.

A ring chimes through the house and a notification covers the top right-hand corner of my screen. It shows Calix and his scouts, waiting, all standing at attention at the front door. I disable the lock and tell them to come in, letting them know I'm in my father's study. Moments later, they enter and salute me with a hard thump to their chest, honoring me as if my title were still valid.

"At ease," I say, and Calix steps forward with a nod.

"It is good to see you well, Commander."

"I have not yet earned my title's reinstatement."

"You are still our commander." The senior scout's voice holds a defiance that warms me, though it should not.

I pull up the portion of the map that shows Kara's faction. "As I'm sure you've been informed by Admiral Malakai, the Council has tasked me with recapturing those who escaped our initial raid, as well as anyone harboring them."

Calix leans back, digging in his heels, bringing his hand to the neatly trimmed salt and pepper whiskers that cover his jaw. "Yes, I am aware."

"Your group will need to locate them and report back your intel." I enlarged the map, focusing on the Healing Faction's territory.

"Start here." I circle Kara's home on the screen. "It's possible the faction will have moved back to their home after months of inactivity. So, that is where we'll begin."

I know this is untrue. No one in their right mind would return to the place they'd just eluded capture, but I need to buy as much time as possible.

"From there, you will split up, traveling to these factions." I circle the Farming and Smithing factions as obvious targets. Because they also neighbor the Healers, I mark the Gold Faction, although they are our allies and would likely not aid the refugees.

"Do not engage with the enemy." I cannot stress this enough. "Should you locate the captives, gather the information you need and return immediately."

I send the maps and information needed to carry out their mission. Uploading it to their comm units, I dismiss the scouts, effectively initiating the operation.

I lean back to survey the room. My father kept a myriad of Old World artifacts in his study. Everywhere I look, there is some tribute to the gods, and the immortal guardians they created.

I walk over to the painting my father has kept hanging on the wall across from his desk all my life. *Procella*, is what he called it. The artist depicted an immortal water guardian as the raging sea. Her arms rise from the sea foam, bringing with them the tide. She is omnipotent in her immortality, and terrifying in her beauty. It is strange to think that she was once an elemental, like me, before receiving Hydris's blessing.

Below the painting is an assortment of hydro artifacts. I lift a small, corked bottle, peering inside at the set of delicate wings on display. No longer than my index finger, the dainty things look like they'd crumple under my touch. They must be another manufactured trinket, meant only for ascetics, though as I examine the wings closer, I noticed a dry patch at the point where they meet. What looks like dried skin hangs from the wings' junction.

Ciel bursts into the room, foregoing formalities, eyes wide when she spots me.

"You're alright. I thought—" She stops herself, seeming to remember formalities. "Commander," she lifts a fist to her chest. I lift my hand to stop her, the honorific becoming a persistent reminder of my stripped title.

"Sir, it is good to have you back."

"It's good to be back, Admiral. I have need for your assistance in a very . . . delicate matter." I'm careful in choosing my words, knowing discretion is of the utmost importance. One wrong move and I could end up on the first transport to the Outer.

"I'm researching tactics to retain the lowers upon capture. Our methods of transport are not efficient, and I think that mirroring the tactics used to subdue our servants may be useful."

I keep my eyes on her, looking for any flinch of resistance. Any inkling that my motives may not be in the best interests of our region. She gives none, so I continue.

"For this, I will need you to procure a collar and sample of the serum used in routine maintenance." Ciel pauses, lifting her brow. She hesitates before nodding. "I need you to understand that this is a delicate endeavor and requires the utmost discretion. Is that clear?"

She takes in a breath, shaking her head. "Sorren, you have always had my loyalty. And after what you did . . ." Her gaze breaks from mine, falling to the floor. "I know it was through your mercy that I was not the one punished. You took my place when you could have just as easily revealed what I'd done and spared yourself all of this." She waves her hand at me, voice weakening with each word.

I lift a hand to her shoulder. "What's done is done."

I do not regret any of it, even if I can't admit it out loud.

"For the sake of discretion, I can give you until the end of the week to get these items to me."

"You will have them before then, sir."

"That'll be all, Admiral."

Ciel bows and turns on her heels to leave, ready to execute her mission. On her way out, she passes Kai, leaning against the doorframe, arms crossed, giving me that damned look.

"Bloody Aelious, Kai. How long have you been standing there?"

He laughs. "Not long."

Pushing his lithe frame from the doorway, he strolls to me as smoothly and quietly as a trickle of water. I rise, hugging my best friend. His hand slaps down on my back.

"It is so good to see you, and in one piece," he says, and I hadn't realized how much I'd missed my second.

"Ah, they couldn't hold me down for a long." I pull back, still holding him by the forearm. "So, what brings you by to the old Astley Manor?"

"Oh, you didn't think I'd find you here? I've come to bring you back to the barracks to live among your soldiers. Your sentence is complete, you've earned it." My hydro friend, always so practical.

"I can't, not until my mission is complete."

His mouth sets in a tight line. He thinks I feel the need to prove myself before rejoining my brigade. My second knows me well, and this has been a common theme in my life. But not this time. I cannot live among the men I have not totally committed to rejoin. I do not wish to be a snake hiding in plain sight. To live among the soldiers as I pretend to seek the escaped captives is a low I will not hit today.

"I need to ask a favor of you." I tread lightly, trying to feel him out before going any further.

"Anything, my friend."

"Could you gather some information for me?"

He raises an eyebrow, drawing his mouth into a lopsided smirk. His knowing ocean-blue eyes look right through my façade. It's the look he gave me as a young cadet at the academy. I would prepare to carry out some elaborate prank on the upperclassmen, right before he evaluated, then gave me his input on how to actually make it work.

It's a look I remember from our first years as foot soldiers. He'd watch me out maneuver my superior officers, guiding them on how to defeat our enemies against impossible odds. Most recently, it is the look he gave me at the Healer raid, when he saw I was straying from the course. My second knew before I did that I would betray orders.

"What kind of . . . information?" He says the word as if it's code for something, and I know it's a long shot, but must try.

"I need the servant records." His slanted eyes narrow on me, his lips open in an unasked question. I press on, hoping to distract him from my actual intent. "I just need to gather some data to prepare for the capture of the escaped elementals."

Kai looks down at the screen. I assume he's viewing the map and almost think I've gotten away with the request. But I'm wrong. He is viewing the monitor that leads to the front door, checking the hallway.

He grabs my forearm with one hand and his own forearm with the other. Pushing water to seep through the pores of our skin and into our comm units, he shorts them. It's a trick he learned years ago to ensure a few minutes of privacy while the systems reboot.

The typically calm hydro fumes. "What in the bloody hells are you trying to do?"

I balk at his ability to dissect the full intent of my request with only the few words I'd given him. "Just as I said. I'm collecting—"

"Don't lie to me, Sorren. I'm only going to ask you this one more time. What are you planning?" He punctuates each word with a seriousness that takes him over the edge. I realize there is no use lying.

"I need to find out what's going on with the captives. Those collars don't just mute their abilities, it's doing something to their minds."

Kai slams his fist on the desk. "For fuck's sake, Sorren. Are you mad? Have you lost your mind? What in the actual hells would make you think you should focus on anything other than the mission which holds the key to your freedom?"

I'm lost for words.

The simple answer of, *it's the right thing to do,* sounds so trivial. The honest answer of, *I cannot betray her again,* sounds so naïve. I do not insult him with either. And besides, who am I to start doing the noble thing now?

"I have to know. I have to know what following my duty has cost these people, what carrying out this mission will hold for the elementals we capture." I try to reason with my oldest and dearest friend, pleading for him to understand this is more than just a grasp at my humanity. I have caused so much damage in my life, I'm only trying to truly assess what I have done.

"When you already know what these people have cost your father? What awaited Nero upon his capture?"

The words sting, and I flinch, pulling my arm from his grasp.

He brings a hand to cover his face, pushing his thumb and middle finger into his temples. "They're just servants, Sorren. The enemy, no less." His hands, still gripping his face, muffle his words.

"They are people first. Elementals like you and me, who have families and ambitions. People who are loyal, and strong," I say, thinking of Kara. "They've been stripped of everything, Kai, their wielding abilities, their deities, and their memories. How can you stand by without even questioning it?"

"Because it is my duty," he says, clenching his fists and digging his heels into the ground. I cannot argue him away from the sentiment.

"Please. I must know. I can't go through with this mission blindly."

He sighs, rolling his eyes, as he so often does, following our arguments. "If I do this, you will abandon these fantasies of atonement for crimes you did not commit?" There are no crimes in war, where all is fair, and the victors are exonerated.

"I swear it."

"Fine. I will get to you the servants' records and we will put to rest once and for all, whatever nonsense has plagued you since the day we rode into that faction."

I nod as our comm-screens blink on, not uttering another word.

CHAPTER 19
KARA

S LEEP EVADES ME. MY eyes refuse to close as my mind races with everything the day has brought. How could we be so foolish? How could they have so easily deceived us? I beat myself up and run myself down, asking how I hadn't seen it before, why I never questioned it.

My mind has grown progressively clear since overcoming my last maintenance. The haze that usually blocked my thoughts and leveled my temperament is wearing off and, in its place, I am afforded a clarity I cannot remember ever having.

I must give the other serving elementals this same clarity. *But how?*

How can I stop this, even for a day?

My mind replays the siphoning. Every needle probe, every word exchanged by the soldiers. I search it all for clues to how I can end this.

An idea comes to mind, but it calls for me to ask for help. I am hesitant. It is a dangerous thing to call others into this risky game. I shouldn't privy them to knowledge that could just as easily damn them as it would set them free. It's a risk to give information to someone who could easily go back to the soldiers who guard us. If the council discovers our plan, they will send anyone involved to the Outer.

Whatever the dangers, I will chance them. Nothing could be as awful as remaining slaves, captives to our minds.

When day breaks, I cross the corridor of our sleeping quarters to find ML Twenty-three. She's already begun her work inventorying the antidotes and remedies we have in stock, humming a light tune I've heard from her a thousand times before.

As she hums, I remember her singing this same song, stroking her fingers along my hair, singing the words rather than just humming the tune.

"Mother, oh Gaia, send protection for me...
Ward off the evils of old...
Grant us a guardian, so we might be free...
Place us in their immortal hold..."

As I say the words aloud, her head snaps up.

"How do you know those words?" she asks, her brows knitting together.

"I—I think you taught them to me." Her frown deepens, as I ask, "Who is Gaia?"

Sorren has told me several times about the mythical land mother, but for the first time, I think I may believe him.

"I don't know, child."

"Do you think we could have a deity, too? Like the hydros and aeros?"

Her brows lift as she shakes her head. "Oh, dear, don't be ridiculous," she says, dismissing my question.

She smiles, waving her hand, summoning me. "Did you rest well?"

I nod. Last night she thought I'd needed rest. I make a note that she seems to remember that conversation, but not the one we had only an hour prior to siphoning. They must inject us with a neurotoxin, but my knowledge of poisons seems to be locked away and unavailable for access. I cannot call on the herbs and potions they must be using to alter us, but Twenty-three's abilities far outreach my own.

"You prepare the maintenance serums, right?" I present the question as innocently as possible.

"Yes, be a dear and tally the avulki," she says, putting me to work. I oblige, without really having a choice. Twenty-three is my superior. When she tells me to do something, I do it.

"So, what do you mix into the serum?" I ask, not looking up from my task. Trying to keep my tone light and conversational.

Her hands stop rummaging through the lines of antidotes she has laid out. She looks up at me, eyes narrowing. "Why do you ask?"

"Just curious. I think I'd like to learn more about antidotes, to improve my healing." She moves away from the jars she'd been tallying, drifting closer to me.

"And why the sudden curiosity in that serum particularly?"

I work my brain for a suitable answer but come up empty. I decide to come clean. The woman cares for me, although I don't know why. She will not let any harm come to me, especially by her hands. She won't tell the guards of what I suspect, so I divulge my theory. I tell her about the extraction and how I believe the memory haze is the byproduct of a neurotoxin.

"Girl, you make dangerous accusations," Twenty-three warns me, glancing around the room, her voice an angry whisper.

"They are dangerous because they are plausible. We are being kept sedated, so we do not question what is plain in front of us."

I can tell her patience grows thin and she will soon cease to indulge this conversation. I try to think fast. "Yesterday, you said you care for me. I know you may not remember. It was too close to your maintenance hour, but if even a fragment of that is true, please extend the tiniest bit of faith to me now."

She does not argue. She does not negate the idea that she cares for me, even deeply. Once I see I may have broken through to her, I press on. "I told you my name is Kara. Do you remember?"

Her eyes widen as she murmurs my name. She says it repeatedly just as she'd done before. I seize the opportunity to continue.

"We cannot trust the Upper elementals. They do not mean us well." I use the words she said yesterday, hoping they will resonate with her. "I have a name. You have a name, too, and we're going to figure it out. But I need your help."

Her brows clench together as if she's trying to figure something out. "I do not know what goes into the serum. They give me unnamed herbs, things I've never seen before. I only process them. I do what I'm told. I know nothing else."

I realize she cannot alter the genetic makeup of the serum. Asking her to dabble and manipulate herbs that she's unfamiliar with is much too dangerous to the elementals that will receive this injection. I franticly search for a different way to stop the siphoning.

"What about the consistency? Could you thicken it?"

"You realize altering the serum could be detrimental to us all? You're asking me to tamper with unidentified ingredients that are injected intravenously. Do you have the slightest idea what a mistake could cost?"

"Do you realize what complacency has already cost us? We are so lost that we don't even know what they've stolen from us."

Twenty-three squeezes her eyes shut, letting out a ragged breath. "Even if I could safely alter the consistency, this serum has a purpose. It helps us adapt to the hydro environment."

I pause before countering, "But what if it doesn't?"

Twenty-three opens her mouth to argue but shuts it without response. I know the idea is radical, but my gut tells me that this is a lie. The Uppers have deceived us in so many things. Why not this? "The aeros are not native to this land, yet they don't require aid in surviving here."

My instincts are telling me to question this, and with so much of my memory lost, my instincts are all I have. "At worst, it will only be for this maintenance. One missed maintenance will not kill us."

At least, I don't think it will.

Twenty-three studies me before answering. "I believe there is a benign gel I can use to thicken the serum, but not by much."

That's all I need. Thickening this serum too much will tip off the maintenance soldiers anyway. The slightest change in consistency will suffice. I have a plan for the rest. "That's perfect."

"But I will only alter this one batch. And we must be the first to receive maintenance. Should something go wrong, this will prevent them from injecting the others."

"Absolutely. Can you alter today's batch?"

She looks outside, gauging the sun, assessing the time. "I believe so. The guards will deliver the raw materials for today's serum by midday. I will adjust the consistency as best as I can."

My triumph is short and sweet. I have hurdled this task, but it is only the beginning. This will only buy us a limited amount of time. Eventually, the maintenance enforcers will discover what's happening, and that puts Twenty-three in danger.

"If they ask you anything, just tell them you've forgotten the processing specifics." This excuse has the best chance of working. They should expect it. You cannot alter someone's mind and cherry pick what they do and don't remember, things they can and can't keep. I pray that excuse will keep her safe, but know that I must work quickly, regardless.

She agrees. "Kara, you will be careful." This comes out as forceful a command as any she has ever given. Though the heat in her voice lessens when the sound of my name registers. "It is a dangerous game you play, and I will not have you sent to the Outer."

I go to her, wrapping my arms around her midsection, burying my face in her wavy brown hair. My newfound clarity affords me no pause in showing the woman affection. I know her. I know her well, and once my body has cleansed itself of the toxin it's been infected with, I will call her name.

Once Twenty-three has agreed to help me, I waste no time racing to the smithing building, leaving without even grabbing a coat to combat the harsh winter wind. Level One hydros drive water pods across the open water to circumvent the labyrinth of pathways leading from one building to the next. As one whizzes by, it splashes another servant and me with icy cold water, forcing the girl to drop a load of linens she was carrying.

"Hydris be damned!" she says, falling to gather the damp clothes.

"Let me help you." I say, folding the sodden pieces in a vain attempt to fix the inconsiderate hydro's mess.

"I need to get these to the barracks. Admiral Malakai will be furious with me." She scrambles from the floor, grabbing the dripping linens I hold out in my arms.

"You're going the wrong way. The barracks are near the city wall. You're heading toward the capitol building."

"Oh no, I've forgotten again." Tears well in the servant's red and puffy eyes. They brim over and trickle over her bruised cheek.

"I'm lost." She sobs, cracking her already split lip, forcing a fat droplet of blood to bubble and fall. "I don't know where I am. I don't know anything anymore." Tears continue to cascade down her face as her arms fall under the weight of her heavy load.

"Shhh." I pull the broken servant into me, clutching her curly red hair as she weeps into my chest. "Look at me." I pull her head back to examine her face. "Did he do this to you?"

Her lips tremble as her fists tighten in my shirt. The servant's breaths are fast and shallow. Her gaze falls from my face. "Ye-yes."

Her words are so low and timid, I feel almost guilty for making her admit them. "How often does he hurt you?"

Her lips part, and a cacophony of sobs fall out. "I don't know. I can't remember," she wails.

I pull her back into my chest. "It's going to be okay. You're not going back to him. Give me these." I bend to take the laundry she's dropped at our feet.

"But he will expect *me*." Her fingers frantically grab at the soggy clothes.

"I will handle it." My recent victory has given me a false confidence that fools me into thinking I can change things beyond my control. "I know someone who will help."

Surely Sorren is in no position to grant favors, but I cannot send this poor girl back to the admiral.

"What's your name? I'll ensure you're transferred. You won't go back there. I promise." Although I have no means of upholding this promise, I will let nothing drag her back to him.

Her eyes widen. "Aelious, bless you." She says, hugging me. "It is Barracks Fire Seventy-eight."

I etch the identification into my memory. I will not forget.

I gather the linens in my arms and turn the pyro back around, pointing at the capitol building. "I will take care of the laundry. Follow this pathway straight to the capitol. Find the infirmary and let Medical Land Twenty-three know you will be transferring to the medical wing."

She jerks her head up and down, fervently agreeing to follow my directions. I pause for a moment, praying to Hydris that Sorren can uphold the promise I've made, debating whether I trust her to make it to the infirmary. I have no more time to waste. With this new task added to my agenda, I must get moving if I want to stop tonight's maintenance. The capitol is only a short distance away, I decide. She can make it.

"I will be back to check on you before our maintenance hour."

She grips me in a hug once more. "Thank you," she says into my chest, her tears further dampening my shirt. "May Aelious bless you."

"May he bless us all. Now go." Turning her, I send the pyro off.

The soggy clothes weigh heavily in my arms, dampening my uniform and sending an intense chill through my body. When I finally reach the smithing building, the heat radiating from it is Hydris-sent.

Even from outside the large metal door, I hear the hum of hammers ring against steel. Time is against me. I do not have any to waste waiting for the pyro to hear me above the zing of his mallets. I breathe in and push the door open, walking to the center of the room. Once he sees me, his hammering stops.

"Terra, you're here early." He places the mallets down, making his way toward me. The same generous smile he has every other time I've seen him graces his face. "Today's package is not ready."

His eyebrows pull up as his eyes land on my dripping load.

"I need a favor. Well, actually, a few favors."

His teeth flash in a roguish grin. "I'm not much for laundry duty—but for you—I'll give it a try." He winks at me, and my chest tightens, pulling my heart into my stomach.

"They're already clean . . . well, clean enough. I only need you to dry them."

"Ah, I see. Sure, I'll string up a line."

"And deliver them," I quickly add.

"To where?" He pauses, lifting an eyebrow.

"Admiral Malakai."

I keep my tone even and conversational as I move to separate the wet laundry.

The pyro groans, looking at a barely healed patch of frost burn on his shoulder. "I'm not exactly his favorite elemental."

I wince, not wanting to put him in harm's way just so that I may avoid the cruel officer. "It's okay. If you can just dry them, I'll deliver—"

"No," he says, his firm tone holding none of the mirth he usually weaves into all his words. "I don't want you going anywhere near him."

"Pyro, I don't want to see you injured."

"Nah, what's another frost burn?" He flexes his arm, displaying a delicious set of finely toned muscles, achieved only through daily hard labor. "I think they make me look kinda tough. What do you think?" he shrugs with a wink.

I trace the swirling brands that curve over each bulge with my eyes, not realizing I'm staring until he huffs a laugh, wagging his eyebrows at me. My cheeks heat, as I'm unable to keep a smile from stretching across my face.

"There we go," he says, gently brushing my cheek. "I'll take these." He grabs the laundry I'd been sorting and puts it aside to deal with later.

"Now, what other favors might I do for you?" His tone dips seductively low, his eyes daring me to look away.

I force myself to swallow, sure the pounding of my heart rings just as loud as the beating of his mallets.

"That's actually why I'm here." My nerves run away from me, and I find the words I need slipping from my grasp. Not because I'm in a mental fog, but because I suddenly fear the predicament I am putting Twenty-three and myself in, by divulging the plan to a stranger.

I race through alternatives in my head and know there are none. If this plan is to work, I must trust the pyro.

He stands there expectedly, waiting for me to elaborate. He will not turn me in to the Uppers. The cornucopia of frost burns and abrasions from hydro streams that blast with too much pressure decorate his skin. They serve as visible evidence he is no friend to the Upper. I have every confidence that if he agrees to go forth with my plan, he will not tip off the enforcers. If only to allow some small havoc to plague their lives.

"I need your help."

"Yes, whatever it is," he says without hesitation, and I'm taken aback. Surely, he must be joking, his playful nature making the best of him.

"You don't even know what I'm about to ask."

His eyes squint in a playful smolder as a devious grin crosses his lips. "What can I say? I'm a sucker for a pretty face."

I roll my eyes; now sure he's being funny. Tapping my foot, I cross my arms until he drops the playful grin.

"Seriously, what do you need?" he says more sincerely.

Taking a breath, I muster the courage I need to press on. "I need you to alter the collars."

I hold my breath waiting for his response, halfway expecting him to run from the room and alert the first Upper soldier he can lasso in the street. But when the sincere look turns to grief, I brace myself for a much harder answer.

"I can't."

That's it. My plan—my hopes—shattered. Defeat must edge itself into my features because he quickly continues. "It's not that I don't want to. Believe me—I've tried."

Shock draws my eyes back to him. "What do you mean you've tried?"

"They inspect the collars I give, check the latches and the cleft. Must not trust me, I guess." He shrugs with a wink.

This pyro is unlike the rest of us. He does not follow in line. He does not move without question. The hard labor of the smithing house and array of Upper inflicted injuries brand him as a troublemaker, just as surely as the decorative burn lines that swirl about his skin.

"We must try. They're altering us and they're using these collars for it. They're trying to make us believe we have no past—no powers—but they're wrong," I say, begging him to believe the outlandish tale.

"I know."

Again, shock reverberates through me. He knows? And as if to answer the silent question, he flicks his wrists, sending an array of flames over his hand, up his arm, and around his shoulders. My jaw drops. I can't believe what I see.

He continues when I have no words. "It started with just a little trickle of energy. The night of the big storm, I saw the lightning hit and remembered wielding that very energy."

Weeks ago, I may have thought he spoke nonsense. I'd call him crazy and maybe very well turn him into the guards for immediate evaluation. A pyro, wielding lightning? Who'd have heard of such a thing? But now, I almost believe him.

"Every day since, I have grasped at the bit of energy inside me and pulled it, cultivating it. Every day, I grow stronger."

I could leap for joy. There is someone here like me. I do not need to convince him or prove that I'm not crazy. He understands.

"Why didn't you say something?"

He cocks an eyebrow. "I said I'm a sucker for a pretty face, not an idiot. I wasn't sure I could trust you to keep this little secret from the guards. The Upper has made terras their pets, convincing you all you're superior to pyros. Is not out of the question for one to spill valuable information just to gain more favor."

Although the words sting, they are true. Our guards have drilled into us that the calmer temperament and nurturing nature of our elemental affinity brings us closer to the hydros and aeros in nature.

Therefore, superior to the pyros, whose temperament is volatile, and element is destructive.

I cast my eyes down, shamed, not that I ever subscribed to the notion, but because I live in the privilege of it. My work in the capitol building does not solicit the back breaking, sweat wrenching labor of the pyros who serve alongside me. And though I didn't ask for the privilege, I'm suddenly chagrined by it.

He moves toward me, bringing my chin up to look at him. "It's okay. We battle an enemy who has grossly unleveled the playing field. But we'll figure this out. Each day, we grow stronger. I feel it. The pain, here," he brushes his thumb to my temple, then brings another hand to my fingertips. "And here. They're memories, trying to come out. That's why you have to let them free. The pain is temporary. It will pass."

But it won't. My pain will never pass. Those memories bear their own set of heartache and sorrow. Whatever I hold back attaches to so much agony, I know it will destroy me.

"So, you remember?" I ask.

His lips turn down in a grimace. "Not everything. Not enough. But some things." His obsidian eyes flicker with the spark of a memory that draws his lips into a smile. His fingers enclose themselves around the pendant hanging above my chest. "Like this."

"What about it?" I ask, eager to hear whatever information he has about me—about the pendant that has adorned my neck for as long as I can remember. "What is it?"

"A promise." His obsidian eyes burn so deep into mine that I can feel the apples of my cheeks flush with heat that has nothing to do with the fires surrounding us.

"A promise of what?" My pulse quickens as I urge him to elaborate.

His brows furrow and his fingers fall from my necklace. "I don't know."

He looks away, and I grip his hand. "But we will. We will remember everything. We just need time to get whatever they're injecting through these collars out of our systems."

"But how?"

"We don't need to alter the collars, just the needles." His brows lift in an obvious curiosity, urging me to continue. "We're thickening the serum's consistency. That alone won't be enough to keep it from moving through the needles if we want to keep the change too subtle to tip off the guards. That slight alteration, combined with lowering the needle gauge, should hold the serum and keep the guards oblivious for a day or two."

He considers my proposal, assessing the obvious risk to him. If the council discovers our plan, he will not get by with the simple excuse of a lapse in memory, like Twenty-three might. Failure guarantees his transfer to the Outer, and I'm guilt stricken for asking him to make the choice.

"I'll do it. I can have them ready for this evening's maintenance."

Relief overtakes the guilt as it is done.

"Thank you," I say, trying to convey just how much this means. What his help can do for all the serving elementals.

"You don't need to thank me. Whatever diabolical plan you have cooked up in that pretty head of yours, make it work, and make it work fast."

I nod, fully aware of the ticking clock, now weighing on my shoulders.

CHAPTER 20
KARA

I RUSH THROUGH MY chores. After spending all morning setting the pieces of my plan in place, I returned to the infirmary for Barracks Fire Seventy-eight. Relieved to find she made it to the medical wing, I spent much of my afternoon healing her wounds because she refused to allow ML Twenty-three to touch her. Some were recent, though many were old and hidden. Each new bruise, cut, and sprain compounded my resolve to end maintenance. Even with the considerable time I spent with her, the redheaded pyro was still a trembling mess when I left her in our servant's quarters to rest.

Unable to stay by her side any longer, I am behind on my duties. For an elemental whose only concern should be their daily tasks, mine going entirely undone will raise a red flag I cannot afford. Just as I am all but through, I race to the infirmary to tidy up.

At the entrance of the capitol building, I recognize Admiral Malakai towering over a young soldier. I barely suppress a growl, though I cannot keep myself from stopping to size him up. He is a harsh man, with nasty red scars marring his face and neck. His tone is abrasive, and his eyes never meet those of a servant, preferring to talk over us than directly. He is not someone we'll soon forget. With or without the maintenance serum, we know to stay away.

"The commander has made a request and I don't know what he's up to, but I think it will hold some interest to you." The younger man talking to the Admiral, a lower-ranking soldier, leans into him, looking around.

They pay no mind as I pass by. Resentment bubbles up with anger in my gut. They won't expect me to remember a thing they say. I can spit on them, but I'm much more interested in what information the younger man has in connection to Sorren.

"Admiral Ciel is looking to collect a sample of the collars and serum for him."

"What in the bloody hells is Sorren up to?" The admiral's gaze drifts to me, and I know I've stayed idle for too long. "Stay close to Ciel. Report back to me when you have something else," he says to the young soldier as I hasten my pace, walking away from the two officers. I cannot afford to draw their attention, not now. But as I leave, another question burns in my mind.

Does he know?

As I approach the infirmary entryway, a cool breeze flows from beneath it, tickling my ankles. I pull the door open, hoping he waits inside.

He does.

Sorren stands in front of the bed he'd laid up on so many nights before. Totally healed from the damage inflicted during conditioning, I admire my handiwork before moving to him.

"What are you doing here?" I ask going to him. I know with his freedom comes a long list of tasks to make up for the time he spent on hiatus. And although my heart had hoped, I never expected him to be back here so soon.

"I had to see you again," he says, bridging the gap between us, taking my hands in his. "There's something I need to tell you." He looks down as if searching for the words. And although I am pleased to see him, I must know if he knew what they were doing to us all along.

So, I don't let him finish. "Did you know they were altering us?" The question is so plain—so simple—it seems comical, relative to the gravity it holds. Sorren's face slackens, his eyes widening, and the guilt that riddles him tells me all I need to know. My heart breaks a little. "You knew."

"Yes. I don't know how or why. That's what I'm trying to figure out."

Does he mean to help us? That question is almost as laughable as the one before. He can't, but my heart longs to believe otherwise.

"Is that why you wanted the collars and serum?"

His jaw tightens. "How do you know about that?" His voice carries a desperate urgency that frightens me for him.

"I overheard a soldier telling Admiral Malakai someone is gathering them for you."

"Damn it." Sorren's eyes shut as his hands clench into tight fists. "Malakai must be having Ciel watched."

He brings his hand to his forehead, sliding it down his cheek, assessing whatever damage the conversation will hold. Shaking his head, he looks back at me. "That's what I need to talk to you about. I'm trying to figure out what they're doing to you. I knew your memory was altered because . . . I've met you before."

His eyes hold on to mine as I balk at the words tumbling from his mouth. His simple words confirm the burning familiarity that I feel when I look into those crystal gray eyes.

"That day in my cell was not our first encounter. We've met before. Under much different circumstances." He can no longer hold my gaze, his falling to the floor.

My mind tries to piece together the familiar puzzle of his eyes. The pounding of a thousand hammers threatens to bash my skull in from the inside, and I squeeze my eyes shut before my mind can implode on itself. Taking in jagged breaths to slow the alarms going off in my head, there is too much to unpack with the secrets his eyes hold. I need my mind clear for this evening's task.

I see the sun has already set and do not have time to talk this through with him—work through whatever mess the recovered memory will leave in its wake. Maintenance hour grows near, and I must be the first to receive the serum. This is my experiment and if it fails, it will fail on me. I cannot allow others to go before me, taking the risk of my actions.

"Whatever it is will have to wait. But I do need your help," I say, thinking of BF Seventy-eight.

Sorren's eyes widen, and he reaches for my hand. "What is it? Are you okay?" The words rush from his lips, and I place a hand on his chest to calm him. Beneath my palm, I feel the thundering race of his pulse.

"It's not for me. I met one of the admiral's servants. He's injured her . . . repeatedly."

A growl rips from his throat, as a flash of ice encases my hand where it intertwines in his. More ice creeps across the palm I have pressed against his chest as the element begins to swiftly overtake the room. "Sorren, it's okay. I've gotten her away from him. She's safe, but she needs to be transferred."

His eyes darken as his glower fixes on me. "I will handle it. Trust me when I say, she, nor any other servant of the Upper, will ever need to fear his hand again." The sinister tone of his voice sends chills across my shoulders and up my neck, stronger than his intense cold could.

"Thank you," I say, resting my head on his chest as he retracts the ice that has escaped him. "I have to go. It's my maintenance hour."

His hand grips mine, urgently pulling me even closer to him. "Don't go. You can't let them—"

"You know I have to. But I'm stronger now, in no small part thanks to you. I'll be careful, I promise." I bring his hand to my lips, placing a kiss on his knuckles.

An icy breeze wraps itself around me, pushing me flush with him. The heady scent of clean, crisp air hazes my mind more than any serum ever could. More warnings blare in my head. Warnings that the gray eyes and icy touch hold danger. That I should not feel the way I do for this man—that I should feel nothing but hate and anger. I ignore them all. Because all I want to do is lose myself in the cool embrace of his arms.

So, when he brings them around me, I let him pull me in. The thick stubble of his beard tickles my cheek as he leans down to place his lips on mine. I breathe him, as if he is the only air I need. He surrounds me and consumes me and awakens a passion I cannot abate.

Heat wells in my core as ice kisses my skin. The cool, hot feel of it drives me insane, and I only want him to pull me closer. I want to feel his hands on every piece of my skin. I want his mouth to taste every bit of me.

My heart races, stealing my breath and dizzying my head as his tongue teases mine. To feel anything after so much time of numbing monotony sends trills of electricity buzzing through my core. When his lips break from mine, he gasps for air, as if he'd consumed me rather than his element. I want him to devour me. I ache to be all that he needs, to sate him in a way nothing else can. When his gray eyes open, looking at me with an overwhelming sadness, my heart plummets. This kiss feels like a goodbye.

"I must see you tonight. I have to know you're okay." His words are rushed, dread and anxiety lacing his tone. "There is something I need to tell you."

He leans his forehead against mine, the long waves of his black hair tumbling beside my temples. His firm hand slides up my neck to cradle the back of my head, as I nod, agreeing.

He lets out a breath. "I'll meet you in this room at guard change."

He pulls back, crystal eyes holding mine with an urgent pleading I can't deny.

"Okay, I'll be here."

The serum should be even more removed from my system by then. I should be able to assess whether I can solicit his help. Right now, I'd be a fool to believe that a few love-drunk kisses and kind words make him anything less than the enemy an Upper officer should be. Once he spills his secrets to me, I will decide if I can trust him with mine.

"Tonight," he says, placing a kiss on my forehead that sends my head spinning once again.

I wave him goodbye as I slip through the door of the infirmary first, so that no one sees us leaving together.

Tonight, I have no trouble making my way to the maintenance room. My mind does not forget the exact path to take, and I am there in minutes. The maintenance soldier preparing the chairs looks up at me.

"You're early."

I widen my eyes, shrugging my shoulders, hoping to look as clueless as they expect me to be. "Am I?"

The man shakes his head, waving his arm. "Come here."

My heart pounds as I sit in the chair, preparing to be strapped down. I border hyperventilation, suddenly terrified they will piece it together, that my plan will fail.

The soldier straps me down. I send prayer after prayer to Hydris so that the deity may have mercy on me. I know the deities hold no love for the terras and pyros of elements different from their own, but I pray Hydris finds clemency for me this once.

As the soldier extracts the needles of today's collar from my neck, I stifle a gasp at the pinch of new ones entering my skin.

Calm yourself.

Anxiety may tip him off. There is no reason for a servant who has done this every day prior to shy away from it now.

Get ahold of yourself. It will be fine.

As a soldier begins the maintenance, I wait for the serum's burn to sear through my veins. But it does not come. More elementals pour through the room, each sitting in a different chair. The pyro crosses my path. Here, much earlier than he should be, I imagine his sentiment may have been the same as mine.

Behind me, the soldier attending my maintenance lets out a frustrated grunt. "Damns be to Aelious. The stupid tech has jammed." He slams a fist on the machine connected to me.

A nearby soldier, having his own trouble with the siphoning, calls back to him. "It was only a matter of time. With all these new enforcers, the rookies don't know how to take care of the damned tech." He gestures to the enormous machine running all the chairs in the room, pointing a glare at the nearest rookie maintenance enforcer.

I don't dare to breathe. I don't dare to show any relief—any emotion at all that may alert them that this is not a coincidence. They use their comm units to call for backup. Different maintenance enforcers and tech experts focus their attentions on the machine. After so much time has passed that serving elementals pile up outside the door of the maintenance room, the maintenance officer lets out a command.

"Shut the tech down. We cannot perform maintenance tonight. Escort the servants back to their quarters while we adjust the unit."

"About time," the enforcer behind me mutters to his comrade.

The rookie next to him says, "I thought that maintenance had to be regular."

"It can hold off a few days. It'll just be hell getting them readjusted. We ought to be fine for at least three days."

The tension holding my muscles taut releases. Three days. I can work with that.

The enforcer snaps the collar back in place around my neck, disconnecting me from the unit at my side.

"Return to your quarters immediately, understood?"

"Yes, sir." I sputter, too eager to escape the room. He gives me a warning stare, then waves me off, dismissing me from maintenance.

In the hallway, I almost skip ahead. I'm so giddy that I don't notice as I run into the back of the pyro who has helped make this all possible.

He turns around, not even trying to stifle the triumphant grin. "You did it." He grips my shoulders, looking around to make sure no one can hear us.

I throw my arms around his waist, so grateful that he's helped me, so optimistic that this wild plan could actually work.

"*We* did it." I hug him and he stiffens beneath my touch. He pulls me back, his deep obsidian eyes bearing into me as the flash of a memory crosses his face. His brow crumbles, and I can tell pain shoots from one temple to another. When he's recovered, his eyes widen.

"Kara?"

He knows my name.

CHAPTER 21
SORREN

I SHOULD NOT HAVE kissed her. I went to the infirmary with the best of intentions, needing to tell her what was happening. Let her know what I'd found out. She needed to know who I was so that she could hate me for the monster I am. Instead, I let her melt into me. I let her believe I was a good man worthy of her affections, when nothing could be farther from the truth.

The list of grievances I've committed against the terra stacks in a weighted column that threatens to crush me. Of all the sins I've committed, growing close to her—kissing her—is the greatest of all. It is also the only one I would repeat time and time again. And it is for this reason I will never deserve her.

Tonight, I will not back down. When I take her to the only piece of land within Central City. Our capital is a floating city that sits in the western area of the Upper Region. It is the area native to hydros. The wall stands on a small sliver of land where two oceans meet. I will return her to her element, and there I will tell her everything. And I know when she learns who I truly am, she will no longer look upon me with warmth.

I can still feel the loathing in her gaze bearing into me from when I first commanded the capture and destruction of her home. The scream that ripped from her throat as I pulled her away from her dying father.

I will never know how I built the audacity to accept any kindness from the woman I have wronged so greatly. Regardless, I will remedy this tonight. Once I confess, she will extend nothing but hate to me ever again.

I waited a decent amount of time after Kara exited the infirmary to leave. She does not need anyone connecting her to me. It could mean danger for her, and the last thing I want is to put her at risk.

I walk across the capitol building in search of Malakai, murderous thoughts filling my head. He is exactly where I expect him to be, heading back from Morgana's office.

The little toad could not hold on to whatever information the foolish soldier fed him. Never mind what he has told Morgana. Damn their consequences. It is time for Malakai's reckoning, and I will all too gladly deliver it.

I stand next to a marble column, remaining utterly still until the officer passes me. When he does, I snatch the air from his body, stopping him mid-stride. He whirls around, clutching his throat. His eyes bulge as they land on me. His face turns an angry crimson before bleeding into purple as he tries to grunt, but nothing comes out.

Malakai falls to his knees, crawling over to dig his nails into my shin. The grip holds no strength as I count just seventy seconds before the admiral passes out. I've seen children hold their breath for longer. *Pathetic.*

Using the air beneath to lift him, I carry the oversized man to an unoccupied room, far away from the policymakers. I take a clearly vacant path to avoid running into any misguided do-gooders. Malakai only remains unconscious for a few minutes, but it is just enough to get him exactly where I want him.

"Sorren, you son of a bitch. When I inform the prime—"

"It looks like you've had much to tell the prime," I say, crouching down to level my eyes with his.

A toothy grin spreads his lips thin across a mouthful of crowded teeth. "You will fall by my hand, Astley; I swear if it's the last thing I do."

"See the thing about your hand . . . I hear you haven't been keeping it to yourself."

His brows knit together, as if he's harmed so many people, that he truly couldn't begin to guess which I refer to. Anger beats against my chest, raw and primal. I clench my fist to prevent it from slamming into Malakai's jaw prematurely.

"The servant girl," I say through my teeth with a snarl.

Malakai smirks at my angry display. "Which one?"

Before I can stop myself, I swing, slamming into his face and wiping the smug grin from his lips.

His mouth falls open as he brings the back of his hand up to wipe the blood from his chin. "You're gonna pay for—"

But I do not let him finish. Once I've had a taste of his blood, I cannot stop myself from punishing him further.

The large man blocks my next punch and hooks his arm around my waist to pull me down. As I fall I grab his head, slamming it into my knee. Maneuvering myself to fall on his shoulder, I twist into him to yank it out of the socket.

Malakai jerks away at the last minute, keeping me from debilitating that arm. I do not use my element against him. I severely out match his wielding ability and want there to be no question of fairness in this fight.

The admiral pushes up on his knees, wobbling to a standing position. Before I can stand upright, he charges at me. I drop, sweeping my leg out to under-kick him. He stumbles and I tackle him the rest of the way to the ground. Once I have him beneath me, I work my fists into his face. Landing punch after punch, his head can hardly recover from one blow before I land another. The only thoughts in my mind are of the last comments he made to Kara, out on the battlefield of her faction town.

You're a pretty thing, aren't you?

I move from his face to midsection, as his arms become too weak to block me.

I'll make sure you're my personal servant.

Punch, punch.

You'll pay for every drop of blood your dear father took from me.

This could have easily been Kara, rather than the poor girl she saved.

When his hands finally drop, I force myself to cease my assault.

My chest heaves as I catch my breath, blood painting my knuckles red.

"You will be sorry for this," he chokes out.

"There are a great number of things I must atone for in this life. This will never be one of them," I say, dragging my hand along his uniform, wiping his blood on the lapel of his officer's coat. "Nor will I atone for your murder, should I ever find out you've harmed another serving elemental."

"You cannot threaten me," he sneers.

"Make no mistake, Admiral. I make no threats. I swear to Aelious that I will drive an ice dagger through your gut so that I might reach in to rip out your entrails, should I ever learn you've harmed a captive." The man's eyes widen as I continue, "I will then wrap them around your throat, and hang you in the city's center, walking to the Outer with a smile on my face."

The idiot officer collects a mouthful of bloody saliva and spits it at me. I raise a hand to freeze it in midair, pulling it to a sharp point and thrusting it back into his shoulder. Malakai falls back with a howl I'm sure will alert anyone nearby, and I know my fun must come to an end.

I restrict his airflow, allowing only enough for the aero to breathe. There will be none for screaming.

"It seems you doubt my commitment, Admiral." I grip the hand I assume he raised to the serving pyro, bending it back until I hear the loud snap of bone.

Malakai's face turns such a deep red that it edges onto violet, his mouth widening into a scream that he has no air to release.

"I have tried playing by the rules. You may be the prime's pet, but you are nothing compared to the son of Nero Astley," I say, for the first time in my life, using my father's name, and owning its privilege. "I will kill you, and no one in this entire realm will give a single shit about it."

I push the icicle protruding from my palm against his neck, the point barely piercing skin, only drawing a small drop of blood. The admiral's eyes roll up and I release the air I'd been holding from the elemental on the verge of passing out. He heaves in his element, cradling his broken hand to his chest.

My comm unit pings and I release his coat, allowing him to stumble back to the floor.

I have just received a summons, and I level Malakai with a glare. Anger boils in my chest at the foolish soldier who betrayed Ciel. It seems Malakai wasted no time in building his alliances and employing surveillances while I was fulfilling my sentence. He has taken his role as the prime's informant farther than I expected, and I cannot allow this to continue in the manner it has. Malakai believes he has only the prime to answer to, and I am all too happy to remind him of his blunder as needed.

I rise, knowing I cannot keep the prime waiting.

"We'll continue this later,"

I leave him on the floor, and the sight of the pitiful aero sickens me. The pathetic officer only seems to enjoy fighting subjects whose hands are tied. As I leave the room, I see him cradling his fingers to his chest, and smile, knowing he will not use that hand for quite some time.

When I've made it to the tall glass door of Morgana's office, she pushes a ribbon of water to hook behind me, wordlessly commanding me to enter. She then uses the ribbon to shut the door, cutting our conversation off from anyone who may be nearby.

"Evening, Madam Prime," I say, thumping a fist to my chest.

"Do you think me a fool, Sorren?" Her thin lips press into a firm line. I suppose formalities are overrated.

"I do not Madam."

"There seemed to be a malfunction with today's maintenance," she says.

Relief washes over me. I think back to Kara's reassurances that she'd had maintenance under control and stifle a laugh. I've never been so proud of anyone. I should have known she'd find a way to upset the process. She is brilliant, and there isn't a thing this region can do to hold her down.

The prime continues. "I find it rather coincidental this has occurred shortly after I hear you've inquired about having a sample of the serum and a collar stolen for personal use." Her voice tightens as she makes false connections about the relief I make no effort to hide.

I do not care. If her believing I had something to do with this sabotage draws her away from Kara's trail, then all the better. She has nothing to actually pin to me.

"I requested the two so that I might study them. I aim to modernize our transport technique."

She waves her hand, absentmindedly pulling a wall of water from the fountain in her office. "Save me the antics. You may have the other policymakers fooled, but not me. I will be watching you."

She stands from her desk, walking around it to meet me. "Tell me, Sorren, how does your mission progress?"

Though she is heads shorter than me, we stand toe to toe, and she is no less intimidating for it. I hear the challenge in her words that demand I produce.

"I have sent soldiers to scout out the Healing Faction and the three bordering factions. They have not yet returned with information."

"You stall, soldier." Though all who serve the military are soldiers, she uses this title to remind me of my rank. A cheap shot that highlights my stripped title.

"I will set up an audience for you with the other policymakers and me tomorrow at midday. You will present the plans for moving forward in your mission." My time is running out. "And since it seems we may have overestimated our ability to rely on you to complete this task, I will name Malakai as your second on this operation."

"The lieutenant is my second. I will not accept the admiral," I snarl.

"That is where you are mistaken, soldier. The admiral will serve as your second on this mission and if you're not careful, he may replace your office altogether."

The sound of trickling water is the only thing permeating the heavy air between us as she allows the authority of her words to resonate. Her threat is not thinly veiled. It is not ambiguous or implied. It is real and apparent.

CHAPTER 22
SORREN

I POUR OVER THE maps and addresses in my father's library. The journals he kept, the canons he wrote. I'm so engrossed in his work that I don't realize when Kai strolls through the door.

"So, you have abandoned a security system altogether." He states the apparent observation.

"We do have these handy comm units," I say, extending my forearm. "You could always . . . I don't know . . . call."

"Yes, but then I lose the element of surprise." He flicks his fingers into the air, spreading them apart. Sprays of water burst from them like fireworks. My dear friend and his love for the element of surprise.

"So, what brings you by this evening?"

He moves forward, reaching a hand into his pocket. When he pulls it out, he drops a small pin disk on the desk. "You asked me for something. I delivered."

He gestures to it, and I realize he's gotten an override disk. It will grant me access to the captive files.

"They are not comprehensive, and only examine high profile and exceptionally skilled captives. They gave the rest basic files with demographic information," he says.

I reach forward, immediately sinking the disk into my father's screen.

"I expect you to uphold your end of our deal as well. Sorren, you'll look through this, and when you find nothing of use, you will put these foolish notions to rest."

I can see my friend worries for me. "I will. But I must know."

He shakes his head. "I may never truly understand you."

And that is so much more than an understatement.

"What did the prime wish to speak to you about?"

I don't dare to tell him about Ciel's task or Malakai's instatement as second in command on the mission I was supposed to enact solo. I don't need Kai worrying any more than he already is.

"She wishes to have me sit before the Council of Policy tomorrow. They would like for me to present my plans and strategy for the mission."

His lips pinch together. He knows me well enough to know I have nothing prepared. "Well, I'll let you get to that. I'm sure whatever you come up with will have them enthralled."

As he leaves the office, Kai turns back at the threshold of the hallway, assessing me. "You're free now. Get yourself cleaned up before meeting the Council of Policy. You look like a feral terra, just escaped from the backwoods of the Lower."

Since my time imprisoned and reconditioning, my hair has grown out from the short comb over that is acceptable of a military officer. The stubble of my beard has grown thick.

I run a hand over my woolen jaw, teasing my friend. "I was sort of liking the look. Think it makes me appear older, more intimidating."

He laughs. "Get a shave and a haircut and let me know once you've met with the council," he says, leaving my father's house.

I spend the entire night poring over the captives' records, looking for any correlations—any clues to why they took such force with this entire faction. I try to understand what their plans are for the servants.

I do not know what compels me to seek a reason to disobey my orders, but still I continue. Skimming through each file, I memorize Kara's as if it holds the secret to life.

I don't know why I torture myself with the thought of her. Looking at her servant record feels wrong. I know I do not deserve to learn anything more about the woman who shared so many unshielded pieces of herself. But I cannot help but peek into the life of the woman I've stolen everything from.

She's one of the handful of L3s serving in Central City. We captured four Level Threes from her faction, two more terras, and a pyro. The council would have considered my mission a great success had I not folded at the last minute.

I continue to read Kara's file, hoping it will give me more insight into this captivating elemental I can't seem to get out of my head. I learn she is next in line to lead the faction . . . after her mother. I slap my palm onto my forehead and drag it down my face. The captive who walked in on Kara and I was her *mother*.

I groan, understanding the woman's protectiveness and distaste toward me. I feel guilty that the two have worked alongside each other for so long, ignorant of their relationship, and add that to my ever-growing list of things to make right.

Scouring the database, I skim through the files on my raid's captives. They hold very little information beyond basic demographics. Most of the faction members captured don't have a file at all.

I scan through and tally up the numbers. They aren't adding up. On the day of the raid, I delivered over seven thousand Lowers to the prime. Totaling the numbers now, it appears that almost half have completely vanished.

Kai has delivered me access to the entire database. I look beyond the elementals I captured and search the others serving the Upper. Still, the missing elementals are unaccounted for.

I think to look for one more record. The Torcher's.

As a pyro in the Upper, there must be something on him. Finally, I come across Jarek's record. I open it, hoping it will reveal some explanation for how he gained his status, why he is here.

His record is pieced together, the information in it choppy and incomplete. The fire wielder did not come to Central City as a servant. He came as an infiltrator. Aether prickles at my fingertips as I scroll through the pyro's file. Jarek was a part of the initial raid on our capitol. He participated in the attack that initiated the Regional Battles, the very attack that led to the assassination of my father.

This is impossible. All Lowers from that attack were sent to the Outer for execution. No Lower should have lived to walk away from my father's assassination. Rage quickens my breathing and grinds my teeth.

How is it that he lives, while my father does not? My hate for the fire wielder compounds into a visceral loathing. I override the confidentiality locks and search for an explanation, finding his imprisonment files and backtrack to access his sentencing and testimony.

I, Jarek Quinlan of the Fire Clan's Smithing Faction, agree to testify thoroughly and truthfully, the account of the Lower attack unit on Central City. The warrior unit, composed of representatives of the Lightening, Farming, Magma, Healing, and Smithing factions, attacked Central City intending to appropriate serving elementals and assassinate Prime Policymaker Nero Astley.

I ball my fists, squeezing my eyes shut, to block out the words. How does he live?

I continue to read the gruesome testimony that granted the Upper leave to execute the elementals involved. It is the only direct vengeance we've gained on my father's death. Apparently, the testimony that condemned his comrades was the same to exonerate him. Though Jarek does claim to have reconsidered in the final hour, working to stop the assassination, it was not enough.

This is how the damned pyro escaped a life of imprisonment, by selling out his comrades. The traitor. I wince as the irony of my words becomes evident. Though, I will not put myself on level with the pyro I despise, almost as much as the admiral he shadows.

At least my treachery is not self-serving. This coward only sought to save himself.

For all his betrayal, the pyro could not escape punishment entirely. His sentencing paperwork simply reads, *Reconditioning*. My stomach clenches, threatening to relieve me of its contents. A book's worth of reconditioning notes spans the screen. After tallying the totals, it appears the pyro served five years of reconditioning.

Chill bumps rise in mini mountains on my skin. Five years of reeducation and torture. Year after year of mornings spent sitting through mind-numbing propaganda, countless afternoons enduring ceaseless pain. I swallow the lump of loathing in my throat and suppress the hint of pity I would feel for anyone other than an active participant in my father's assassination and my own torture.

My mind races. The prickling of dread crawls up my spine at the thought of what my punishment could have been. The already impossible sentence could have been so much worse. It is a sobering reminder that the treacherous games I play have stakes I may be unable to bear.

How could one man survive so much torment? And for what reason?

Jarek Quinlan has successfully completed 60 months of reconditioning, and it is my recommendation that he be allowed to rejoin our society as a reformed elemental. He has displayed a comprehensive understanding of the Upper Region's superior nature, and an eagerness to devote his talents and loyalty to the region.

Jarek is a shining example of our ability to rehabilitate the Lower elementals and should be celebrated as a grand success.

I shut the files.

Just like so many of us, this pyro is a pawn in the council's relentless games. There is no reason to read further.

Just as well, my comm unit pings with an alert. I look down and the message that projects into the air above my comm sinks my heart into my stomach. It's from Calix.

We've located the targets.

I am stuck. My plans steadily collapse at those simple words. I need more time to figure a way out of this. Against my better judgement, I call the scout.

"Calix, I need you to stand down."

"Sir?"

"Report directly to my father's manor. Do not return to the capitol before we've met."

There's a long pause. Calix pulls a heavy hand down his salt and pepper beard before answering. "Understood, sir."

"I will see you here after midday tomorrow for your briefing. There, I will give you your next orders."

"Yes sir," he says, disconnecting the call.

I continue to pour over the records deep into the night, searching desperately for anything that can help me. When I finally close the database, I see guard change is only a short time away.

I look in the mirror and decide to take Kai's advice. I cut my hair and shave my beard, so my disheveled appearance does not work against me in tomorrow's meeting with the Council of Policy.

Before I leave to meet with Kara, I don the officer uniform I wore the morning of my raid on her home. It will help me to move her through Central City with little suspicion. Even more, when I tell Kara who I truly am, I want her to have no doubt in my words. The council has removed my medals and honors from it, and all that's left are the faded outlines highlighting my degraded status. But at heart, it is still the same.

When I am through, I grimace at my reflection. This is exactly how I looked the first time Kara and I met.

I leave the manor, making a quick detour to the hydro gardens before meeting with Kara. Though she may want nothing from me once I've told her the truth, I can't help myself. Once I've grabbed what I need from the gardens, I make my way to the infirmary.

I push the air below me, rising to my old room's window. It's dark, and I don't see any movement inside. Once I tap on the glass, Kara comes up to open it. When she swings the glass open, I pause, waiting for her to assess me.

Her eyes widen as her gaze moves from my neatly combed over hair to my clean-shaven jaw.

"Sorren." My name comes out barely above a whisper, and my heart rate speeds in anticipation of her piecing it all together. As I expect her to lash out, finally seeing who I truly am, her lips curve into a smile. "You look handsome."

I open my mouth, but don't know what to say as relief washes over me.

"You're okay," is all I can manage.

Whatever she did truly worked. They did not catch her; there was no maintenance. I pull her into me, still hovering outside the window, so relieved she's okay. Kara pulls back smiling, nodding her head.

"Come on, let's get out of here." I want to take her as far from the capitol building as I can. "I want to show you something."

She grabs my hand, pushing forward to peek out the window. Looking down, her gaze snaps back up to me. "And how am I supposed to get down there?"

I grin, holding my hand out. She looks back down before bravely taking it, and I help her out of the window, sitting her on the ledge.

"Put your arms around me," I say, wrapping my hands around her waist. When she does, I gently pull her out of the window and into the nighttime. Her fingers grip my neck as she peeks at the ground below with a gasp.

"Eyes on me," I say, as I slowly bring us down. "I have you."

When we land, I hold Kara for a beat longer, not ready to relinquish her warm weight in my arms. As she makes no movement to free herself from my grasp, I believe she is in no rush either. We stay, just like this, looking at each other, the knowledge we've received from the day painting each other in a new light.

"Where are you taking me?" Her voice is low and breathy.

"It's a surprise. Follow me."

CHAPTER 23
SORREN

I GENTLY PLACE KARA on the ground and take her hand, leading her to the wall. As we walk across Central City, her gaze darts around, taking the nighttime landscape in.

"I've never been out here at night before. Servants aren't allowed out of their quarters following maintenance."

My stomach turns at the thought, and I want nothing more than to take her away from this place for good. The closer we get to the city wall, the lower the streets sink below water. I freeze the liquid beneath our feet to walk above it, not wanting to bother with splashing around.

"Gods, it's so beautiful."

I steer her, keeping her on the path as she continues to look down, rather than in front of her, transfixed on the glowing waters below. The bioluminescent plankton inhabiting the waters of Central City bask the pathways in a bright blue light.

"Wait until you see the beach."

My mind races with what may happen, how she may react to the truths I plan to tell her. A part of me wants to hold on to this charade for as long as possible. The sickening part, the one that has allowed so many transgressions already. I bury that. He is not who I aspire to be. He is not who she deserves.

When we reach the edge of Central City, I slip Kara through the grate in the stone wall that allows water from the ocean to pass through, rather than lifting her over. I want her to know where she can access the opening, even without me. When she makes it to the other side, she halts with a gasp.

Before us, the sea stretches out in an endless spectacle of glowing waves. Kara bends, scooping up a handful of sand. She studies the tiny particles of land. With the twist of her wrist, she wields the sand, pulling it up, forcing it to spin and whip in her palm. I see the shift in her. For the first time in months, she's able to truly access her element, finally reunited with the land.

She rushes further onto the beach, bending into the sand like it's a long-lost friend. Crouching on the shore of the vast oceanscape, she places her hands on the ground and pulls green stalks from the white sand. I stand for a moment, watching her revel in her power.

She is beautiful, as her fingers glow green, and her smile broadens with every stalk she pulls from the ground. When she finally looks back at me, she stands, dusting the sand from her clothes. Her eyes find mine and a smile spreads across her lips.

"Thank you for bringing me here. This is amazing." She gestures out to the ocean before us.

"Would you like to see it from higher up?"

Her brows lift as she looks back at the rolling waves, then nods, taking my hand.

I gently take her arms to wrap them around my waist, then move to scoop her up, securing her against me. I fan my hand out, using it to manipulate the air. Wind circulates around our feet, pushing up our legs, blowing and ruffling the fabric of her dress. As I lift us from the ground, her hold on me tightens.

I keep the ascent slow—the floor of air gradually thickens as we lift from the ground.

Wind swirls around us, pushing our bodies farther and farther from the sand. I check on her every few feet, looking down to see her face. "Are you still okay?"

She gives me a wordless nod, looking back to the ground, then clutching me again.

"Eyes on me." I bend my forehead to hers, nudging her to look up, rather than down.

When she does, her gaze does not leave mine for the remainder of our assent.

Once I'm satisfied we've reached the perfect height, I stop, wielding my element to form a compacted platform for us to sit on. When Kara's gaze breaks from mine, she looks over at the sea with a gasp. Her mouth falls open, watching the dark waves outlined with light crash into each other, causing luminescent ripples. Seeing everything from a vantage point she never has before.

"What do you think?"

She answers me, never pulling her gaze from the sea. "I think I'm looking at the most magnificent beauty in this entire realm."

The sight of her deep golden skin, painted pale and luminescent in the moonlight, is breathtaking. Her fingertips still glow from the flood of her essence. Her bright emerald eyes, wide and shining with marvel, send a wave of longing through me, and I know exactly how she feels. "So do I."

I etch this image of her into my mind. It is how I will envision her when she is long gone, and no longer mine to look upon. I will keep it with me forever.

Kara turns her gaze from the sea to me, smiling, the faintest pink staining her cheeks.

"Let's have a seat." I lower to the makeshift platform.

Her gaze shoots down, as if she's just realized that we are suspended in midair. "Is it safe? There's nothing beneath us."

"Go ahead. It's solid, I promise."

Once I've positioned myself comfortably on the platform of air, she follows me down. Slowly crouching into a squat, Kara pats the platform, confirming it's solid, before sitting next to me. She brings herself flush with my side, leaning her body against mine and laying her head in the nook of my arm and chest. I'm sure it's for security, but I revel in her proximity, regardless.

I reach into my pocket, pulling out my plunder from the hydro gardens. "I got these for you."

I carefully unfold the bundle, and while they are not smashed, the bright purple berries are far from prime condition. "They aren't much, but I figured they would be a pleasant deviation from seaweed."

Kara gasps. "Those look delicious." She plucks one from the cloth and pops it into her mouth. Her face lights up as she chews.

"Gods Sorren," she says, grabbing another four. "These are amazing."

"Here, take them all," I laugh, relieved the berries align with her tastes.

We sit in silence as she gobbles up the last of the berries, watching the waves hug the shore. It doesn't take long to lose myself in the beauty of it. As the waves travel forward, a wall of neon blue light rushes, then falls against the sand. The glow grips onto the ground, as if the ocean clings on for dear life, before being dragged back into the deep.

"This is my favorite wielding skill; there is no better escape than this. I remember the first time I ascended. It was the day I presented as a Level Three, just as I had received word of my father's passing." I continue to watch the sea, unable to meet Kara's gaze as I bear my vulnerabilities to her.

"Nero was always so disappointed that his only child never presented as anything more than a Level Two. Hell, he was disappointed in just about everything regarding me. He died disappointed . . ." Kara places her hand on my knee, squeezing it, reminding me she is here with me so that I do not get lost in the memory's heaviness.

"I didn't even get to bury him. A small part of me was actually relieved that he was gone. I thought that maybe, with him, died this obsession to prove myself—my worth."

I hang my head in my hands, raking my fingers through the neatly combed strands of hair. "How foolish. Since then, I've fought more than ever. Like some cruel, sick irony, his disapproval haunts me from the grave. No matter what I accomplish, what I conquer, how hard I work to climb, it is all credited to him, his legacy, his station. He built all this, and I have sullied his legacy, and just about lost everything I've worked to attain."

"Sorren, what happened?"

I take a deep breath. "I was ordered to lead an attack on a group of terras. The orders were to take all living elementals from the town, but I didn't . . ."

Her expression breaks, and I am sure she remembers. "What happened to them?"

"I let them go."

She looks at me, seeming to stare deep within me. As she goes to speak, her face crumples in a pained expression I've seen on her so many times before. She rubs her temples, shaking her head, as if she can shake the pain away.

My hand is on her back in an instant. "Kara."

She touches my chest, the features of her face smoothing. "I'm okay."

She keeps her eyes closed for a beat or two more, before opening them to look forward. "Why did your father hate the terras so much?"

I think for a moment, wanting to give her the most honest answer I can. "It was a culmination of things. I think he was resentful of the Lower's power over us. They held control over the food and medicines we were so desperate for."

Kara shifts, looking up at me as I continue. "I think that caused him to blame the terras for some of the tragedies in his life. His parents died during a pandemic before I was born. The terras withheld medicines that could have saved thousands. They demanded exorbitant payment for the remedies we so desperately needed, but my father did not come from wealth, so his parents did not receive the cure that would have saved them."

"Gods Sorren, I'm so sorry."

I shrug. They died before I was born, so I don't honestly have much to mourn. "It was the same with my mother. When she died, my father blamed the terras, though I don't know what they could have done for her. Still, he insists they let her die . . ."

Kara nods, looking at me. "I'm from the Lower, aren't I?"

My pulse pounds with the revelation, the heavy whooshing of blood thundering in my ears, drowning out the sound of the sea. "Yes."

"I was a healer." This is a revelation she's made already. Still, I nod, holding my breath for her to make more connections, but she does not. She only looks at me, her deep green eyes soft and filled with understanding. "I'm sorry for what my people have done. I'm sorry you've been alone all this time."

The truth of it stabs me, and I cannot speak. For my entire life, I've been desolately untethered. It wasn't until this terra grounded me that I'd ever felt at home anywhere. I clench my jaw, looking forward, focusing on the crashing waves.

I feel her gentle hand caress my cheek, tilting my head back toward hers. Once she has my focus, she looks into my eyes, holding my gaze. "You're not alone anymore." Her fingers slide up my jaw and into my hair. "I promise you will never be alone again."

Her words slice into me, the sweetest agony I've ever experienced. How can this woman see me so wholly? How can she reach into the core of me? Sift through all my deepest pains and insecurities, touch them all and set them free. For the first time in my life, I do not feel alone. The terrifying reality of that comes crashing into me as I realize I am about to lose the most precious thing I have ever had.

I can already feel the void the loss of her affections will leave. It will destroy me. It will leave me more broken than any reconditioning from Malakai, any disappointment from my father, any unmet expectation of my brigade. Kara came into my life and filled a void I didn't know existed. An emptiness I was born with that was never meant to be filled.

As her fingers loosen in my hair, I grip her hand, terrified of losing her touch. Need wracks my body and forces a shudder through my bones for the woman I could never deserve. And when she moves in to place her lips on mine, I devour her.

I breathe her in more intensely than my element. When she pushes herself closer to me, I wrap my arms around her. Sliding my hand up her back to bury into the brown waves of her hair, and my other hand to wrap around her waist, gripping her hip. Pulling her even closer into me, I feel the rapid rise and fall of her chest.

She bites down on my lip, forcing a groan from my throat, and I pull back, giving us both a moment to catch our breath. Our heavy breathing turns to white mist between us, and I don't know if I've dropped the temperature, or if it is just the winter air chilling the atmosphere.

Kara touches the frost I left on her lips, allowing it to melt on her fingers, and smiles up at me. "Let's go for a swim."

I can't help the laugh that escapes me. "Isn't it a bit cold for a terra to go swimming?"

She smiles. "After my time here, I think I can handle a little cold water."

Anger settles in my chest at what she implies. "What do you mean?"

"I've spent my fair share of time in solid ice." She shrugs, and I must suppress the growl forming in my chest. "The worst was when one of the aeros caught me staring at the tribute at the city's center."

I know which one she speaks of. It is the tribute my father dedicated to Procella; a guardian Hydris blessed with immortality.

"He thought I had been staring too long, rather than getting on with my chores. So, he said if I was so intent on spending my day staring at the tribute, I'd get my fill of it. Then he froze me there for a few hours."

Rage bubbles in my core. How disgustingly hypocritical. I am just as repulsive as whatever aero she speaks of now. My anger simmers into distressing guilt as I recall wrapping Kara in a block of ice the morning I took her faction.

How many people had I ordered frozen in the elemental device as a means of convenient restraint?

I take a breath, running a rough hand through my hair. How could I have messed things up so terribly?

Again, Kara sees right through me. "It's okay. It wasn't a big deal. At least it got me out of the afternoon's chores. And I got to study the tribute longer." She sighs. "There was just something so familiar about the woman. Like I'd seen her before . . ."

Kara looks down at the waves, a small smile curving her full lips. "Enough of that. Let's go."

I rise, offering her my hand. She grips it, pulling herself up and into my arms. I lower us slowly, making sure to place her gently back on the ground.

As Kara bends to remove her shoes, I give her privacy by turning to take off my own. I remove my officer's coat and slacks, folding them in a neat stack on the sand, keeping my undergarments on. I can air dry us both when we leave the water.

I turn, searching for Kara, but all I see are her garments, lying in a messy pile on the sand. I scan the water, and when my eyes find her, a chill runs through my body.

Kara stands in the middle of the sea, her bare backside bathed in pale moonlight, washing her skin in a soft blue glow. Each glowing wave crashes against her in a luminescent burst of color, cresting at her waist, then pulling back to reveal the firm curve of her rear.

I try to swallow, but my throat runs so dry that I cannot. An unfamiliar heat flushes through my body and pours down into the pit of my stomach. She turns to look at me over her shoulder, and the swell of her breast becomes barely visible, the luminescent glow of water dripping from her like rain.

She tilts her head, bidding me to come join her. I move forward, suddenly achingly aware of the blatant stiffness in my boxers.

There isn't a thing I could do in this world to suppress my body's response to her. With each step I take toward her, I feel my need compounding. It strikes in my chest and pulses through my groin, achingly desperate for release.

I am so distracted that I don't realize I'm not sinking into the water. Each step I take freezes the liquid beneath me, forming an ice platform beneath my feet. I am losing control of my element, and take a breath to rein it back in. Kara giggles, and the sound of her sets me at ease, sending another bolt of lust through my veins.

I clench my fist, retracting the cold and sinking into the water. When I finally reach Kara, my body is so tense that I'm sure one touch from the woman will completely undo me.

She appraises me with hooded eyes, looking up at me through a curtain of thick lashes. Placing her hand on my chest, the mere feel of her on me has me ready to explode. Then she says, her voice low and seductive, "I believe you are overdressed, Commander."

CHAPTER 24
KARA

THE RIPPLES OF HIS abdomen are painfully clear through his now soaked undershirt, but I still want to feel his bare skin against mine. I slowly move my hand up and down his broad chest, keeping my gaze locked on his for any sign that I've gone too far.

There is none.

"Is that so?" he replies, his voice tight, the Adams apple in his neck bobbing as he swallows. "Well, we can't have that."

I smile up at him, using my tongue to dampen my bottom lip before taking it between my teeth.

"Allow me to help you with that," I say.

I wait for him to nod before sliding my hand down and under his shirt, slowly dragging it up the bare skin I've been so desperate to feel. Keeping my movements slow, relishing each hard bump of his abdomen, I run my fingers along the slight line of hair running up the center of him. It runs from his pectorals to navel, and I'm eager to see exactly how far down the patch goes.

When my hands reach his chest, I feel the rapid beat of his heart, and it leaves me breathless. I push the shirt up, and he crosses his arms to grip, then pulls it the rest of the way over his head. I take

223

the moment to revel in the sight of him. Bare chested, his already pale skin glows practically translucent in the moonlight.

He balls the shirt in his hand, and I feel the air around us swirl, forming a dense pocket that he uses to thrust the garment onto the sand. I slide my hands down his frame, bringing them to the elastic of his boxers.

I don't know where this strange new boldness comes from. Maybe it is the heat of need making me delirious. Maybe it's the surge of power I feel being so directly connected to the land. Whatever it is, makes me feel powerful and bold.

As I slide his boxers down, they get caught on the hard length of him, and the air escapes my lungs. Sorren lifts his hand to my chin, pulling me up with a gentle tug, smiling. "No need for that."

I want to protest, but his cool mouth meets mine, and I lose all thought.

His hand slides from my chin down to my neck, then shoulder, as his other hand wraps around to the small of my back, nuzzling me into him.

Ice creeps up every part of me that his fingers touch, but I don't feel cold. I'm much too hot for his elemental device to bring anything but comfort to the burning ache raging inside of me.

I bring my hands to his face, pulling him into a deeper kiss, wanting him to devour me, needing to feel his tongue on mine and his air give me breath. Intense need shoots through me, sending a tingle down my core where a needy ache settles at the bottom of my sex, and all I want is for this man to be mine.

I don't care what he's done. Damn any warning signs or meddlesome intuition. I need him. As surely as I need my element, this man belongs with me, and I will never let him go.

As the waves crash around us, he lifts me up, melding me even closer into him. I wrap my thighs around his waist, feeling the impossibly hard length of him press at my aching slit through the thin fabric of his boxers. I pulse with need and would do anything to remove the barrier, keeping him from me.

"Sorren," I beg, and the word comes out muffled against his lips. I can feel myself clench at the touch of him and know that even if we were not submerged in water, I'd still be soaking wet. "Please."

"Gods, Kara, you'll be the death of me." He rests his forehead against mine. And I know I could die a thousand times and still make my way back to him. I feel him connected to the very essence of me, and it is a connection I can never let go.

"Sorren." My words come out breathy and unsteady. "I think I'm in love with you."

He pulls back, looking at me with wide gray eyes. "Kara, you can't mean that."

An urgency flares through me. I'm not going to let him do this. I'm not going to let him pull away, not again. "Don't tell me what I mean. Sorren, I know what I feel."

"But—"

I raise a finger to his lips. "Don't run from me. Please."

His eyes plead with me to understand. "I don't deserve . . . If you knew who I truly am . . . "

His jaw flexes, and I can see it so much clearer now that he's cut the stubble away. He shakes his head, and I bring my hands up to steady him.

"I know who you are. I see the truest parts of you . . . and they are what I love the most."

His nostrils flare as he lets out a shaky breath, bending down to meet me. "Gods Kara, I will never deserve you."

Then his lips crash against mine, heated and urgent. His fingers dig into my skin with a desperate force, as if I'm being pulled away, and it's all he can do to hold on to me. When his tongue strokes mine, it feels cold as ice. His mouth moves to my jaw, leaving urgent icy kisses down my neck where I feel his tongue against my jugular. My pulse beats hard, pounding against my skin, my heart thundering in my ears.

I tighten my thighs around him, squeezing to release the pressure, but the ache does not abate. It only grows in a swirling turbine of need that shoots straight through me. I dig my nails into his back, raking them down his shoulder blades.

Sorren growls into my neck, wrapping his hands around my ass. Squeezing until I gasp, he pushes me up until my chest is level with his face.

He takes one of my nipples, hard from the cold, into his mouth, pulling it gently between his teeth. I cry out, gripping his hair and pulling him closer to me, silently begging for him to take more of me in. He laps the hard rosy peak further into his mouth, then releases it with an audible pop. He slides me back down the center of him, dragging my clit over each hard ripple of his abdomen until his lips meet mine.

The bold caress of his tongue sends chill bumps over my skin, and I shiver against him, my body surrounded by cold, yet thoroughly consumed with heat. I break my lips from his, but his mouth moves down my jaw and chin, never lifting from my flesh.

"I need you, please." My words sound much needier than I intend. Trying to push myself down onto him, I wiggle just above the tip of his arousal. He groans, squeezing my ass, stopping me from sinking lower. I grunt, frustrated with my lack of release.

"Please Sorren." I take his bottom lip between my teeth, tugging before I release it. "I need you."

"No, wildflower, not yet."

I whine, sure I'll die from all the pent-up need swirling in my core, until he brings his hand to slide around my thigh. He drags his fingers across my pelvis, then slides them down until they glide across my slit. I swallow a gasp, stunned by the shock of it, digging my fingers into his skin, pulling him closer.

When he brings his fingers back up to circle the tiny bud at the tip of my entrance, I can't help the guttural moan that escapes me. It is all the invitation he needs to continue in those slow, maddening circles until my breath comes out in quick shallow huffs. Just when I'm on the edge of hyperventilating, he plunges his thick finger into my center, forcing me to cry out.

He is so cold against the hot core of me, the contrast drives me wild. When he drags his finger in and out of me, I thrust my hips, meeting his tempo. He brings his head down to my neck, placing his cold lips on my skin, dragging his tongue in the same maddening circles as his fingers.

I clutch tighter to him. "More."

I want him. And I want him more intensely than I want land or air, or any other element this world has to offer.

Then his thrusts stop, and before I can protest the pause, I feel a second finger nudge at my slit. He gently pushes it inside me, stretching me around him.

"Gods Kara, you're so tight."

He tentatively begins to thrust, bringing his thumb to rub against my clit. The dual sensation of it undoes me. I rock my hips against his fingers, riding his hand with unbridled lust. I grind until the thrusts grow rapid. Tendrils of electricity shoot through me, pushing every nerve ending I have, and sending a tingle through my entire body.

The swirling energy building in my core feels like power. It is seductive, as it is overwhelming and strong. My breathing hitches as Sorren pulls his head back to look into my eyes.

His gaze penetrates me like no other part of him can, and every muscle in my body tenses. With each maddening circle, he winds the tension in my core tighter, until it is coiled like a vine viper, poised for attack. Until it steals my breath, and the thrumming beat of my heart becomes rabid.

When he whispers, "Come for me, wildflower," I am undone.

My release crashes against me like the waves of the sea. It comes in a flood of energy that rips through my chest and shoots through my fingertips in a blinding green light. The ground beneath us quakes as I cry out his name, my body trembling in an electrifying shudder as he clutches me to him.

By the time the last tremors of ecstasy run through me, I collapse onto him, thoroughly exhausted, unable to lift my head from his shoulder. Sorren slides his fingers from me, leaving a cold emptiness that wasn't there before.

Wrapping his arms around me, he carries me to the beach, laying me on the sand. I lay back for a second, looking up at the beautiful nighttime sky, before Sorren stoops to kiss my forehead. "Let's get you dressed before you freeze."

A sudden shiver shakes my body, and I don't know if it's from the late winter wind, or his breath on my skin. He takes it as confirmation and gently lifts me up to slip my dress over my head. I lift my black necklace, securing it back around my neck, and finish dressing. Once he's put on his own clothes, we lay back down on the sand.

He tucks me into the crook of his arm, resting my head on his chest, then drapes his officer's coat over me, shielding me from the chill.

We lie there, silently looking up at the stars, until we fall asleep.

CHAPTER 25

KARA

BRIGHT RAYS OF SUN warm my face as a steady pulse drums below my palm. I feel the slow rise and fall of Sorren's chest beneath my cheek and smile, remembering last night.

When I open my eyes, I see my fingers have turned into thin vines that lay across his chest in flowery ropes. It takes a moment for me to retract them, and I gasp at the realization that I suddenly remember how to.

I lift from him, the steady flow of aether running strong through my veins.

"Sorren." My voice is light, giddy with the feel of familiar power coursing through my fingertips. With my direct connection to the land below me, the aether's pulsing seeps into my skin and intertwines with my essence. Now that the last of the maintenance serum has emptied from my body, I have no trouble calling to the power that has been mine all along.

More bubbles beneath the surface of my skin that I'm almost afraid to summon it. I look down, taking the delicious sight of him in, appreciating the neat trim of his hair, though it is no longer carefully combed over, but rather messy from last night's festivities. He's shaved the thick beard that had so often brushed my cheek, making him look years younger.

When he opens his eyes to meet mine, the crystal gray irises strike something deep within me.

He is right. I have met this man before.

Sorren sits up once he notices my body stiffen. He stays there, looking at me in that uniform—with those eyes—and the flood of a memory comes cascading down.

The last time I saw him like this, sand and a pretty oceanscape did not surround us.

We were surrounded by chaos and a sea of blood.

As the pieces of this long-overrun puzzle come together, a lump forms in the pit of my throat. It grows large, with sharp corners and edges that sting me and make me choke back a sob that threatens to bubble to the surface before I even know why.

The first time this man held me in his frozen embrace, I was not surrounded by his arms. His element encased me. The horror of it all settles on me as I remember being wrapped in ice while everything around me burned.

Something in me breaks as adrenaline rushes through every cell in my body. My pulse picks up and raw, searing hatred settles on my chest.

As I recall the man, I just looked upon so dotingly, I remember all that he took from me. Like a flipped switch—the turning on of tech, or the transfer from night to day—it all becomes clear.

All the pain, all the hurt, all the rage that had laid dormant beneath the surface—that I'd held tight under lock and key—pushes its way to the forefront. This time I do not hold it back. I let the pain and rage overtake me. I allow it to fuel me and release the power I know I hold.

His eyes widen as the beach sand elevates, ready to heed my command. The ground trembles, and I can hardly contain myself.

As if to calm me down, he scrambles to his feet, speaking the name he has no right to. "Kara, I can—"

I push the sand forward, aiming to bury him alive. He throws up a force field of air, blocking my attack. I slam my fist on the ground, breaking it apart to swallow him up, pushing even more sand atop him. Although I can feel the raw essence rush through my core, the techniques I'd spent so long cultivating are still hazy and uneasily accessed. So, I throw what I can at him, needing to see him bleed.

"Kara, wait!"

I hear none of it. He has done enough talking. He's had weeks to talk. There has been so much said between us, and not once could he tell me the truth.

My powers come at me in a rush, and I scramble to take hold of them. This is not like the wielding I remember. The gentle coaxing of my element. The element I wield is pure aether, and it bends at my command. I push thorns from my palms to throw at him. I grasp the rope of essence wielding in my core, willing it to shoot through my fingertips and wrap around his neck.

He should have told me.

He should have never let me . . .

Anger and rage consume me until all I see is red. I strangle him with the thick ropes of my vines, but it is still not enough. I wish to break him with my bare hands. *How could he?*

I search the land for a weapon to wield that will end him. I find rocks and boulders, erecting them from deep within the ground to catapult in his direction.

"How dare you? What kind of sick game?" I yell between shots. "Is that what this was? A game to you."

I run to him, bringing with me a blanket of soil I will suffocate him with. He breaks the wall of dirt apart with a swift brisk wind and when I've pulled out all my tricks, I run quickly, aiming to wrap my hands around his throat.

"Kara, stop. Please let me explain."

"What is there to explain?" I do not slow my attack to hear his empty words. In my time here, he's given me so many words, and none of them were truth.

It makes me sick to think of how easily I fell for his lies. How easily I fell for *him*. Never questioning, never giving heed to the warnings my mind tried to give me. I ignored it all. I did this.

Another wave of rage rushes over me and my fist slams into his jaw. The crack of it satisfies me like nothing else.

"So, taking my home and my people were not enough?" He ducks, dodging my next swing. "You have already won. Why'd you aim to break me even more?"

I rage, needing to hear his answer, needing to know why. "Do you so thoroughly hate me? Do you resent my people so much that you aim to steal everything from me? And when there was nothing left to take, you take my heart, only to break that too?"

"No, I never wanted to hurt you. You must believe me."

A manic howl bubbles from my throat, and the sound of it frightens even me. "You insult me, aero."

"My feelings for you have always been genuine. Kara, please believe me."

I'm so angered by his words that I bring my open hand up to slap across his face, bloodying the lips he used to kiss me and so much more.

"Lies! That's all you've ever given me. Lies then and lies now." My voice breaks. I try to hold on to the rage—the hatred and the anger—because beneath them lies something so much more painful.

Behind my wrath is hurt. Beneath my bloodlust is a broken heart that I am ashamed to even have. As deeply as I hate the man before me, I hate myself more. How easily I fell for the enemy. I'm sickened by the dishonor I have done to myself and my people. So much so, I cannot aim my wrath at him any longer, when it more suitably belongs to me.

He watches it all play out, quietly giving me time to process. As he witnesses my breakdown, a look of pity softens his eyes, and I recognize that, too. It was the look he gave me as he watched me cry at the foot of my father's dying body.

I choke out a sob, fresh waves of grief washing over me. A wail rips from my throat, as the gravity of all I've lost weighs on me. I hiccup my sobs, barely able to breathe between them.

My father is dead.

He may still lie on our town's floor. Grief maddens me until I'm crazy with it. No one person can handle so much pain. I'm sure I'll die from the sheer experience of it. Sorren moves in to comfort me and I shove him away.

"Don't you touch me. Don't you dare—" My words are broken by sobs. Regret rakes sharp claws down my chest as I wish I'd left the memories locked away quiet and asleep. How much I long for the serum that would bring my mind peace.

"You don't ever get to touch me again. You are a liar and a fraud, Sorren Astley, and I will hate you until the day I die."

I leave him, because just looking at him brings me a heartache I cannot handle, not on top of everything else. I sneak back into the city through the gate, and when I'm sure he does not follow me, I sag along the wall and cry.

I cry for all that I have lost: my father, my faction, my freedom. And while I'm sure no one is around to see; I cry for the love that was only a figment of my imagination. A love I was certain was real. One I would have sold my soul to the deities to protect.

Why did it have to be him?

I'm not sure how long I sit there, letting myself weep until my body shakes and my head throbs. I cry until my tears are dry and nothing springs from my eyes. When I've composed myself, I know I must go to the pyro and tell him what I have learned.

I can't allow grief to consume me. I must press forward. My people are hurt and kept captive. If I don't use this clarity to save them, then we truly will lose everything.

When I reach the smith building, I do not hear the ring of mallets. I'd fear the pyro is not there, had the heat surrounding the building not been so intense. I open the door to find him wielding the hearth's flames. Upon hearing me, he draws the flames forward, creating a barrier between him and the intruder. When he sees it's only me, he extinguishes the wall of fire.

"Kara," he greets me with the name he remembered just last night.

My name was all he could recall, and he couldn't remember how he knew it or me. We thought a good night's rest and a little more time to rid his body of the serum might get us the answers we sought. But I do not need answers from him. I have my own. Looking at him now, surrounded by the flames—I remember. "Cinis."

His brows furrow, then lift. A surprised "Yes," falls from his lips. "That's my name."

He smiles, excitement raising his tone, and I cannot believe I did not recognize those obsidian eyes and golden blond curls before.

"You're Cinis Stallard, of the Fire Clan's Smithing Faction." I clap my hands together, relief washing over his features. That's all he needs, as the veil that seemed to block his memories somehow falls. He rushes to me, lifting me up in his embrace.

"Yes. Yes, Kara of the Terra Clan's Healing Faction." He leads me by my waist, twirling me in the air, placing me down to my feet to grab the obsidian pendant around my neck. "Kara, my dear, my betrothed." The smile that stretches his lips pulls back to show his teeth.

"Y-yes . . ." I'm barely able to push the whisper of the word past my lips.

Guilt riddled, I cannot meet his gaze. A betrothed he will reject once he knows the level of betrayal she's served him. Betrayal in readying to leave him and her faction behind the night of the attack. Betrayal in finding release in the enemy's arms while he fights the spell they had us all under.

Shame heats the apples of my cheeks, and I can feel them reddening. Cinis mistakes the blush for something else, pulling me into his embrace, again promising me everything will be all right.

He traces a hot finger along my cheekbone. "How could I have forgotten you, my Kara." And I know that he would have been better off keeping it that way. But there's no time for guilt. Only time for action. With both of us clear minded, we can surely figure out how to save the faction.

"We have to help the others."

He nods, looking down at me. "We don't have much time. The siphoning will resume soon enough. Our window is closing. We must act fast."

"We'll need Twenty-three's help. I'll go find her. Maybe I can spark her memory as well. She'll help us," I say.

"Okay, talk to her and this evening I will meet you both in the infirmary so that we can discuss our next steps."

I agree as he pulls me in for one last embrace, holding me so tight I'm sure he fears that once he lets me go, he'll risk losing me again.

"Kara, be careful," he breathes into my hair, kissing my forehead and sending another ripple of shame through my body.

I leave him, seeking the older terra I know can help us free our fellow Lower elementals.

Twenty-three is easy to find. She follows her regular schedule, tending to her afternoon duties with diligence. I'm eager to see what the lack of neurotoxin has done for her memory, anxious to watch her freed terra powers flow out.

I find her in the inventory room pouring over the herbs and roots that she's given to make the serum, putting all her concentration into her work as she typically does. When she hears me walk in, she lifts her head and, just like the others before, I know exactly who she is.

"Mom." Hot tears spring from my eyes as I run to her, throwing my arms around her shoulders. She stiffens, still confused by the emotional display, but I'm too overwhelmed to give that much concern.

I cry into her hair, "You're okay," so relieved to see her alive and before me. I remember the day they transported us to this miserable place. I thought she'd been killed. I knew for certain we'd left her behind, dead along with my father.

Her body relaxes, and she wraps her arms around me, rubbing my back as I let the sobs flow out. When I've settled, she pulls me back to look at my face, confusion furrowing her brow.

"It's me, Kara. Your daughter." Her brows pull even closer together. I can see she tries to remember, but just cannot grasp the memories to convince her mind my words are true. I don't understand, she did not receive the neurotoxin last night. She should be better. She is a stronger wielder than Cinis or I. Of anyone, she should have recovered quickest. My heart breaks a little that my mother does not know who I am.

"Mom, don't you remember me?"

'I'm sorry, I do not," and it comes like a punch to the gut. She runs her fingers through my hair as she had so often done to comfort me before. The gesture is so familiar—so comforting—that I decide it is all I need, at least for now.

"Don't fret, dear girl," she says, her fingers still stroking my hair. "There's still so much that I do not remember. I've gained so much clarity since my last maintenance that I'm sure, given more time, I'll remember."

I wrap my arms around her even tighter, so much closer to having the mother I thought I'd lost back.

Although she hasn't fully recovered her memory, it is not something we can wait for. I tell her all that I know, almost grateful for her memory's disconnect. It horrifies her to hear what happened to our faction—what happened to us. Still, she does not have that deep connection to our faction that she would have, had her memory been clear. What she displays is not a fragment of the grief she would have should she remember who she truly is. For this reason, I don't tell her about Dad. I cannot handle any more heartbreak, at least not today.

She discounts nothing I say. She accepts my words for truth and agrees to help me. That we aren't perishing in the hydro territory is proof enough for her to continue.

"Cinis will meet us here this evening so we can devise a plan to get the other elementals out. We can't squander the little time we have before they resume maintenance."

"I agree," she says, her eyes narrowing on something affixed at the top of my head.

She brings her hand to a strand of my hair, but when she pulls it back, I see it is not hair. It's a thin, willowy vine. I jerk my hand to the crown of my head, reaching for the root, feeling that it goes into my scalp. I gasp.

This is not like the vines that grow through my fingers or the thorns I had thrown from my palm. I did not summon this, and I cannot make it go away. The worried look etched on my mother's face sends me further into panic.

"What is it?" I ask.

Her eyes haze and I can tell she searches her mind for an answer. "This is not good." Worry riddles her tone. "This is a sign."

"Of what?"

"A sign of the immortal."

CHAPTER 26
SORREN

IT IS DONE. Now she knows, and hates me, as it always should have been. She's finally cleared to see the monster hidden among her—the great deceiver.

Her words play on repeat in my mind, taunting me, exploiting every truth I have never wanted to face. Now she's lost to me forever. She was never truly mine to begin with. I could never deserve her. But for things to go so unequivocally wrong . . . I couldn't have prepared myself for how quickly her sweet look of reverence would turn into one of pure hatred.

The weight of all I've done crushes me. I will never expel the look of raw anguish that twisted her features, from my mind. Her sobs were a torture more acute than any Malakai could ever hope to inflict. I cannot atone for this. I have cost her too much and will never make it right.

I splash my face with water, chilling it with my element, looking up at my bloodied lip and swollen jaw. An insignificant penance to pay for all I have done. After I allowed things to go so far last night . . . The girl deserves a pound of my flesh for how thoroughly I've wronged her. In truth, I'd willingly give it all.

And for all her rage, I cannot help but find joy in seeing her come back into her powers fully. They had not permanently altered the elemental abilities she is so blessed with. The moment she remembered me—and all I had done—it appeared as if she'd awoken from a curse. The terra wielded her element with the same strength I'd witnessed the first time I'd met her.

Since that day in my cell, I've longed to see her so powerful. Today she stood before me once again, a beacon of chaos and beauty. I run a wet hand through my hair, smoothing back the freshly cut strands. I must still take great care to look presentable before the council today, needing whatever advantages I can scrape up. I cannot repair the tears in my uniform, ripped in this morning's scuffle. I can only patch them and work with what I have.

I journey to the council hall. When I reach the colossal glass entryway, I consider the last time I stood before these doors. I'd entered under very different circumstances and somehow quite the same.

Entering the council room today, the policymakers will once again decide my fate. Hopefully, I can convince them my work has been diligent enough to buy me more time to figure everything out before moving in on the faction. I muster my gall and push the glass doors open, walking to the center of the crescent-shaped table gathering the Council of Policy.

"Sirs and madams of the council," I address them formally.

"Sorren Astley, you have been called here today to update the council on your progress toward capturing the terras and pyros you allowed to escape." The prime policymaker stands.

"The mission progresses accordingly. Upon the completion of my reconditioning, I sent out three scouts to locate the escaped faction members."

"And have we received word from these scouts?"

"No," I lie, desperate to buy more time, "but their last updated coordinates indicate they're due back to Central City today." Although it is a betrayal to my father and my region, I cannot allow this mission to succeed.

"It appears you may stall, Sorren." The vindictive arch of the prime's eyebrows sets me on edge.

Just as she goes to speak, the doors of the council room push open and Malakai steps through, with my scouts in tow.

"I apologize for my tardiness." He bows his head to the council, his eyes and cheeks swollen. The bruises and cuts I gave him decorate his already marred face. Morgana looks past him and to the scouts he has in tow. Her lips curve in a wicked grin.

"Thank you for joining us, Admiral," she says. "Please share with us what you've brought."

My pulse hastens as the prime bids them to come forth.

"The scouts have returned with an update on our targets. They reported to Astley Manor, rather than the Capitol Building," Malakai says, eying me.

"What a treat. Now we may all hear the debriefing. Soldier, what is your report?" She gestures to Calix.

His mouth turns down in a grimace, his eyes dart to me, before returning to the prime. "Madam Prime," he says with a bow, "we have located the escaped faction."

All my plans come crumbling down. I have lost the time I thought I'd have to figure a way out of this, and all the hope I held for regaining my office. With each upset, it's becoming clearer that I will need to choose.

"There are several refugees taking up shelter in the Fire Clan's Smithing Faction. The fire faction is severely armed and keeps the Healers well protected."

"And how many do you estimate?" she asks.

"By our observations, we believe there are approximately three thousand Healing refugees."

Three thousand? I couldn't have imagined so many Healers would escape the raid. Now that I see the fate they've evaded, I am grateful so many got away. The policymakers look at me with expressions ranging from shock to rage, and it is clear they do not share this sentiment. Still, I had not expected the terras to be so foolish as to hideout in a neighboring faction. I'd hoped they were smart enough to continue running to stay on the move and not get caught. Least of all, caught so quickly.

"That is excellent news." The prime claps her hands together, her vindictive smile aimed at me. "Sorren, how will you proceed?"

This is a test. They all wait for my response.

"We will move quickly. I will begin rounding my troops to move in on the Smithing Faction. This faction is skilled and specializes in weaponry. Their trained warriors are plentiful. They will not be an easy defeat, and I will need to take some time to prepare a—"

"You have taken too much time already. I'm beginning to think you're incapable of handling this mission," she challenges me. "It is for this reason I propose we allow you some help. Admiral Malakai will function as your second in command for this operation. He will aid in the strategy required to capture this faction."

This means my final call is one he can challenge. Unlike last time, where I outranked him. The second in command's most notable function is to challenge the lead.

"You will deploy on this mission in three days. Not a moment later. Do you understand?"

"I do."

I have three days to understand what is happening to the captives and navigate how to conduct this mission under Malakai's watchful eye.

Time has slipped through my grasp like the sand in an hourglass. I have wasted the little time I've had with foolish notions of fixing everything and helping everyone. Now, all my options have been exhausted and I can no longer hope to find a way to both save Kara's faction and retain my office.

I have three days to right the wrongs I have committed to either my region or to Kara. I can only choose one, and no matter how I succeed, I will still fail.

CHAPTER 27
KARA

After leaving Twenty—*Mom*, I rush through my chores while searching the city for my faction members. There're so many serving elementals in Central City. I recognize the terras and pyros from many of the Lower factions. The dark skin and gold-streaked coils of the Gold Faction bustle among a sea of blond-haired pyros from the Magma Faction. I look for my people first but am blown away by the diversity of captives. They've collected a plethora of elementals from all seven of the Lower factions. I must temper down my sympathetic heart. I must remember that, depending on how limited our resources for escape are, my obligation is to the Healers first.

Of all my people, I look for Rae specifically. I remember seeing her the day of our capture. She must be here. My eyes seek to touch every servant, but none are my pyro best friend.

On instinct, I begin a prayer, asking for aid in finding Rae. Then the thought strikes me that in my time serving the Upper, I have only prayed to Hydris. The homage I'd given in my time here was for Hydris alone. Gaia's name never crossed my lips or entered my thoughts until the first night I healed Sorren.

I am embarrassed, and ashamed, that I could forget my deity. But above those feelings, I am angry. My deity allowed my people and me to worship another. Did our homage mean so little to her she did not care whether it went to someone else?

My people have suffered. My faction is all but destroyed. Does the mother of all terras care so little for us she would allow our thorough defeat and capture? She would stand by while they made us believe we had no powers, no level, and no goddess. I don't know whether it would be worse to learn that she saw our suffering and did nothing, or that she does not exist at all.

Regardless, she does not need my prayers, and she will never receive them again.

By the time I'm able to complete my duties, the day is done, and I hurry to meet my mother and Cinis in the infirmary. Cinis beats me there, and when I arrive, he is trying to jog Mom's memory, with little success.

"Kara." He stands.

"Did anyone see you come in?" my mother says.

"No."

"Good, we must be quick. There is not much time before they scan the building and send all lingering servants to their quarters." She continues, "Whatever we choose to do, we must act tomorrow. They are looking at the serum."

Anxiety wiggles its way into my chest, tightening it at the sudden time constraint. Only a day to plan and execute the retrieval. I had hoped for at least a few days.

"They have exhausted all troubleshooting for the machine and instructed me to adjust the serum," she says.

"Once they've adjusted the serum, they will move to the collars," Cinis adds.

"We must, quickly and efficiently, get as many people out of the city as possible," I say. "I scouted the city today, looking for elementals I recognize as Healers. There were thousands of our people captured." I think back to the magnetite fence holding most of my faction. "But looking around the city, and considering how many elementals are serving, there can't be that many of us still here."

I may not recognize everyone, and there are, of course, elementals I've missed, but it still doesn't explain the gap in numbers. Search as I may, I could not find Rae and many other lower-level elementals. The day they captured us, I remember seeing so many young children chained in the transporters, but when I look around the city, I see none of the Healers.

My stomach turns at the thought of how many of my people are still missing. Could the council have sent them to the Outer? There's no reason for young children to be sent to a prison region. My people may serve outside the city, but that's contrary to protocol. They only hold servants within the walls of Central City.

I rack my brain trying to figure out where the additional elementals could be but cannot dedicate too much focus to it. Now, I have my hands full with the many right in front of me, relying on us to rescue them.

Cinis speaks up, "We can take them by transporter. The enforcers are planning to attack another faction."

My heart sinks at his words—at the thought of others facing the horrors within these city walls. It is not only our responsibility to release my captured faction members, but also to stop the impending attack.

"I don't know the specifics. I only know they are preparing large transporters to hold captives. If we could get our hands on a transporter, then we'll have the space we need to get our people out and the tech to do it quickly," he says.

I consider his suggestion. It's brilliant, save for one minor problem. "How are we going to man the transporters? We don't have access to their energy supply, and our collars will not have entry to the transport hangar or any of the ships."

At each maintenance, the enforcers program our collars, giving us access to the areas we need. A servant's schedule is consistent and well planned out. Our collars either grant or restrict access to certain parts of the city based on our duties.

"Leave that to me. I'm working on an unlocking mechanism for the collars. It wasn't something I could do before because the enforcers checked them during maintenance, but with the extra time, I think I'm close to something."

The tightness in my chest unravels as I see we may actually have a shot at this.

"And we don't need their energy," he says, bringing his fingers together, then apart to demonstrate. "I have my own."

Miniature bolts of lightning pass along his fingers as I remember the ability unique to Lightning and some Level Three pyros. The ease by which he wields the lightning is mind-boggling, and I cannot help but gape add it.

"I've always been able to wield lightning, but it's different now. It's . . ." he searches for the word. "Easier, somehow. It's like I can control it, where before I only coaxed the aether," he says, bouncing lightning from one hand to another. "Since my powers have come back, they feel stronger—bolder—I can run the transporter."

I feel it, too. The pain that tingles behind my fingertips—the rush of energy that pushes through my veins is so much bolder than it has ever been before, it frightens me.

My mother considers this before speaking. "I can alter the serum. I know how now. What they'd given me before was unfamiliar because it's nothing we've ever used. I've been studying the genetic matter of the plants they ask me to process into the serum. What they have grown is not of Gaia," she says with a stony look that sends worry lines into her thin lips. I stifle a scoff at the mention of our inutile deity. Whatever the Upper has devised to put into this serum is not natural to our world.

"Then what is it?" Curiosity burns at the back of my tongue.

The blood drains from her face as I find myself afraid of what is coming from her lips. "They have somehow intertwined the herb with elemental essence." A shiver runs through me as I look over to Cinis whose mouth hangs open in a gape.

"How is this possible?" I say, just as much to myself as her.

"I don't know. This is very much outside my scope. I have regained much of my knowledge of poison study. I can replace the ingredients with others that will maintain the consistency and appearance of the serum. This should buy us at least another day."

She proposes to create a placebo. I take a breath, ready to say no. It's too dangerous. If she's caught, they will certainly send her to the Outer. If we do not effect this plan, or if it does not work, she will be vulnerable. There's no insisting that she forgot the procedure, no claiming there was a mixing mistake. This is a deliberate ingredient change and she will suffer for it if I fail. "You cannot."

She holds up a hand to stop me. This is not her asking permission. For this reason, she is the leader I will never be. I can't risk her. I know the consequences, and I cannot put my selfish desires to protect my only living parent aside for the greater good of our faction. But she can. And she will.

I sigh, knowing that I do not have a say in the matter. Sick, because my lack of say is probably for the better. The only thing I can do is make sure this works.

"At tomorrow's maintenance hour, I will begin gathering elementals," I say.

I have regained essentially all my memory. My mind is clear, and I will recognize our faction members. By tomorrow, I should look somewhat familiar to them as well.

My powers are strong enough so that I can protect the group I will gather should things go wrong. Though, I must be tactical in how I collect them. Our last retrieval lays heavy on my mind, and I can tell that it is at the forefront of Cinis's as well.

In our last rescue attempt, the serving elementals did not aid us in freeing them. They fought us through every part of the mission until we were forced to retreat. Now, I understand why. Though, it doesn't stop tears from prickling my eyelids at the thought of my cousin Caelum, whose death was my fault.

I have felt the haze of whatever poison the Upper feeds through these collars. Now that I've lived without my memories, I am horrified at what my cousin must have felt in his last moments. It guts me knowing that he died so afraid and confused, with his final memory of me as his murderer.

We cannot risk the defiance of these elementals. We cannot risk one of them tipping off the guards to our plan. "I'll be strategic in how I choose who will come. I will make sure they're willing, only letting them know to meet us near the hangar. They cannot know we mean to escape until the deed is all but done. If they remember me and trust me enough to go, then they should be a safe choice. But if they do not, simply meeting by the hangar won't be enough for them to alert the enforcers of anything."

This is our plan. Cinis and my mother have until sundown tomorrow to switch out the serum and complete the unlocking mechanism. At sundown I will corral our people. I will either shepherd them to freedom or death.

CHAPTER 28
SORREN

MALAKAI HAS TAKEN ON his new role as my second with annoying zeal. We spent the night and the better part of this morning ironing out our attack. Neither of us acknowledged the injuries that made it impossible for him to stand over the battle maps or mark up our operation plans with his dominant hand. Regardless of his wounds, Malakai ensured I left no stone unturned and enthusiastically challenged my plans every chance he had.

My inability to commit to our region has cost my dearest friend. Although Malakai has not taken his place as my second in command, it is degrading to Kai for another to be named second on this mission.

I have put so much at risk—not only my good name—but Kai's as well, in his association with me. My whole life, I thought I knew my place. I believed it was to uphold my father's legacy. To supply the Upper with the labor they need to fulfill his vision. To help create a region self-sufficient and not reliant on trade with the Lower. I thought it was my place to strengthen the Upper, but when all I have done is undermine it, I don't know what my place is anymore.

Everything in my father's house serves as a steadfast reminder of his hopes that I would carry on his life's work. I shudder to think what he would have to say about me now.

I have readied the soldiers we will take on this mission, all vetted by Malakai. The sting of this check serves as a harsh reminder of what else is at risk should I fail. If Malakai gains command of the Western Area, there will be no limit to the immoral and harsh measures he will take to fulfill the prime's every sadistic whim.

Malakai has already begun preparing our transporter ships. In planning, he highlighted the mistakes and lessons from our previous raid. We've readied extra transporters to hold the captive elementals. We need the additional capacity to accommodate the added captives from the Smithing Faction. The Council expects us to ensure no Lowers will escape.

We've already loaded the main ship with the supplies needed for the journey and capture. We will deploy more soldiers to complete this mission. The Smithing Faction is no easy defeat. Not only are the Smithers a larger group than the Healers, but their warriors are more skilled in combat. If I sabotage this operation, I will sentence so many of my soldiers to death.

I'd like to think we are prepared, but I cannot confirm that all my soldiers are behind this cause. So many of their disapproving eyes haunt me. I can still see the shadow of trepidation in their expression at each command I gave so many months ago. Just as I'd been pressured into following orders at all costs, my command forced many of them to defy their own moral code and press forward with the mission. A command I will soon subject them to again.

I must see this as an opportunity to redeem myself. I cannot place the betrayal of Kara over the betrayal of my entire region. As the memory of her soft lips and smooth skin wiggle into my mind, regret tightens my chest. Thinking about her body wrapped around mine, remembering how it felt to hold her in my arms on the sandy beach under the nighttime sky, weakens my resolve.

I push the treacherous thoughts away. I cannot hold her esteem higher than my father's. There is an entire brigade counting on me, whose lives I put at risk in allowing the terras to escape. Whatever soldiers I lose in retrieving the escapees, I'm acutely aware their deaths are entirely on my hands. I must execute this mission with flawless precision. I owe my soldiers that much.

I search my father's database, combing through its maps, studying the notes on this missing faction. I fill my head with strategy, so it's not distracted by foolish notions of honor and benevolence. I dive so deep into his database that when I come across the locked file, I'm sure I've gone deeper than I ever have before.

Most of my father's files are DNA protected, but this one has additional encryptions. Could this be something he did not want even me to see?

I dive into it hungry for some guidance from the prominent leader. I already know what he'd expect from me, but if I can uncover some strategy—some knowledge that will aid me—that will spare any of my soldiers on this mission, then I will be grateful for it.

Several authentication encryptions protect this file. The first is DNA. I press my palm to the biometric lock system. This time, it pulls more than just the inconsequential bit of blood it typically does. The sting of essence flowing through my palm shocks me, and I quickly yank it away, but the system seems to have gained all it needs. The monitor hums to life, glowing brighter than before, bringing me to the next authenticity indicator.

A red beam shoots from the screen, scanning my face and body, then sweeping the entire room. Once it registers clearance, I hear the automatic clink of the windows and doors bolt. Anticipation prickles at my fingertips as the final encryption pops up.

The screen goes black with only a small window to enter a password. *Damn it.*

The files are password encrypted, and I haven't the slightest clue what it could be. My father must not have meant for me to see this, or else the password would be one of the several clever words or combinations I try. They all fail.

I search the recesses of my mind for a clue. Something—anything—that will grant me access to these files. A storm rages outside. The wind pushes sea waves to crash against the windows of my father's study. It reminds me of the painting Nero hung on the wall directly across from his desk.

Looking up, I study the immortal painted in the sea. She rises with the mighty wave, her face and limbs emerging through the sea foam, her power unbridled and immense. A quiet word flows through my mind, *Procella*.

It means sea storm, and of all my father's devotion to the immortals, his incessant study and raving over them all, he worshipped her.

I type the letters, holding my breath for another denial. But when the screen blinks and the file opens, I cannot recover from what I see.

Father, what have you done?

CHAPTER 29
KARA

THE NEXT DAY FLOWS by as if it rides on the back of an aero's breeze. It is swift and unyielding, and I struggle to get ahead of it. There's so much to do before the maintenance hour.

As maintenance will resume tonight, we must make our leave now. The enforcers will busy themselves, siphoning elementals. Corralling them together and settling them again will be more difficult now that two days have passed since our last maintenance. We must take advantage of this distraction. It's the only one we will have.

Throughout the day I rush through the chores that must be done, but only those which will draw attention if missed. The others I do not bother with. After tonight, whether our plan succeeds or fails, I will have no use for the chores or the soldiers' good graces.

When I finish my duties, I set out to the smithing building. As the sun nears the horizon, it basks the canals of Central City in a bright orange hue. I will forever associate that color with the probing of needles and searing burn of thick serum coursing through my neck.

I hug the satchel to my chest. It holds clothes I stole from the launder earlier today. They were an easy swipe. The outfits are unremarkable and I'm sure no one will miss them. The casual clothing of Central City elementals will provide us with camouflage. They are a stark contrast to the monochromatic beige linen the servants wear. When my mother and I execute the plan, these clothes will help us move unnoticed.

I push the large metal door of the smith building open, not bothering to knock. The ringing of metal fills the air and would muffle my knock had I wanted to. Thick sweet smoke fills my lungs as I move through the entryway. I take a few steps inside the building before I see Cinis.

He stands there in Upper clothes, but my eyes immediately dart to his neck. I stare at the bare bronze skin, magnificent and free of his collar. The swirling brands that climb up his shoulders and to the base of his skull are fully visible.

A wide grin spreads across his face as he says, "It worked."

"I can see that." I'm unable to contain my excitement as I bounce on the balls of my feet. The first piece of this plan has already fallen into place.

I bring my hand up to touch his uncovered skin, hardly able to believe he's succeeded. I run my fingers along the brands I'd traced so many times before. The familiarity of the touch distracts me from how intimate it is. Cinis smiles down at me, heat blazing behind his gaze. He wraps his warm arms around me and pulls me into his chest. Guilt burns deep within my stomach as I remember how Sorren held me in this exact way. I remember how content I was to lie there in his arms. So *happy* to be surrounded by him. I was such a fool.

I back away from Cinis, unable to wrangle the guilt I hold from finding such comfort with another. He lets me go, moving to his workbench to grab a small metal device. "Are you ready?"

"Yes." I've been ready to get this thing off since the day they closed it around my throat.

He brings the mechanism up to my collar. It's no larger than a pair of scissors and fits neatly into his hands. There are two metal pieces at the end, that curve. He hooks them on the inside of my magroginite clasp, taking great care not to nick my skin. Aligning them with the needles, just as the maintenance soldiers do, he wiggles the device until I hear a click. He squeezes the mechanism together, and it pulls at the magroginite. With one more click, the band opens, and I take in a breath at the sting of needles still lodged in my neck.

"Hold still, for just a second." Cinis says as he gingerly pulls the needles from my veins.

When I feel the slow trickle of blood, I know it is done. He presses a gauze to my neck to stop the bleeding. It will not take long for it to clot. They're only small puncture wounds. Though, I make a mental note to get hemoxi for the others. My hands fly to my throat where I have not felt bare skin in months.

Cinis bends to wrap me in a hug. "We're that much closer. In just a few hours, we will be free."

He looks at me, his hand wandering to the pendant still hanging above my chest. He places the unlocking mechanism in my hand. "Here, take this. Give it to your mom after you unlock her collar.

Tell her to meet me at the hangar. She can unlock the elementals who are joining us."

It's time for him to head to the hangar. I know he can pull this off. I know he's capable of breaking into and starting the transporter, but that does nothing to ease the anxiety I have at the risk he takes.

"Please be careful," I beg, wrapping my arms around him in a tight embrace. I do not pray to Gaia for Cinis's protection. At this point, it almost seems like bad luck.

"Don't worry about me. I'll be fine. You must be careful. Do not talk to anyone you feel is unwilling. Be quick. I know you want to save everyone, but we just don't have the resources or the time. Get who you can, and we will come back for the others."

No, we won't. His words are only nice sentiments. A hoax to get me to comply with his pleas for safety. We could not recover the serving elementals before. I have no illusions that my faction will be as strong as it was several months ago. We've lost so many people and the elementals we do have left are weakened. There will be no way we can come back for anyone we'll leave behind. And anyone we leave, we knowingly sentence to a life of servitude.

I don't bother arguing with him. I don't want to worry him any-more than he already is. So, I nod, pretending to agree, changing into my Upper disguise. When I am respectfully camouflaged, I tell him goodbye for what could be the last time and leave the smith building.

As I walk the streets, I'm grateful the tide has receded, leaving a clear pathway for me. It helps me to blend in with the other

Uppers. When the tide rises, covering the pathways in water, the aeros freeze it to walk on top. The hydros part the water, but terras and pyros can only splash in it. Nothing would give me away sooner.

On my way to the infirmary, I pass several of my faction members. I can't help but direct them to the hangar. I should not deviate from the plan. I should wait until my mother joins Cinis so that she can help him receive the elementals. But I cannot risk missing them later. Each elemental counts, and I won't willingly leave someone behind. Each person I direct to safety could pick up another to join them. If one of those elementals could be Rae, I'll be forever grateful.

By the time I make it to the medic room, the sun has all but disappeared from the sky, and the maintenance hour is already upon us. As I open the door, I remove the satchel that holds my mother's change of clothes.

"You're here." She lets out a huge breath, her palm resting on her heart. Looking up, she stares at me for a quiet moment. Her eyes widen as her jaw goes slack.

"Kara."

My heart skips at the familiarity she uses when saying my name. I try to calm myself, not getting too overexcited. She knows my name. I've told her, and she's remembered. This is not the first time she's called me by it, but it is the first time she's called me in this way. Seconds tick by as she says my name again, this time incredulity lacing her tone.

"Mom?" I say with the slow caution of someone approaching a feral animal.

"Yes." Tears dampen her hazel eyes.

"You remember?"

"I remember. Oh, my Kara." She rushes to me, folding me in her arms, hot tears trickling down her cheeks, falling on my forehead. This is a victory. In this tiny moment, I feel like I have all I need. I hadn't realized how much I missed my mother while she had been next to me all along.

"Kara, I'm so sorry. You were right here the whole time, and I didn't even—"

"Don't." I stop her, not wanting her to harbor any guilt over this circumstance they put on us. "No one remembered. It's okay. I have you now. That's all that matters."

"What about your father? Have you seen him?"

The question slams into me, crushing me under the weight it holds. Sharp grief stings my eyelids as the tears I've held back pour over. I cannot look up to meet her gaze. I can hardly make myself break the news.

"Dad's not here." I pause, not knowing how to tell her. Not knowing how to make my mouth form the words, *he's dead.*

"Dad didn't make it."

And when I finally look up at her, despair twists her brows, grief parting her lips.

She shakes her head. "What do you mean—" she stops herself. "No."

She stumbles back, bracing herself against the bar behind.

"No," she repeats as if she can simply will it to be the truth.

More tears cascade down my face as I choke back a sob. The grief of my father hits me anew in the face of my mourning mother. I try to push back the tears, knowing she needs me to be strong, but I cannot. The only thing I can do is wrap her head in my arms and pull her into my chest, letting her weep against my broken heart.

When the gut-wrenching wails of my mother slow into muffled sniffles, she looks up at me. Using the back of her sleeve, she wipes the tears streaking her cheeks and chin.

She forces a smile that has no place in this moment and brings the backs of her fingers to my face. "It is okay. He is with us."

She wipes the tear flooded emerald eyes my father gave to me, running her hand down the wavy brown hair I inherited from him, too. I lean into her hand, seeking some strength from it. She pulls me to her and kisses my forehead.

"There is no time to waste," she says, her tone holding no more inflection than a dead man's. "I could not alter the serum. Maintenance enforcers monitored the process to ensure the serum was correct." Her shoulders sag at this additional defeat.

"It's okay, Mom. The plan will work, and we will leave this place before sunrise."

She nods; her face remains placid. "The guards will gather all the serving elementals soon, so we must be swift."

Her hand moves to my neck, newly freed from the collar that previously adorned it.

"I have Upper clothes that will help you blend in, and this." I pull the unlocking mechanism, bringing it to her collar. As I fumble with the lock, trying to fit it into the grooves just as Cinis had done, I explain it to her. I instruct her on how to unlock the collars of the elementals that will go to the hangar.

When I hear the first click of the lock release, I sigh, tension uncoiling from my shoulders and chest. When the second click sounds, she gasps from the pain of the needles that tear from her skin. I tenderly remove them, being careful not to cause her any additional pain. When the collar is off, I blot her neck with hemoxi to stop the bleeding. Her hands also fly to the bare skin she has not felt in months.

She quickly changes into the clothes I brought, pulling me in for another hug before we say our goodbyes.

"Kara, promise me you will be careful. I cannot lose you, too." Her voice breaks, and I squeeze her even tighter to me.

"I promise."

All the other parts of our plan have fallen into place. Now it is time for the last step, and arguably the most dangerous. Gathering the elementals.

My mom leaves the room and I follow out. She heads to the hangar and on her way, she will gather the elementals out in the city. Meanwhile, I'll make my round through the capitol, gathering the ones inside and those heading toward maintenance.

The first elemental from my faction is one I know very well. I almost stumble in my rush to get to him before stopping myself, forcing my lungs to take deep, slow breaths. I must remain calm. I cannot afford to tip any enforcers off, not now. Slowing my walk to him, when I finally reach the familiar elemental with curly brown hair and a warrior's broad shoulders, I confirm that it's Emrick.

Looking over my shoulder to make sure no one is near, I call his name. "Emrick."

He looks at me, eyes wide. "How do you know that name?" The intensity of his gaze burns into me.

"It's your name."

He regards me for a moment, piecing something together. This encourages me to continue. "It's me, Kara, Rae's best friend. Have you seen her?"

The flash of recognition that flies across his face simmers as he searches for the memory that seems to flee him.

"I know Rae," he says, trying to convince himself just as much as me.

"She's your love." I don't mention the baby. I can see his mind is still in a haze and don't want to bombard him. He nods, as if remembering, or at least agreeing. His eyebrows clench. I know he does not remember fully, but he's trying. This is enough for me to trust him.

"Emrick," I say his name again for good measure. "I need you to go down to the transport hangar."

The crease of his brows furrow. "Why?"

"I can't say. I know you don't have a reason to, but I need you to trust me. Go there right now. We have friends there waiting. They will explain everything to you, I promise."

He regards me for a moment and nods. "But what about maintenance?"

"Don't worry about that now. Please, just go to the hangar. You can go to maintenance after," I say, knowing Mom and Cinis will not let him leave.

He rubs the side of his collar, wincing as he considers another maintenance after so many days of rest. "Okay, I'll go," he says firmly, as a group of servants catches his attention.

"Hey, Sixty-four, Seventy-eight, you guys come with me," he calls to the group.

"Where are we going?" one says.

"Don't worry, just come with me. I'll explain on the way." Emrick nods at me and turns to lead the others away. I let out a breath and my chest decompresses at this tiny victory.

I continue gathering my faction members. Some shake their head at me and insist they must go to maintenance, but others grasp at that spark of a memory. I understand why they seem to trust me when I've given them so little reason to. The words I say are the first piece of truth they have heard in months, and they recognize it. I do not know them all, but I know who we truly are, and they recognize that.

I am discrete in pulling elementals away from maintenance. In my efforts, I can hear the enforcers stumble through this first procedure after days of rest. They struggle to maintain the servants, and each who leaves the room is so sedated they can barely walk. The council has deployed additional enforcers. They help escort, and even carry, the servants back to their quarters after the procedures finish. This allows me to make such progress in my corralling. There is already too much going on.

As I swiftly try to gather all the elementals I can, I also direct those who are not with my faction. Smithers, Farmers, and Magma elementals all serve in the city, and I cannot leave them behind either. Once the maintenance hour draws to an end, I can no longer count how many elementals I have spoken to. Still, I'm pained by how many I abandon. I wish I could reach them all, praying that Rae has somehow found her way to the hangar. I hope that my mother has gotten more but know this is the best we can do.

"You've killed him!" I hear a woman scream from the maintenance room.

I flatten myself against the wall to better hear what's going on.

"Will you shut her up! She's going to excite the others," an enforcer says. "Bag him up. You took too much. Damn rookies," he curses, and I don't understand what's happening.

I can't stay here and try to figure it out. I can't save any more elementals. I need to leave.

As I make my way toward the exit, a wall of water erects before me.

"It appears we have a troublemaker on our hands."

I freeze. I know the voice behind me. It belongs to the prime. The wall of water wraps itself around me, crushing me in a liquid restraint. She pulls me to her.

"A concerned servant has alerted policymaker Aquil that you are directing servants not to go to the maintenance." Her words are calm, though they are laced with all the venom of a zelem bloom. "Now, why would you do that?"

As the condescending question hangs in the air along with the fat droplets of water she suspends throughout the space, I cannot talk my way out of this.

So, I don't.

I command the stone floor to break apart, pulling it from the ground and hurling it at the prime. She shrieks, obviously not expecting me to hold any power. When the stone slams into her, she drops me from my watery binds, and I scramble away. She calls for more guards as another wall of water stops me.

I grasp for my element, but it is fleeting. In the hydro city, there's not much soil, and too few land elements for me to grasp and control. I drop to the ground where I've broken apart the stone. Beneath it is concrete where I'd hoped would be dirt.

The city lies directly atop water. I will not find any soil here. The hydro's wall of liquid races toward me and I extend the vines of my fingers to wrap around her. When I've got her in my grasp, I pick her up and slam her against the wall. I'm immediately hit with another wall of water, this one coming from a nearby soldier.

Another block of water slams against me, pushing me to the ground. I clutch my throat as all the air escapes my lungs. An aero pulls his element from me, suffocating me where I lay. As more guards close in, the prime stands from where she'd fallen, regaining her composure, and walking toward me.

Guard after guard hurls their element upon me. They wrap me in ice and keep me restrained. The prime approaches me. The snarl on her lips lets me know I'm about to die. Then she looks at my head, her mouth falling open just before her eyes narrow in a glare.

She snarls. "This cannot be."

She brings her hand to my hair, wrapping her fingers around the same willowy branch my mother noticed earlier. Yanking it, she jerks my head forward, then drops it as soon as she confirms it's connected to my scalp. She pulls out another. More have sprouted unbeknownst to me. She drops her hands, throwing her head back in a cackling laugh. I fear she's gone mad with the way her manic chuckle shakes the room.

"You have got to be kidding me!" she screams.

Composing herself, she commands a guard to come forward. "Retrieve Admiral Malakai. Let him know we found the missing essence. The girl is immortal."

Sparing me one more glance, hate blazes through her deep blue irises, and reddens her pale face. She commands the soldiers forward, and they drag me away.

CHAPTER 30
SORREN

WHEN THE FILE OPENS, it reveals a labyrinth of plans and data. My father has neatly organized studies and statistics—blueprints and strategies—articles and addresses. They all lay out before me, and I realize father meant for me to see it after all.

Nero had always wanted to see me elected as prime policymaker when his work was finished. Although we do not name successors as the Lower does, he groomed me for the role and our region welcomed it.

The screen displays everything I need to carry out his mission. The wealth of information is so abundant, I don't know where to start. I could study this for the rest of my life and still walk away with questions.

I search through the files and find his tech. Our monumental strides in technology and medicine have always been a mystery to me. How one reign could produce so many advancements in such a short amount of time is an aberration.

Laid out before me are the blueprints for all the tech he designed. Intricate sketches and scales litter the screen. Designs for all the tech produced by the Upper are written out and anatomized. They are the same proofs that are given to our region's engineers for replication and mass production. But these hold slight deviations from the plans I've seen before. These blueprints account for an additional mechanism.

The plans I've seen outlining the replications have only detailed the receiver—never the power source that goes into it. I search the special protocol for the implement, reading through files mentioning an energy source, though it's never well defined. I persist through the data, seeing things I'd rather forget, like the medicine trials and tech testing.

When I come across the detailed outline that completes the fabrication instructions, I find the power source. It looks strikingly familiar, though I cannot place where I've seen the tubes before.

I trace the outline, an answer teasing at my memory, until finally it slams into me and stops my fingers mid screen. Maintenance uses these tubes.

When elemental essence is harvested using the tool's attractant, it's aether becomes an independent catalyst, separate from the elemental.

I scroll through the data, my eyes glued to the text detailing an energy source which seems to come directly from the very essence of elementals.

Ice crawls across my fingertips, and I do not realize it encases my hands, until the pads of my fingers are no longer recognized by my father's screen. I read the text repeatedly until the lines blur and the words no longer make sense.

I shut my eyes, unbelieving—rejecting the possibility. This is impossible. One cannot extract an elemental's essence. But as I think back to my father's encryption, and reread the notes, I know it to be true.

The protocol lays plain in front of me. An uncontrollable shiver rips through my body as I review my father's failed attempts in the early days of his experimenting.

It is unclear where he got the knowledge to extract essence, but he refers to a mysterious *they* throughout his notes. Whoever *they* are, were not explicit on the specifics of extraction. Father only received the knowledge of what can be done with the essence, and some tool to facilitate the extractions. I scour his notes for the specific apparatus used, but I cannot find anything. As hard as I search, all I come across are his test notes.

Despite my aero nature, I break out in a cold sweat, my stomach turning as I read over failure after failure. Poor innocents from the Lower, captured and stolen, used as test subjects for his sadistic experiments. I read through years' worth of trials before finding an elemental who finally lived through the extraction.

I see it was the successful siphoning of Lower elementals that prompted the influx of tech. Advancements on top of each other were made and marketed to the Lower. It was his intent to trade for labor. To ensnare the Lowers with machines brought to life by their own essence.

I drag a rough hand through my hair. It's all here—every plan outlined clearly for me to see. Notes on medicines infused with aether that heal more powerfully than any herb or root clutter the screen. I study the conversion of essence, each machine taking a finite amount designed to last the duration of the machine's life.

He details how to distribute the siphoned aether. A portion is to be set aside for the tech and medicines we continually produce. Some go to the council of policy.

I read that over again.

Why would the individual policymakers need essence? What use would they have for it besides what my father had detailed in his notes?

I search for the answer, but I cannot find it. There's a discrepancy between the amount siphoned and the amount distributed. I calculate there is still some aether remaining from all that's siphoned from the captives. What are they doing with all this?

I've always known about his vision of a supreme society—a superior Upper. He has shared them with me since I was old enough to listen. I continue to read his communications to the Council of Policy. There are parts of his plan that were never told to me. From what I can tell, he only shared them with the council.

Laid out in phases, he instructs an action plan for achieving his goal. I read the first phase and recognize it immediately. The plan was to always trade the tech for labor; it was his design. He needed to capture Lower elementals to siphon their essence. During this period, they only took minimal amounts of essence. He details the procedure learned from his early days of experimenting, to not take too much, only half a vial's worth. The second part of his procedure gives directions for administering a neurotoxin. Small doses maintain the serving elementals in a mental fog.

I pale, thinking back to the servants I'd come across on my rare visits to the manor. They'd always seemed a little off to me. I'd assumed that all Lowers were a bit air-headed and daft. I could never have imagined they were being altered. Still, in that state, they were not nearly as incoherent as today's servants are.

I remember the breakdown in communication the Lower claimed started the war. As I continue to read my father's directives, I see it was intentional. The Upper sought to diminish communication between the servants and their families. It minimized suspicion as the Upper continued to raise the dose of neurotoxin and the amount of aether siphoned.

My skin prickles as I feel the blood drain from my face. I shut my eyes, praying to Aelious that I've read phase two wrong. When I open them to read it again, my heart stops. I did not misread.

In order to gain all that is due to us, we must incite war with the Lower. Only then can we take what is rightfully ours and cast down the elementals who dare to subvert us.

The war was part of his plan. It was not a spontaneous initiation on the Lower's part, as we'd all been led to believe. My father and the Council of Policy intended to start the war to subjugate the Lowers. To fuel this superior new Upper, they required laborers to work and provide essence. All this, they would gain in the Lower elementals.

I sit back in the chair, not wanting to read anymore. He died for this. I can't help but wonder if he knew this war would cost him his life. I don't feel a bit of shame that I am glad for it. How much more damage could he have inflicted had he survived? I'm sick knowing the same blood that ran through him runs through me. Furious that I was a willing part of this sadistic scheme.

I piece together the vast change from the servants I remember and those I see now. Somewhere along the line, the protocol for siphoning changed. With no more need for caution, the dose of the neurotoxin has tripled, and the amount of essence siphoned—doubled. This explains why servants only work in Central City and are kept away from the rest of the region. The council will not extradite the serving elementals to the rest of the Upper until they have won the war. Until phase three.

I read the address given by my father to the Council of Policy. I cannot understand how the body entrusted with upholding justice could all support this devious plan. How they could allow him to head such atrocities. What could he have promised them substantial enough to partake in this?

In his address he outlines the grand new Upper. He illustrates the importance that the serving elementals play in this new world. The confidence with which he addresses the council is sickening. His words are so sure he will be victorious in the war, and successfully enslave all the Lowers, that they become arrogant.

He serves this address as a lecture, as if he speaks to eager students he wishes to mentor. He seeks to win them over with his foolproof plan. Nero convinces them that enslaving the Lower elementals will be no more difficult than training an unruly pet.

"Follow me, and I will ensure both the cooperation and even loyalty of our enemy."

He speaks about the neurotoxin and siphoning of the captives' essence. He assures the council this is necessary to keep them powerless and ignorant of any abilities they once had. My father argues that if they are unaware of the power they possess, they will not attempt to access it.

The reminder sparks my memory of the encounter with Kara in my cell. The L3 terra had been convinced pyros and terras held so little power that we could not classify them at levels.

"If our enemy is told they are and have always been powerless, they will believe it," he says. "They will not attempt to improve their abilities, because they will assume the feat to be futile."

He proposes we pit the two elemental groups against each other. Pyros against terras and vice versa.

I'm not ignorant of the favor my kind has put on terras above pyros. I, myself, am guilty of looking at terras as more relatable than their fiery counterparts. I read now this was deliberate. Exploiting the pyros' volatile nature. Stereotyping them as brash and violent. Dangerous. While considering the terras' nurturing nature to be superior to their counterparts. Giving them easier jobs and more favorable work conditions.

'This will ensure the terras' loyalty to the Upper—if they believe themselves to be favored.'

He proposes it will lessen their likelihood of teaming up with the pyros they believe to be inferior. And I am abhorred to say, he was right.

My stomach turns. Bile rises at the back of my throat, called upon by the sick game my father and his counterparts played with these elementals. All this time, I thought I'd been fighting the war from the front lines. Out in the battlefields, where we shed blood. I could not have been more wrong.

The war was never there, only the retrieval. The actual war takes place in the minds of the captive elementals. This small test group serving in Central City proves that much. The Upper uses their minds as a war ground, and they have all but won.

I slam my fist on the desk, enraged that I provided so many elementals to this horrific agenda. I should have known what was going on. I should have looked harder and made myself more aware. Instead, I focused on my career and my duty and my pathetic hopes of making my father and region proud.

I am just as much to blame, if not more, than any policymaker sitting on council. I have personally supplied more than half of all the serving elementals, and I'm set to be the demise of so many more.

I jump from the desk, realizing there is no time to waste. I will stop this extraction. I must stop the mission that I have prepared my brigade to go on in less than one day's time.

Remembering the servant files I'd studied, one of the Level Threes stood out. One of the L3s was not from the Healing Faction. He was a native of the Smithing Faction, the one we will be attacking. I must go to him. I know it's a long shot. If he does not remember himself, I may not receive his aid, or he will be useless. But if he does remember himself—and me—I could risk so much more.

I put those concerns aside. Risks be damned, I must stop this. But first, I must disable the transporters. They cannot carry out this mission. I close the file, unlock the room, and race toward the transport hangar.

CHAPTER 31
KARA

ICE CREEPS OVER MY mouth as I struggle to scream. The harsh cold burns my skin, sending a convulsing shiver through my body. The aeros have made this ice colder than what encased us after they attacked my faction. They cool it to a temperature that aims to debilitate me.

I thrash against my icy bindings, rocking against the soldiers who drag me behind the prime. I must escape. The elemental who tipped Policymaker Aquil off told him where I directed the elementals to go. It will only be a matter of time before they find out what is happening at the hangar. I must warn Cinis and my mom.

As the aeros drag me down the long corridor, I search my surroundings for even a remnant of my element. I desperately look for something to grab hold of. When I come up empty, the only thing I can resort to is the marble floor. Unable to touch it, I force all my focus into disturbing the stone. I can feel the aether in a way I never have before. It's a tangible rope that I command rather than coax.

It is so apparent to me, that I can see the thin coppery-gold strands of it hanging in the air. My temples and fingertips throb as pressure builds. Suddenly, the floor beneath the prime cracks, splitting open and breaking apart. I waste no time harnessing the pieces of broken rock, thrusting them toward her and my escorts. She whips around, pulling water from a nearby fountain, using it to intercept the rocks.

"Can't you idiots contain her?" she says, venom spewing from her lips. "Never mind, I'll do it myself."

She steps toward me, gripping my face in her hand. She squeezes my jaw with her thumb and forefingers, wedging the digits into the joints until my mouth pops. She pulls me to her, intently focusing her eyes on mine.

I try to fight, but the struggle seems to escape me. My vigor lulls. I am in a trance; the fluid of my body rocks like the lazy waves of the sea. Even worse than my siphoning, she controls me—mind and body. She sings a siren's song, though no sound ever crosses her lips.

I think back to our capture when they initially collared and restrained us. I remember the terrifying immortal who stood, beautiful and deadly, above our magroginite containment. I finally understand how they could subdue thousands of elementals at once.

When all the fight in me has died, and I no longer thrash against my bindings, she pulls me into the maintenance room. She takes no care, throwing me into the nearest chair. The ice around me melts, but I am no threat. The hydro's siren song sedates me without the use of a needle or serum.

She uses the chair restraints to tie me back, cuffing my hands, ankles, and head. I let the steady rock inside my body calm me, unable to fight it.

The temperature of the room drops dangerously low. In an instant, I see my breath grow white before my eyes. Frost forms on the room's slick metal beams, and I fight back a shiver.

"This is the woman?"

I hear the terrifying tone of a man's voice come from behind me. The inflection is extraordinary. I've heard it before and will remember it for the rest of my life. The sound is akin to ice scraping across glass, otherworldly end unsettling.

"Yes, My Lord." The prime policymaker bows before me to the creature standing at my back. They've strapped my head, keeping me from turning to look upon him. An icy hand grips my shoulder and I jump at the cold, dead feel of it.

"Let's have a better look at you," the creature says.

He rounds me, coming to stand in front of me. I immediately recognize the monster, although I've never seen him this close. He peers at me, only inches from my face. Examining me like a specimen on display.

The intrigue is mutual. I cannot part my glance from the grayish blue skin that covers him. Frost coats parts of his arms and cheek. His skin wrinkles and creases from the dry air he encompasses. The man looks ancient, and I know very well he could be far older. I'd never quite believed in immortals until the day I saw him stand above the magroginite cage, wielding the wind like Aelious himself.

The creature places his hands on my temples and if my head weren't so tightly secured, I would shrink back from his touch. Energy buzzes from his fingertips and my head throbs in time with my pulse.

Essence weaves itself through my body and rushes to my head. It pushes itself at my temples and burns to be set free. I grunt from the pain, but the monster's eyes only narrow in concentration. When he finally releases his grip, the power and pressure welling in my head collapse. I take a deep breath, centering myself as he backs away from me.

The creature's eyes narrow as his jaw flexes in an angry scowl. "What did you do?" he shrieks. "How did you harness their essence?"

"I don't know what you're talking about," I say. The creature is truly terrifying, as he aims all his wrath toward me.

"Do not lie to me." He raises the back of his hand and slaps it across my face. Pain explodes fiery hot across my right eye and cheek. My lip throbs as I can feel the trickle of blood trail down my chin.

"How did you harness the essence?" Frost creeps across every surface of the room as his anger heightens.

"I don't know what you're talking about," I cry, begging him to believe me. "I have not harnessed anyone's essence. They have only stolen essence from me." I glare at the prime who has headed the siphoning.

He must be mistaken. He must know they have only been taking essence from us, never giving it.

282

The creature checks his anger, stepping toward me. "You have made yourself into an immortal, girl."

I flinch as he raises his hand again, but instead of bringing it down across my face, he reaches for my hair.

"And it seems you've already used some of your immortal power," he says, picking out the branches that grow from my scalp. I squeeze my eyes shut, not understanding his words. I do not have immortal essence. No one can simply grant themselves immortality. Until seeing him, I didn't even think immortals were real.

He drops the branches of my hair, setting his face to an impassive scowl.

"Morgana," he calls to the prime, "extract the essence, and prepare it for the Outer."

My pulse races as the creature walks past mean to leave. "And this time, make sure there is none left. She will have no use for it, as we will have no use for her."

The cold recedes with the monster from the room. He has given his orders and sentenced me to death.

CHAPTER 32
SORREN

I RACE TO THE hangar. There's little time to waste. I have commissioned two transporters to prepare for the mission. If I am to dismantle this operation, it starts there. It is no minor risk I am taking on. This is complete and utter treason for me, and anyone I involve.

To sabotage this mission, I must deprogram the ship. I've uploaded the transporter's blueprints to my comm unit. I will destroy the power source to debilitate the units altogether. This will give me enough time to steal a pod and warn the fire faction of what is coming.

When I approach the hangar, I run a mental check of all the guards I know should be on patrol tonight. There should be at least one guarding each entrance and two others guarding the transporters themselves.

I approach the hangar door and lift my palm to the biometric lock pad. No light scans my hand. The device only releases a gentle smoke. I inspect it further and see it's fried. I push against the massive metal door, sliding it open with a heavy grunt. My guard is on high alert. No soldier would simply leave the transport hangar unlocked and open for anyone to walk in.

I creep into the hangar, keeping my back to the wall. Dozens of transporter ships, carriers, and pods park in the colossal garage without a single soldier to guard them. When I've made it midway across, I come to an unconscious hydro, slumped in the corner. I bend over to home in on his breathing. I can feel the flow of air pull into his mouth and circulate through his lungs. He lives. I slow my breaths to an inaudible level.

I listen for the sounds of an intruder but hear nothing, not even the shuffling of the other guards on patrol. Something's happened to them. I am not here alone.

I take great caution in making my way to the first transport ship—remaining vigilant—expecting an ambush. I survey the area around the massive vessel and find the two remaining guards that patrolled it. They also lay unconscious on the floor. Ice creeps up my fingertips and along my forearms.

I hear the clunking sound of metal hitting the ground and spin to face whatever is behind me. A young girl scrambles backwards, scurrying behind the transporter. I run to follow her. As I round the large ship, I catch sight of hundreds of elemental servants huddled together at the entrance of our first transporter.

There are so many captives. What are they all doing here? I notice their necks, all bare of collars. They mean to escape. Shock clouds my mind, halting me from making another move.

I balk at the sheer numbers they have amassed. This is Kara's work, I know it. Pride wells in my chest for the brilliant and re-sourceful terra. She is the strongest elemental I've ever encountered. There could be no better leader for these people, and I was a fool to think I could ever deserve her.

She must have intricately planned the organized exodus for it to go so unnoticed. But how did they expect to make it out of the city devoid of proper fuel? Surely, none of them know how to operate the large transporter. I can help them. I can help them escape and warn the Smithing Faction.

As I open my mouth to speak, a large ball of fire hurdles toward me. I dodge it, feeling it pass so close to my skin that it melts the frost accumulating on my shoulder.

"Yield! I mean to help you!" I shout at my attacker, not wanting to engage in combat.

The man steps forward, his hands engulfed in flames. I know this man. I take no time to place him as the Level Three pyro from the Healing Faction.

He throws his head back, laughing as if we'd shared an absurd joke. I wouldn't believe me if I were in his position either, but before I can explain, the pyro hurls more fire at me. I block his attacks, pushing a pocket of cold air to encircle him and cool him down. This gives me just enough time to speak.

"I mean no harm. I came to dismantle the transporters. I will not stop you if you wish to go."

The pyro stares at me, his brows lifting. When he opens his mouth to speak rather than lift his hand to fire off another attack, I know he means to humor me.

"And why would you do that?"

"Because I know the truth. I know the truth of what the Upper has been doing to you and what they intend to do."

His eyes narrow as if he's trying to place me. If the gods have any mercy, he won't. "And what do they intend to do?"

"They seek the Smithing Faction. They will capture them and those they are housing. Then they will return them here to serve."

The pyro pales as his horror-stricken face searches mine. "How do you know this?"

"Because I planned the attack."

Murmurs break out across the crowd. Panicked whispers turn into a sea of muffled protests. When the pyro's eyes stop searching mine, they narrow in a glare.

His jaw clenches and he says, "It's you."

So much for the gods' mercy. He engulfs his entire body in a massive flame. He remembers.

Before I can open my mouth to explain, he hurls large balls of fire at me. One after another, I dodge them, trying not to engage.

"If you'll just let me explain."

He encircles me in a ring of flames. Ignoring my protests, he grows the flames higher. As my body temperature rises, I cannot play peacekeeper any longer.

I blast a strong wind through the hangar, knocking out the flames and pushing over all who stand nearby.

"I'm here now, please believe me—"

The pyro sends another wave of flames, cutting me off. I spin the air around, blocking them.

He reaches a supply rack, grabbing a large metal chain. When it touches his hand, a red glowing heat illuminates the links. My abdomen recoils on itself, an automatic response as flashbacks of the last pyro who wielded a heated chain bombard me. He draws the chain back, whipping it at me as another fireball comes hurling toward my core. I move to evade it, leaving my neck wide open. The cord wraps itself around my throat, burning through the skin it touches.

I try to cry out, but the chain compresses my airway. I don't want to harm the pyro, but if I don't stop him, he will kill me. I force icicles from my palms and aim for him. One cuts his hand, forcing him to drop it.

As I stagger away, my breathing is labored. I stammer, but as soon as I stand the accompanying terras and pyros attack from behind. I am blessed that they cannot use the full extent of their abilities. If I weren't so busy fighting for my life, I'd have time to wonder why the pyro seems to wield his so effortlessly.

According to my father's work, this shouldn't be possible. He should not have gained back so much of his essence. My father studied the regeneration of aether. Anytime we use our essence, it depletes. Wielding aether comes at a price to our energy stores, but it regenerates just as our blood does. Once enough essence has been siphoned to lower an elemental's level, there's no record of them regaining it. The elementals who claw at my legs and arms, struggling to hold me still, don't possess a fraction of the power this pyro does.

A trail of flames blazes behind him as he walks toward me. My only defense is to remove the air from the room, to suffocate the flame and my captors. As I do, the elementals surrounding me begin to cough and wheeze, struggling to breathe. The pyro's eyes widen when he figures out what I have done. When the blacks of his eyes glimmer, I know he means to harm me without flame. I brace myself as the hangar door bursts open.

A woman scurries through, and I recognize her from the infirmary. She's the Healing Faction's leader, and when her eyes fall on me, she holds the same burning hate that she did the night she found Kara and me.

When the pyro sees her, he drops the heat he had been wielding. "Have you found her?" he asks.

Her gaze darkens, never leaving me. Something else compounds the hate her eyes hold. Recognition, and I know that if she holds the same power as the pyro, this is going to hurt.

"What's he doing here?" I see her hands flex. I imagine she searches for her elemental power. It's my good fortune that it never comes.

"I want to help," I quickly shout before the pyro can say anything.

"Help?" She rushes to me, bringing her hand down to strike my face. "Had it not been for you—" Her eyes widen as she remembers something, and I can only guess what it is.

"Why her? What kind of game—" Pain fills her eyes, and I can only imagine what she's thinking right now. I want to tell her that all my feelings were genuine. That it was not a game, it was not an act. It wasn't even intentional. But all I can do is hang my head, ashamed because she is right. It should not have happened.

The pyro moves forward. "Who are you talking about? What has he done?"

He's hungry for answers, but the terra looks at me, then back at him, shaking her head. She waves him off and I cannot figure out why she's spared me his additional wrath, why she does not tell him what I've done.

"They have Kara," she says and my breathing hitches. If they're escaping, she needs to be here. She must get out of Central City and away from the capitol.

The pyro becomes frantic. "What happened? Where is she?"

"A servant tipped off policymaker Aquil. The prime has her."

"We must get her. We cannot leave her with Morgana," I say.

The pyro spits. "*We?* You're not going anywhere. I will handle this."

"You need me. I can help."

"And why would you help? Why should I trust you? I should kill you where you kneel."

"Cinis," the terra leader says, and he pauses. She regards me for a moment, deciding whether she can trust me.

"I know Aquil. I know where we can find him." I plead for them to let me help, looking at the terra, hoping she will hear the sincerity in my words. "Let me take you to him. Please—if anything happened to her—" I cannot finish. The thought alone sends me into panic.

Her eyes soften, and she shakes her head.

The pyro's glare narrows on me. "And why do you care so much?" His suspicion carries a strange tone. Possessiveness, jealousy?

The terra cuts him off. "They're holding Kara inside the capitol. Because enforcers fill the place, we will need his help. You are the only one of us who can effectively wield, Cinis. We can't help you retrieve her. The aero knows his way around the capitol and has better access than we do. He can get us to the policymaker. We don't have time to waste."

"We cannot trust him."

"He comes." She looks at the elementals holding me down. "Release him," she says with all the authority of a faction lead. And they obey.

I fall as they push me forward, releasing me from their grasp. As I raise to my feet, she turns to address a terra man at my back.

"Emrick, you keep them safe. Keep them quiet and close together. Stay aboard the transporter and if we do not make it back within an hour, run." She rests her hands on his shoulders. "You have strength in numbers. You cannot let them take you back."

The man nods. "They won't take me alive."

Her lips thin into a straight line. "We will return."

She turns back to Cinis and I. "We must hurry, who knows what they're doing to her."

And my throat tightens. Because I do.

CHAPTER 33
KARA

THE PRIME ROUNDS ME as she prepares for the extraction. The immortal's presence is still fresh in my mind. The evidence of his visit leaves behind melting icicles that cling from the ceiling and walls. It reminds me of the first extraction they performed. After they captured my faction and pushed us into a magroginite cage, like wild animals.

"You have something that belongs to us." Morgana approaches me with a metal collar and anger flares in my core. Cinis had only just freed me from the damn thing. How can fate be so cruel? As she locks the device around my neck, the cold hard feel of metal on my skin causes me to buck against the siren song she still sings to keep me lulled.

I never imagined I'd be back in this servant's collar. The same sickening feeling I had the first time the enforcers placed it on me outside the metal cage, courses through me. I become claustrophobic and desperate to free myself from it.

"No use fighting, girl. Just let yourself go. Release yourself and it will all be over soon." Her words are slow and calm. Her voice comes out as a hum, smooth and rhythmic.

She is right. If I concede now, everything will be over, my life included. Still, I cannot seem to part myself from the suggestion of her words. It's as if my body rocks against itself, slow and steady as the rolling waves, convincing me that what she says is best.

The bite of needles stings my flesh, and I brace myself for the serum. When she turns the machine on, her siren's song stops. The fluid in my body no longer rocks and waves, and I can ground myself in my own thoughts.

As fluid flows through the needles, it sears its way through my veins. It wraps against the essence flowing within me and pulls. I focus on the flow of it and feel its makeup. The serum contains aether, but it is not mine. This aether is omnipotent and powerful, and I will take it for my own.

My mind goes back to what I'd first felt inside the walls of that magroginite cage so many months ago. Everything is so familiar. The same needles bite and pull at me. My heart rate spikes, just like it did before, as my essence rushes to every cell in my body. I remember Cinis and I frantically pulling the tubes from each other's necks and the immense pain that followed. The agonizing rush of raw aether surged through me then, and I feel it now.

That same pain ricochets through me, but instead of debilitating me, it strengthens me. Instead of shutting me down, it opens me up. I take control of the aether being pulled by Morgana's serum. They will take nothing else from me. I yank it back, ripping it away from the serum's grip. As essence floods back into me, I release my body to it, allowing the aether to wield me, rather than the other way around.

When I feel the stab of essence dart through my fingertips, I do not stop it. I do not quell it. I harness it and set it free.

I latch onto the metal binds, strapping me down, pushing my power to connect with them. Once I connect, I break them down and pry them open. The chair latches break apart instantaneously, and I do not take the time to marvel at my sudden ability to wield metals in a way I never have before. The second my hands are free, I reach for the collar that encloses my neck.

Essence sprays through my fingertips so abundantly that the moment I pry my hands to the needles within my collar, they disintegrate. Quickly, I thin my index finger into a vine, pushing it into the lock and unlatching the collar completely.

Morgana's head turns to me in a snap. She sucks in a gasp as I do not waste any time wielding the marble beneath her feet. I slam my fist to the ground, breaking apart the floor under her, down to the cinder blocks that hold us above the water. I hoped there would be solid ground below us, but again, I'm disappointed to find only more of her element.

She pulls the water up from the ground, flooding the room. I push vines from my fingertips and hands to wrap around her. Once they enclose her body, I lift her up and slam her against the floor.

She drops the wall of water she's been wielding. A high-pressure stream shoots at me, knocking me off the ground and pummeling against my stomach. I scramble away from it as it peels the flesh from my abdomen, ripping apart the shirt that offered me the slightest protection.

She screams for the enforcers, and they rush through the door. I push a slab of stone from the floor to barricade against the entrance, giving me more time alone with her. The essence that coils in my core and pushes through my palms is more powerful than I have ever wielded before, but I do not question it. I harness and focus it on her.

She lifts her hand, palm facing me. When she closes her fingers and twists her wrist, I can feel the water in my body pool to my throat. She is drowning me in my own fluids, and I have no element to grab on to. I desperately scan the room, searching for any remnants of the land I wield. I drop to the floor, throwing my hand in the split. Submerging myself in the water, I reach for the ground below, knowing that beneath the sea there is soil. If it is too far down, I cannot grasp it, but I have no other options but to try.

I push all the energy I possess down through the water, reaching for my element. When I feel it connect, I pull up with all my strength. Water and soil erupt through the split, pouring into the room. The muddy sand moves at my command, and I bury her in it. She sprays her way through, but I do not slow my attack. The moment she escapes, I pile more on top of her. I reach down to pull more sand from beneath the concrete column. Although I know it holds this room's foundation, I do not stop until I feel the space tremor.

As Morgana gets up, I wrap vines around her, securing her in place before burying her under more sand. The guards at the door push their way through and a blanket of ice covers the room.

I turn back to see Admiral Malakai leading the group of soldiers who have forced their way into the maintenance area.

I focused my attacks on Morgana because I know I do not stand a chance against the others single-handedly. I try to wound her, to debilitate her. I break apart the floor until there is no stone left, only split and cracked concrete that crumbles beneath our feet. I propel the stone at the soldiers and the prime, burying her even further.

An icicle pierces my biceps, and I hiss as blood trickles to the floor. The floor beneath us begins to crumble and fall into the sea below. We have only a few more minutes until the room and surrounding area collapse.

The admiral looks at the pile of debris the prime lies under and knows he must make a choice. He can either capture me or save the prime and his men before we fall to the sea.

I do not wait for him to decide. I throw a vine to latch on to the beams hanging on the ceiling. From them, I swing over the crumbling floor. As the admiral rushes to the prime, directing his men to secure a path and dig her out, I climb from the room and swing out by the vines extended from my hands. But when I land in the hall that is also trembling on the edge of collapse, I am met by what seems like the entire Upper army.

CHAPTER 34
SORREN

W E RACE THROUGH THE pathways of Central City. The canals are silent. No boats pass through the channels at this hour; no hydros ski across the water. I'm grateful the terra and pyro do not wear collars so that they draw even less attention. I know where Aquil will be. On the eve of our mission, he will be in his office preparing for tomorrow's council meeting.

We must find him if we want to know what's happened to Kara. Aside from that, I have my own questions for him. So much of my father's work remains a mystery, and Aquil has been a policymaker for longer than I've been alive. He sat through my father's addresses and voted on all his policies. Aquil will give me the answers I need, or he will die silently.

As we approach the capitol steps, Cinis protests. "She will not be here. Maintenance hour's long over."

"But Aquil is here, and he knows what has happened to her." I don't tell them it's likely Kara is here. If Morgana had truly gotten to her, she would surely take her to the torture chambers below the capitol or the extraction room in maintenance.

They follow me as I lead them down the quiet corridors. Although the terra knows her way around the capitol, she keeps her head down to go unnoticed. Even without their collars, they're still distinguishable as lower elementals. A keen eye will notice the water that splashes rather than yields to them, or the wind that labors their walk and chills their skin.

We climb up to the north wing where the policymaker offices are. I go down the hall where Aquil's office sits. When I peer down to see a light shine through the crack of his door, my shoulders relax. He is here.

"You two hang back. Let me go in first to see if I can get what we need from him without causing a disturbance."

"You think we're fools, aero?" the pyro points a black finger at me. I take his hand, rubbing it to see if the charcoal tipped digits will come away clean. He yanks his hand back to examine them for himself.

The terra gasps, "Not you, too, Cinis."

"What is this?" he asks her.

"I don't know for certain, but I think it may be a mark of the immortal," she says, gripping his hand.

Cinis snorts. He looks down at his fingers and shakes his hand, rubbing it against his pant leg. We both know there isn't time to worry about this now.

I insist on going in. "I want to see Kara safe just as much as you. We have the best chance if I can get the information I need from him without him suspecting us of foul play." I look at Kara's mother, and she nods. "You can stand at the door if you don't trust me."

"I will," he says.

I straighten my clothes and walk into the official's office.

"Policymaker Aquil." I raise a fist to my chest and tilt my head in a slight bow.

The policymaker stands to greet me. "Commander, come in." he regards me, taking in my disheveled appearance. No amount of dusting off can hide the charred holes the pyro burned into my uniform. "Well, soon to be Commander, that is. What can I do for you?"

"I heard someone tipped you off about a terra advising the servants to skip maintenance hour and converge."

The policymaker lifts a brow. "Yes."

"Would you know if they found the woman, or what they've done with her? I'd like to question her myself."

"Isn't this a little outside your scope? Shouldn't you be preparing for the mission?" The policymaker shakes his head. "Never bother. She is being taken care of."

I ball my fists, washing my knuckles white.

"What do you mean? What have they done to her?" I take great care in steadying my tone, not letting the slightest ounce of emotion flow through. But it is no use. I need to know that she is okay.

"Sorren, forgive me, but that is not any of your concern."

"Of course, it is my concern." I look at the clock. We waste valuable time, and I cannot continue with this dance for much longer. "Now tell me where she is," I demand.

"Soldier, I suggest you leave my office now before I report to the council that we have made a mistake."

The pyro bursts through the door, slamming it against the wall as he enters.

"That's enough. We tried it your way, aero. Now let's try it mine." His hands engulf in flames as he runs toward the policy-maker.

Aquil glares at me, and his expression calls me a traitor louder than his voice ever could. But I cannot back down now. I have chosen my side and established my alliance. There's no turning back. When the hydro erects a geyser of shooting water beneath the pyro, I freeze it, preventing it from injuring him.

I wrap the official in ice to keep him from continuing his attack. The pyro circles the room, lighting little fires, setting everything he touches ablaze.

"Now you will tell us what they have done to Kara," he says.

"The prime has finished her. Don't even waste your time."

Icy rage shoots through my core so raw and uncontrolled that I break him from the ice to grab him by the throat.

"What have you done?" I say with venom in my voice.

Aquil's brows shoot up in mock surprise. "What have I done? No Commander. It is what *we* have done, and what we will do," he says, reminding me I am just as much a part of this as he. That I have contributed just as much, if not more, than anyone else to my father's legacy.

I am guilty. While I was unaware of Nero's plans, this policy-maker knew them all along. I must know why. "Why did you do it? What did he promise you that was worth the blood of an entire region?"

Aquil's expression shifts, and he knows exactly what I'm referring to. He shakes his head. "It is a shame you do not possess the gift of your father's vision."

"My father's vision was a curse. It has brought only destruction. He fed our region lies and used us as pawns in his sadistic plan."

"I am no pawn, boy."

Just as I'd suspected, he was fully aware and onboard. "Why? What's in it for you?"

"Your father's vision was brilliant. Through his work, we can establish a unified government. One system to coalesce the realm. Both regions ruled by the Council of Policy."

The sheer greed of it is like a punch in the gut. Of course, he'd promised them rulership. They'd sold out the Lower elementals so they could gain more power. I look back at the terra and pyro accompanying me. The pyro has stopped lighting fires, his jaw slack, eyes narrow, trying to make sense of the sadistic person my father was.

My fingers wrap tighter around the policymaker's neck. "What have they done with her?"

The policymaker chokes as I loosen my grip. "Morgana has taken her."

Anger courses through me when Aquil stops there. I need more answers.

"What does she intend to do with her?" As my rage increases and boils over, a throne of ice forms beneath my feet. It raises me from the ground, picking the policymaker up even higher. When he does not answer, I push cold through his body. Frostbite creeps up his fingers and hands, traveling along his arms.

He makes gurgling sounds as I loosen my grip, giving him one more chance to talk.

"She's harvesting her essence. She means to send it to the Outer." The policymaker's broken words jumble through the gargling sound coming from his throat.

This doesn't make sense. "Why would she send it to the Outer? Who is she sending it to?" And the mysterious *they* pops into my mind. I watch the policymaker for an answer that he is reluctant to give. I urge him on with the push of my element, freezing his limbs until they're black and frosting over.

"The immortals."

I nearly drop him. I take a second, evaluating him, deciding whether he aims to fool me with this nonsense, or if he speaks the truth. The fear in his wide eyes convinces me he tells no lies. In my father's notes, there was so much information about the immortals. I remember him obsessing over them when I was growing up, but they still never felt like more than a ghost story to me. Until now.

"That is all I know."

"What use could the immortals have for essence? Why would Morgana send it?"

The policymaker shakes in my grip, moving his head back and forth, choking out gargled words. "I do not know. I swear to Hydris, this is all I know."

I know he speaks the truth. Which means he is no longer of value to me, or Kara.

I tighten my grip around his neck, pushing the cold deep into his veins until they ice over. Black frostbite creeps over his skin until every inch of him is cold and brittle. I toss him from the ice throne we have erected. When his body hits the ground, he shatters into a thousand pieces that clink against the stone floor like porcelain.

"They're holding her in maintenance. We must go."

The pyro gathers his element into him, then pushes it out through his palms. In a second, the entire room is ablaze and the dead pieces of Policymaker Aquil fuel the fire. We rush from the room, and I look down to see that the black of his fingertips has spread to cover his knuckles. With the fresh thought of immortals on my mind, I see this as a sign. I stopped to examine them, lifting his arm.

"When did this start happening?" I ask.

He yanks his hand back defensively, cradling his arm to his chest. "I guess when I started using my powers again. Maybe when I fought you, when they were stronger."

Before I can say another word, the ground around us tremors. We turn the corner to see a portion of my brigade occupy the corridor just outside the maintenance room. The floor beneath us cracks, and I hear a sound like demolition coming from the chamber.

Thick vines wrap around the members of my brigade, lifting and slamming them against the wall. Tiled stone flies in a storm of rocks, assaulting the air and water wielders. Centered in the chaos is Kara, fighting her way through the horde. She holds her own against the accomplished soldiers, fierce in her army of one.

CHAPTER 35
KARA

I CANNOT PAUSE MY wielding to assess the surrounding area. Soldiers pack every inch of the previously empty corridor. I'm surrounded, each of them aiming their element at me. When I've wielded all the land elements available in this constrictive corridor, I search for a different weapon to wield. Extending a vine from my hand, I grab hold of a metal bar affixed to the wall. I yank it, throwing all my body weight into removing the fixture.

When the cold metal bar reaches my grasp, I swing at the soldiers moving in on me. I propel the rod across the space in front of me, connecting it with the nearest encroaching soldier's face. I swing again, letting them know I will not go down without a fight. If these assholes mean to take me, I will make sure they go down, too.

A wave of water flows through the crowd and wraps itself around me. Just as it lifts me from where I stand, a powerful gust of wind pushes through the corridor. It knocks down the group of soldiers as if they were nothing more than terra stick-dolls.

I wrap my vines around a beam in the ceiling to keep myself from blowing away at the sheer force of this arctic blast. As the soldiers stumble upon one another, we all crane our necks to spy the aggressor.

I let out a strangled whimper as I see *him,* standing tall above the chaos.

Sorren.

He stands in front of my mother and Cinis, all three poised to attack. Panic quickens my breathing, as I realize, with my mother and Cinis here, there is no one left to protect the others. I should fear that Sorren has captured them. That he's finally enacting his grand plan to destroy everything I love. But as his stance seems protective in front of them, I can't make myself believe he means us harm. The fool I am.

The attack ceases for a moment. I can't spend my time wondering how those three came together. I wait for him to reveal his true intentions. He could be here to help me, but I don't allow my heart to hope.

His eyes meet mine, and for a brief second, I am lost. I did not think I would see him again. Part of me wishes I hadn't. The other part—the treacherous part—flutters, watching him stand above the fallen soldiers.

He throws a pocket of air around me, protecting me from the brisk gusts, never slowing his wind. He sends gust after gust of air flowing through the corridor, never allowing the soldiers a moment to recover themselves.

I brace myself for what's coming next. There is no way for me to know his intentions. He might very well be here to aid in my capture, but as he walks to me, I grow calm rather than anxious.

Once he reaches me, his eyes find mine, and everything I'd suppressed since remembering him comes flooding in.

He silently mouths, "Please trust me." And I am a fool, because I do.

He takes my hand in his, slowing the wind he wields to a calm breeze, and the gesture makes me self-conscious in front of my mother and Cinis. It's then that I notice the nasty burn in the pattern of a chain wrapped around his neck. I wince, wondering if Cinis inflicted the injury.

"Hold," he says to the group, commanding them with all the authority of his office. The soldiers look stricken. Their gazes frantically shift from their commander, back to the destroyed maintenance room.

Finally, a woman stands. She's of a tall, athletic build. Half of her straw-blond hair balls in a knot atop her head, the rest she has shaved to the scalp. She raises a hand to her group of soldiers and nods at Sorren in a show of support. I believe she is an admiral, and the soldiers who look to her command must be her unit.

They give Sorren their attention as he addresses the crowd.

"The council has deceived us. We've kneeled before a throne of lies and served it innocent blood. The very people we vow to serve and protect have inundated us with falsehoods they used to manipulate and play us as pawns. In my time here, I have learned the truth about our region's leaders. I have learned the truth about my father."

The soldiers listen, showing respect for Sorren's position. As he continues, the admiral and her group move toward us. It is subtle, and I remain on high alert to make sure they do not mean to attack.

"I have failed you all in leading you into a mission we knew was wrong. I have allowed duty to blind me and forced you all to ignore your own moral code for the sake of following orders. We have wronged our Lower brethren on so many levels. We have blamed them for inciting the war that my father had planned all along."

Murmurs erupt across the group, but Sorren speaks through them, raising his voice to maintain authority. "My father started this war as a ploy to gain Lower labor. The advances he made were born from the blood of our Lower brothers and sisters. The elementals we deliver to Central City do not simply serve. We alter them. We inject them with poison to muddy their minds and siphon their essence."

Gasps ricochet across the corridor. I hear the words, *lies* and *impossible,* repeated from different voices. The admiral steps from the crowd to speak.

"It is true, I have seen it," she says as she continues to move toward us until she's standing next to Sorren. In front of Cinis and my mother, her unit surrounds us. "We don't suppress servants' powers, we steal them. The council plays a dangerous game and uses us to do their bidding." As she finishes, the crowd erupts.

"Ciel?" he murmurs.

"You think you were the only one with questions?" the admiral replies, her hushed words getting lost in the crowd's uproar.

Sorren speaks, raising his voice to rein them in. "Tomorrow, we will deliver thousands of elementals to that very fate," he says.

I clutch my chest, not believing what I hear.

"My brothers and sisters in arms. I beg you to reconsider. I will not aid the council in acquiring slaves for their selfish gain. What they're doing is reprehensible, and I will no longer take part in it."

For a long moment, the hall is silent. The soldiers exchange confused glances, facing their own internal struggles.

A voice rings out above the others. "Traitor!"

Sorren's hand grips mine. I know he prepares for battle as ice creeps across our fingertips. Mine thin into vines in response, readying for a fight.

Trained soldiers surround us, ready for combat, and we don't stand a chance against them. As the soldiers from the middle of the crowd surge forward, their elements in hand, the soldiers around us attack. I take a second to register that they are fighting their own brigade rather than us. As more race forward, the admiral leads her group to rush them, blocking their attack, shielding us from the elements they wield.

Chaos ensues all around. Sorren pulls me behind him as he throws up a wall of ice to protect us. Meanwhile, I break apart the floor beneath the attacking soldiers' feet and stone them with fragmented pieces.

As fighting continues all around, it is difficult to tell a friend from foe. The soldiers of Sorren's brigade are indistinguishable in every way that matters. A group of them form a barrier around us, taking on the soldiers who fight to break through. A crack of lightning ricochets through the corridor, blasting through the ceiling, causing it to crumble and fall onto the soldiers beneath. Another lightning bolt strikes, and it can only come from Cinis.

I look across the corridor to see him in front of my mother, protecting her from the ensuing elementals. I rush to her, knowing she cannot wield her power.

When I reach her, I erect a stone wall from the floor, blocking the icicles that seek to pierce her flesh. I wield thick thorns tipped with poison and shoot them at my opponent.

More soldiers pour in and the few that fight with us are losing ground. A line of fire blazes through the hallway, heating the aeros and slowing their attack.

As a group rushes toward us, I throw my vines to grab hold of the already disintegrating ceiling, pulling it down to fall on top of them. Despite our efforts, we are no match for their numbers. We do not stand a chance unless more soldiers decide to come to our aid.

Sorren is once again next to me. He assesses the unfolding battle, and I can tell by the lines of his face that he's decided.

"They know about the hangar. They know you are directing elementals there. It's only a matter of time before they attack. You and your mother must protect the captives that hide there," Sorren says. I look over at Cinis, who pushes white-hot flames from every pore of his skin.

"But what about you and Cinis? You need to come, too. We need you."

"No, we'll stay here and hold them off. It'll give you and your mom the best chance of making it to the others," he says through gritted teeth. He bears against the wall of ice he's erected to protect us from a hydros stream.

I shake my head.

Cinis throws another bolt of lightning above Sorren's ice wall, slowing the ensuing attack.

"Go, now, they will listen to you. You are the leaders of their faction. You will corral them better than we could," Cinis pleads with me. "It's our best chance, go."

I look at Sorren and know it's decided. They're right. We must save my people first. He fans his hand out, forming a pocket of air around us. Once it encloses around my mom and me, he pushes us through the crowd and through the corridor. When the pocket releases us, I grab my mother's hand and pull her from the hall. We race from the capitol. I stay vigilant. I'm my mother's only defense should someone follow.

The tide slows our pace, and I curse the freezing water that rises to our ankles. Swearing, I'd be happy to never see another puddle again. We slosh through the streets, ignoring the passersby who grumble and stare at our splashing.

Once we've made it a considerable distance from the capitol, we slow to a stop as my mother rests her hands on her knees, bending over to catch her breath.

When she's recovered herself, she stands, placing her hands on my shoulders. She stares deep into me and begins to speak.

"My daughter. You will lead our faction. This is the role you were born to take, and I know there's no one better equipped to shepherd our people than you. This has been proof of that." She gestures to my hands that still hold a slight resemblance to the vines I'd wielded. I don't know why she's telling me this.

"Mom, you're our faction's lead," I say, not yet ready to have this conversation with her.

"But it will not always be that way. Kara, you must promise me that when my time comes, when Gaia takes me from this world, you will take my place as lead. Our faction needs you. Promise me this." My head shakes as the finality of this seems so absolute. As if she is watching her own death unfold.

"I promise."

She hugs me to her, and I grip my fingers, digging into her shoulder blades, fearing that if I let go now, I will lose her forever. We run the rest of the way to the hangar. It is empty and quiet, and I give a panicked look at my mother.

"Where are they?" They should be here.

My mother hushes me. "They're hiding," she whispers as she looks around, searching for an invisible enemy.

As her mouth opens to say another word, a barreling wind wraps around her, lifting her. I reach for her as a block of ice slams against my head, knocking me over. My vision spots. When I blink my eyes into focus, Admiral Malakai stands above me.

CHAPTER 36
SORREN

A FTER PUSHING KARA AND her mother out of the attacking crowd, I can finally relax, though just in the slightest. Although Kara can hold her own, we were quickly becoming overpowered, and I'm glad at the very least I could get her out of this mess.

Soldiers pile on top of one another in the cramped corridor. Elements fly every which way, most focusing on my unlikely comrade, the pyro.

I switch to a defensive strategy and focus my efforts on blocking the attacks aimed at the fire wielder. Of the strange battle between brothers and sisters in arms, the pyro's the only clear-cut *other* among us. I'm also an easy enough target. They're all my soldiers, so they recognize me, but the man covered in flames sticks out like an ember among ash.

As he pulls lightning bolts from the sky, he does not seem to lose energy like he should. As I grow weaker with each attack, threatening to exhaust my element at any moment, he only grows stronger with each strike. I cannot take long to marvel at his power as the surrounding corridor crumbles.

The last bolt strikes through the ceiling. It pierces the floor, pushing the foundation and all the elementals who stand above it into the sea below. More of the soldiers who fight with me surround us, pushing us from the attacking soldiers. As we scramble away from the disintegrating foundation, another band of elementals round the corner of the next hall.

I look up and pray that my eyes deceive me. Standing, front line, leading the small group, is Kai.

I drop the ice I've been wielding, taking in the look of confusion on my friend's face. He looks back at the scene behind us—then to me—then the pyro. His eyes narrow on Cinis as he pulls up a sweeping stream of water from the open floor below.

It whips across the hall, aiming for the fire wielder. I freeze it before it reaches him, then send a gust of wind to push it from its trajectory. Confusion contorts the features of Kai's face as he looks at me with knitted brows. I spin the air in front of me, making it obvious that I seek to protect the pyro. The look of betrayal Kai aims at me stabs deeper than anything else could.

"What are you doing?" he yells across the corridor. "Move out of the way, Sorren."

I stand in front of Cinis who is wielding at my back, holding off the attackers alongside the members of my brigade, who stay loyal to me.

"Stand down, Kai."

His mouth hangs open as he searches for words to fill it.

"What have you done?" His eyes grow wide as the gravity of my treason sinks in. "You would betray your own region?"

"It is our region who betrays us. They are stealing the essence of the elementals we capture. Kai, I saw it all. You must believe me," I beg my best friend and second in command.

"We have a duty. We have pledged fealty, as you've so easily discarded," he says, flexing his fingers, drawing them into fists.

All that we've worked for—all that we've stood for—thrown to the wayside in a matter of hours. My best friend has been fighting a losing battle. He's tried to keep me on a straight path since we'd attacked the terra faction. His shoulders drop as he realizes there's no use now.

"Sorren, abandon this madness, please. There's still time for you to redeem your station."

But that is a lie. There's no turning back now, even if I wanted to. I spin the air around me even faster, solidifying my decision, making it clear to the man I call best friend.

Kai's mouth sets in a hard line as his jaw flexes beneath his warm beige skin. "So, you've decided. This is where you stand."

And his words come out as more an accusation than a statement. My answer comes as a powerful gust of air, knocking him and his small group over. Before he hits the ground, he's already sprung a geyser of water from the sea below. It shoots through the floor beneath Cinis and me, extinguishing his flame. I freeze the jetting water and thrust it forward at the group. More elementals charge at our backs and my soldiers lose ground in holding them off.

I dry Cinis, and he pushes more flames ahead at the attacking elementals. More soldiers pour in through the corridor and if we don't do something, they will surely defeat us. Our groups have separated themselves. Those who stand with me from those who stand against. My allies form a tight circle around the pyro and me, and I scramble for a way to get us all out of this.

Cinis forms an inferno around him, piling up the flames of this fire, pushing them forward toward our mutual enemy. I form an air pocket, pulling everything from it but the oxygen mixed inside. When I have successfully separated the gas, I push it into his blaze. It combusts in a fiery bomb that bathes our attackers in flames and destroys what is left of the already crumbling corridor.

Cinis pauses to assess me, impressed by the manner my element enhanced his. The manic way he looks at the gargantuan flames puts me on edge. We scramble away as the floor and walls around us crumble and fall into the sea. I grab hold of Cinis as I use my element to thrust us over the falling ground. When we reach the side Kai is on, he does not give me any time to recover before wrapping me in a blanket of water. As he cuts off my air supply, Cinis pulls lightning down from the heavens to strike the soldiers standing with him. I use what energy I have left to pull the air from Kai's lungs, debilitating him, and causing him to fall.

"I don't want to fight you, Kai."

"You have made your choice, traitor." His voice is laced with pain. His words sting more than any hydro's stream could. He moves toward me with all the unfeeling mechanicalness of one of my father's machines. I know he does what he believes is his duty, but I cannot let him stand in the way of me doing what is right.

Cinis calls over to me. "We must get to the hangar. They have no way to use the transport. We need to get out of here."

Kai runs toward me. Distracted by Cinis, I do not expect the blow Kai lands on my chin.

"I will not let you do this to yourself!" my friend shouts, and I drop to the ground, sideswiping him with a kick that topples him over. He lands on a bed of water that pushes him back up to stand. Once his left hook connects with my cheek, it throws my head back.

I do not want to hurt him. His hands wrap around my neck, and I thrust my forehead into his nose. A waterfall of blood follows the cracking sound that the bones make. I kick my foot forward, landing square in the middle of his chest. He flies backward, falling.

I reach down to help him up, but when I do, he throws a whip of water that slaps against my neck and head. As I fall back, he continues to attack me. I look over and see that Cinis is being overpowered as well and know we must get out of here quickly. Wave after wave slams into my face, cutting off my air supply. I use the energy I have left to wield icicles I thrust at Kai. One pierces his forearm, and he drops the blanket of water he's confined me in.

When he falls, I enfold him and the soldiers that surround him in a pocket of air. I lift them up and slam them against the wall. They fall to the ground like dolls, some of their limbs contorted into impossible angles. Kai lies in the heap of soldiers. Eyes closed and jaw slack, I pray to Aelious he is only unconscious.

"We have to get out of here," Cinis says.

Ciel comes behind him. "He's right, Commander, we must go. We can cover your backs, but we must leave now."

I grip the admiral's forearm, unable to properly express my gratitude. "Ciel, your support . . ." I cannot find the words to convey what this means.

She waves me off. "Are you kidding? Do you know how long I've waited for you to get your head out of your ass? Now go, so I can save it," she says with a laugh, small turbulence of wind forming in her palms.

As the group of soldiers aligned with us stand their ground, the hydros and aeros who seek to stop us, close in. Cinis sends me a nod, silently conveying what we need to do to make it out of here.

Again, he conjures a large ball of flame as I wield oxygen from the surrounding air. We throw the explosive into the line of attacking soldiers. As it detonates, it sends them flying every which way. The combustion rocks the hallway, demolishing the remaining walls and foundation until the entire area crumbles into the sea. We run from the demolition, knowing if our speed slows in the slightest, we will be sacrificed to the waters below.

As the floor slips from beneath our feet, I push my allies forward with the last gust of wind I can muster, propelling them to safety. Once we've reached solid ground, we flee from the capitol.

I cannot look back. I cannot stare at the deathbed I've lain my best friend in, or at the soldiers I have commanded and betrayed. I can only move forward. So, we run to the hangar, praying we make it there before Malakai's soldiers.

CHAPTER 37
KARA

THE ADMIRAL REACHES DOWN to pick me up by the collar. He raises me level with him.

"Going somewhere?"

The stale odor of his breath wafts through my nostrils, with his face only inches from mine. I thrash against his hold, kicking him in the stomach. He drops me, gripping his abdomen. I fall on my back, hitting the floor with a loud slap.

A massive block of ice hurls toward me and I rollover, twisting away right before it crashes to the ground. Jumping to my feet, I brace for the attack. His hand reaches out to strike and I duck, landing another blow to his abdomen. As he clenches his midsection, I thrust my knee into his groin, doubling the large man over. I quickly swing my leg over the back of his neck, then slam him to the ground, crushing his face on the stone floor.

His fingers catch me as I move to stand, pulling me down with him. Bringing the back of my elbow to connect with his ear, I kick his chin before scrambling up and away. His thick, callused fingers wrap around my ankle before I can take two steps. He yanks me back, slamming my head to the ground with a thud.

Once I fall, Malakai slams his elbow into my shin, aiming to break it. I cry out, and my mother runs toward me, horror contorting the lines of her face. I slam my fist against the ground, causing it to send a ripple, tripping her before she can reach me.

"Stay back," I say.

It isn't safe for her. She cannot wield. If she tries to take Malakai on, she will not survive. Twisting to turn over from my belly, I connect my knee with his temple, knocking him off me. I thrust my heel into his face as his head flies back. Sweeping the ground beneath me, I shoot the broken stones at him.

He spins the wind to defer the flying projectiles. Daggers of ice form in both of his palms as he swings his arms, slicing them at me. I wrap a vine around his wrists, flinging him backward, but he only regains himself and charges me with more force and anger than before. I slam my foot against the ground, sending another ripple toward him. It trips him as he runs, and I take the pause in his attack to grab hold of my own weapon.

With no more land elements to wield, I yank the metal bar from a shelving unit against the wall. As he charges at me again, I thrust the tip into his chest. Although it does not pierce his flesh, it sends him sprawling back. I swing the bar, connecting it with the hard flesh of his arm.

A loud crack echoes through the space, signifying the breaking of bone. I take another swing, aiming for his head, but he catches it with his left hand and yanks me forward. When I fall into him, he wraps his arm around my neck and squeezes it so tight I fear my head will pop off.

I claw his arm, scratching—frantic to free myself from his head-lock. From behind me, I feel pounding as his head thrusts forward into mine. He shakes, trying to ward off whatever hammering attacks him. With my ability to take in air completely depleted, my vision begins to blacken. I fight so thoroughly to maintain my grip on consciousness that I lose hold of my element.

The admiral thrusts me away from him. As I fall, I see him reach back, clawing at his attacker.

It is my mother.

She clings to his back, her teeth sunken into the side of his face and her fingers pressed firmly into his eye sockets. As I fall, my head slams against the wall, blackening my vision.

Blood trickles down my neck and onto my back. An assailing gust of air rips through the space, and I hear the crunch of her bones smash against the floor. I blink my vision into focus and see her body lying at an impossible angle on the ground before me.

The piercing throb of my head keeps my limbs from moving as quickly as they should. I fall over, crawling toward my mother. She turns her head to look at me. As she coughs, blood drips from her mouth. She tries to make a sound, but it only comes out as a gurgle. She mouths her last words to me, and I read her lips.

"I love you."

My chest constricts until I cannot breathe.

No, no, no.

My skin grows cold and damp. This cannot be real. I wrap my arms around her, gripping her to my breast.

Not her.

I struggle to breathe against the weight baring down on my ribcage—crushing me.

"I love you, too, Mom. Please, don't go. I love you." My heart slams against my chest and pounds in my eardrums as I beg the last living parent, I have left to stay with me just a bit longer. Tears cascade down my cheeks and on to her fading face.

A deep voice screams out my name. "Kara!"

Blinking through the blur of my tears, I see Sorren and Cinis at the entrance of the hangar. They rush toward Malakai as I look down at my mother.

Don't leave me.

She blinks up at me for the last time before her eyes close and the slow rise of her chest falls.

She is gone, and I can't do a thing to save her.

CHAPTER 38
SORREN

ONCE WE'VE REACHED THE hangar, we find Malakai at the center of the room. He's bent over, cradling his face in his hands. His eyes are bloody, and it appears someone has taken a chunk of flesh from his cheek.

I pull the air from his lungs, suffocating him. A swift death is much too merciful for the miserable bastard. He doubles over, clawing for the air I've taken away from him. I wish for nothing more than the time it will take to administer a slow and torturous end, but I know I will not receive it.

Malakai's soldiers are close in suit. We saw them approaching as we made our way to the hangar. Ciel and the others stayed back to hold them off. The precious time I take teasing him with death only puts my soldiers at more risk. It only further endangers Kara. I must get her out of here.

Cinis approaches, touching a fiery hand to Malakai. He lets the blaze creep over every inch of skin until he's completely coated in it. Malakai's body flips and twists against the blaze which consumes him.

His mouth opens in a scream, but nothing escapes. There's no air left in his lungs to fuel the sound. He only burns.

Cinis maintains the fire long after Malakai's limbs cease to twitch. The blaze still burns once his skin is black and the stench of cooking flesh fills the air.

Once we finish him, I take a long look at my sworn enemy, laying crumpled, burned to a crisp on the floor. His end was not nearly satisfying enough, but it will have to do.

I follow Cinis to Kara as she kneels on the ground rocking her now dead mother against her breasts. My heart breaks for her, but I know it is not my place to offer comfort. I do not deserve to take those liberties with her. So, I stand watching Kara fall apart, unable to do nothing but silently disintegrate with her.

She cries into Cinis as he wraps his arms around her, cradling her head to his chest. The familiarity of their position makes me wonder how well they knew each other before our attack.

A loud banging on the hangar wall pulls me from my thoughts. I peer outside to see the battle has already reached us. The elementals of the Upper army are relentless in their attack, swiftly overpowering the members of my brigade who hold them back.

Kara remains on the floor, eyes dazed and unfocused as she clings to her mother. She cannot fight, she will not move. One look at the chaos ensuing and I know we don't stand a chance. I must get Kara out.

"Cinis, they're here," I say, and he looks at Kara, hugging her to his chest, lifting her chin to meet his eyes.

"You must let Zimara go," he whispers to her so intimately that rage begins to fester in the pit of my stomach. I calm the jealousy I have no right to and move to the far wall where the control station is located.

I unlock the command desk, thankful my comm unit still has its accesses. We do not have time to move the ship. Not without being shot down by the ensuing army. The only thing we can do is save Kara. I open the hanger as if preparing for takeoff. The far wall and roof split, clearing a path for trajectory. Once it's open, it is already too late. The Upper soldiers pour into the hangar, heading straight for us.

Cinis springs from Kara, running into the fight. I flee to her, hating myself for what I must do.

"You must go. We can't win this. You need to escape and warn the Smithing Faction the Upper is sending more soldiers."

She looks at me. Eyes wide, clutching her mother even closer to her, she cries. "No. I will not leave her."

The sickening déjà vu of this moment will haunt me for the rest of my days. She is not thinking clearly. Grief consumes her, and our time to act is dwindling along with our options.

I pull her from her mother, prying her once again from a parent she watches die before her. The shriek of her scream rings in my ears as she throws her fists at me, clawing to get away. I hold steadfast until I can envelop her in a pocket of air. She thumps her fists against the invisible walls of the prison I've encased her in.

I know it is selfish of me to lay this on her, but I cannot die without telling her at least once. I can't let her go on thinking this was anything less than real. So, I say the words that have been burning on my tongue since the first night she kissed me in the infirmary.

"I love you," I shout through the walls of the air pocket I've sealed her in. "I swear to the gods, Kara, I love you, and will until my dying breath."

Her shrieking ceases, her fists fall, and she stands looking at me for a long moment, mouth open and unmoving. I take in the sight of her one last time before pushing the air beneath her and raising her high above my head. With the thrust of my palm, I use all my remaining essence to propel her from the hangar and pass the wall of Central City. When it is done, I collapse, totally depleted of any power to wield.

As the soldiers push their way through the hangar, they home in on Cinis. The elementals throw everything they have at the skilled pyro. I cannot help him. My element has been entirely depleted. As the group of aeros freeze the space, removing all its heat, the hydros submerge the pyro in a bed of water. And with Cinis, the rest of my brigade falls.

Four hydros hold me by my arms and neck, securing me on the ground.

They push Cinis down, burying his face in the floor next to me as four more aeros secure him. Additional soldiers, two aeros and two hydros, stand guard around us. Through the corner of my eye, I see the soldiers raid the transport ship, carrying out the hiding captives that never stood a chance.

Once they've captured us all, I hear the hollow clink of booted heels thrum against the floor. They stop before me, kicking my face up with the tip of their boot. I lift my head to see Morgana.

"Take these two to the holding cells. Lock them up and wait for my command," she says to the soldiers holding us. She bends down to bring her face close to mine and whispers, "I cannot tell you how long I have waited for this day. To watch you bleed. To see you die by my hand. Sorren, this will not be swift. You will suffer, and I will relish your pain."

CHAPTER 39

KARA

Sounds were muffled inside of the air-filled globe, but I heard him loud and clear.

"I love you."

The words rang in my ears as he pushed me up and out of the hangar. I flew through the air, propelling away from him, from Cinis, my faction members, and my mother. As I soared over the city, I saw the horde of soldiers breaking through the hangar and knew that I'd left them all to their death.

Once the pocket of air holding me descends, I look down to anticipate where I'll land. Sorren far overshoots the city wall, sending me past it and into the sea. As I fall into the water, the force of my impact sends water dozens of feet into the sky, tossing me around my air-cushioned chamber.

When the air pocket releases me, I plunge into the cold ocean. Below the water, everything is quiet. In contrast to the muffled sounds of my air pocket, there are none here. I look up toward the water's surface at the faint light of the morning sun shining through.

I float in that space—the in-between—until my lungs burn for oxygen, and I can no longer rest in the peace of the silent sea.

Kicking up, I struggle to bring my head to the surface and open my mouth to take in a breath of air. As soon as I do, it fills with more salt water as another wave crashes into me. Sorren and Cinis and the rest of my faction are likely already lost to the ensuing soldiers.

My mother . . . My mother is dead.

She died protecting me—died saving me. If I were as strong as she believed me to be, I could have saved her. But alas, I can protect no one.

Wave after wave crashes over me, burying my head underwater. I want to let the current take me. I want to let the salty liquid fill my lungs until I no longer feel pain. Until I no longer feel anything.

Coughing out water, I take in a quick breath before another surge hits. The relentless waves of the ocean are a vast contrast to the calm depths that lie just below. The current twists and turns me until I lose all sense of direction. I no longer face the shore and do not have time to search for it before another wave engulfs me.

Water covers me faster than I can tread above it. Each time I open my mouth to breathe, more saltwater fills it, rather than the air I desperately need. My heart races from the constant treading, and my lungs burn with the empty abandon that fills them. As I struggle to kick my legs faster, working to get my head above the surface, a cramp twists the muscles in my calf.

My legs jolt out once more before stopping.

I am tired.

I am tired of fighting, tired of struggling. Tired of pain, sorrow, and loss.

There is a dark humor in my overriding determination to stop the siphoning. My desperation to rid my body of the neurotoxin is the cruelest irony I can imagine. I found peace under the influence of their serum. Peace I have not felt since the days I played with stick dolls and lay under the falling leaves my mother rained down for me. My body may not have been free, but my mind was placid—my heart unburdened.

I let the current pull and push me further into the deep, welcoming the burn in my lungs, as it will be the last pain I have to endure. This world has stolen too much from me. Why should I walk through a life that so many others cannot? To be alive while so many are dead. Emi, Caelum, Dad—Mom. It's wrong, and I cannot find the point in it.

I could not save them. Each died at my feet, and I stood there helpless for all. If life is only filled with loss and sorrow, then what's the point?

I force my mouth shut, as it begs to open. My body works against me, and I fight not to breathe in the ocean around me. There's no one here to save me now. And I cannot find the desire to survive any longer. All my struggle, all my pain, has been for nothing. I have helped no one.

As I float here, tossed by the sea, the serving elementals I'd tried to help are being recaptured and certainly destined for the Outer. For all my help, I have only brought more hardship.

The stab of guilt fights the burning of my lungs for claim of my chest. If I let go now, I leave everyone to certain death. The serving elementals, Sorren, Cinis—my faction.

My mother's last request slams itself against my heart, demanding to be heard. She told me to lead the faction, as if she could see a future I can't. If I let go now, there will be no one to warn Cinis's people, and mine. And of all the lives I've lost, of all the mistakes I've made, this will not be one.

I fight to control my convulsing limbs, kicking my feet as the rest of my body thrashes against itself. The silence of the ocean now blares alarms in my ears. They ring so loud it's deafening. I must make it to land.

As my mouth opens to fill with water, I break the surface, and take in the damp salty air. My lungs sting as they expand, filling themselves with a greedy desperation I could not stop if I tried. I tread frantically, spinning around to search for sand. The shore is not far, only a short swim.

As another wave crashes against me, I swim with it, allowing it to carry me closer to the beach. I must be strategic with my breathing, taking in the precious bouts of air as they become available.

My body convulses in the cold water, and my lungs constrict. My arms and legs cramp, threatening to debilitate me and send me back to the depths, but I fight through it. I have endured pain and know this is only physical. In a sad way, pain has become such a constant for me, that I find comfort in the familiarity.

As the last wave pushes me to shore, I dig my trembling fingers into the sand, commanding it to roll and pull me onto the beach and away from the tide. My breathing becomes rapid as my chest seems to move up and down in time with my thundering heart.

I turn my head to the side, coughing out mouthfuls of seawater before collapsing onto the land.

The struggle to shore has exhausted my body, and my limbs refuse to cooperate in lifting me from the ground. Aether still buzzes through my veins, so I use it to command the sand to lift me. I harness my power and use it to wield my element. I must return to the city and free the others.

I mold the sand to form a throne beneath me, commanding it to carry me forward until I have recovered.

My people need me.

As raw elemental power surges through every cell of my body, I know I am strong.

I will not relent.

CHAPTER 40
SORREN

THE HYDROS ENCASE ME in a pool of water. This is entirely unnecessary. I used all my energy to send Kara off. There is no essence for me to wield now. I must wait for my body to replenish itself.

I turn my head to see Cinis completely encased in ice. And although there are four elementals on each of us, maintaining our bindings, four more stand at the ready, should we escape.

We will not escape. It is over.

We trail behind the massive group of serving elementals that are carted off with us. They were so close, only hours away from freedom.

As we approach the capitol building, I see the full extent of the damage. Most of the building lies in a heap of rubble, barely protruding from the water's surface. What remains of the structure seems highly unstable. They lead us through the entrance, anyway. They do not intend to keep us in the capitol.

The prisoner cells lie below the capitol, deep in the sea's heart, nestled against the single strip of land bordering our city. Of all that was destroyed, I know they stand still.

As Morgana's soldiers force the serving elementals down the narrow stairway to the cells, I cannot help but feel a stabbing guilt for letting them down. My soldiers also file into small cells awaiting punishment. What a deep and unsettling failure it is to know that because I could not succeed, those who believed in me must pay the ultimate price. I will go down in history as the Western Area's worst officer. I have dishonored each soldier of my brigade, failing those who stood with me, and betrayed those who stood against me.

Enforcers shove and secure the others into their cells as the guards take Cinis and me past them. As we pass the last row of cells, my stomach knots. This route is familiar. I know where we're headed. They are bringing us to the conditioning arena.

As our guards open the massive set of double doors, the stench of stale blood and the musk of sweat assaults my senses. My core clenches as they shackle me to the chains I'd spent so much time in before. This time I have a companion. They lock Cinis in a set of manacles on the other side of the arena to await conditioning.

I hear the heavy doors open once more and know the administrators of our punishment approach. I feel the blaze of his fire light beneath me before I even see his face. My tormentor has returned. The miserable pyro who doled out Malakai's bidding stands before me once again. I hear the clinking of Cinis's chains.

"Jarek?" Cinis looks at the pyro, squinting his eyes into focus, ensuring that what he sees is accurate. "Jarek," he says the name again, frantic in his urgency. "By Pyris, is that really you?"

I see the briefest twinge of grief flash across the torcher's face before he settles it back into an impassive glower. "No."

And although I know that to be his name, he denies it, never making eye contact with Cinis again.

Two enforcers come in to administer questioning. They want to know about our plans. They ask about what happened to Kara. We say nothing, glad to take their punishment, rather than betraying her and the others.

I know Cinis has affected Jarek. He takes his anger and anxiety out on me, raising the fire, licking at my core. He lashes out at me with a heated chain, delivering whips with careless abandon. With our refusal to respond to their questioning, there is little point for this session. He does not seek to rehabilitate or recondition. He only seeks to injure.

Across the arena, my comrade does not receive any leniencies. His aero enforcer fashions blocks of ice from his fists and pounds them against the pyro mercilessly. When the doors open again, the pounding stops. The conditioning enforcers halt and stand to attention. I can only assume Morgana is near.

People at our back clamber through the room as I hear metal drag across stone. They fashion something in the arena's corner I cannot see.

The hollow click of booted heels confirms my suspicions.

"Take them down and secure them to the chairs," she orders.

At her command, the administrators release us from our chains, dragging us to the station newly assembled in the corner.

They throw us into the chairs, strapping down our wrists and ankles. The guard handling me pushes my head against the headrest and pulls another strap across my forehead to secure me in place. I feel uneasy and claustrophobic in these new binds. Something about them is exponentially worse than the shackles hung from the ceiling at Malakai's order.

"Hurry, you idiots. We need to have this done before there are any distractions," she says to the enforcers.

The prime rounds us, holding two collars in her hands. At the sight of it, Cinis thrashes against his chair. I can tell she finds pleasure in his frantic display because she moves to him first. When she closes the collar around his neck, he lets out a throaty yell. She looks at him with a rueful smile. "There, right back where it should be."

She comes to me with an identical collar, bringing it to my throat. "Dear misguided Sorren. You sympathize so greatly with the Lower it is only fitting you share in their fate."

She snaps the collar around me, and I feel the bite of two needles dig into my veins. The pain catches me off guard as the hard metal presses against the burn wounds Cinis inflicted earlier and I suck in a breath at the shock of it.

Morgana turns to face the unit, and I am not sure whether she directs her comments at me or Cinis. "Your little girlfriend destroyed our maintenance room. But never bother, we have other means," she says, hooking the collars up to a piece of tech. "We simply needed to go back to the basics. It seems that our collars and serum had been tampered with."

She turns to look pointedly at Cinis. "Did you believe we had no other means? Do you believe you were the first to make these collars, or your cohorts the first to manufacture our serums?" She shakes her head, letting out a taunting chuckle. "You fools. We maintained our supplies long before you arrived, and we will continue to do so long after you are dead."

She looks at me. "And let me assure you. You *are* dead."

She programs the tech connected to our collars and I feel the vibration from the frequency it emits. A low hum comes from the machine right before the burn of the needle singes my skin. I grind my teeth as whatever serum she has flowing through the needle pours into my veins.

Something within the serum connects to me, burning with blatant familiarity. Whatever it is, feels like an ornate part of me that has just found its way back, filling an empty space within me I hadn't known existed.

My body's essence comes alive and floods each of my nerve endings in sharp, painful bursts. Worse than Jarek's burning chain, the aether blazes inside me. It connects with something in the serum and pulls. My heart races as raw essence swirls around me, ripping me apart from the inside out.

"What in the gods?" Morgana gasps as a thick layer of ice covers me and my restraints.

I feel my element spread beyond me. Aether hangs in the surrounding space. Wispy tendrils of coppery gold beg me to reach out and grasp them. As I lift my arm through the ice, the restraint binding me shatters in a brittle, frozen mess.

When I touch the aether, it rushes into me in an agonizing sweep, unlocking something within my core that consumes my body in blaring white pain. I cry out, a sound so guttural that Morgana races to the tech, scrambling to shut it off.

The door slams open behind us and I hear the panting of someone who runs to the prime.

"You must stop," he says between heaving breaths. "*He* is here," the man sputters.

Morgana frantically continues to fumble with the tech, right as the room's temperature drops to a dangerous low. I glance over at the pyro across from me. Ice creeps along the floor and crawls up the machines at our sides. Morgana shrinks back as a wickedly ethereal voice addresses her.

"What is the meaning of this?"

The voice is not of this world. It does not hold the deep vibrato of a man's tone. This voice shrieks and whispers. It sounds like ice and has a harsh edge to it that leaves me anxious.

Morgana bows. "My Lord, I was only harvesting their essence. Preparing it for *you*." Her voice is shaky and timid. I can tell the creature draws near because he brings an intense cold with him.

The prime shrinks back. "The pyro. He's tampered with the collars. He aimed to steal a transport ship and take away the serving elementals. The commander was his accomplice." Her voice falters with the last part.

The creature's intense cold moved directly behind me. "What happened here?"

Morgana stutters, "I—I don't know. We performed everything according to protocol. Something happened when we injected the serum. I've never seen this be . . . before." Her words break apart as she tries to control her shivering.

"Interesting," the creature says.

She moves to Cinis, gesturing to his black hands. "This one also displays signs of the immortal."

I do not move my head, but peer through the corner of my eyes to see black has crept up past Cinis's wrists, completely covering his hands.

The creature moves forward, blocking my vision, bending over to examine his hands. My breath hitches at the sight of him. He is not of this world. His back is turned to me as he faces Cinis, but I see the aged blue gray of his skin. Ice coats his shoulders and arms. I know immediately what he is.

Before me stands an immortal. My father was right. I thought I recognized the signs in Cinis but seeing an immortal only feet away from me rocks everything I do and don't believe.

With the pass of his hand, he freezes the strap of Cinis's wrists with no noticeable effort until it is frigid and breaks apart as he lifts the pyro's hand. Cinis lets out a grunt at the intense cold and I send a silent prayer to Aelious that he can hold on a bit longer. The creature brings his hand up to examine it.

"Fascinating," he breathes, "tell me how you did it."

Cinis shakes his head against the strap holding him in place. "I don't know what you're talking about."

"I'm talking about the essence you stole from me." The creature talks in riddles I struggle to decipher.

He addresses Morgana. "And where is the woman? Where is her essence?"

Morgana bends at the waist, bowing her head down.

"She got away, My Lord. She overpowered us and escaped. But we—" The prime's eyes widen in terror as ice scrawls up her chest toward her chin.

"*Excuses*. Find her and bring her to me."

My heart thumps against my chest. They speak of Kara. I pray she's somewhere far from here. I fear that for all my efforts, it may not be enough.

The creature releases his invisible hold on the prime and she collapses, clawing the ice from her chest.

"Secure them in a cell until I am ready to take my leave." He looks down at the prime on the floor.

"But My Lord, I have not yet siphoned them."

His shrieking voice booms. "And you shall not!" She cowers at his words. "You had your chance, and you failed. I will take them to the Outer with me. Now, do as I say and secure them in their cells."

I strain my head to look at him, thinking he may turn, but all I see is his back as he leaves the room covered in a blanket of frost.

With the creature gone, Morgana slowly rises from the floor, dusting herself off, as if to maintain some semblance of dignity. She sends a command over her comm unit for our escort.

Soldiers unlock Cinis and me from the chairs we are bound to, removing our collars and restraints. Again, four aeros attend him and four hydros are on me. As they lift me from the chair, they take me by the arms, dragging me toward the door. More soldiers wait outside to escort us. Kai heads the small unit.

My jaw slackens at the sight of my friend. My body releases a tension I didn't know it held. I send praise to Aelious for sparing him. My deepest fear was that Kai would not make it out of the rubble. That I had killed my friend. But he stands before me like a ghost, and I have never been so grateful.

Once I push past the initial shock of seeing him here in front of me, I inspect him, wincing at the extent of his injuries. A bandage reaches from his shoulder to wrist. Crusted blood lines his face and neck, while bruises of varying colors decorate his skin.

I did this.

He commands the guards forward. He turns to lead them, and I notice he limps as he moves. Only a short time ago, our situation would have seemed impossible. Laughable, that in just a few months I would be here, a traitor and a failure. How far I have fallen.

The man I've called brother now leads me to my cell where I will await death. His march is slow and his limp obvious. This is my doing. I have injured him and it's just one more thing to hate myself for.

CHAPTER 41
KARA

I RIDE THE SAND and stones, commanding them to propel me forward to the part of the wall closest to the hangar. Approaching, I command the sand to gently set me on my feet, testing my weary legs before applying my full weight to them. As I step away from the platform that has held me up, I press my palms against the stone wall, creating a large opening that I plan to use again later. Stepping through it, the city is empty. It's been evacuated of the citizens who walk it from day to day, with only armed guards patrolling the streets and canals. No doubt a result of today's upheaval.

I slip into the frigid water. Although I'd rather never submerge myself again, I have little choice. With no foliage to hide behind, this will be much easier to go unnoticed. I remain cognizant of the hydros whose element I'm immersing myself into. I stay close to the buildings, trying to swim in their shadows. It's much quicker to cut across the canals rather than trying to follow the walkways. I must be swift. I need to get to the capitol building, but I must go to the hangar first.

Listening for patrollers, I creep into the full metal garage. It is quiet, a stark contrast to the war zone it was such a short time ago. The only two individuals left in the empty building are the Admiral and my mother.

They lay only feet apart, each long taken to their final rest. I could spit on the man who murdered both of my parents but know he does not even deserve that from me. Instead, I go to my mom, stooping to lift her head and run my fingers through the thick chestnut waves. It is something she'd always done that brought me comfort, and although I know I cannot comfort her, I feel a strange obligation to try.

I lay her head back down on the concrete floor, patting her to let her know I will be back, that I won't abandon her. Not like I did my father.

I move to the transporters, checking the one we'd prepared for our journey. It sits untouched, still ready to carry my people to safety. There is still hope to get them to freedom. I move swiftly to the dozens of other aircraft in the hangar. I know if we want the slightest chance at escape, I must disable anything that might aid the Upper in reaching us.

We must work quickly to escape Central City and reach this Smithing Faction. Every minute we have to warn and prepare for the inevitable attack will be precious. I work through the power sources on each aircraft, seeking the natural metal that lies within the wires. I manipulate the copper and nickel until they are non-functional, bending and breaking them beyond repair. By the time I reach the last one, I've already lost too much time.

I go back to my mother, who is still on the floor. Gently lifting her up, I stagger beneath the added weight. Draping her over my shoulder, I leave the hanger and return to the beach. Though pulling her body through the water is significantly easier than carrying her, I still struggle to complete my journey. I wrap a vine around her body to tow her behind me as I swim, pushing through the pain until I make it to land.

Once I reach the wall lining the beach, I fall onto the sand, using it to help carry us the rest of the way. Reached a suitable burial place, I position my mother on the side of me and I dig my hands into the land, searching for any plant matter I can use as a burial wrap.

I must work quickly. There are hundreds of others counting on me to break them free, but I cannot neglect this. Although I no longer hold faith in Gaia, my mother did. Her soul longs for a proper burial. While I do not honor my deity, Mom will not find rest unless she is reunited with hers.

When my essence grabs hold to the remnants of a seedling buried deep below the sand, I pull it to the surface. Long strands of seaweed spring forth and I grimace at the subpar burial wrap.

I will it to grow taller and wider, hoping that will help the material adequately cover my mother. With great care, I wrap every inch of her limp body, smoothing the damp seaweed over itself, layer after layer until she is thickly and tightly bound. I graze my hand along the material to smooth the layers in a motion that becomes methodical and almost therapeutic.

Now staring out at the vast oceanscape, barren of any vegetation, I wonder if my mother's spirit can produce beautiful greenery where there is none. She deserves to rest eternally in a lush forest amongst the trees and shrubs she would thrive in, but here is the best I can do.

I look at my mother's tightly wrapped body for the last time, lean on to her, gripping her in my arms. I'm not ready to let go. I'm not ready to do this without her. All the mistakes I've made, all the opportunities I've missed, weigh heavily on me now.

There is so much I have yet to learn from her. So much I could have learned while I sought to run. It was time wasted when I did not know there would be so little time left.

I pull a hand away from her to bury it in the sand, moving the land beneath her body. I do not trust Gaia to take back my mother's essence and redistribute it to the land we wield. Why would she bother with a dead elemental when she did nothing for the living? But I let the land swallow my mother anyway, because I cannot bear the thought of her simply laying atop it.

My heart aches at the thought this may be it, and just as I am not ready to part with Zimara Nadir, neither should the land. So, I let the sand swallow her up, burying her deep within, so her body does not surface and get taken by the tide. I sink her as deep as my reach can go and secure her in the element she so masterfully wielded.

When my mother is gone and the only thing that remains of her is a plot of upturned sand, I stand and walk away. My people need me, and unlike Gaia, I cannot forsake them.

I use the sand to propel myself forward, surfing it like a wave. I follow the wall along the perimeter of Central City until I reach the capitol. The back wing of the capitol sits against a rocky plot of land. It's the only part not submerged in water, and I know that's where the prisoner cells are located. I remember my first meeting with Sorren there. The walls of his confinement were dirt and rock buried somewhere deep below sea level. When I find the precise spot, I stop.

The essence that flows through me is powerful. I tap into a strength I have never known, sinking my feet into the ground below, commanding it to consume me. I've watched my mother pass through land so often, but I've never actually tried myself.

I call on that power now, commanding the land to open and swallow me up. To welcome me into its core and allow me to move through it. As the ground swallows me inch by inch, I take a deep breath, allowing it to cover my face.

When I'm deep within the soil filled with rocks and sand, I realize I did not need to take in the additional air. The soil breathes with me, feeding its oxygen to me, and I move through it as if it is an extension of the ocean, fluid and forgiving. I do not bother to open my eyes. I don't need them to see. One with the soil, I can sense everything around me.

Searching for the prison cells, I seek a disturbance in the natural form of the island. When I find it, I use all my concentration to push through. A layer of stone lines the wall of the holding area. I begin with my hand.

Maneuvering through the rock is not as effortless as the soil was. The rock is less forgiving. My movements are more confined, but I can still push through. I stretch my hand out until I feel the wide-open air just beyond the stone. When it has successfully passed, I push my shoulder, then head through.

The corridor I enter is empty, though the shouts and rumblings of the many prisoners it holds fills the space. I push through without care to do so quietly. No one can hear my movement above the upheaval. I shift the rock and dirt to allow the rest of me to pass before neatly securing it back in place.

I know where they will keep Cinis and Sorren. He will be in the same place he was the first time we met in Central City. The solitary cells. They're blocked off in the corridor below everyone else. They are separate and heavily guarded.

When I reach the corridor adjacent to where they keep Sorren and Cinis, I sink into the stone wall separating us. This stone is quieter than the grumbling wall I'd come through to enter the holding space. It is a smoother, more refined variety than what lined the area's exterior. Still, it rumbles and chips, opening for me, before allowing me to pass. I do not go all the way through, stopping midway to wait. I hear the muffled sounds of the guard speaking and know I found the right place when one calls Sorren's name.

Using my index finger and thumb, I push open a crack in the stone that allows me to survey the room. I let out a soft breath when I see Cinis and Sorren there—*alive*—relieved I have the right cell, and they are still okay. Ten guards in total stand watching the two, and I pluck them off one by one, starting with those closest to the wall.

A hydro stands within reach of me. I quickly push my hands through the stone to wrap around him, pulling him back into the wall, keeping my hand over his mouth as the rock moves and shifts around us. Grabbing for another, I quickly pull him in as well while the stone creaks and crumbles around. I can hear the muffled sounds of the guards calling to each other.

"What was that?"

I move quickly, picking off more as they focus on the shaking and shifting stone around them.

"What in the hells is this?" one says.

"Must be a tremor. Hold on." They are so focused on the quaking room that they still have not realized so many of them have gone missing. I pull in another and another before they even understand what's happening.

"Where in four bloody hells is Tar?" one says.

By now, I've pulled six guards into the stone. They stand beside me, petrified and defenseless. I should feel pity for the poor souls that will soon suffocate inside the crushing elemental device. But I cannot summon the emotion. This is war, and I have already lost too much to pity anyone.

"What in the hells is going on?" The voice moves closer to the wall, a hand scratching at it. It's gained their attention and I won't be able to pull in anymore from here. I allow myself to sink down into the soil of the island below, drifting forward, treading only a shallow distance beneath the floor surface. I look up again to peek through the stone. The guards all face the wall as they hear the muffled grunts of their trapped comrades.

I reach my hands through the floor, grabbing the ankles of an unsuspecting guard. When I pull her down, she is silent, save for the loud rumble of the stone giving way to swallow her body.

When I grab the next guard, he yelps, and I know I must be quick. I no longer worry about stealth as I reach up to grab the next. Pulling him through, the other runs and I propel myself from the ground.

He trips over himself when he sees me shoot from the stone. His wide-open eyes match his hung jaw to contort his face in an expression of pure horror. As he scrambles for the stairs, I extend a vine to wrap around his torso and mouth, pulling him back to me. When he slams against my chest, I wrap my arms around him and push him down into the ground with me. When the land has swallowed us up, I push away from him and rise once again through the stone floor. This time, the room is empty.

I make it to Sorren's cell first, knowing he can tell me how to free him and Cinis. When I approach the bars, he meets me with urgency. Though his eyes are wide like the guards', they don't look at me in horror. "What was that?"

"I've picked up a few tricks since we last spoke," I say, waving him off. Unable to continue, because it reminds me that the last words he spoke to me were, *I love you.*

His eyes soften, and he lifts his hand between the bars to my face. He gently brushes a smudge of loose dirt from my cheek. I should slap his hand away. Instead, I relish the cool soothing of it.

"Kara," he whispers so gently that the sound threatens to break me. "Why'd you come back? You should have run."

"I'm not running anymore." I've spent too much time running, and it's done me no good. We are who we are, and any time we spend running from that is a waste. My people need me, and I will fight for them with everything I have.

His eyes soften, worry throwing a deep crease in his brow. "You shouldn't have come here."

"I came back to save your sorry ass. We need your help and your soldiers. This doesn't mean I don't still hate you." Although I try, my words hold no heat.

"Of course not." He shakes his head. The ghost of a smile turning his lips tells me he does not believe the lie any more than I mean it. And although I may not hate him, I can never forgive what he's done.

Chapter 42
Sorren

Even as she stands before me, I can't believe it. I put my hands on top of hers just to make sure she's real. To convince myself she is not some sort of delusion brought on by too much blood loss, heat, or exhaustion.

"How do I get the cells open?" she says.

"I need a guard's comm unit." I point to my arm to demonstrate.

She kneels to the ground and sticks her hand past the stone as if she's reaching for loose dirt. I've seen nothing like it. A Level Three can easily pass through soil—but to pass through stone with the same ease is unheard of. Still, I watched her pull guard after guard into the immovable material, wielding it as if it were only mud.

She sticks her hand in so deep that her cheek presses against the floor. When she pulls up a hand, I grimace, seeing it is attached to a still very much alive body beneath the floor's surface. A shiver runs down my back as I wonder how long they will survive trapped down there. She pulls the limb over, handing it to me as if it is free and unattached to my former comrade.

"I need his other hand to work the comm."

She reaches back into the ground to pull up the other hand with all the ease of plucking turnips. Once I have both hands, I use the guard's fingers to type in the commands of his comm unit. Gripping his wrist, I feel the flutter of a faint pulse, and know he will not last much longer. A sliver of guilt wiggles its way into my psyche. Although they act as my captors now, we served the same agenda just a short while ago.

With a little programming, Cinis's and my cell doors pop open. When I'm free, the only thing I want to do is run to Kara and wrap her in my arms, but I dare not approach. No number of extenuating circumstances can change what has happened. Nothing will alter what I've done. She takes a long look at me, then turns to go toward Cinis's cell.

"Kara, you're okay." He rushes to her, and when his arms fold around her in a deep embrace—the way mine long to—I know they are more than just acquaintances. It stirs a turbine of jealousy in my core. One that has no right to be there in the first place. I do not deserve her and should stop no one from giving her affection. Still, I cannot stand the way his limbs fold around her, almost possessive of what my heart has already claimed.

"*Eh em.*" I clear my throat, shamelessly breaking up the too-intimate reunion. "We must move fast if we want to free the others."

Whatever that *thing* was, plans on taking us to the Outer. We need to get my soldiers and the other elementals out before that happens.

Kara quickly breaks from the embrace. Awkwardly avoiding eye contact with the both of us, she divulges her plan.

"If we can get the elementals out of their cells, I can open a tunnel to the beach. From there, we can take them to the transport ship."

"Is it still intact?" I ask.

"Yes, I checked before coming here. It's still prepared for the journey."

My excitement quickly dies as I realize, "I cannot power it on. They have stripped my comm unit of all its privileges." I raise my arm, showing her the embedded tech that is only good for tracking me now.

Cinis speaks up. "I can power it." He looks down at Kara. "Just like my glider back home. My essence is stronger. I can do it."

I remember the lightning he wielded so effortlessly. The plan is shaky, but it's all we have for now.

We climb the stairs, creeping into the corridor that holds my soldiers and the other elementals. We are stealthy, and stalk in silence as we move along the walls of the prison. Just as we make it into their cellblock, a group of guards walk past. Before they see us, Kara grabs Cinis and me, pushing the three of us into the stone.

I shudder at how wrong it feels to be wrapped in rock. Not a piece of my body can move. The rough edges scratch at every inch of my skin, and I can barely breathe through the slightly porous material. I have never been claustrophobic but am manic for escape now and pray it comes quickly.

When she pushes us back out from the rock, chills run over my skin and send an involuntary shiver along my body, as if my limbs want to prove they are free. I feel a pang of sympathy for the guards that are still trapped in the stone. I remind myself they've made their choice and they must live and die with it, just as we will, should this plan fail.

Once we've made it into the cellblock, we quickly survey the room. I count the guards. Only a few dozen. I must free my soldiers to help protect the elementals who can no longer wield their element. With my soldiers' aid, we should move out of the prison with no problem. I nod to Cinis and Kara, signaling them to move forward. We must strike while we can still catch our opponents off guard.

They take my signal and charge forward. Cinis sets ablaze everything he touches, and Kara grasps at the only remnant of her element abundantly available. Throwing stones from the wall, she propels them at the guards. She ropes her vines to corral them into Cinis's flames. As the two enact their mayhem, I grab hold of the nearest enforcer. He is a hydro and I quickly pull the air from his lungs until he passes out. I drag him to the cell that holds my soldiers, forming an air pocket to serve as a force field between me and the attacking elementals. I use the unconscious guard's comm unit to unlock their cell and the elementals within pour out. They run straight into combat like the soldiers they are.

Pride swells in my chest as I watch how many of them have joined in this fight. Even more of my brigade's soldiers joined Ciel's unit in defending us at the hangar. I am so grateful that I can offer them a chance at freedom now. That this decision may not have cost them their lives.

Though they are still few, their skill more than makes up for it. To have even one of my soldiers choose to stand by me—choose the path of righteousness over the path of duty—is more than I could ask for. But here before me, hundreds fight, risking their lives to right the wrongs we unwittingly committed.

Once they succeed in holding back the guards, I call Kara. "Open the tunnel. Hurry, I will release the others."

Cinis aids my soldiers in holding off the guards as I move to the captive's cells, opening the bars and releasing them. I can tell the captive warriors apart from the civilians. Although they can no longer wield their elements completely, they rush into battle regardless. The one they call Emrick runs straight into combat, headfirst, no weapon to wield except for a large rock clenched in his fist.

Kara stands at the north wall, pushing through it. From it pours sand and mud—rock and soil. I usher the captives through, pushing them to follow her. Hundreds of Lower elementals file through the tight tunnel leading to their freedom. Several of my soldiers work to organize the evacuation, keeping it orderly and calm to avoid a stampede. I hear the storming footsteps at the top of the stairwell and know the guards have called for backup.

We cannot let them down here. They cannot follow the captives through the tunnel. As the soldiers have all but defeated our opponents, I command them to follow the other elementals through the tunnel.

"Cinis, we must block the stairwell." It's clear we're in accord. He moves to the mouth of the stairwell, wielding the largest fireball I've ever seen.

"Gas me up!" he yells, and I gather an equally sizable air pocket, again, separating all but the oxygen from it. We push our elements to the top of the stairwell, and when they meet at the chamber entrance, they explode. The reaction sends a world-shattering tremor through the entire space, so intense we're knocked back by the force of it.

Water pools into the prison as the submerged part of the building lies exposed. I wield the wind to push the water back, forming a barrier between my soldiers and the rushing current. Though the aether feels different in my grasp—stronger, more intense—it's not enough to deter the flood. My hydro soldiers stand with me, and together affectively dam the water, but I cannot ask them to remain by my side.

As the guards are all but defeated, I command the last of my soldiers to move through the tunnel, my last effort to get them to safety. Cinis takes care of the remaining enforcers while I struggle to push back the flood alone.

When the last of my soldiers crawl through the tunnel, I finish destroying the prison's entrance.

"Go now. I'll hold the water to keep it from flooding the tunnel," I tell Cinis.

"What about you?" he says.

"Don't worry about me. Now, go!"

He climbs through the wall's opening as I hold back the last surge of water. I use more power than I should possess to break down the remaining barriers of the prison entrance. With the area all but destroyed, no one will follow us now. Water continues to rise as I race to the tunnel. Kara has already sealed it. She had to.

Water already reaches my chest and would have flooded the tunnel, endangering all those who escaped through it. I let out a deep breath, satisfied that I have succeeded in this one thing. Kara and the others are on their way to safety. The captives have the protection of my soldiers and the faction warriors, who are commanded by Ciel and Cinis. They are all led by Kara, who I know will usher them to victory. Though this does not begin to correct my wrongs, it is enough for me to die content.

I lean against the wall as the water rises past my chin.

A hand wraps itself around my waist and pulls me through the mud barrier. Passing through the dirt is slimy and suffocating. When we fall through it, I land in the open space of the tunnel. I look back to see Kara smiling down at me.

"I couldn't very well leave you behind, could I?" And especially now, her smile is the most beautiful thing I've ever seen.

CHAPTER 43
KARA

SORREN LOOKS UP AT me, caked in mud and dumbfounded. I can hardly believe he thought I'd leave him behind. There are already so many elementals I'm leaving in Central City. The thought alone is disheartening, but I must take who I can and come back for the rest. Thousands of my people will suffer inside these city walls until I can make it back to the Lower for help.

"Come on, we have to hurry. The others are all almost through the tunnel." More than half of everyone who's escaped has already made it to the beach. I race ahead, gesturing for him to follow. It's easy for me to climb through the tunnel of my making, but behind me, Sorren is struggling to sludge through the soft mud. I move to the side, allowing him to go ahead of me, filling the tunnel as we move through it to ensure no one can follow.

As the first rays of sunlight stream through the tunnel opening, Sorren surges forward, stumbling through. I follow him and emerge to see hundreds of elementals scattered on the beach. Our elementals.

Pride surges through me as we are so close. I can almost taste victory; I can almost see home. For the first time, I allow myself to entertain the thought that we may make it out of this alive. That we may get all these people to freedom—that all will not have been in vain. I rush forward, letting Sorren's soldiers and mine know where we're headed.

"Stay along this wall. There's an opening near here. Pass through it and it'll take us to the hangar."

The crowd continues forward. Moving so many people is slow, but we're making good time.

As we move on, the wall opening comes into view and we pick up our speed. We are so close. The wind on the beach whips so forcefully, I have to look back at Sorren to make sure he does not wield it. When I see his face is just as baffled as mine, I panic. The temperature drops, and a sinking feeling settles in the pit of my stomach. There's something familiar about this. I scan the beach, looking for *him*.

When my eyes find what they seek, my heart plummets. Coming from behind us, over the city wall, is the creature from before. He rides the air just as I surfed the sand. I race to Emrick.

"Get them through the wall and into the hangar. Load them onto the transport ship so that when we come, you are ready."

"What is that thing?" he says.

"I'll explain later. There's no time for that now. Get them onto the transporter." I drill the last words into him so that he does not even dream of deterring from them. He cannot stay behind to help me, Cinis, or Sorren. Emrick must get our people to safety.

Sorren commands the same of his soldiers and Admiral Ciel. To protect the Lower elementals who cannot wield, to get them to safety, and destroy anyone who gets in their way. He pulls a few to stay behind with us and I'm grateful for it. I know Cinis and my powers are greatly enhanced, but this creature wields his element like nothing I've ever seen before.

As the monster moves in closer to us, I whip the sand, commanding it to propel the escaping elementals toward the wall. It pushes them in the most unceremonious way, and they fall, scrambling at the opening I'd created only hours prior.

I let out a breath as they escape through it. Turning, I stand with Cinis, Sorren, and his soldiers to face the immortal.

An electrifying energy buzzes through my fingertips. My essence pushes at me, trying to force its way out in anticipation of the fight. As the creature approaches, debilitating cold sweeps over us. It overtakes me faster than I can fight it, as a blanket of ice covers everything. The cold is so intense, time seems to stand still.

I look around and feel my eyes widen at the pure shock of it. Everything stands at attention. No birds fly across the sky. Rushing waves halt where they crest, frozen in rigid arcs. The soldiers at Cinis's back stand petrified in the last movement they've made, stuck within an encasement of ice. The only things free to move are Sorren, Cinis, and me.

As the immortal creature descends toward us, his iced-over eyes lock on Sorren. The intensity of the wind that swirls around him whips my hair back and forth but does nothing to the stilled soldiers flanking us.

The creature approaches Sorren, and I brace myself to defend him. He looks down, studying the commander. Long, silent moments pass before the shrill of the creature's voice rings out to address Sorren.

"Son," he says, and the look on Sorren's face changes from defensive to pure shock. He searches the creature, his eyes widening as he finds what he seeks. His mouth opens then closes, unsure of the word he's about to release. When his shaky voice calls to the monster, I am left speechless.

"Father?"

CHAPTER 44
SORREN

THERE ARE LITTLE TO no remnants of the man who was once my father. His skin is a pale blue, bordering on gray. It is dry and cracked, aging him far beyond his years. The raven hue of his hair is completely gone, bleached as white as the once-gray irises of his eyes. He does not hold the deep and authoritative voice my father commanded so many with. This creature shrieks and shrills. Ice builds along the edges of his form, covering random parts of his body in the thick frozen crystals. And I shudder at the fact that he finally looks as frigid as he used to be.

Although nothing of the creature is familiar, I know it is him all the same.

"Father, I thought you were dead." I cannot hide the hurt in my tone, although I'm ashamed of it and know the outward display of weakness will disappoint him.

"I did die. And now, I will never die again." The cryptic message is infuriating in its ambiguity.

"What happened? How did you become *this*?" I gesture to him, and he steps closer, his tone growing casual.

"I achieved immortality, son, by taking what I desired and letting no one stand in my way. I built this region from the ground up. All my work—my studies—my sacrifice, for this."

"You stole their essence. I read your files," I say, unable to conceal the venom in my voice. But rather than an outward denial or the decency of feigning shock, my father shrugs, unfazed—unapologetic.

"It was necessary. That is how we achieve and maintain our immortality."

He speaks in plurals, and it takes me back. "We?" The lines of his eyebrows rise as he seems surprised by my question.

"Yes. I, along with the other immortals, the guardians of the Outer. I had hoped you would heed all those teachings afforded to you in your youth. I see now that it truly was a waste."

My father was obsessed with the immortals. Growing up, he constantly drilled me on facts about them, never missing an opportunity to teach me more. I always thought them to be silly children's stories as real as the ghouls that go bump in the night.

"Besides, without the Lower elementals' minor sacrifice, we could not have made so much progress."

Kara practically growls behind me as I catch sight of a flame tipping from Cinis's fingers.

My father seems unfazed as he continues. "I had always hoped you would carry on my work, son. There is still time. There is so much we can still do."

My throat tightens. I thought my father to be dead. Having him stand here in front of me now is mind-boggling.

I'm conflicted about everything I want to say. So much time has passed, so much has happened. So much has changed. I tussle between wanting to tell him all I have accomplished in my career and in my life—and in wanting to hate him for all that he's done, all that I have seen.

He moves to stand directly in front of me, lifting his hand to the crown of my head. "All this time, I thought you'd been a defect. That you'd rejected your mother's blood. If I'd only known your true nature, simply needed to be activated . . ." He murmurs, looking at something in my hair, no longer speaking to me.

I move from him, and crouch to peer at my reflection on the iced over ground. A bold white streak runs through my jet-black hair. I pull a strand out, sure that the reflection plays a trick on me. When I pull out strings of white coated in mud from the tunnel, I don't know what to make of it.

"Come with me, son." He uses that word like an honorific, saying it more in this brief conversation than I'd heard him say over several years. He hooks me on to it, reeling me in. "Immortal blood runs through you. I can help you wield it."

"But how?" I say, unable to believe what he says is true. Even as denial rushes through my thoughts, the bold caress of an aether stronger than I've ever felt strokes my palms.

"Ah, there is so much for me to finally tell you. I can explain everything. The things that happened in the past, our plans for the future. I can tell you about your mother." He dangles the last bet in front of me. Tempting me to bite. "I always hoped that after you ruled the Unified Regions, you would join me in immortality in the Outer."

The air in my lungs escapes me as I struggle to process what my father proposes. A chance to rule by his side. A new opportunity for redemption; the chance for answers to questions I'd never dared ask. The real possibility that I will make my father proud. That I will live my destiny in upholding his legacy as a proper son should.

"There is still so much for me to teach you, all of you." He looks past me to Cinis and Kara. "I can teach you all to wield your immortal powers. Come with me to the Outer and you will live like gods. The elementals will serve you just as you have served the deities you honor."

My mind reels at how quickly this is all happening. My father, back from the dead, stands in front of me, offering me the thing I've craved most my entire life.

I look back at Kara as he extends his offer. Her eyes narrow and I know her answer before my own.

CHAPTER 45

KARA

I LISTEN TO THE creature's words and am appalled. The casualness of his tone as he talks about stealing my people's essence is sickening. When he offers to take the three of us with him to the Outer, I want to rip out his tongue so that it is the last offer he ever makes.

Sorren looks back at me, the thick white streak of hair showing a sharp contrast to the black strands that fall around his face. I didn't notice it in the tunnel, where it was dark, and mud covered him. Now it registers as a clear sign of immortality, just as Cinis's and mine.

I can tell he is completely and utterly lost. He seemed so boyish standing before his father, eyes wide and jaw slack. It is only now that I see how young he truly is. The weight of his station and the decisions he must make typically age him. The stony expression that remains fixed on his face makes him look old beyond his years.

Right now, he looks young and unsure and my heart aches for him, knowing how deeply he wants to please his father. I think back to all the late-night conversations with him, lamenting over the missed opportunity to live up to Nero's expectations. I remember how completely he longed for the man's approval.

That's why I must act. I cannot trust Sorren to deny his father. I cannot trust him to aid us in stopping Nero.

Cinis moves in the corner of my vision. The furrow of his brow and intensity of his eyes tells me he feels the same. He gives a pointed stare to the ground, then back at me, and I know what we must do.

I quickly drop to the ground, slamming my fist through the ice and into the sand with all my weight. It sends a colossal tremor running through the beach, splitting the land open, pulling the ice and sand into its expanse. We scramble away as the sand slips away beneath us. Cinis draws lava from the opening, sending it into an efflux that shoots straight up, and the creature knows we mean to attack.

The wind around us swirls so swiftly that it takes all our effort to stay put. As the molten lava bubbles to the surface, Cinis surges it forward to cover the immortal. His shrieks pierce our ears as the creature cries out, burning under the magma. When Nero hardens it with a freeze, Cinis pulls lightning from the sky as easily as plucking flowers from a vine. When it strikes the sand, it creates large disks of natural glass. They are similar to the orbises Cinis gifted me, circular blades made only in the Smithing Faction. I wrap my vines around the weapons and wield them just as he taught me all those months ago.

I slice at the immortal who cripples me with an intense cold. As my blades cut through the immortal's skin, they come away clean. No blood pours from his wounds; they just gape open before filling with ice.

Cinis moves back to the break in the ground, erecting more lava from the land. I swing another glass blade at the immortal, but he simply freezes it and allows it to shatter upon impact. Sorren stands in the middle of it all, his face crumpled in a tortured grimace, and I realize I may have put too much faith in him.

Suddenly he moves to the lava that Cinis pulls. He throws his element into it, freezing the magma until it is hardened stone. The rock they create is fertile, and I wield it with ease. The immortal is stronger than anything I've ever come across, but so am I.

I allow my immortal essence to overtake my body. The rush of it pushes through my cells and ignites every part of me until I am bursting from the seams with it. When I pour my essence into the lava rock, it buzzes with the life of my aether, growing and compounding on itself. The rock grows more than a dozen feet in the air, unfolding from itself. I suck in a breath as I can see two arms and two legs form from the solidified magma I wield.

When it finally unfurls, standing at its total height, I see what I have created. It is a monster, and it waits for my command. The immortal sends shards of ice aimed at Cinis. I pull the rock monster in front of him, protecting Cinis from the blows. When I push my creation forward, I command it to swing, knocking over the immortal.

Cinis throws more lava to coat Sorren's father as I swing my fists in time with the monster's, directing him to pummel the immortal. Sorren controls the wind that his father wields. Although he was an accomplished wielder before, his abilities are stronger now. He slows Nero's squall enough for us to continue our attack.

The immortal covers Cinis in a thick case of ice, then sets his sight on me. He envelops my rock monster in a pocket of air, pushing him back several feet. His hands lift, wielding the surrounding air, but before he can attack me, Sorren plunges an icicle into his neck.

Nero's eyes narrow with a demonic rage as he rolls around to grab Sorren by the collar, lifting him above his head.

"You fool. You think to use my own element against me?" With his other hand, he pulls the icicle lodged in his jugular. No blood escapes him. There is only a gaping hole.

"You imbecile. You seek to kill an immortal?" His father mocks him.

As Sorren looks past, he says, "No, just to distract you."

Cinis runs at Nero, massive flames in hand, engulfing the immortal in his element. He drops Sorren as he hurries to extinguish the flames. I send my rock monster charging forward, and with a blow to his abdomen, the immortal flies back several feet. Cinis covers him in molten lava once again as Sorren removes the air from his father's vicinity.

Still, the immortal breaks his bindings, sending a freeze that sweeps across the beach again, caging us all in ice. As we wiggle from our encasements only seconds from release, the immortal turns on us, focusing on Sorren.

"You have always brought me disappointment. But today you have earned my hatred."

As Cinis and I break from our ice bindings, the immortal lifts himself into the sky and flees, soaring through the air like a bird of prey.

Sorren watches him as he disappears into the distance, more broken than on the days I found him hanging in the conditioning arena. I should go to him, but I'm afraid now isn't the time. As I release the aether that controlled my rock monster, it crumbles into a pile on the ground. Back into the magma rock from which it came.

Once the immortal is gone, the sea waves melt and begin to crest again, the tide creeping across the shore. I look back and see the soldiers who stood with us wiggling in their petrified state until they can move fully.

Sorren addresses his soldiers, finally breaking the silence brought on by his father's last words. "We must get to the hangar. The elementals should all be onboard, and we have no time to waste. We must leave immediately." Then he walks toward the opening in the wall.

We race to the hangar, the last leg of our journey, before we are finally free from this hellish place.

Once we approach the transport, we enter to find our elementals are not alone.

CHAPTER 46
SORREN

W E OPEN THE DOOR of the hangar, walking into total chaos. Hundreds of elementals scatter about. There are a handful of Upper enforcers trying to stop the captives from boarding the ship. I recognize that the enforcers only mean to hold them off. I know a larger group follows close behind and we only have precious moments to escape before facing a full siege.

My father's last words still ring fresh in my ears. I'm a traitor.

I am many things, but the title that will benefit me most is Commander. Surveying the hangar, I assess our situation. Picking out the Upper guards, I evaluate how many and which of my soldiers it'll take to hold them off. I recognize the attacking soldiers. They are from Kai's unit, and I know he is not far behind.

Amongst the mayhem, I see the terra they call Emrick. He does his best to load the elementals into the transporter, but they're frantic among the fighting.

I call to Kara. "Get the elementals on the ship. We'll handle the guards."

She snaps into action. She will be the best to get them calm and ordered. With her mother gone, she is their leader, and although

371

they may not remember yet, some things are simply instinctual. She was born to lead her people. They know it just as well as I.

Cinis has already covered himself in flames, aiming an attack at the nearest group of Upper guards. "Cinis, start the transporter. We have no time to waste. We must get out of here."

He takes a tentative look at the group around, contemplating whether he trusts me to take care of the guards single handedly. He must have decided in my favor because he hurries up the transport and onto the ship. There are only a few Upper enforcers left in the hangar and my soldiers are quickly overpowering them.

I know the guards are not who we must beat. Time itself is what we fight. I call my top air wielders to flank my sides and send the rest of my soldiers into the transport.

When Kara's finished loading the elementals, she comes back out to stand on the transport deck, backing me up.

"Stay there and hold," I call to her.

The remaining aeros flank my sides, and together we push our essence to form a large air pocket that we use to engulf the remaining upper soldiers. We thrust them just outside the hangar and I give Kara the command. "Shut the hanger."

Without hesitation, she pushes the metal slab shut, closing them out.

The transporter buzzes to life, and I blow out a sigh, relieved Cinis has powered it. Kara wields the hanger's metal top to open. The takeoff hatch parts the roof and crushes the metal wall. I rush my soldiers to go into the transport behind her. With that piece exposed, we have little time to escape before the hangar floods with soldiers once again. I follow the last of my soldiers, preparing to board the ship, when a thick blanket of water wraps around me, turning my body around.

As it spins me, I face Kai, still bruised, and bloodied from our previous encounter. My heart sinks and after all I have done; I do not have it left in me to fight him.

In such a short time, I have destroyed everything I ever wanted. My station is gone, my home is lost. The dream of carrying on my father's legacy is dead. And although I regained my father for the briefest of moments, I have lost him forever as well.

I have destroyed everything, and I cannot harm my friend. Not again.

Stepping away from the transport door, I will not attempt to get on, but I won't let Kai stop them, either. I will surrender if it means him letting them go. There is no more fight left in me. I step forward, reaching my arms out to my former best friend, the man I called brother. Ready for him to cuff them and take me away.

He reaches his hands for my forearm, and when he grips it, he sends a powerful stream of water through my pores. I jerk back at the pain of it, but he holds tighter. It feels like thick iron needles pass through every pore in my forearm, digging into the flesh and burning it. I look down at his hand. Below it, lights flash and flicker until they die.

"My com unit."

"So, they can't track you. Tell the hydros on your ship to do the same."

I don't know what to say. I only stare at him dumbly, then back at my arm.

He grabs my arm, again pulling me into him, bringing his other arm down on my back. "Live well, brother."

This is goodbye.

"Come with us." Kai is a good man. He does not belong as a pawn in their heinous scheme.

"Sorren, I will not pretend to understand what has caused you to abandon your home and duty. But this is one time I cannot follow you."

"I hope you soon see, and when you do, I will be here." I release my best friend—my brother—and board the transport.

CHAPTER 47
KARA

S ORREN STUMBLES THROUGH THE door, and I quickly shut it behind him. He races to the command board to meet Cinis. Now that Cinis has powered the ship, Sorren types in the coordinates and prepares to take off.

The slow rumble of the ship lifting sends us all stumbling. We grab on to any nearby wall or sturdy fixture we can find to stabilize ourselves. I see the bright blue ocean before us from the glass front of the transporter. As we rise past the roof and over the city, I see the Upper soldiers race toward the hangar.

Cinis says to Sorren, "We must hurry. They'll be on our tails in a second."

Sorren frantically types commands into a large comm board before him.

"I wouldn't worry too much about that," I say with a smile, finally relieved that I have something to smile about. They turn to me, eyebrows raised, expectant.

"Why is that?" Sorren says, the ghost of a smile tugging at the corner of his mouth.

"I disabled the other transporters. They're not going anywhere now."

Their mouths hang open and Cinis pulls me into a hug. "You're a genius."

He's grateful for the extra time to warn his faction of what's coming. The hug is nothing more than friendly, but it still makes me flush, especially in front of Sorren.

Sorren busies himself with adjusting the comm board. He puts too much focus into the small buttons he presses, seeming to place extensive effort into not looking at us.

Cinis braces me as the transporter lunges forward. I let out a heavy breath as the ship flies ahead. Tears well in my eyes as we soar high above the sea, putting more distance between us and Central City. My body relaxes, and I breathe in deeply, feeling as if it's the first time I've been able to since arriving here.

We did it. We are finally free. And though I know the largest task still lies before us, I relish this small victory.

Sorren's brows furrow as he brings his hand up to my shoulder. He passes his hand along the ripped sleeve, exposing my skin. When I look down, I gasp. Where skin should be, a small patch of lavender quartz glitters along my shoulder cap. I scratch it with my nail, thinking it will flake off but find it is just as deeply embedded in me as the wispy branches in my hair, connecting—I suspect—straight down to the bone.

Cinis brings up his blackened hand to touch the rock that has replaced my skin. I grab his arm. Black has crept along his fingertips and past his wrist.

"What's happening to us?" I breathe.

"You've accessed your immortal abilities. Immortal powers do not give without taking something in return." Sorren looks at me, a strained pain creases the lines of his face.

"There must be some remedy for this," I say, the thought of Nero's modifications turning my stomach.

His eyes soften and fill with worry. "I don't know."

My grandmother will know. She's the most adept healer in the realm. My heart lightens at the thought of Corinth. She is all that I have left. To see her again and wrap my arms around her and feel like I am home is all I want. Although, there is no home left to return to.

I stare out at the elementals aboard the ship. So many have gathered with us. Elementals of all types and backgrounds stand together in this transport, but Rae is not among them. Regardless of how many we've rescued today, knowing there are thousands more locked in the walls of Central City keeps me from feeling content.

They all look to me as if I hold the answers, as if I can lead them. This time I do not look away. I do not turn my head and hide my face. I address them.

"Our journey has been long and hard, but it has only just begun. I do not have all the answers to what happened to us in Central City, but I have help in finding them." I look to Sorren and continue.

"We're going home, whatever that means, wherever that is. Now that we know what the Council of Policy is doing, we will not rest until we've stopped them. We will not relent until we have freed all our fellow elementals. Right now, the Upper plans to attack the Smithing Faction. We pledge allegiance to this faction. They have sheltered and protected our family who escaped the initial raid." I turn to Cinis, absentmindedly clutching the pendant around my neck. It is a harsh reminder of the promise I made to him and my people. A promise I cannot break.

"So, that is where we will go. We will warn them and stand by their side as we defend our region."

Thousands of faces look up at me, and Sorren who stands at my back.

Behind me, he reinforces me with his own words. "Soldiers of the Western Area. We are Upper soldiers no more. You have sacrificed more than I could have asked of you in facilitating this evacuation and stand to sacrifice even more. But Aelious and Hydris smile upon us, even when our own region does not. Because they know as well as we all do that no matter what element one may wield, no one is expendable." He turns to me as he continues, "Kara, leader of the Terra Clan's Healing faction." My chest tightens as he says the title, raising his hand to thump his chest. "I pledge my fealty to you. I swear to fight by your side until we have freed the last captive elemental from the Upper, and the threat of this is sure to never happen again."

As he stands at my side, the remaining members of his brigade thump a hand to their chest, taking a knee before us, pledging their allegiance to our cause.

There are so many others I leave behind. So many, who will continue to suffer at the hands of this abominable region. I will not forsake them. The Upper will pay for their crimes against us.

I know the Upper army will soon fix their transporters and be fast on our trails. Let them come. This time, we will be ready.

Once I am through, there is nothing I won't take from the region who has committed such atrocities. There will be no suffering as acute as what I plan to inflict. And when we return to their soil, they will know the true meaning of war.

Follow Kara, Sorren, and Cinis as they narrowly escape the Upper and navigate their way through the Lower Factions in Of Chaos and Ruin.

Thank you for reading Of Chaos and Beauty. I truly hope you enjoyed Sorren and Kara's story and would consider leaving a review so that you can help other readers find their story.

Not ready to leave this chaotic world of elementals? Want to know how Kara and Cinis's arranged engagement came to be, as well as the events leading up to Sorren's attack on Kara's faction? Of Chaos and Fire is the series prequel, told from the point of views of Kara and Cinis. Read it for free here.

ELEMENTAL KEY

Below is a non-comprehensive list of each elemental's attributes relative to the story thus far.

Terras: Land Wielders

- Notable Holidays

  - The Turning of the Leaves (Autumn Equinox)

  - The Blooming (Spring Equinox)

- Deity: Gaia

- Burial Rituals: The departed are wrapped in leaves or other plant matter and buried in the ground. This is to ensure that Gaia can re-disperse their essence and they can live on through the soil and foliage they command.

- Lower Region: Terra Clan Factions

  - Healing Faction

  - Farming Faction

- ○ Mining Faction

- Abilities (varies by level and faction)

  - ○ Plant manipulation

  - ○ Soil manipulation

  - ○ Rock and metal manipulation

  - ○ Grow fingers/limbs into vines

  - ○ Burrow/tunnel

  - ○ Magma manipulation (shared ability with Pyros)

  - ○ Cause tremors/earthquakes

  - ○ Grow size/change chemical properties of plant matter

  - ○ Earth detection (can sense things in the land)

Pyros: Fire Wielders

- Notable Holidays: The Lantern Festival

- Deity: Pyris

- Burial Rituals: The departed are cremated.

- Lower Region: Pyro Clan Factions

  - ○ Welding Faction

- Smithing Faction
- Lightening Faction

- Abilities (varies by level and faction)

  - Fire generation and manipulation

  - Lightning generation and manipulation

  - Heat generation and manipulation

  - Magma manipulation (shared ability with Terras)

  - Dehydration

  - Heat resistance

  - Self-combustion

  - Flamethrowing

  - Fire Breathing

  - Elevate opponent's body temperature.

  - Infrared vision

Hydros: Water Wielders
- Notable Holidays: The Tide/Moon Festival

- Deity: Hydris

- Burial Rituals: The departed are weighted and returned to the sea.

- Upper Region: Hydro Territories

  - The Western Area

  - The Southeastern Area

- Abilities (varies by level and faction)

  - Water Generation and Manipulation

  - Ice Manipulation (shared ability with aeros)

  - Hydrokinetic Surfing/Walking

  - Tidal Wave Generation

  - Underwater Walking

  - Whirlpool Generation

  - Water Pressure Generation

  - Dehydration

  - Self-Liquification

  - Underwater Breathing

  - Siren Song

Aeros: Air Wielders

- Notable Holidays: The Wind Festival

- Deity: Aelious

- Burial Rituals: The departed are laid to rest in ice tombs. This is to ensure they are preserved for the day Aelious returns to awaken them.

- Upper Region: Hydro Territories

  - The Upper Northen Area

  - The Northeastern Area

- Abilities (varies by level and faction)

  - Air Manipulation

  - Air/Wind Amplification

  - Aero-Telekinesis

  - Ice Manipulation (shared ability with aeros)

  - Air Surfing/Walking

  - Aerokinetic Flight

  - Wind Generation

  - Air Detection

- Tornado Generation

- Air Pressure Generation

- Breath Manipulation

- Cold Air Manipulation

- Gas Manipulation

- Air Shield

- Deoxygenation

LOWER REGION FACTION KEY

Below is a non-comprehensive list of each Faction's attributes relative to the story thus far.

Terra Clan: three factions made up of predominantly land wielders.

- Healing Faction:

    - The region's healers

    - Specialize in medicines and poisons

    - Faction Leader: Zimara Nadir

    - Kara's home faction

- Mining Faction:

    - Also known as The Golds

    - Have a proclivity for manipulating the precious metals

- Mining all metals and rocks

- The only Lower faction to ally with the Upper

- Farming Faction:

  - The region's farmers

  - Specialize in Agriculture

Fire Clan: three factions made up of predominantly fire wielders.
- Welding Faction

  - The region's welders

  - This faction sits on an active volcano and mainly uses magma for welding.

  - Cinis's mother's home faction

  - Superior Warriors

- Smithing Faction

  - The region's smithers

  - Main exports are refined weapons

  - Cinis's home faction

  - Superior warriors

- Lightning Faction

  - The region's energy suppliers

  - Inhabitants have a proclivity for wielding lightning.

ACKNOWLEDGEMENTS

T HIS BOOK WOULD NOT have been possible without the love and support of so many people. Thank you to my husband for always supporting my dreams, no matter how fanciful. Thank you to my mother for always encouraging me to reach for the stars. Thank you to my beta readers who painstakingly read through each unedited and incomplete version of this manuscript to help me create the final piece you have before you. Thank you to my editors, who are story, syntax, and proofreading geniuses. And thank *you*, for taking a chance on me and the work I've poured my heart into.

About the Author

Meghan Rhine is a product of the generation who sent countless letters to the Hogwarts Admissions Office, fell in love with sparkly vampires, jumped onto Dauntless trains, and volunteered as tribute in the reaping. She now resides deep in the bayous of Louisiana, where she reigns as queen of the wild things (three adorable little wild things). There, with her husband and three sons, Meghan lives her life fueled by coffee and sarcastic humor, one day hoping to work for the secret part of the government in charge of alien interactions.

Visit her on the web, and get free books, first looks, giveaways, and more, by subscribing to her mailing list.